Ambassador Death

Michael O'Gara

This is a fictional work coming from the author's imagination. Any similarity to actual persons, events, places, organizations and companies, is purely coincidental. Some actual general geographical references are used to create authenticity.

ISBN: 978-0615733128

Heartland Indie Publishing LLC

Chapter 1 – Chance Meeting

Cassandra was uneasy and sensed the tension around her. She was sure there were many armed men and women close by and probably snipers and rapid response teams. She couldn't help herself because old habits die hard and ones that kept you alive die hardest. Cassandra found herself continually scanning and looking for threats, just one thing that seemed out of place.

Cassandra thought that sometimes her background was a blessing and sometimes a curse. In public settings like this and in these circumstances, she couldn't decide which.

Cassandra resisted the urge to touch her weapon. Technically she shouldn't be armed, but she was. Being unarmed in this situation would have driven her mad.

It was the day before the inauguration of her father and she was sitting very publicly to the right of her father. She was at a concert that was a part of the festivities leading up to his formal swearing in. Also attending with President Elect Craig Crossing were his wife Dorothy, Cassandra's younger twin Cal with his wife Maggie, and Cassandra's younger sisters Katie and Molly.

Cassandra sat thinking that in spite of the unfortunate events that had resulted in the abrupt end of her career, it would have come to an end anyway with her father's election. It was just one of those things that one had to face in life. Cassandra half enjoyed the concert and half kept a wary eye out for trouble. After the concert, the family made nice with many dignitaries and then went back to their hotel suites.

Cassandra slept well and was up very early the next morning doing a vigorous workout followed by a three mile run with two young Secret Service Agents who were able to keep up with her blistering pace. At five feet ten inches tall, Cassandra's long legs and superb conditioning gave her a stride that had won her many track races in college. In spite of the activity she was still dressed and ready for the formal breakfast before the rest of her family.

Anyone who was anybody attended the inaugural day events starting with the formal breakfast. All of Washington's powerful and privileged were here. Cassandra had no trouble fitting in due to the fact she had studied up on the key players and was able to call most of the important attendees by name. It was a combination of cultivated skill resulting from her field training and a good mind she had been blessed with by two very intelligent parents.

She was taken to her table at which was standing the Chairman of the Joint Chiefs who greeted her.

"Good morning."

Cassandra smiled and said, "Good morning, sir."

"This is a proud day for your family and the country."

Cassandra replied, "Yes, sir."

The table was seated and introductory remarks were made regarding her father and there was polite applause and then an invocation. The food was served.

It was not lost to Cassandra that the officers sitting at her table were all very high ranking military officials. They were discussing the situation in Mexico. One of the officers, an Admiral who was the Vice Chairman of the Joint Chiefs, asked her in Spanish what she thought of the situation in Mexico.

Cassandra recognized the Highland American Spanish and replied fluently in Spanish with the correct variant, "Sir, the situation though somewhat stabilized seems to be still in a state of flux, somewhat worrisome, and very dangerous."

Cassandra noted the officer smiled at her and said in English, "Do you speak other dialects?"

"Sir, I can manage Caribbean, South Pacific American and Central American, as well as Peninsula Spanish."

The Admiral said, "Very impressive," in the Central American dialect.

Cassandra replied in the same dialect, "Thank you sir. I was fortunate to have some opportunity to practice in country."

The Admiral smiled and said in English, "Your accent changes with the dialect and I would have thought you were native to the region."

"I take that as high praise, sir. Your Spanish is impeccable."

The Admiral smiled again, "I could see how you would fit in anywhere in South America. Your Mediterranean complexion would also help you blend in."

"Yes sir. I get that, of course, from my mother."

The topic of conversation changed and Cassandra sat listening and assessing. She wondered what this was really all about. She should have been sitting with her family and there was obviously a purpose to this meeting.

The Chairman caught her off guard when he suddenly said, "Why do you think you are sitting with us?"

Cassandra didn't break stride, "Sir, I was waiting for someone to tell me why I was seated with this elite group and not with my family. There are too many variables, sir, for me to make a good assessment as to why that is."

The Chairman laughed and the others smiled or chuckled. The Chairman said smiling, "We wanted to pump you for information."

Cassandra replied, "Sir, my father is far too smart to tell me something you gentlemen were not already privy to. He knows I would do my duty and tell you unless he directly ordered me not to do so and he cannot do that yet as he has not been sworn in."

The Admiral said, "She has you there, Sid."

The Chief of Staff of the Air Force asked, "Is it true that Roger is going to be your father's nominee for Secretary of Defense and that's why he is retiring."

Cassandra said, "Yes sir."

The Chairman smiled and said, "There you have it gentlemen. The President elect has our backs." He turned to Cassandra and smiling said, "Thank you, Cassandra. You have put our minds at ease."

Cassandra smiled, "Respectfully, why is it I suspect you already knew the answer?"

Those at the table broke out in smiles. Cassandra was glad these officers found her amusing. The breakfast meal was very enjoyable and when they had finished the President elect and his family rose to leave and Cassandra said to the officers, "Please excuse me, gentlemen."

The Chairman smiled, "Of course."

Cassandra gave the men at the table her most charming smile, "It has been a pleasure, sirs."

As she walked away the Admiral said, "I can see why she was recommended for the special assignment."

The Chairman said, "Yes, she is very bright and I understand a very dangerous and competent operative. She could operate in diplomatic circles and at the same time deal with the generals."

The Admiral said, "Yet they would have to deal with a woman and that would have the right effect given their machismo. They will have to deal with her because of her father's position. The opposition will hope she'll fail so they will probably vote in favor of her appointment."

The others agreed.

Cassandra joined her family and left for the ceremony. She enjoyed the inauguration. The music started the festivities and then there were the Call to Order and the invocation. The Vice President was sworn in first and then after more music her father was given the Presidential oath. Cassandra was very proud of her father as he gave his inaugural address. After the benediction and national anthem, Cassandra joined the family as they witnessed her father signing the required papers. They then left for the congressional luncheon.

It was a somewhat formal affair, but this time Cassandra got to sit with her family. She sat between her mother and her brother. She was to the right of her brother and Maggie his wife sat on his left. Her brother leaned over and asked, "Did the chiefs give you a hard time this morning?"

Cassandra said, "Not in the least. It was a thoroughly enjoyable meal. The gentlemen treated me well."

After the luncheon, the inaugural parade was held. It was a grand affair and Cassandra thoroughly enjoyed the pomp. As a member of the President's family she got to be on the reviewing stand to watch the rest of the parade pass. It was then she realized the significance of her father's position. She also thought that the military certainly knew how to parade.

After the parade finished, the family went to their quarters to prepare for the evening formal ball. It was a very grand affair. The family followed the President into the building. Cassandra knew she was drawing attention in her gown. She looked like a famous model rather than a warrior and her female endowments were evident. At the same time, it could be said she was modestly dressed. Cassandra was glad she had gone to the expense of having her gown specially tailored.

She was able to circulate and meet a number of people including some of those she'd had her photo taken with when she had received the Medal of Freedom for her work on border protection. She had an entirely enjoyable time and danced with several senior Senators and Congressmen as well as some of her father's closest allies and some of those who would be serving in his administration. She also met the wives of several members of the Joint Chiefs. She was resting when Roger and Kirsten came to her.

Four Star General Roger Shires (Retired) was the former Director of National Intelligence and her father's nominee for Secretary of Defense. She and her family had recently spent their Christmas vacation with Roger and Kirsten. The smart money was that his nomination would fly through the confirmation process.

Kirsten said, "This is quite an affair, Cassandra."

Cassandra smiled, "Indeed. I am having a good time."

Roger said, "I see you were networking."

Cassandra said, "Yes sir. I have it on good authority the Joint Chiefs are happy with my father's choice for a nominee for Secretary of Defense."

Roger smiled, "Is that so?"

Cassandra smiled, "As if you and your old comrades at arms hadn't already discussed it, sir."

Kirsten laughed and Roger smiled before saying, "You know how it is, Cassandra."

She replied, "Yes sir. You can take the man out of the military, but not the military out of the man."

Kirsten smiled, "That was a very nice play on words."

Cassandra replied, "Thank you, Kirsten."

Roger shook his head in disbelief, but he was smiling.

Kirsten looked at her husband and said, "Roger, let's dance," and Roger took her glass and put it on a nearby table and they went to the dance floor.

A man Cassandra didn't know suddenly was beside her, "May I have the honor of this dance?"

Cassandra looked at him and smiled. She had a reaction she had never experienced before. There was an attraction between them that was almost electric. She knew he was experiencing it. He was a handsome man and perhaps five or six years her senior. He had the accent of a well educated native Spanish speaker. He was about the same height as she, but she perceived he had a military background because of the way he stood. She also suspected he was very fit.

She said, "Why certainly, but first you must introduce yourself."

The man said, "My pardon señorita, I am Alejandro Garcia Ramirez, Ambassador of Mexico to the United States. Please just call me Alejandro."

Cassandra replied, "I am Cassandra Crossing. Please call me Cassandra."

The Ambassador offered his arm and Cassandra took it. Cassandra could almost swear there was almost a spark of electricity when they touched. Alejandro was a very good dancer and he complimented Cassandra, "You dance very well."

Cassandra smiled and teased, "I'm not sure how much of a compliment that is. The waltz is not a difficult dance, especially when one has a partner as accomplished a dancer as you. The Tango is a different matter."

Alejandro smiled as he whirled Cassandra around the floor. When the dance finished Alejandro asked, "May I get you a drink?"

Cassandra said, "That would be nice."

Cassandra took the Ambassador's arm and he led her off the dance floor. He asked, "Would champagne suit or would you like something else?"

Cassandra said, "Champagne please."

Alejandro smiled, "Certainly. He flagged a waiter and took two crystal champagne flutes and brought one for Cassandra.

Cassandra nodded and said, "Thank you, Alejandro."

Alejandro said, "I will be returning to Mexico soon. I hope before I go that we could perhaps have lunch?"

Cassandra asked, "What is the purpose of the luncheon?"

"It is purely social, Cassandra."

Cassandra asked, "I don't wish to seem insensitive, but are you married, Alejandro?"

She hoped he would say no.

A sad look crept into Alejandro voice and he said, "I was, but my wife died. I am," he paused, "What do you call it in English?"

Cassandra said, "Widower."

"Yes, I am a widower."

Cassandra said with a smile, "In that case, I accept."

A man came and spoke to Alejandro in Spanish. Cassandra assumed they did not realize she spoke Spanish fluently.

The man said, "You are the Ambassador and you should see to your official duties instead of pursuing an American woman."

Alejandro smiled and said in a firm, but calm voice, "It is precisely because of my position that you should show respect Diego."

Cassandra watched the older man bow his head slightly in acknowledgement.

Alejandro turned back to Cassandra and switched to English, "How may I contact you?"

Cassandra gave him her cell phone number and he repeated it to her. Cassandra confirmed he had repeated it correctly.

He said, "Good. I will call you. I must go now and see to my official duties."

He took her hand and kissed it and Cassandra knew her face was becoming flushed. What was happening to her that she was acting like a school girl? She nodded. The Ambassador left and Cassandra rejoined her family. Her parents had just come back from dancing. Her father smiled.

"I saw you dancing with the Ambassador of Mexico."

Cassandra said, "He invited me to have lunch with him."

Craig said, "That is a very interesting development." He said it in a way that Cassandra knew it was the President making the comment.

Cassandra responded, "Indeed. It will be interesting to see what his motive is."

Craig looked at his daughter, "It could be purely social. My daughter is a beautiful woman."

"Perhaps, father, but I think there is more to it than that."

Her father just nodded in agreement, "Talk to Roger before you go."

Cassandra said, "Yes, father." She enjoyed the rest of the evening, but she did not get to interact with the handsome ambassador again.

Cassandra was up early the next morning and exercised rigorously as she usually did. Afterward, she showered and got ready for the day. A message came from her mother inviting her to join the family for breakfast. On the way, Cassandra received a call.

The number was a Mexican one and she assumed she knew who was calling and answered, "Good morning, this is Cassandra."

"Good morning, it is I, Alejandro. I would like to take you to lunch today."

Cassandra said, "I would like that. Where do you propose we lunch and I'll meet you there?"

Alejandro suggested a place to meet at twelve thirty. Cassandra agreed and then put Alejandro's captured number into her cell.

The family breakfast was very pleasant and when they had finished eating her father said, "I had better go. I have a long commute to the office."

Cassandra smiled and her mother laughed. Craig kissed Dorothy and left for work.

Dorothy said to her daughter, "Your father told me the Mexican Ambassador asked you to lunch."

Cassandra nodded, "We have a date for today."

Katie interjected, "He is very good looking."

Cassandra said, "He is that."

Cal added, "Be careful, sis. Those Latin men are very passionate."

Maggie elbowed her husband playfully and she was smiling.

Cal asked, "How are things going with your former team?"

"I talked to Dave day before yesterday and things are going very well. They still haven't heard who will be replacing me."

Cal smiled, "There is a rumor that Dave will be acting for quite some time. Certain people want to see what he is capable of."

Cassandra said, "I see."

Cal said, "Well, I have to get to work and Maggie is going hunting for a permanent place for us to live."

The couple got up and kissed everyone goodbye and left.

Cassandra excused herself and phoned Roger. She went directly to meet with him and Chas Elliot who was nominated to be her father's Secretary of State. They had a lengthy conversation.

Cassandra arrived for her luncheon date five minutes early. She was dressed in a very expensive business suit with very tasteful and understated jewelry. Alejandro was already there waiting for her. She was shown to his table and as she approached he stood up.

Alejandro said, "I did not expect you for some time yet, Cassandra."

Cassandra said with a broad smile, "I do not believe in the rude practice of being fashionably late."

Alejandro smiled back, "How refreshing. Would you like a glass of wine?"

Cassandra thought that his smile could melt an iceberg. She said, "Please."

They ate an enjoyable light meal of baked Tilapia over a bed of seasoned rice. The conversation centered on the inauguration. After the meal, the waiter brought coffee.

Alejandro asked, "What do you think of Mexico's military?"

Cassandra said, "If you ask that question, I'm afraid you might not like the answer."

Alejandro said, "I would like to know your assessment"

Cassandra sat back, "Parts of the Mexican military are corrupt and undependable. Not only is their loyalty to the elected government suspect, but they are undisciplined and some units have participated in killings, torture, rape, and beatings. Mexico's National Human Rights Commission has documented such cases. Most recently some substantial portion of the army has been in open rebellion against the elected government."

Alejandro was leaning forward with his arms on the table, "Do you think the US aid to the military loyal to my government will continue?"

Cassandra said, "Well the southern border is now sealed very tightly and the drug flow into this country has been reduced to a trickle. I've seen the latest figures on how many former addicts are volunteering for treatment because they can't get street drugs. If you were a politician here would you send funds to the Mexican military for a drug war that we've already won? Especially knowing the military is corrupt and increasingly dangerous in their decision making. In fact, as a Mexican politician would you want the present military supported unconditionally until things become more stable? I do not expect an answer to that last question. If the support is to continue, relationships as well as the situation will have to improve."

Alejandro sighed and said without commitment, "I think you understand the situation. The larger part of the military is still loyal to the government."

Cassandra leaned forward and said, "How can you say that Alejandro knowing as you probably do about the special cargo and the rebellion of certain units."

Special Cargo was a code word for nuclear bombs that had been smuggled into Mexico and interdicted by U.S. covert operations.

Alejandro was shocked and whispered, "You know about that?"

Cassandra said, "Yes. It is also public knowledge how many dirty bombs we intercepted at the U.S. border. The special cargo that went missing or was destroyed in Mexico is not public knowledge. Why wouldn't I know given the position I held?"

Alejandro said, "It was naïve of me to suppose you didn't know." He paused before saying, "It was a close thing and brought my country to the brink of collapse."

Cassandra said, "We thought no one in Mexico would be foolish enough to chance provoking a war with us. That thinking was obviously wrong. The destruction of our Embassy in Mexico City almost provoked a strong military response. It was after all sovereign territory of the United States and some thought an act of war as the Mexican Government did nothing to stop it."

Alejandro said, "Unfortunately the government at the time was in no position to take action. You know what happened when the police tried to intervene."

Cassandra paused and looked at Alejandro, "It was the death of those policemen that kept things from getting worse. That villain Castillo brought us to the brink with the result of awakening many of our leaders to just how unstable your elected government has become."

Alejandro was wearing a poker face which meant he was troubled, "Was it really that close a thing?"

Cassandra said, "I believe we were very close to war. If one of those bombs had made it to a major city..." She did not finish the sentence and shrugged.

Alejandro said, "I suppose I can understand that. I did not know about the special cargo until very recently."

Cassandra thought that Alejandro might be lying. On the other hand his government was struggling internally for survival and did not find out about the special cargos until after they had been destroyed or captured.

Cassandra said, "I understand things are still unsettled in Mexico."

Alejandro shrugged, "I am going home to participate in the work to stabilize the government."

Cassandra said, "Good."

Alejandro looked up quite shocked at her reaction.

Cassandra added, "I hope others listen to your voice of reason. It may be difficult to rebuild the goodwill between our countries, but not impossible. In this country, we have overcome our financial difficulties and that is good as the Congress now sees a need to strengthen our military; especially in the south."

Alejandro just nodded, "I see. Perhaps you will be able to come to Mexico and visit me sometime."

Cassandra said, "I would welcome the day it will be possible."

She wondered to what degree this strong attraction between them could be a danger. She did want to see him again, but she did not know if he could be trusted.

Alejandro said, "I must be going. Thank you for the enjoyable lunch and the enlightening conversation."

Cassandra said, "It was a pleasure, Alejandro."

Cassandra got up and Alejandro reached for her hand and she let him take it. The electricity was still there and she could feel her pulse rate increase at his touch.

Cassandra said, "I will pray for your success, Alejandro."

"Thank you, Cassandra."

He left and Cassandra sat back down and finished her coffee thinking about the conversation. She left and reported back to Roger. Cassandra returned with her assigned Secret Service Agents to the White House.

Cassandra was taken to the residence where her mother said, "Did you have a nice lunch, Cassandra?"

Cassandra replied, "Oh yes."

"I expect your father shortly."

Cassandra asked, "How are my sisters doing?"

"Katie is doing well at her studies. Molly is too. Katie is going to intern for Senator Bright this summer. Tonight we are having a family dinner here. Cal and Maggie are coming."

Cassandra said, "I really need a shower. I think I'll go freshen up."

"When you are done, come and have coffee with me."

A half hour later Cassandra was dressing to go see her mother when her cell rang. There had been a bidding war on her condo that she had put up for sale and her attorney had an offer well above the list price. She agreed to fax him approval to sell. Cassandra had listed the condo knowing she would no longer need it. She would not be living in New York and her very desirable condo would increase her fortune. Cassandra hand wrote a note and arranged for it to be faxed. She then went to see her mother.

Her mother told her about her settling in as First Lady. They had some laughs and enjoyed each other's company.

Dinner that evening was entirely enjoyable. Cassandra enjoyed seeing her sisters and they all shared their recent experiences. Cassandra slept like a baby that night and rose long before the alarm and exercised. She showered, dressed, and was ready to report.

Cassandra walked from the residence to the Oval Office. Her father was already at work. She was shown in and her father greeted her.

"Good morning, dear."

Cassandra kissed her father on the cheek and said, "Good morning, father."

Chas Elliot the Secretary of State said, "Good morning, Cassandra."

Cassandra said, "Good morning, sir."

Roger said, "It is good to see you, Cassandra."

Her father said, "Please have a seat. We have a special assignment for you that is going to be both delicate and dangerous. It involves Mexico."

Cassandra replied, "Sir," and took a seat.

Her father nodded to Roger, "Go ahead, Roger."

"Our intelligence indicates that seven of the twelve military regions are now firmly under the control of the Mexican President. The three regions that were under the control of Senior Castillo seem somewhat reluctant to come back into the fold. Certain officers are afraid they will be tried for treason which they should be. We expect that stand off will not easily be resolved. Two other military regions that were under the influence of another drug lord have not been purged. During a period of lawlessness, certain loyal Generals of the Army took the opportunity to unleash their troops on the drug cartels; leaders and members were summarily executed including some turncoat officers. Their properties were of course seized and the drug fields burned. There were some ugly firefights. The Generals were very unhappy with Castillo's attempt to nuke parts of the Mexican Army and seize power. They are determined to permanently rid Mexico of the cartels and any future threat to themselves. There was a lot of bloodshed and the media here reported very little of it, mainly because they couldn't get there."

Cassandra said nothing as she surmised Roger had more to tell her.

Roger sighed, "The Mexican President and his Cabinet realized how close they came to total collapse of the government or war with us. They are moving quickly to regain control of the country with a sense of purpose never before seen. Those officials who were suspected of being in the pockets of the drug cartels are just disappearing. The word purging comes to mind."

Roger paused and looked at Cassandra.

She asked, "What is to be my role, sir."

Roger said, "That is complicated. We have been asked to re-establish an embassy in Mexico City, but we have our doubts regarding security and stability. Still, we want to comply. We have identified a suitable site, which is to say you defensible, and have purchased it. We have special permission to bring in an extraordinary amount of Embassy security, but we are reluctant to send in people from Chas's Department until we know the lay of the land."

Cassandra asked, "Where do I fit in?"

"You have worked out of Embassies during your intelligence operations so you know something about what an embassy needs. You are also capable of getting yourself and your people out of Mexico if things go sideways. At the same time, your relationship to the President makes our serious intention clear. If you accept, you will be on diplomatic status as Special Envoy to assess the situation and report directly to us. What we really want is your recommendation regarding economic and military aid."

Cassandra nodded understanding, "I see."

Chas smiled, "The President has ordered that the Chief of Station of the CIA in Mexico is to take his marching orders from you. You will also be in command of all military assets in country. We will not appoint the Ambassador until you give the all clear. The Ambassador, before he leaves, will be told it would be very wise to accept your advice as though it was an order until you are reassigned."

Cassandra asked, "Just how big is the security team they are allowing us to bring in?"

Roger answered, "It was agreed that two augmented companies and their equipment would be permitted to enter the country in order to provide security. They will be airlifted into Mexico City International Airport. The troops will offload their vehicles and equipment and be escorted by Mexican Military to the Embassy site. Our people will secure the Embassy site and establish communications. Once you are in place and you will gather intelligence and report on the situation. You will determine if and when it is safe for diplomats and their dependents to be flown in. In the meantime you will be our representative there.

The military unit providing security will be well enough armed that in the event of attack they could reasonably hold the Embassy until a relief force can get you out and mobile enough to make a run for it. On another note, your friend Alejandro Garcia Ramirez is now Secretary of the Interior."

Cassandra said, "That is an interesting development."

Roger said, "Exactly. The advance contingent will leave the day after tomorrow and you will go in with the troops. Six CIA field Agents of your choice will accompany you. You will be given confidential briefing material to study. You will also be given discretionary funds for your operations. It is all in your briefing material. There is a special contact number in the file whom you may contact if you need anything further. Communications from the Embassy will be encrypted and you will report as you see fit."

Cassandra said, "I see."

Her father asked, "Will you do it?"

Cassandra looked her father in the eye and said, "Yes sir."

Chas said, "May God bless your endeavors, Cassandra."

Cassandra replied, "Thank you, sir. I will certainly need His help."

Chapter 2 – On Mission

Cassandra was very pleased with the force that had been assigned to the Embassy. This was not the normal marine detachment. Her review of the records indicated the two companies were commanded by a combat tested Major and two veteran Captains. All of the other officers, NCOs and their men had seen combat. They were all top notch.

It was obvious this group had been assembled as if a fight was imminent rather than just possible. The military leader of their party, Major Bob Sharp, was an experienced combat veteran and a rising star. The security team was a hodgepodge of marine snipers, Navy SEALs, Army Rangers, as well as exceptional soldiers and marines. The team offered an operational flexibility that was quite unique.

Cassandra had reviewed the combat loading that had been organized and was much impressed. They would have a lot of trucks and combat vehicles in transit to the Embassy and far more than were normally necessary for two companies. The Major had prepared for an extended siege and continuous combat operations during that period. As he had access to unlimited materials, he had requisitioned everything he could think of that fit into the agreement with the Mexican government and that might extend his men's life expectancy. She was impressed.

Her small civilian plane arrived at the military airfield two hours before departure of the military transport planes. The apparent civilians with Cassandra unloaded their packs and brought Cassandra's baggage. She carried a back pack and was dressed in sneakers, slacks and a loose blouse under which she wore a custom ballistic vest and her handgun. Her back up weapon was in an ankle holster. This was not a casual picnic outing and the danger was great.

Cassandra was directed to where Major Sharp was organizing things outside of a hanger and went with her two most senior people. The Major's soldiers and marines were sitting on the tarmac with their gear. As Cassandra marched toward the Major an alert NCO alerted the commanding officer. The Major and other officers greeted her.

Cassandra said, "Good afternoon, gentlemen."

Major Sharp said, "Good afternoon, ma'am."

"Major. I see you have things well in hand."

"Yes ma'am. We will leave on time."

A Sergeant Major came in a rush and pulled up short. He saluted.

Cassandra turned to Major Sharp and said, "Major, as we are entering what could be considered a combat zone, would you advise all ranks to dispense with military courtesy. I have no desire to be shot again just because I happen to be standing next to you."

Major Sharp smiled, "Yes ma'am, with pleasure." He turned to the sergeant major, "Please pass the word, Pat."

The sergeant major said, "Yes sir."

Cassandra said, "There are five gentlemen and a lady with me who are civilian personnel of the embassy who are going to catch a ride with us. The big one is Mr. Sloan and the other is Mr. Thomas."

The Major said, "Yes ma'am. I was told you were bringing some spooks." He turned to the civilians and said, "Pleased to meet you gentlemen." The major offered and shook their hands.

Cassandra said, "I was very impressed with the items you arranged for our little visit south of the border with one exception."

The Major asked, "What was that, ma'am?"

Cassandra smiled, "What if we need a kitchen sink?"

The Major laughed as did the Captains with him.

Cassandra asked, "Where can I get something to eat. I haven't eaten."

Major Sharp said, "Captain Moore, please show the Envoy to the officers' mess."

"Yes sir. Please follow me, ma'am."

Cassandra followed the Captain to a jeep and they sped off. When they got out of the jeep, Captain Moore continued to lead the way and Cassandra followed. When they entered the building, a Major, who had been drinking beer with his meal said, "This is for base officers only, Captain."

Cassandra said in a forceful voice, "Major, on your feet."

The Major looked at Cassandra and said, "Where did you meet this fine looking woman, Jake?"

Captain Jake Moore replied, "This is the Special Envoy to Mexico and daughter of the Commander in Chief."

The Major jumped to his feet, "I'm sorry, ma'am. I didn't ..."

Cassandra interrupted, "You certainly didn't and you are a disgrace to your uniform, Major. Tighten your tie and tuck in your shirt. Have you been drinking, major?"

"Yes ma'am."

Cassandra said, "Who is your commanding officer."

"Lt. Colonel Winslow, ma'am,"

Cassandra said, "And what would your C.O. say about your conduct this day, Major."

The Major was now looking straight ahead, "He would have my ass in a sling, ma'am."

Cassandra continued, "Do you usually disrespect brother officers visiting your base in the way you did my captain? Would your C.O. approve?"

The Major said, "No ma'am."

Cassandra asked a question she already knew the answer to, "Where is your C.O.?"

The Major said, "On leave, ma'am."

"Who is in charge while the Colonel is away?"

"I am, ma'am."

Cassandra said, "So you are drinking on duty, Major?"

The Major was now apparently mortified. He saw the end of his career before him.

Cassandra said in a low voice, "Major, if you give me your word as an officer and a gentleman that you will never again be disrespectful of junior officers unless they need a, butt chewing, I will not put you on report. Do you give me your word?"

"Yes ma'am."

Cassandra said, "Good. Now please arrange for someone to bring us a sandwich and a cold beer."

The Major looked with disbelief at Cassandra who said, "The proper response is 'yes ma'am'."

The Major smiled knowing he'd just been had, "Yes ma'am." He hurried away and then came back to report, "The Special Envoy's order will be here directly."

Cassandra said, "Why don't you join us, Major. I take it you know Captain Moore."

The Major said, "Thank you, ma'am. Captain Moore and I served together in Iraq."

Cassandra said, "Where are you from, Major?"

"I'm Wisconsin born and raised ma'am."

Cassandra struck up a conversation with the major and they had a pleasant if short meeting and lunch. She knew it would be a long flight so Cassandra used the toilet before leaving the building. Cassandra shook hands with the Major as they left and everyone was smiling.

As they drove back to the hanger Cassandra asked, "Does anyone call you Jacob?"

"No ma'am. They call me Jake."

Cassandra just nodded.

As promised, the aircraft loading was accomplished with time to spare and soon the contingent was ready to take off. Cassandra was used to such rides and fell asleep sitting upright, much to the amazement of the others in the uncomfortable seats. She woke as the planes made their approach into Mexico City. Suddenly their plane made an evasive maneuver and Cassandra knew from experience what was happening. Someone had fired at the planes; probably a shoulder fired surface to air missile.

Cassandra said it without conscious thought, "So much for an uneventful entrance."

The remark brought chuckles from the marines closest to her.

The plane went straight into the airport and landed safely. It taxied and then the gate went down and the platoon leaders led their troops off the planes and they took up defensive positions as vehicles were offloaded. Cassandra watched the entire operation and decided this mixed team was very good. A Mexican Officer came to meet them and went to Major Sharp and addressed him in Spanish, but Cassandra was too far away to hear the conversation. Major Sharp came to Cassandra.

Major Sharp said, "Major Reyes told me his troops are ready when we are loaded. He seemed a little perturbed when I told him we would have guards with each of the trucks. I told him the Special Envoy had ordered me to do it."

Cassandra smiled, "I guess Major Reyes had plans of his own for our cargo."

Major Sharp smiled and said, "Yes ma'am."

Cassandra pulled out her portable GPS, "Have you been to Mexico City before?"

"No ma'am"

Cassandra spoke quietly, "Major Reyes may try to lead us off the main expressway. Make sure our combat vehicles corral the transports so they cannot follow him. No matter what route the Major takes we take the most direct route. We will not go onto the secondary roads. Make sure we have someone in the cab with each driver. If they try to divert they may be relieved of their truck at pistol point if they refuse to stay on the route. I'd prefer we didn't shoot any Mexicans if we can avoid it."

Bob smiled making note of the "if we can avoid it" comment. He answered, "Yes ma'am." He hurried off to give the order.

The Multi Gun System platoons offloaded their combat vehicles and took up positions in front of and beside the Mexican transport trucks into which they were putting the combat loaded pallets using forklifts. Cassandra saw Major

Reyes looking her way. It was obvious he had not expected the combat vehicles or such a large number of them.

Bob Sharp said, "Ma'am, we should be out of here within a half hour."

Cassandra nodded. She and Bob watched the captains supervise the off loading and loading. They watched as some of Bob's troops jumped onto each loaded truck.

Bob looked at his watch, "We'll still have daylight when we get to our destination."

The CIA operatives were keeping close to Cassandra. As long as they were with her they wouldn't get left behind and neither would the important luggage they were responsible for.

When the time came to leave, Cassandra climbed in one of the combat vehicles with Bob and the CIA agents grabbed rides with various vehicles. They set out. About halfway to their destination the lead Mexican vehicles took an exit ramp, but none of Cassandra's vehicles or the transports followed them. Several other Mexican military vehicles left the convoy.

Cassandra said, "Give the order to lock and load Major and do it on an open channel."

Cassandra anticipated the Mexican major was listening in on their communications. She took a chance and hoped that Alejandro still had the same cell phone with him. She dialed his number and he answered, "Good afternoon, Cassandra."

Cassandra replied, "Good afternoon, Alejandro. How are you this fine day?"

"Busy, but I am never too busy to talk to you. How is the weather in Washington?"

Cassandra paused because her pulse rate was increasing, "I don't know, but it is warm in Mexico City."

Alejandro said, "You are in Mexico City?"

"Yes. I am with an advance group going to our new Embassy."

She could hear Alejandro laugh, "Your father is very devious, Cassandra. This is a pleasant surprise. I thought you would come with the Ambassador. I will meet you at the Embassy."

Cassandra said, "I don't think that would be a good idea as much as I would enjoy it. I may be busy fending off the unwelcome advances of one Major Reyes. I am afraid he is not an honorable man."

Alejandro said, "You are well advised not to trust him. He is a traitor. I have to go now as it is urgent I find out what happened to the men who were supposed to meet you. I will tell the President you are in the country."

"Thank you, Alejandro. When we are settled perhaps we could have another pleasant luncheon. There are some very good restaurants near the new embassy, if I remember the area correctly."

Alejandro said, "Of course. I look forward to it."

The call ended and Bob was looking at her.

Cassandra smiled and said, "That was Alejandro Garcia Ramirez the Minister of the Interior. We may not have to fight our way to the embassy, but be careful just in case."

Bob said, "Yes ma'am."

The trip was taking some time because they had to travel from the airport east of the city through the city to the western side. The new embassy was located in the richest neighborhood in Mexico City, Lomas de Chapultepec. It was relatively near the Polanco neighborhood where many Embassies had been abandoned. The U.S. Embassy would be the first major embassy to be re-established.

The U.S. Government had purchased a walled in urban mansion with relatively large grounds for Mexico City. Cassandra had a copy of the building plans that had been in the briefing materials she had been given. They arrived to find the gates had been forced open and the place was not guarded as had been promised. Some soldiers were loading furniture onto a truck and were surprised to see the combat vehicles surround them. Their weapons were not close at hand because they had been carrying out the loot.

Bob was giving orders as the troops and transports took up positions. A squad entered the building ready for a fight as the unarmed Mexican soldiers outside were taken into custody without a shot being fired, though one officer had his face introduced to a rifle butt. The hands of the Mexicans were being bound behind their backs with plastic ties. Cassandra dismounted with the major. He ordered the last two armored vehicles to block the gate and that was done. The troops were taking up defensive positions and the armored vehicles had surrounded the main building. The Mexican drivers were looking very nervous.

Cassandra turned to Bob, "I think it would be wise to round up the drivers and sit them on the lawn. Do the same with the soldiers who were stealing our furniture, but keep the two groups separated."

Bob said, "Yes ma'am." He gave the orders.

The fifteen Mexican military drivers came at gunpoint.

Captain Cable came to Cassandra, "You were right. They all had to be forced at gun point not to leave the expressway."

Jake came and said, "The embassy is stripped bare and the walls have been spray painted with not so friendly anti-American slogans."

Cassandra watched the men on the grass being roughly searched. An officer was brought out of the building his hands tied behind his back with plastic ties.

The officer said, "You have no right to detain me. I am a Mexican Army Officer."

Bob said, "Actually, Lieutenant, you are on sovereign soil of the United States and you were caught committing theft of government property which is a federal offense. You have provoked an international incident."

Bob turned to Cassandra and asked, "Ma'am, do you want me to get him on one of the planes going back?"

Cassandra said, "No, I think Secretary Garcia Ramirez would prefer to have the opportunity to have his people interrogate these men."

The reaction of the officer was immediate and it was obvious he spoke English. Cassandra decided to take a risk and said to him, "Unless of course you would like to tell me what the plan was. That might keep you and your men from being stood against a wall and being summarily executed."

Cassandra noticed the men they had in custody had suddenly become very tense as word was whispered between them about what had been said. The officer put his head in the air and it was obvious he was not going to talk. Cassandra turned to one of the civilians with her and said, "Mr. Sloan, would you and Mr. Thomas take this Mexican officer inside."

Without a word they lifted the officer up by his arm pits and carried him inside handling him roughly. Cassandra decided to let the men in the grass stew for a little while. She said, "Major, please make sure the grounds are secure and have the outbuildings inspected. I'm going to have a look inside."

Bob said, "Sergeant Kinsey, take two men and go with her."

"Yes sir," Kinsey responded and pointed at two of his men and motioned them forward.

Cassandra entered the main building and found the damage wasn't as bad as she had expected. Only two of the downstairs rooms had been spray painted and it was clear they had interrupted the progress because an open box of paint spray-cans sat in the middle of the floor. She examined the main building and found all the furniture had been stolen along with everything that wasn't nailed down. Cassandra went onto the flat roof and found she had a commanding view of the grounds and beyond.

She looked at the Sergeant and they traded a look. Cassandra smiled, "Good fields of fire from up here."

Sergeant Kinsey turned to one of his men and said, "Emory go tell Captain Cable we have excellent fields of fire from up here. Tell Kersey to bring a heavy weapons squad up here."

The man hurried away.

Cassandra went downstairs and into the kitchen. The Mexican lieutenant was now blindfolded. Cassandra winked at Sloan and said, "Take him down to the basement so his screams won't be heard."

The Lieutenant didn't flinch. Cassandra had to give him credit. She motioned to the Sergeant and he was manhandled downstairs.

Cassandra went to the refrigerator and saw what she wanted. She took the meat package out and handed it to Sloan, "One of you squeeze some of the blood from this meat onto the floor and make sure you get some on your shirt than go grab a soldier who looks terrified and bring him in here. See what you can find out."

Stan Thomas looked at his colleague and said, "I think she's done this before, Greg."

Greg said smiling, "Once a spook always a spook."

Cassandra said, "Play nice, but see what you can find out."

Greg said, "Yes boss."

Cassandra went outside and Bob came to her.

He said, "I don't like this."

Cassandra said, "I know. Let's prepare for a night assault."

Bob said, "I hear the embassy roof has a commanding view."

"Yes. One of the heavy machine guns up there could do a lot of damage. Let's break out some of those special airplane greetings and get a couple up on the roof as well."

Bob said, "The basement will make a good bunker."

Cassandra said, "I've been down there and it only has two ways out and that worries me. I'd rather be in the open."

Bob laid out the aerial view photo map on the hood of their vehicle and the two captains came over. Bob said, "We've set up fields of fire to cover the walls." and pointed.

Cassandra said, "Bob there are floodlights all over the place. Let's find out if they work."

Bob turned to Captain Cable, "Justin, have that checked out."

"Yes sir."

Mr. Sloan came out to report, "Ma'am, the plan was to steal our supplies and strand us so the theft here could be completed. The Mexican vehicles were just going to peel off and disappear while the troop carriers took us in a roundabout way to the embassy."

Cassandra said, "They must think we're stupid and I'm not sure it was that innocent."

Sloan said, "I also have my doubts. They work for Major Reyes."

Cassandra said, "Let's get photos of them all and take their boots. We'll keep them and their trucks here and see who comes to collect."

The compound was already a flurry of activity. One company was standing guard while the other company unloaded and set up. Three soldiers were busy in the kitchen preparing meals and sentries were on the roof. They were just about to go to eat when a sentry alerted to the approach of a convoy. Among a number of military trucks was a limousine.

Cassandra ordered, "Keep the soldiers sitting and bring up the officer." At the gate the limousine stopped. Her phone rang and she answered.

"This is Crossing."

It was Alejandro, "I am at your gate. May I come in?"

"Of course you may, Alejandro."

Cassandra ordered, "Let the limousine in."

She realized she was looking forward to seeing Alejandro for reasons other than business.

The two combat vehicles blocking the gate moved and the limousine drove in. One of the accompanying military vehicles started to enter and Cassandra said, "Let that one in, but the rest can wait outside."

Cassandra went to meet their guest. The rear door of the limousine opened and Alejandro got out and an officer was with him. All the Mexican military captives remained on the ground and did not try to stand to attention. Alejandro and the officer with him ignored the men.

Alejandro said, "Cassandra, it is so good to see you."

Cassandra was facing the seated troops and when Alejandro embraced her she saw the looks of alarm on the soldiers' faces. The emotions the embrace triggered also alarmed her, but she had a practiced poker face.

She said, "I hadn't expected to see you again so soon, Alejandro."

Alejandro said, "May I present Colonel Mendez."

The Colonel saluted and Cassandra offered her hand and they shook. Cassandra said, "I'm pleased to meet you, Colonel."

The Colonel said, "The pleasure is mine, Excellency."

Colonel Mendez was a small man who stood about five seven and probably weighed a hundred and forty pounds soaking wet, but he had an air of authority and confidence that more than compensated for his slight build.

Bob was now by her side and she said, "Secretary Garcia Ramirez and Colonel Mendez may I present Major Sharp who is charged with embassy security."

Bob saluted and the Colonel returned it and then Alejandro offered his hand and shook Bob's. The Colonel did likewise.

Cassandra said, "Have someone bring chairs inside."

A nearby junior officer left to see it was done. Neither Cassandra nor Bob Sharp had to give an order.

Cassandra said, "Please, let us go inside."

They went inside and Alejandro asked, "The embassy has no furniture?"

Cassandra did not miss that he saw the profanity spray painted on the wall.

Cassandra said, "The soldiers on the lawn, instead of guarding the building, were looting it. We only have what's left in the last truck that they didn't get out before we arrived. We haven't unloaded it yet."

Alejandro just nodded and said, "My people will take the soldiers off your hands."

Cassandra could tell it was as much a request as an offer. She said, "Of course, Alejandro. I'm sorry to inconvenience you."

Folding chairs were brought into the living room and they all sat down.

Cassandra said, "I would offer you a drink, but alas our wine cellar is empty. Instead I offer my apology. Could I offer you some coffee?"

Alejandro said with a smile, "Yes, please."

Cassandra said, "And you Colonel?"

"Please."

The Sergeant standing behind Cassandra went without being ordered in anticipation of what was to be done. His action was not lost on the colonel that the major had not given an order.

Alejandro said, "I am glad your father sent you, Cassandra. It will make things much easier."

"I hope so, Alejandro. Our countries have been friends and allies too long to let a few thugs, traitors, and drug dealers come between us. I hope to be able to help."

Alejandro said, "Colonel Mendez has recently become the commander of this military region. His superior was an unfortunate casualty of the recent internal problems."

Cassandra said, "I look forward to a friendly and productive relationship, Colonel."

The coffee was brought in metal military canteen cups because there were no proper cups as all the china had been stolen. They all prepared their coffee and when they were sipping, Cassandra sat back waiting for the big question.

Alejandro said, "I know why the embassy is being reopened, but why did they send you, Cassandra? It is unusual for someone of your rank and influence to be sent on such an assignment even as special envoy."

Cassandra smiled and said, "Alejandro, I would not be so frank if we were not friends."

A thought flashed through her mind that she would have him be more than a friend. She pushed it back in her mind. She did not know if they were playing a diplomatic game or if Alejandro could be trusted.

Cassandra continued, "My mission is to assess the political, economic, and military stability here and make a recommendation as to any economic and military help which you might find useful. I have special skills and knowledge that a career diplomat would not have. The assessment and negotiation is very important."

Alejandro laughed, "It is refreshing that you are so direct. I will of course help in any way I can. In a like manner, Colonel Mendez will be happy to help you. He and I attended Heróico Colegio Militar together and I trust him completely."

Cassandra looked at the colonel and said, "That is high praise, Colonel."

The Colonel made a grand nod with a smile.

Cassandra said, "I am eager to start discussions with your government and I will appreciate your help."

Alejandro said, "The president is eager to meet you. Perhaps we can arrange that next week."

Cassandra said with a smile, "Yes, of course."

"How long will it be before the ambassador arrives?"

Cassandra smiled, "I must ensure the embassy is ready and that may take a little longer than I expected."

The thought crossed her mind that the longer she was here the more chance there was to see Alejandro.

Alejandro said, "I understand. You will do well to be vigilant. Things here are not yet as stable as we would like and there are still criminal elements about."

Cassandra nodded, "I understand and thank you for the warning."

Alejandro replied, "I think you would have been vigilant in any event."

Colonel Mendez offered, "You seem well prepared to defend the embassy."

Cassandra replied, "Within the limits agreed to."

The Colonel nodded, "Of course. Your soldiers were wise in the choice of equipment."

Cassandra said, "I think so. These are dangerous times as you know only too well, Colonel."

"Indeed. It is unfortunate, but true."

They had finished the coffee.

Alejandro stood and said, "I will leave you now. Call me day or night if you need anything."

Cassandra stood and said, "Of course, Alejandro."

The Colonel handed Cassandra a business card, "I am also available if you need anything of a military nature."

Cassandra said, "Thank you, Colonel."

They went outside and Major Sharp ordered the prisoners up. They were marched to the street where they were roughly loaded onto trucks by the soldiers under the command of Colonel Mendez.

Alejandro embraced Cassandra and whispered, "I look forward to a social meeting."

Cassandra felt her pulse throbbing and she felt heated.

Cassandra said, "I do too. There are many good restaurants in Mexico City."

Alejandro let go of her and she saw she had the same effect on him as he had on her.

When they had left Bob looked at Cassandra, "That was certainly educational, ma'am."

Cassandra said, "Watch and learn, Bob. The best wars are the ones you don't have to fight."

Bob replied, "I agree whole heartedly."

Cassandra called a meeting of the senior officers as well as Mr. Sloan and Thomas. Once everyone was assembled she said, "It is obvious things are not as settled as we were led to believe. Mr. Sloan and Mr. Thomas as well as their people are familiar with the City. I want to find out just how bad things are. I will send four of them out and it would be better if they went separately, but they need back up. Those going with them will take diplomatic passports. If it is as bad as I expect, the passports will not be of any use if they get caught so they must not. Who do we have who speak Spanish, can gather intelligence, and are adventurous enough to volunteer?"

It turned out they were able to send out four three man teams in civilian attire and could have sent more. Each team was given currency out of the special funds so they could hire transportation, pay bribes, and pay for incidentals. After dark, they slipped away unnoticed out of the compound.

Cassandra sent an encrypted message to her mentor's office. The body read, *"Situation not as stable as reported; situation is deemed dangerous. Gathering intelligence, but have secured looted embassy without a shot. Have established contact with Alejandro and regional military commander. Advise you do not, repeat, do not send embassy staff at this time. C."*

Overnight the companies in the compound worked and slept in rotation. Cassandra slept well and woke early and did her exercises. The hot water was not working so she had a cold shower. Downstairs she found two sofas and a chair in the living room. It was sparse, but better than what had been there the day before. She could smell breakfast being cooked.

She went outside to examine the progress that had been made overnight when she ran into Captain Cable.

Cassandra said, "Good morning, Justin."

"Good morning, ma'am."

Cassandra said, "You'd better get some sleep Justin; you must be tired."

He responded, "Yes ma'am," and left to get some much needed rest.

Cassandra approved of the dispositions and it had been done so the place had not been torn up and for the most part the embassy appeared to be lightly guarded, but it was anything, but. She was at the back of the house when she received a radio call.

There was a car and a military vehicle at the front gate. The Lieutenant on guard did not know the persons and would not let them enter without authorization. Cassandra ran into the house at the same time Bob was coming out the front door. Cassandra bounded up the stairs to the roof. She arrived just as the car and military vehicle sped away. She watched the vehicles for some distance until they were out of sight.

The Lieutenant came to the roof with Major Sharp. The Lieutenant said, "Ma'am, it was Major Reyes and he said he came to pay his respects and apologize for yesterday's misunderstanding. I told him I would radio the Major who would check with Colonel Mendez before authorizing entry. The Major then sped away. He was not on embassy property, so I ordered no action."

Major Sharp said, "Well done, Kelly."

Cassandra said, "Yes Lieutenant, very good."

The Major add, "You are dismissed."

The Lieutenant left.

Bob asked, "What do you think that was all about?"

"He came looking for his missing men. When Kelly mentioned Mendez, Reyes knew they had been handed over."

Bob nodded understanding, "He didn't stay around to be scooped up by Mendez."

Cassandra said, "Exactly."

A radio call came in, "Recon team one has returned."

Bob said, "Send them to the embassy to report."

Cassandra and Bob met them in the living room. Greg Sloan and the two men with him were obviously tired.

Cassandra said, "What did you find out, Greg?"

"There is a strip between here and the airport that is very well controlled. The neighborhoods around us are patrolled and generally under government control, but still dangerous. North of here the situation is very unstable. There is a curfew in effect and there is a shoot on sight order after curfew. The government is still searching for small dissident military units.

This Reyes guy is on the government's most wanted list. Apparently he hijacked the unit that was supposed to provide our escort and killed the soldiers. He then replaced them in hopes of getting us.

Reyes isn't the only loose cannon. Crime is rampant now that the drug trade has been shut down. The price of drugs has gone through the roof and so has crime. If it weren't for the Army, the place would be a total nightmare, but it is still touch and go. The police were all fired because the government couldn't sort out who was corrupt and who wasn't. Two of my 'in country' operatives are dead, and not because they were operatives, but just because they lived here."

Cassandra said, "Get something to eat and some sleep, then write up a short report to send to Washington."

"Yes ma'am."

Team three showed up ten minutes later and their information confirmed what had been learned. To the south things were worse, but not because of organized resistance, but just outright criminal activity. The military curfew was very serious and there were no foreign journalists in the area and the internet had been shut down. Team two showed up and reported that the Centro district and to the south the Condesa -Roma district was firmly under government control and the area to the west was generally pacified.

The remaining recon team did not show up until after lunch when a taxi dropped them off at the gate. They reported that the south east part of the city was a nightmare after dark. The government was moving harshly to suppress the criminal element, but commerce was breaking down.

By mid afternoon, the reports had been combined and a summary sent to Washington. At three o'clock Alejandro called Cassandra.

Cassandra answered, "Hello, Alejandro."

Alejandro said, "Hello, Cassandra. The President would like to meet with you. If you will agree to come, I will have an escort sent for you."

Cassandra said, "Of course I will come, Alejandro, but I do not have any formal dress appropriate for an audience with the President."

"These are unusual times Cassandra. The matter is urgent."

Cassandra said, "Of course."

Fifteen minutes later, the convoy arrived. Cassandra had already sent a message to Roger advising him of the meeting. Cassandra decided as a sign of trust she was going alone. She did put a military radio in her back pack.

Colonel Mendez came with three armored vehicles and four civilian trucks. He was allowed in the front gate and drove up to the building to pick up Cassandra.

Colonel Mendez made a motion like a slight bow and said, "The President sends his regards. He awaits you."

Cassandra said, "Thank you, Colonel. It is good to see you again and I place myself in your care."

Cassandra climbed into an armored military vehicle with the Colonel. They had no sooner started on their journey than the Colonel asked, "Do you have a weapon on your person?

Cassandra smiled, "Of course."

Colonel Mendez smiled, "Good. One should always be prepared. Have you been here before?"

Cassandra smiled, "I have. It is a unique and beautiful city."

Colonel Mendez was interrupted and Cassandra heard him giving urgent orders which were broadcast on the radio. Cassandra knew instinctively what was happening and opened her mouth and grabbed onto the seat as suddenly their vehicle overturned with the sound of the explosion. The soldier opposite her was lying unconscious on the right side of the vehicle which was now down. Cassandra undid her seat belt and dropped down. She grabbed the man's rifle and locked and loaded grabbing extra clips and stuffing them in her waistband and throwing her back pack off her shoulder.

The door opened from the outside and Cassandra shot the man who had opened it. Major Reyes fell backward a hole in his forehead. Cassandra then fired on full auto spraying indiscriminately at the two soldiers who had been with Reyes. She jumped out ejecting the empty clip and reloading in one swift motion. The place was bedlam. They were only blocks from the embassy.

Cassandra took cover behind the door of the vehicle. An attacker moved to fire inside the vehicle and she shot him before he had a chance to shoot. Rounds were clanging off the door and vehicle. Cassandra knew she had to get out of there. She looked in the vehicle and saw Colonel Mendez was unconscious and bleeding from a nasty gash on his head.

Cassandra made a decision and struggled to pick up Colonel Mendez. Using a fireman's carry, she ran in the only direction where there were no attackers. She was in good shape, but after a block her legs were burning. She stopped and hid behind a massive concrete gate post and laid the Colonel against it. A car was coming down the lane toward the gate and the automatic gate opened. Cassandra stepped out into the lane and raised her automatic rifle. The man driving stopped the car.

Cassandra yelled in Spanish, "Get out, leave the keys, and go back to the house!"

The man complied and Cassandra picked the Colonel up and loaded him into the back seat then got in the driver's seat and sped away. She entered the street and turned away from the area of the attack. She circled around at a high rate of speed the tires squealing at each corner and approached the embassy. She slammed on the brakes in front of the embassy walls and jumped out. She wrestled Mendez out of the back seat and using the fireman's carry ran the twenty or so yards to the front gate. She had a rifle in her right hand and her left was keeping Mendez on her shoulders.

The guards at the gate recognized Cassandra and moved the vehicles so she could just get through. A soldier took Colonel Mendez and Cassandra collapsed against a vehicle tire and sat down. Every muscle in her body was screaming and she was having difficulty breathing. The veins in her arms were standing out and the muscles were swollen. She could still hear small arms fire in the distance although it was diminishing.

Cassandra was trying to catch her breath. A sergeant asked, "Are you all right, ma'am?"

Cassandra nodded, but said nothing. The sergeant kept looking at her and it was making her uncomfortable. She got up and walked slowly toward the embassy. Bob was running down the drive.

"Are you all right?"

Cassandra said between gasps, "Yes. How is the Colonel?"

"They are treating him now. What happened?"

"It was an ambush. I was able to get away with Mendez and I commandeered a car about a block away from the attack site. It was a mess. I have to make a call."

Cassandra pulled her cell from her pocket, but it was broken. She said to Bob, "Let me have your cell."

Bob handed it to her and she changed the SIM cards and called Alejandro.

He answered, "Cassandra?"

"Yes. We were ambushed by Reyes. I was able to get Colonel Mendez here, but he is unconscious. I won't be making the meeting."

Alejandro said, "I advise you to stay there. It seems some remnants of the opposition are making another attempt to overthrow the government. Right now we have our hands full. I will give the President your apologies."

Cassandra answered, "Please do." The call ended.

She could hear more firing in the distance and now artillery could be heard in the distance.

Cassandra said, "Bob spread the word the government is under attack so anything could happen."

Bob turned to a nearby sergeant, "Tell the captains what is happening. I want everyone on alert and at their post."

The sergeant hurried off.

Cassandra went inside to the living room where a medic was stitching Colonel Mendez's head wound. Cassandra had not realized she had a significant amount of the Colonel's blood on her. She sat down.

Bob asked, "How bad was it?"

"Bad. The vehicle I was in was on its side from a blast. Most of the soldiers weren't belted in and were seriously injured. I think I was the only one wearing a belt. The Colonel was standing trying to give radio orders when we went over. Mendez was the only one I was able to save."

The medic came over and examined Cassandra. He asked, "Your muscles are strained. How did that happen?"

"It's from carrying the Colonel. Luckily, he's a relatively small man and as it was I was stretched to get him out."

The medic nodded and gave her two pills.

Cassandra asked, "What are they? I can't afford to be doped up."

"It's just aspirin, ma'am."

Cassandra nodded and someone handed her a canteen and she took the pills saying, "Thanks." She paused then said, "I have to make a report."

A sergeant came rushing in, "Captain Moore sent me to tell you some of the Colonel's men have shown up. They were disarmed and allowed into the compound and the wounded are being brought here for treatment. The soldiers have asked to speak to the boss lady."

Cassandra heard moans and noticed Mendez was awake. A medic had used smelling salts to get him conscious. The Colonel was obviously wobbly and a medic was checking his eyes with a pen light.

Three wounded soldiers were brought in and the medics started working on them.

Cassandra said, "I will go talk to Mendez's men."

Cassandra went outside where five of the Colonel's men were assembled. The officer approached her and she recognized him.

He saluted and Cassandra said, "Thank you, Captain."

The Captain said, "Señora, we thank you for your brave defense of our Colonel. Is he all right?"

Cassandra said, "I think he has a concussion and his head wound is being treated. Your soldiers are receiving medical attention as we speak"

The Captain motioned to one of his men who brought Cassandra's back pack.

The Captain said, "You left this when you rescued the Colonel."

Cassandra said, "Thank you."

"May I see the Colonel?"

Cassandra said, "Follow me."

The Colonel was half sitting when they went into the room. The Captain saluted and said, "My Colonel, with your permission we will return to engage in defending the nation."

The Colonel nodded and motioned the Captain forward. Cassandra could not hear what they were saying, but the Colonel was looking at Cassandra. He nodded and the Captain saluted and left. The Colonel smiled at Cassandra and then put his head down and lost consciousness.

The Captain turned to Cassandra, "We will be leaving now to return to our unit to fight."

Cassandra said, "I understand, but the Colonel is not in any condition to go with you. We will take good care of him and your men."

The officer said, "Gracias."

Cassandra added, "We still have Mexican Army trucks here. You may take what you need and we will return your weapons."

The officer said, "We are indebted to you."

Bob was standing nearby and called out, "Sergeant Abernathy, take the captain and his men to their transportation."

"Yes sir."

Cassandra decided it would be unwise to go outside, so she sat down watching first aid being administered. She laid the rifle she'd confiscated on the floor and sat against the wall. She was going over in her mind how she would report this.

Bob interrupted her thoughts, "Are you all right?"

Cassandra looked up, "Yes. I was just thinking about this. It is unbelievable this is happening here."

Bob nodded and went back outside. Cassandra could hear small arms fire and artillery in the distance. It was not a good day for Mexican democracy.

Chapter 3 – After Action

Cassandra sent a report on the day's events to Washington and then called a meeting. Bob and his Captains as well as Greg and Stan came.

Cassandra started the meeting with, "We need to know what is going on."

Greg said, "All, but one of the radio stations are down and I don't know how reliable the reports are, but they are saying the fighting is mostly to the south of the city. It makes sense given that is where most of the gunfire is coming from."

Stan said, "I don't see that we have any choice but to go back out. I received reports by cell from two of my contacts here and they seem to confirm the bulk of the fighting is to the south."

Bob asked, "Why would they attack the convoy here."

Cassandra said, "They were probably after me. They don't want us here or the government getting aid. Killing me would really muddy the waters. I think the looting of the embassy was meant to intimidate us more than it was about the loot. It's not over yet."

Bob said, "Well, I guess it's the same teams as last time, but they will all recon to the south."

Stan interjected, "I suggest we send one team to scout the local area. That ambush was not the kind of thing I'd want to see happen again."

Bob said, "That is a good idea."

It was agreed the teams would leave at dark.

After transmitting a report to Washington, Cassandra finally got to go shower and change. She knew it would be difficult for her to do that after dark as they would not have the lights on.

The electricity was operating sporadically in their neighborhood, but most of the expensive homes had emergency generators and lights. The Embassy's emergency generator was started, but they did not turn any lights on.

Cassandra was on the roof looking out over the city. There seemed to be flashes indicating conflict to the south. It was eerie. As the night went on, the clashes did not diminish.

Cassandra found she was sore and took two more aspirin and slept with her weapon beside her on the floor of the small suite she had claimed. She woke to the sun shining into the bedroom. She found she was stiff and sore. She brushed her teeth and hair, put on clean slacks and blouse. She noticed her shoes were stained with blood. She pulled out a pair of cross trainers from her luggage and put them on before going downstairs.

Early morning breakfast was being cooked in the kitchen and delivered to the team members at their posts. Cassandra was hungry and was drawn by the smell of the food. She didn't realize it, but she was still carrying the Mexican weapon she had picked up the day before. She leaned the weapon against the living room wall.

She went and talked to the corpsman who was keeping an eye on the wounded. Colonel Mendez was asleep.

Cassandra asked quietly, "How is the Colonel doing?"

"Good. We woke him every hour all night without a problem. It ended up we had to put some more stitches in his scalp because the wound just wouldn't stop bleeding."

"How are the others?"

"They should be alright. Only one wound was serious."

Cassandra nodded, picked up her rifle and left to get something to eat. She walked into the formal dining room to find men sitting on the floor eating quietly. She walked through into the kitchen and got some hot food. She took it out the back door and after praying sat on the ground with her back against the building quietly eating.

She was almost done when Jake came and sat beside her. He bowed his head and prayed over his meal.

When he finished, Cassandra said, "It was a quiet night here, but not to the south."

Jake nodded and said, "The fighting was sporadic all night long."

Bob came out and said, "Three of the recon teams have returned. Stan called in by cell and they will shelter in place until tonight. He said every things A-1, but it would be too dangerous to exfiltrate in daylight. He didn't report in detail because he needed to keep it short."

Cassandra nodded, "Thanks. I guess we should go hear what everyone has to report."

At the meeting, Cassandra learned that indeed the fighting was to the south of the city and the rebels were being driven back but slowly. The government was not in complete control of the Federal District let alone the country.

It was reported the area between the Embassy and the Central District was generally under government control as now was everything within the Federal District. However that did not mean the District was safe. Small units of rebels were causing problems so that the government could not send all their forces to the south.

Criminals had tried to take advantage of the situation, but the government was reacting to the criminals as though they were combatants. There were no trials just firefights and executions.

The meeting ended and Cassandra prepared and sent an encrypted report to Roger in Washington. It read, "Situation here very unstable and dangerous. Pockets of violence still exist in the Federal District although large scale rebellion apparently put down by the government. Fighting continues in the south. One recon team plans to exfiltrate from the south tonight. Will report further when it returns."

Two hours later Cassandra received a short message, *"C. Our aerial reconnaissance correlates with your report. Hold! Dad."*

Cassandra smiled at the personal nature of the message.

Cassandra went outside and sat on a low garden retaining wall. It was a sunny day and Cassandra realized she had lost all track of time. What day of the week was it? She thought it really didn't matter. They were in danger and some of her group might die and in fact there was no guarantee they wouldn't all be killed. Cassandra also presumed a lot of innocents would fall victim to the fighting in the south. She got off the wall and knelt in the grass and started praying. She didn't realize she was praying out loud until she finished and several voices said, "Amen."

Cassandra looked up to find over a dozen soldiers getting off their knees. She stood up and stretched because her muscles were still stiff.

A sergeant came to Cassandra, "Ma'am, Colonel Mendez would like to see you."

Cassandra replied, "Thank you, Sergeant," and headed into the house.

She found the Colonel sitting in the dining room floor eating.

Cassandra said, "Hello, Colonel. You are looking better today."

The Colonel smiled, "Yes I am, thank you. Please sit with me."

Cassandra sat on the floor. The Colonel looked at the rifle she was carrying.

"Is that what you shot Reyes with?"

Cassandra nodded.

"I understand you saved my life."

Cassandra said, "Yes, Colonel."

"Thank you."

"You are most welcome."

The Colonel said, "I think under the circumstances you should call me, Carlos."

"All right, Carlos, I will but only if you call me Cassandra."

The Colonel smiled, "Of course. I will consider it an honor. I need to get in contact with my people."

Cassandra took out the cell phone she had in her pocket, "It may still be working."

The Colonel put down his food and tried it then said, "No service," and handed it back to Cassandra.

He picked up his food and started eating again.

Cassandra said, "After you eat, we'll see if we can establish radio contact with your headquarters."

"Thank you, Cassandra. Are you and your people going to fly home?"

Cassandra shook her head, "No, Carlos. We are staying. I do not intend to leave unless I'm ordered to do so and I do not see that happening. Friends do not abandon their friends when the going gets tough."

The Colonel just nodded understanding as he chewed. They both sat in silence until the Colonel finished his food and stood up. Cassandra followed into the kitchen where he returned the mess kit and said to the soldier who had cooked, "Thank you."

The soldier "snapped to" and said, "You are welcome, sir."

Carlos said, "Cassandra, perhaps we can now see if we can contact my headquarters?"

Cassandra brought him to the radio room and Carlos told the operator the bandwidth to broadcast on. He was able to broadcast in the open and had a short conversation with his headquarters all of which Cassandra overheard and understood as did Cassandra's operator.

After the communication ended Carlos said, "They are sending for me, but they will not broadcast when or how in case someone is listening in. They will contact us when they are very close."

Cassandra said, "Then we will be on alert."

Carlos said, "I would like to go outside into the sunshine."

They walked out to the garden and sat down. Carlos said, "Do you know what is happening?"

Cassandra said, "The Federal District seems to be generally under your government's control, but there is still danger from some small units. I think they are trying to create enough problems to keep some of the army units here. There is continuous fighting in the south and it is my understanding the north is pacified."

Carlos smiled, "Pacified. I like that word."

Cassandra nodded.

Carlos said, "I am glad you are staying. We will remember our friends when this is all over."

Cassandra just nodded, "It seems events are keeping me from meeting your president." She smiled while looking directly into Carlos' eyes and said, "I have to stay until he stops avoiding me."

Carlos laughed, "I will tell him that. He will no doubt find it amusing."

Cassandra handed the rifle she'd been carrying to Carlos, "You may need this and we have our own here."

Carlos said, "Thank you," and took it. "What will you do if attacked?"

"Kill all the attackers and defend the embassy."

Carlos smiled, "What if they come in force?"

Cassandra said, "If they come with a force large enough to take this place then it will be that your government has fallen. I will have no reservation about calling for air cover."

Carlos said, "Your father has your military supplying us with satellite reconnaissance."

Cassandra simply said, "Good."

Jake came to them, "Colonel, some of your people are approaching and waiting for our clearance to come into the compound. We'd like your verification."

Carlos got up, "I guess it is time for me to leave."

He and Cassandra followed Jake to the front gate.

Carlos verified the vehicles were legitimate and they were allowed onto the grounds. Soldiers were bringing the wounded out to the vehicles. Carlos kissed Cassandra on both cheeks and then got into an armored vehicle. The convoy drove off.

The last recon team arrived ten minutes after Carlos left. The team was taken to be fed, but Stan just grabbed a coffee and came to report to Cassandra. She was in the garden sitting at a wrought iron table.

Stan said, "Good morning."

Cassandra said, "It is good to see you, Stan."

"It was a very interesting trip."

"What did you find out?"

Stan took a sip of coffee before speaking, "The army is very hard pressed. They are running low on ammunition for their artillery and we think the air arm is running out of bombs. Apparently their production and supplies were disrupted by sabotage. They seem to have lots of small arms ammunition and of course fuel is not a problem. As a result of the shortages, the army's advance has almost come to a grinding halt."

Cassandra asked, "How reliable is your intelligence source?"

"Very. It comes from inside the army and we verified by observation that the army is conserving ammunition during firefights when the use of concentrated artillery would certainly turn the tide. There have to be problems with military supplies. Apparently Castillo is running the rebellion and he is threatening to blow up Mexico City with a nuke if the generals do not withdraw. The military is not taking him seriously."

Cassandra asked, "What do you think? Does he have another nuke?"

Stan shrugged, "I could not verify it either way. What I can tell you is that the outcome of the battles in the south is far from certain. Castillo is getting a lot of help from somewhere because his forces are still using their artillery and a few tanks unreservedly and that is how they are holding on. The Mexican Army can't use their airplanes and that has made the situation worse for they have most of the combat aircraft, but aren't using them."

Cassandra said, "Is it because they don't have pilots or they are out of munitions?"

Stan said, "I don't know, but I think it is a shortage of munitions. It would be hard to find out."

Cassandra said, "Then I'll have to ask."

Cassandra went to the communication room and sent an urgent message to Washington. A half hour later she was drinking coffee in the garden when the reply came. Cassandra went back to the radio room for a voice communication over an encrypted channel.

Roger came on the line, "Hello, Cassandra."

Cassandra replied, "Hello, Roger."

The radio operator was quite taken aback by the obvious familiarity between the Special Envoy and the Secretary of Defense.

Cassandra added, "I'd venture to guess you are quite busy these days."

Roger said, "Indeed. Your father sends his regards, but he is in a meeting at the moment as a result of your last report."

Cassandra asked, "What do you wish me to do."

"Try to arrange the meeting you proposed. In the meantime, we are working to answer the question you posed about another special cargo. We'll have to get back to you on that."

Cassandra said, "Thank you. What about the planes?"

Roger said, "We have noticed a diminishing air presence in the conflict."

"Do you think it is a question of munitions?"

"We do. They should have more pilots than planes to operate."

Cassandra asked, "Then why haven't they asked for help?"

"That we can't figure out and we are hoping you can clarify that through a face to face."

Cassandra paused, "I'll see what I can do."

Roger said, "Good."

The transmission shut down and Cassandra asked the radio operator, "Do you think you can reach Colonel Mendez for me?"

The answer was, "Yes, ma'am. I have been monitoring their frequency."

Cassandra blurted, "Have you been keeping notes?"

The operator said, "Yes, ma'am," and reached for a yellow lined pad and handed it to her.

She read through the time and dates and a synopsis of the transmission. It became clear munitions were a problem.

Cassandra said, "Keep monitoring this frequency. Keep detailed notes. Can we set up another radio for around the clock monitoring of the channel?"

"Yes ma'am."

Cassandra said, "I need to talk to the major."

Cassandra thought she could kick herself for not thinking to do this. Bob showed up and arranged to have continuous radio and TV monitoring. Cassandra arranged to rotate her CIA personnel to assess the data being monitored and once they had that taken care of she put in a radio call to pass a message to Colonel Mendez.

The message passed on simply said, "The special lady needs to urgently talk to the boss. Please tell Alexander."

Cassandra figured that Carlos would figure out the meaning easily. If not, he would probably radio back. Cassandra was waiting when Bob came to see her.

"We have a visitor, Cassandra. It's one of the embassy staff that was able to escape and go into hiding. He found out we were here and came."

Cassandra said, "Lead on," and got up. She followed Bob to the dining room where an unshaven and disheveled man sat on the floor eating.

Cassandra said, "Hello, I'm Cassandra Crossing."

The man stopped eating and wiped his right hand on his dirty slacks and offered his hand saying, "I'm Anthony Sagan, but everyone calls me Tony. The man took a tattered passport from his front pocket and handed it to Cassandra. She passed it to Bob.

"Please send a message to Washington that Tony has turned up. His family will want to know."

Bob turned and talked to the closest sergeant who hurried away.

Cassandra sat down beside Tony, "You've done well to evade and survive."

Tony hung his head and said, "I was lucky to survive. I took a weapon from a dead marine and fought my way outside. I was able to escape with two women. One was shot in the back as we ran away from the embassy and the other died when the building we were hiding in was struck by an artillery shell."

Cassandra could tell the man was close to his breaking point and changed the subject by asking, "What did you do at the embassy?"

"I worked in consular services. I helped people who had lost their passports."

Cassandra nodded understanding.

Tony asked, "How many other survivors have shown up?"

Cassandra said, "You are the first."

Tony sighed and started crying. Cassandra put her arm around him as he sat sobbing. Bob was back and stood watching awkwardly.

Cassandra said quietly, "Tony will need some clean clothes and toiletries. Would you see if someone can round him up some please, Bob."

Tony wiped his eyes, "I'm sorry. It was awful. They just shot and killed unarmed people with no reason. There were so many dead including women and children. Whole families were in the lobby. Some of my friends died."

Cassandra said, "You can help us. We have no confirmation of those who were killed. You can start a list of those who you know died. First though, you need a shower and some sleep. Tomorrow you can start to work."

Tony said, "Thank you," and got up and one of Bob's men led him upstairs where he could shower.

Sergeant Abernathy came to Cassandra, "You will be glad to know Corporal Mayer got the hot water working."

Cassandra said with a smile, "Please thank the plumbing genius for me."

Abernathy smiled, "Will do."

Greg came into the room and sat down beside Cassandra and handed her a note. It read, "Alexander would like to take you to lunch at the white house tomorrow at the same time as the last luncheon."

Greg said, "I take it that's a code for you are going to meet your friend?"

"Yes, I have a meeting tomorrow afternoon at Los Pinos; the presidential residence. Is there a civilian car around here?"

Bob said, "We didn't find one and I don't think that is the way to go. I think we send a guard."

Greg said, "I think that would draw unwanted attention. I think Cassandra is right. We should go in maybe two civilian cars with perhaps six security men." Greg looked at Cassandra, "I'm going and Stan can keep watch here."

Cassandra nodded.

Bob said, "Where are we going to get two cars?"

Greg said, "Buy them just like everyone else does."

Cassandra said, "Remember they will be diplomatic vehicles so purchase accordingly."

Greg said, "Understood. Are the cells working yet?"

Bob said, "No."

Greg asked, "What about the land lines?"

"Our guys say the lines are dead."

Greg said, "Then I'd better start walking."

Two hours later Greg came back driving a new Mercedes. He left with one of the men and came back with a BMW. Greg went into the embassy building and found Cassandra making notes on the kitchen table.

"Boss you have to come see what I brought home."

Cassandra followed him out the front door. She looked the cars over and smiled looking at Craig.

Greg said, "I got them for a lot less than it would cost at home because I was paying in U.S. dollars. Apparently everyone here is afraid of the peso at the moment."

Bob was inspecting the cars.

Cassandra said, "That solves our transportation problem. What was it like travelling to the dealership?"

"No problem. Things seem pretty calm at the moment."

Cassandra said, "Do you think you could get us some furniture. We could stand to use a lot of beds for the guys to sleep on. What do you think Bob?"

Bob said, "The men would appreciate regular beds."

Greg asked Bob, "Can I borrow three of your guys to go in civilian clothes to help me?"

Bob smiled, "No problem, if you have the clothes. We'd all like to sleep in a bunk."

When Greg left, Bob asked, "You brought cash with you?"

Cassandra said, "Of course. You planned your part and we took care of our part."

Bob smiled, "But you made sure we did our part before we left and I didn't think to check yours."

Cassandra smiled.

Greg came back before dusk with three trucks full of furniture. Some of the embassy security troops unloaded steel bunk beds from the first truck and a few men started assembling them. After all the beds were brought inside some of the troops started unloading double beds for the third floor and some steel office desks as well as several sets of kitchen tables and chairs which were set up in the ballroom for a mess and finally unloaded furniture for the living room. There were also a lot of folding chairs and several unmarked boxes.

It took less than thirty minutes to unload the trucks and send the drivers on their way. Bob had beds distributed throughout the basement and first story so the sleeping troops wouldn't all be in the same place in case of attack. The troops were all smiling and cutting up as they now had some creature comforts. The boxes were the last things to be unpacked and the troops smiled to find they contained cutlery, plates, mugs, coffee makers, and packaged coffee.

A delivery truck pulled up to the main gate and three large heavy boxes were unloaded and brought to the kitchen along with a dozen large bags of charcoal and one hundred and fifty bottles of Mexican beer. The boxes contained three hundred steaks; more than enough for one for each person in the compound. The back patio's brick grill was fired up and the steaks were unpacked. The staff would have to be fed in four shifts, but nobody would complain because they were getting a real meal and not the prepackaged field rations. It was a good meal because everyone ate fresh food.

The night passed without incident. Late the next morning, Cassandra and her small security detail left to meet the President. At their destination the security was tight and there were troops and armored vehicles visible in key locations. Cassandra was expected and she and her party were passed through. Cassandra left her security detail with the cars and was accompanied by a military officer to the waiting room outside the main room where the meeting would take place.

Alejandro was there and came to meet her with, "Good afternoon Cassandra," and kissed her hand. Sparks flew between them and they both realized it.

Cassandra smiled and said, "Good afternoon, Alejandro."

Alejandro said, "This way please," and led her into the study where the President was. Alejandro said, "My President, may I present the Special Envoy of the United States, Her Excellency Cassandra Crossing."

The President who was sitting in a large leather chair stood and offered his hand, "I am pleased to meet you, Envoy Crossing."

"The pleasure is mine, Mr. President."

The President smiled. He was not at all what Cassandra was expecting. She had seen photographs, but she had never met him. He was a man of average build and height, but there the use of average stopped. He had an air of easy authority and she could tell he was a charismatic man. Most women would probably be enthralled with him for he was a very good looking. She knew the president was in his early fifties. He had the touch of grey in his wavy long hair which made him look very distinguished.

The President said, "Please have a seat, señora."

Cassandra chose a chair facing the President and said, "I would consider it an honor, Mr. President, if you would call me by my given name, Cassandra."

The President smiled, "Of course Cassandra and you may call me Enrique."

Cassandra said, "Thank you for the honor, Enrique."

The President asked, "What can we do for you, Cassandra?"

Cassandra smiled, "Perhaps it is what we can do for you, Enrique. I suppose I should now present my credentials."

Enrique said, "It is just us and under the circumstances we can do away with formalities. Consider them accepted and approved."

Cassandra said, "Thank you. Enrique, may I speak very directly?"

Enrique smiled, "That would be a pleasant change; diplomats usually are not direct."

Cassandra nodded agreement, "Yes, but I must admit I am not the usual diplomat."

Enrique laughed lightly, "You amuse me, Cassandra."

Cassandra said, "Good. Friends should get along and I would hope we could be friends."

Cassandra could tell she had Enrique interested.

He said, "But of course. Our countries have been friends and allies for a long time."

Cassandra said, "I meant unofficially more than officially."

The President looked at Alejandro and back to Cassandra, "That implies a certain amount of trust."

Cassandra says, "It does."

The President said, "As a friend what would your expectations be?"

Cassandra said, "Just a friendly relationship. I do not expect either of us would agree to something that is not in the best interest of our countries."

Enrique nodded agreement and said, "Please go on."

"As a token of our friendship I would like on behalf of my President to gift you a sizeable amount of munitions to help you in your fight against the insurgents."

Enrique looked at Alejandro and back to Cassandra, "I am told you were an intelligence-operative."

Cassandra said, "That is true."

"I am also told you saved Colonel Mendez from certain death."

Cassandra said, "That is also true, Enrique."

The President looked at Cassandra, "What else do you know about our current situation?"

Cassandra had decided to be bluntly honest, "It seems you are short on artillery munitions. You also have a lack of munitions for your airplanes. We were surprised that you did not ask for our help sooner."

Enrique said, "Quite frankly, we were offended that you undertook military operations in our country without our knowledge. I understand your concerns about the special cargo, but it would have been better to consult with us. Our national pride was hurt and our pride does not allow us to be beggars."

Cassandra said with what she hoped was the right amount of humility, "On the first point, I understand and apologize. In our defense, at the time we did not know who would have knowledge of the attacks if we told you before hand and if the information would be leaked about the special cargo. On the positive side, we did save the lives of millions of Mexican citizens. I apologize for the harm our actions caused, but we ask you to weigh that against the good we did."

Enrique smiled and said, "I accept your apology. Still we do not want to be seen as beggars going to the Americans with our hat in our hands."

Cassandra said, "I understand. Then we will sell you the munitions you need at our military's delivered cost and you may pay us later in oil when you have defeated the insurrection. It becomes purely a business transaction, but between friends."

Cassandra hoped she was providing a way for Enrique to save face and maintain a strong position.

Enrique asked, "How will the munitions be delivered?"

"I propose we fly immediate supplies into the airport here and the rest will come by ship with a naval escort, if that is agreeable."

Enrique said, "It is agreeable. I will have a list prepared of what we need urgently and what we will need in the coming weeks. Security will be a problem. Our forces have their hands full."

Cassandra asked, "How may we be of assistance?"

Enrique asked, "Would you be agreeable to providing security at the airport to guard the property of the U.S. Government until we can take delivery. Of course, you will need to increase your security detail, but that will be temporary."

Cassandra smiled broadly, "I can see the wisdom in your plan, Enrique. How large a security force do you think we will need?"

Enrique said with a broad smile, "I think a battalion with some light armor would be sufficient to deter any banditry at the airport."

Cassandra said, "We would also need forklifts and trucks."

"We will make them available from the airport."

Cassandra said, "I will contact my superiors about this. I must get approval for the security force, but I will argue for it."

Enrique added, "Tell your father we will be appreciative of your government's cooperation."

Cassandra sighed, "I have a delicate matter and a favor to request, Enrique."

"What is it, Cassandra?"

Cassandra said, "The bodies of those killed at the embassy, we would like to bring them home for burial. There are probably others in hiding and if they are discovered my country would appreciate their return."

Enrique said, “That is agreeable. I will have it seen to. I cannot guarantee we will be able to recover all the bodies, but you have my word we will do our best. You can bring them out on the same airplanes that deliver the munitions.”

Cassandra said, “Thank you.”

Enrique said, “Now that the business is completed, let us have lunch.”

Enrique led them to a small dining room where they had a delightful lunch. It was there that Enrique asked in Spanish, “*Do you speak our language, Cassandra*?”

Cassandra responded in Spanish, “*Of course, Enrique*.”

Cassandra could tell Alejandro was surprised. The conversation would now be in Spanish.

Enrique asked, “*How is it that Alejandro did not know this*?”

Cassandra said, “*He never asked. His English, as yours, is very good so I just followed his lead.*”

Enrique laughed, “*Alejandro, you have a lot to learn about American women*.”

Alejandro looked at Cassandra and smiled, “*I have a lot to learn about women; they are such a mystery.*”

The President laughed then said to Cassandra who was smiling, “*Alejandro is so modest. He was quite the ladies man until he met his poor departed wife.*”

Cassandra said, “*I can believe that.*”

Enrique said, “*He seems to be interested in you, Cassandra.*”

“*It has not escaped my notice, Enrique,*” Cassandra replied glancing at Alejandro.

Enrique laughed again, “*You are such good company, Cassandra. Our official records do not indicate you have ever been in Mexico before, but I suspect you have been. Is my guess right.*”

“*Yes. I have been here many times and sometimes for an extended time.*”

Enrique looked at Cassandra, “*Your Spanish is excellent and you sound like a native speaker so I am not surprised. I suppose at one time it was just as easy to come this way as to go north."*

Cassandra said, "*Yes.*"

Enrique said, "*You were very successful in closing the border.*"

Cassandra said, "*You can thank Mr. Castillo for that.*"

Enrique said, "*Yes. His ambition to become dictator changed a lot of things.*"

Cassandra said, "*The world will be better off when he leaves it.*"

Enrique said, "*I would very much like to help him on his journey.*"

Cassandra laughed lightly, "*We are agreed on that.*"

Enrique added, "*Unfortunately we can't seem to pin down his location. We get conflicting reports of his whereabouts.*"

After lunch Enrique walked beside her back to her vehicles. Along the way Enrique said, "*If it is agreeable, I will have Colonel Mendez bring a liaison officer to stay with you.*"

Cassandra said, "*That is agreeable and will be very helpful.*"

She and her security detail were escorted back to the embassy by several armored vehicles which peeled off when her security detail entered the embassy grounds. The cars pulled up to the front of the embassy building where Bob was standing waiting for her.

He asked, "How did it go?"

"It went better than I hoped. I have to contact Washington. Tell the gate that Colonel Mendez will be coming with a liaison officer."

Cassandra went inside and immediately contacted her father. A half hour later, she was on an encrypted conference call with her father, Roger, Chas and the Chairman of the Joint Chiefs. A plan was agreed to in principle.

It was late afternoon when a small motorcade pulled up to the Embassy gates. The vehicles were passed in and Cassandra went to meet them at the front door. Colonel Mendez got out with a middle aged man in civilian clothes.

Cassandra went to Carlos and embraced him and said in Spanish, *"It is good to see you again, Carlos."*

Carlos said, *"Cassandra, may I present Captain Diego Vargas-Ramirez."*

Cassandra said, *"I am pleased to meet you, señor."*

Vargas-Ramirez said, *"The honor is mine Doña Cassandra Crossing."*

Cassandra said, *"I am glad the President sent someone from CISEN. We will be able to cut through much red tape. Welcome."*

CISEN or the Centro de Investigación y Seguridad Nacional translates as the Center for Research and National Security; Mexico's security agency. Cassandra had an instinct for recognizing operatives, but she had direct knowledge of this man in particular.

Diego smiled, *"Yes, I understand we have a background in common."*

Cassandra said, *"Yes, but since I have become such a public figure my duties have changed."*

Diego changed to English and said, "Yes, but once a, how do they call it in English, yes a spook then always a spook."

Cassandra laughed and responded in English, "I can see we will get along just fine, Diego. Diego let me introduce you to my head of security Major Sharp."

The two men shook hands.

Cassandra said, "Please come in gentlemen."

They went into the living room and Cassandra could see Diego looking at the spray paint on the walls.

Cassandra said, "You will have to pardon the walls, but the press of other business has not yet allowed us to redecorate."

Diego smiled broadly at Cassandra's humor and asked, "You did not find it offensive?"

Cassandra smiled, "I understood the motive, so it is of no consequence. What I find offensive is when someone starts shooting at us."

Diego smiled and said, "I agree with that."

Carlos interjected, "Have you talked to your father?"

"Yes. Please tell the President it is agreed. The plans on our end are already started. The first planes will be ready within forty eight hours of my sending your list on. As soon as we have the arrangements completed on this end, the flights can start."

Chapter 4 – The Unexpected

Carlos took some documents from his briefcase and said, "This is the paperwork to accredit you, to allow your security to take charge of the airport for purposes of protecting cargo going to the military, and the agreement to purchase the artillery and aircraft munitions along with a private letter from my President to yours." He pulled out another paper, "This is the list of our needs."

Cassandra looked the list over and said, "Very good."

She turned to Bob and handed him the list which he passed to a sergeant who left to transmit it.

Cassandra said, "The most dangerous time will be the initial flights until we have sufficient security on the ground. We need to scout the location."

Carlos pulled out a map of the airport and laid it on the coffee table, "Given there are no commercial flights coming into the airport we have many options. This building is currently empty and next to a taxiway. It has toilet and shower facilities that were used for air crews and passengers. We suggest that be the temporary barracks. We further suggest this other building be used for storage."

Cassandra looked at Bob, "Isn't it too close?"

Bob said, "I agree it is just too close to the place where our men will be billeted. I suggest we off load directly to trucks and have constant flow of trucks taking the offloaded cargo directly to the battle front or air stations. We can schedule flights so the planes are arriving and departing in sequence. If any cargo is intercepted between the airport and the front lines it will be only a small part. I don't like the idea of storing any munitions within buildings."

Cassandra looked at Carlos, "Could that be arranged?"

Carlos said, "Yes. We will use commercial trucks driven by soldiers as well as military trucks."

Bob said, "We can do the offloading right here," and pointed to the map.

Carlos said, "If there is a delay the loaded trucks could be dispersed throughout the airport.

Bob said, "That is a good idea."

Carlos said, "Then we have a plan."

Cassandra said, "Yes, but I'd like some of our people to get a look at it on the ground and get agreement from the people who will actually be conducting the operation."

Bob asked, "When can we scout the airport?"

Carlos said, "We can go now."

Cassandra said, "Bob, who do you want to go? I'll stay here."

Bob said, "I will go and I'll take Justin and a squad of my guys to make an assessment report."

Cassandra saw Colonel Mendez and Diego watching the interactions. She asked, "Is that agreeable, Colonel?"

"Yes."

Cassandra turned to Diego, "Would you like to accompany the major or stay here with me?"

Diego replied, "I'd like to go. My knowledge of the airport might be useful."

Bob said, "He's right."

Cassandra nodded agreement, "Then it is agreed."

Fifteen minutes later the little convoy left with a new addition; two U.S. armored personnel carriers transporting Bob's squad and Diego. Cassandra went inside and reported to Washington on what was happening and her suggestions for additions to the list Colonel Mendez had given her. She told them Major Sharp had left to do a site assessment at the airport.

The military had some specific things they wanted to know that they could not get from the satellite surveillance. Cassandra made notes and after the communication ended she reached Bob on an encrypted radio and asked him to address the questions.

It was dark when Bob returned to the Embassy compound. His vehicles pulled onto the Embassy grounds, but the Mexican vehicles stopped on the street long enough to drop Diego. Diego got out carrying a bag and came to the embassy building where Bob assigned him officers' quarters then went to the radio room to forward his report. Afterward, Bob and Diego came to see Cassandra, who was sitting in a folding chair on the roof thinking. Bob took the vacant chair beside her and Diego one opposite her.

Bob said, "The first few flights will be the most dangerous until we get more troops on the ground. I radioed our site report. Diego was very helpful. My squad stayed to keep an eye out for trouble. I suppose they will send a colonel in to command the battalion. Will I report to him or you?"

Cassandra said, "To me."

Bob said, "Understood, though a colonel may find that difficult."

Cassandra said, "Don't worry about that. I have been delegated command of all resources here."

She also knew the man who would be in command.

Bob said, "Yes, ma'am."

Cassandra added, "I'm sending one of my civilian people back with a diplomatic pouch on the first plane that arrives. I'd like three of your men to help Stan make sure it gets to the airport. I'm also sending Tony home. They are sending me four more civilian employees so we'll need to send both cars."

"I'll assign three very good men."

Cassandra said, "A battalion will start arriving tomorrow afternoon to guard the airport. Your responsibility will be embassy security. We have to get this place respectable."

Bob said, "It's not good that no more survivors have shown up."

Cassandra said, "No it isn't."

Diego added, "There is still hope, Excellency."

Cassandra nodded and smiled, "Thank you, Diego." She paused and said, "It is late and I'm tired. Please excuse me gentlemen, I will see you both in the morning."

Cassandra got up and went to her room and crawled into bed. She slept fitfully waking several times from nightmares about the missing embassy staff and dependents. The next morning she rose early and exercised then showered. She was drinking coffee in the kitchen when her phone rang. She looked at the phone and saw it was Colonel Mendez calling.

"Good morning, Carlos."

"Good morning Cassandra. Would it be acceptable if I come to see you?"

"Of course, when do you want to come?"

Carlos asked, "Are you available now."

"Yes."

"I will see you shortly."

Cassandra picked up her radio and called the front gate to advise them the Colonel was coming. She also advised Bob and Diego. It was less than an hour later that the colonel came to the Embassy. He had about thirty soldiers with him. It was unusual that there was a commercial bus in the little convoy that was passed onto the embassy grounds.

Cassandra came out to meet the Colonel with Bob and Diego. Carlos got out of an armored vehicle with the captain who had returned Cassandra's back pack. Cassandra greeted the colonel.

"Hello, Carlos."

Carlos said as he embraced Cassandra, "I am glad to see you under happy circumstances."

Cassandra smiled at the captain, "Good morning Captain and thank you again for your thoughtfulness in returning my pack."

The captain smiled and bowed his head in acknowledgement.

The bus doors opened and disheveled civilians started exiting the bus.

Carlos said, "They are some of the embassy personnel and dependents that escaped. "

Cassandra blurted enthusiastically, "God bless you and your men Carlos," and hugged him and it was not the formal embrace they usually exchanged.

She let go of Carlos and looked at the survivors.

There were thirty or so civilians; men, women and children. They were dirty and looked stressed. Most had large dark circles under their eyes. It was obvious by the way their clothes hung on them that they had experienced some weight loss. They were milling around and Cassandra went to them and raised her voice.

"Welcome to the new American Embassy. You will be safe here. We will get you fed while we arrange transportation back home."

That brought excited comments and the group started hugging each other and celebrating.

Cassandra exchanged glances with Stan. Stan knew what needed to be done. He rushed away to get organized to interview the survivors and put together an initial report to send to Washington.

Soldiers came and started talking to the rescued people. Many of the civilians were sobbing and a few of the women broke down altogether; relieved that they were finally safe. Jake took control and assigned soldiers to get the civilians situated.

Cassandra started walking toward the embassy with Carlos. His captain followed behind them.

Carlos said. "Various units discovered your people hiding in different parts of the city, but didn't know what to do with them until they got the president's order."

"Thank you for getting them back safely, Carlos."

A woman approached Cassandra and Carlos and interrupted, "I'm Marilyn Mayhew. I am the first secretary."

Cassandra smiled and offered her hand, "I am pleased to meet you, Marilyn."

Marilyn Mayhew was a career diplomat and she didn't know who the young woman dressed so informally in a blouse, slacks and cross trainers was. Marilyn decided the young woman's age and the fact she was wearing a side arm meant she could not be anyone of consequence.

Marilyn raised an eyebrow and said officiously, "I am Ms. Mayhew. I demand to see the ambassador."

Cassandra smirked, "My name is Cassandra Crossing. I am the Special Envoy to Mexico. The ambassador is deceased. We are in the process of arranging your return to Washington. In the meantime, there will be a lot of questions about what you went through. One of my people will talk with you."

Ms. Mayhew was somewhat taken aback, "You are in charge?"

Cassandra said, "Yes. Now you must excuse us, Ms. Mayhew, as the colonel and I have business. Please join the others."

The woman hesitated before leaving and joining the group of survivors.

Carlos looked at Cassandra and said, "The previous ambassador must have trained that one."

Cassandra said, "I take it you knew the ambassador?"

Carlos smiled, "Between friends, I tell you he was a pompous and officious man, rest his soul." Carlos made a sign of the cross then continued, "The president could not tolerate to be around him and that affected our relationship."

Cassandra sighed, "I'm sorry, Carlos. I hope the new ambassador is someone you will be able to work with. It is important that we have a good relationship."

Carlos nodded in agreement, "We have discussed just that thing."

"Carlos, would you do me the honor of joining me for breakfast? It will be soldiers fare, but well prepared."

"It will be my pleasure, Cassandra."

Cassandra asked, "Have your men eaten?"

"Not since last night."

"Then if it is agreeable, I will arrange breakfast for them as well."

Carlos smiled, "That would be appreciated."

Carlos looked at his Captain who nodded and hurried off without a word passing between them.

Cassandra led Carlos into the dining area, "Please have a seat Carlos and I'll arrange food."

Carlos nodded and took a seat as Cassandra went to the kitchen. She advised the staff there that they would have the rescued civilians to feed as well as about thirty Mexican soldiers. The Sergeant in charge said they'd get right on it and suggested as they had some steaks left they might cut them into breakfast portions to serve with eggs and fresh bread to the Mexican military who had rescued the civilians. They would cook bacon and eggs for the survivors. Cassandra smiled and approved the suggestion.

When she returned to the table, she found Bob and Carlos talking. Carlos was giving Bob a report on the military situation. Cassandra sat and listened.

"Since we are no longer concerned about conserving our munitions, we are making significant progress in pushing the enemy southward. We are still mopping up small pockets of resistance and banditry, but we are confident with the munitions being supplied we will be successful in putting down the rebellion in a matter of weeks. We believe the enemy has left behind small units to carry out attacks behind our lines. We are searching them out, but with some difficulty."

Bob commented, "That is likely to take awhile."

"Yes," Carlos answered with a shrug, "but the outcome is now inevitable."

Bob nodded and Cassandra wondered if it was in agreement or just acknowledgement. She was not so certain the outcome was inevitable. Carlos gave them more specific information regarding the situation as they ate.

Cassandra asked, "Bob, has Washington been advised that our friends have rescued some of our people?"

Bob said, "Yes. A list of names has probably already been sent. I requested to return the civilians on the transports bringing the troops, in accordance with your statement to the survivors."

Cassandra said, "Good."

Carlos asked, "I understand the first flights will arrive as scheduled."

Cassandra smiled, "Yes, Carlos. They should start landing in about two hours."

"The president has asked me to be at the airport to greet them."

Cassandra said, "I think I should go as well. It will ease the way as I have worked closely with the commander of the battalion."

Carlos smiled, "I would welcome the company."

Cassandra turned to Diego, "Would you care to accompany me, Diego?"

Diego smiled, "But of course, Excellency."

Cassandra said, "Bob, perhaps you could spare two armored vehicles to accompany us. The incoming troops will be less concerned with our little convoy if the embassy cars are accompanied by U.S. troops."

Cassandra looked at Carlos who smiled and nodded agreement. A sergeant delivered a message to Bob who read it and looked at Cassandra, "The civilians will be taken out on the return flight."

Cassandra said, "Good. Then everything is organized. Why don't we have coffee in the garden before we start on our journey?"

Bob said, "I'll be there as soon as I arrange your escort."

Cassandra nodded and the rest of the party went to the garden. Once seated, Diego was the first to speak and he did so in Spanish, *"Excellency, I am curious as to why you are so gracious?"*

Cassandra knew what he asked was not what he really meant. A coffee tray was brought to the wrought iron table at which the party was sitting and the soldier started pouring coffee for the little group. Cassandra waited until the coffee was poured and the soldier left before responding.

"Diego, I really believe that it is in the best interest of both our countries to have the most open and friendly of relationships. For my part, I intend that my personal relationships with your leaders be at least cordial, constructive, and honest. I truly hope for more. I want us to

be true friends who can and do trust each other. I am willing to wait to earn that trust. Well at least waiting for as much time as I am here in an official capacity."

Carlos said, "*What does your intelligence tell you about our progress?"*

Cassandra said, "*I have not sent out any reconnaissance once we were reasonably assured of our safety. As for the other, I know you are privy to the satellite reconnaissance my government has provided you."*

Carlos nodded and looked up as Bob returned to the table, "Everything's arranged. We can leave just as soon as the civilians are fed and on the bus."

They spent some time talking about more pleasant times. After everyone had been fed, a sergeant came and said the civilians were on the bus.

Carlos smiled, "With your permission Cassandra, let us be on our way."

Cassandra nodded in agreement and the party got up and left. Cassandra climbed into one of the embassy cars with Diego and Carlos. Stan was in the front seat with the driver. The drive to the airport was uneventful and there was a significant amount of traffic on the roads now. It was a sure sign life in the city was returning to some semblance of normality. The convoy arrived at the airport fifteen minutes before the military planes were scheduled to arrive.

The civilians were offloaded from the bus and led into one of the passenger lounges to await aircraft boarding. Cassandra went with them. The air conditioning in the terminal building was now operational and it was quite comfortable.

Cassandra had the survivors seated and said, "Military transports will be arriving shortly. You will be leaving on them when they depart, but that may take some time. In the meantime try to make yourselves as comfortable as possible."

The survivors started clapping and one woman came and embraced Cassandra, "Thank you."

Cassandra nodded and left the survivors in the care of two of Jake's men and went outside with Stan.

Jake was talking with Carlos as Cassandra approached, "The planes will land and the security force will unload in quick time to form a perimeter. I respectfully suggest that I station at the skirt of the taxiway to meet the first incoming plane. I also suggest you accompany me and the Special Envoy to meet the battalion commander who is likely to be on one of the first planes in."

Cassandra added, "We'll take the embassy cars onto the skirt as well."

Carlos said, "That will be acceptable. We can arrange an orderly turnover of the airport. We have set up our security in the closest repair building and we can go there to talk."

One of Jake's men, Sergeant Calvin came running up, "Sir, they are ahead of schedule and ten klicks out on approach."

The group hurried to their vehicles and drove to the agreed spot to wait for the planes to land. Cassandra and her group got out of their vehicles with Carlos and Diego. One Mexican military vehicle had accompanied them.

The first plane landed and taxied to disembark close to where the little group was waiting. The rear gate came down and two combat vehicles drove off and men jogged down the ramp and started for predetermined positions. A small group was headed toward Cassandra's people. Jake and his men snapped to attention and saluted.

Matt Brite returned the salute and approached Cassandra and said, "Madame Special Envoy," and saluted.

Cassandra said, "We are happy to see you, Matt," and embraced him.

Matt laughed, "It is good to see you, Cassandra."

Cassandra spoke in Spanish, *"Matt, this is my friend Colonel Carlos Mendez who commands the Federal Military District and Diego Sanchez my liaison with Mexican intelligence. This is Captain Jake Moore of the Embassy security detail. This is my friend Brigadier General Matt Brite."*

Carlos saluted and said, *"General."*

Matt returned the salute and responded in Spanish, "*Colonel, I am very pleased to meet you. Any friend of Cassandra's is a friend of mine.*" Matt turned to Diego, "*I think you and Cassandra have much in common.*"

Diego smiled and said in English, "*So it seems, General.*"

Matt offered his hand and the two men shook. Matt looked at Jake, "It is good to see you again, Jake."

"Thank you, sir," Jake responded.

Carlos changed the conversation to English, "We established a headquarters over there in a maintenance building. My men have been instructed to withdraw as your men take up positions."

Matt said, "With the Special Envoy's permission, please lead on, Carlos."

Carlos said, "Of course, General."

The second plane had landed and taxied and was offloading as the third plane approached the airport. There were soldiers taking up positions all around the airport. A platoon was following them as they headed for the maintenance building.

At the building, the security platoon with the general broke into squads and one hurried off to make certain the building was secure. Jake's armored vehicles had followed them to the building and two of the General's showed up and took up positions as the party entered the building. Through the hanger doors, they could see another cargo plane had landed and was off loading. Soldiers were jogging toward the perimeter buildings of the airport and combat vehicles were rushing to take up positions.

Chairs were brought for the party to sit on and Matt waited for Cassandra to sit and then took a seat. When they were all seated Matt asked, "When will your trucks arrive Carlos?"

"They have been assembled in a parking lot close by and are ready on very short notice."

Matt asked, "Do you have helicopter pilots available Carlos?"

Carlos said, "General, I'm sorry, but our helicopters are on combat duty."

Matt looked at Cassandra, "I guess I let the cat out of the bag."

Cassandra shrugged and asked Matt, "When will they arrive?"

"They are coming on alternate planes after the first two loaded with munitions off load."

Cassandra said to Carlos, "I arranged for four helicopters for use by the embassy. Right now we have no use for them, so I would appreciate it if you would keep them operational." She smiled at Carlos, "You might wish to arrange for pilots for four helicopters and door gunners. I thought you might like to have them to fly air cover for your munitions convoys to make sure the helicopters stay in operating condition."

Carlos smiled, "I will be extremely pleased to see they are kept operational." The Colonel smiled and added, "That is a very generous and appreciated loan, Cassandra. The President will be very appreciative as am I. At the moment, we have more pilots than aircraft."

Carlos looked at one of his officers who hurried away to make arrangements without being ordered.

The group had a ring side seat as the planes landed and unloaded their troops and cargo. A truck had finished refueling the first plane that arrived.

Stan came into the hanger and came up behind Cassandra and said, "The survivors are ready to get on a plane home."

Cassandra nodded and said, "Excuse me please, gentlemen, while I say goodbye to our folks headed stateside."

She walked to one of the embassy cars. The men watched Cassandra leave.

Carlos asked, "Have you known Cassandra a long time, General?"

"Yes, Carlos. I met her some years ago when I was serving abroad and that is about all I can say. She is a remarkable woman."

Carlos said, “Did you know she saved my life?”

“No, but nothing she does would surprise me based upon my past experience.” Matt added, “Well, things are going so well it does not appear we have a lot to do.”

Carlos looked at Matt and said, “Good planning sometimes has that result, General. No?”

Matt smiled, “Sometimes, Carlos. Why don’t you call me Matt?”

Carlos smiled, “Of course, Matt.”

Another Mexican Army Colonel approached and saluted Carlos who returned the salute as did Matt. Carlos introduced him to the General. Carlos said, “The Colonel will be in charge of arranging the convoys.”

It was not lost on Matt that there were obviously Colonels and then there were Colonels like Carlos whose influence was far beyond his rank. Matt turned to his Executive Officer, “Ben please co-ordinate the transport with the Colonel.”

“Yes sir.”

The American Colonel turned to the Mexican Colonel and they left to coordinate the off loading of cargo. Several forklifts driven by Mexican military men had appeared and headed toward where the cargo planes were parking. Hanging on the side of each of the forklifts was an American soldier who was a specialist in combat loading and spoke Spanish.

Carlos got up, “Well Matt, the airport is for the time being under your command. I will accompany Cassandra back to her embassy.”

Matt smiled, “Thank you, Colonel.”

Matt stood up and the men shook hands.

Carlos and his aide followed him as he walked to his vehicle and drove to meet Cassandra. Cassandra had finished saying her goodbyes to the survivors and was returning to her car as Carlos arrived. Carlos got out and approached her.

Cassandra said, “I think it is time for me to return to the embassy, Carlos. I just have to wait for the new vehicles Washington has sent for embassy use.”

Carlos said, "I and my men will of course accompany you to the embassy."

"Thank you, Carlos. Would you and Diego care to ride with me back to the embassy in one of the new vehicles?"

Cassandra had not sooner gotten the words out than two large black SUVs came across the tarmac to pick up the party. They were followed by Jake's armored vehicle.

Carlos looked at Cassandra smiling, "I suppose the new vehicles are armored."

Cassandra, looked at Carlos smiled and said, "I certainly hope so or Washington wasted a lot of money and effort to get them here."

The return trip to the Embassy was uneventful. Carlos and Cassandra talked about the changes that were occurring in the city. Stan and Diego listened as the Colonel shared where they could find furniture suitable for the Embassy building and even recommended a contractor who could be trusted and would do good work.

The four embassy vehicles entered the embassy compound followed by Carlos' vehicle and Bob's armored vehicles. The rest of the Mexican Army vehicles parked on the street. Once out of the vehicle, Carlos said, "Cassandra, I apologize, but Diego and I must report to the President, so we will leave now with your permission."

Cassandra smiled, "Of course, Carlos. Give my regards to the President," then paused before adding, "and to the Interior Secretary of course."

Carlos smiled and said, "Of course," and then went to his vehicle and left.

Cassandra turned to Stan, "Did you make note of the businesses Carlos recommended."

"Yes."

"Perhaps tomorrow we could purchase furnishings."

"Consider it done."

Bob came to meet Cassandra, "How do you think it went?"

"Smoothly, Bob. I think I'll go freshen up. If you will excuse me gentlemen," and with that Cassandra went into the building and headed to her room. The electricity was on and the central air was working and Cassandra thought it felt good. She went to her room and showered. She was delighted to find the water was still hot. Refreshed, she put on clean clothes and went to the rooftop.

She found Jake's men had brought up one of the umbrella tables and some chairs from the garden. She went and sat down. She thought about what would come next. Soon it would be stable enough to bring the Ambassador from Washington. She did not know how wrong she was nor how that would complicate her life.

Stan showed up with Greg and the new embassy employees who had come in on the plane. Cassandra had specifically requested this group.

Cassandra said, "Take a seat gentlemen and lady." The little group took seats around the table and Cassandra greeted them, "It is good to see you all again. We have a liaison officer from Mexican security who is very sharp. His name is Diego Sanchez."

Another of the group, Mike Moore, asked, "The Diego Sanchez?"

Cassandra nodded, "Yes. Izzy and Rory you will be part of my personal security detail for when we are off the grounds. Diego will of course assume you are CIA, but in this case it doesn't matter. Amanda you will serve as my personal assistant and that will give you the opportunity to observe things I might miss and watch my back. Mike, with your business degree background you will be serving as my Administrative Attaché. We have to get this place up and running so there is a lot to do. The work will give you the opportunity to see how the city is really functioning."

The group looked at the newcomer who had come onto the roof. Bob came to the table and Cassandra introduced him.

Bob said, "I'm pleased to meet all the resident spooks."

The group looked at Cassandra who said, "Bob knows pretty much all that goes on around here."

Bob added wryly, "Including the baggage they brought that I have under guard."

Cassandra said, "Our next issue is to figure out how we turn this into a working embassy. I would like you to put your heads together with Bob and his people to figure out security within the building. I think we will use the third floor as we are now for residences and the second floor for temporary offices. We need to better arrange quarters for the troops as we will eventually need to use the entire main floor for entertaining and offices, but I'm open to suggestions. Perhaps we can turn the outbuildings, including the garages, into troop accommodations and use some of the spaces here for officer's quarters. We have a substantial budget for construction and acquisition, but remember we can't have the place looking like an armed camp. At the same time, I want it to be one."

It was Greg who said, "I suggest we buy the place next door. It would be cheaper than building and give us more room right away."

Cassandra asked, "What makes you think it is for sale?"

"There is realtor's for sale sign in front of it."

Cassandra said, "Mike, it will be your first task to research that."

Mike nodded, "Sure thing, boss."

Greg said, "Mike, you'll have to be careful about that. It goes for all of us. Cassandra is no longer just in charge. She's a diplomat and we have to act as such."

Mike said, "Understood."

Cassandra asked, "Is there anything else?"

Bob said, "I'll move some of my guys downstairs, ma'am."

Cassandra nodded then said, "Then why don't you all go get settled in."

The group was dispersing when Cassandra's phone rang. It was Alejandro. "Hello, Cassandra."

"Hello, Alejandro. It is good to hear from you."

Alejandro paused, "I ask you to accompany me to dinner tomorrow evening at the president's home. It will be a formal affair."

"I'd be delighted, Alejandro."

Alejandro said, "I will come for you at five if that is acceptable?"

"It is."

"I will see you then, Cassandra."

The call ended and Cassandra sat thinking about what she would do next. It was late in the day, but possibly she could resolve her dilemma this evening. She had Amanda come back. She explained her dilemma and Amanda went off to make some calls.

Greg came carrying the "diplomatic case" that had come on the plane from Washington. He handed it to Cassandra who said, "We'd better go inside before I open this."

Inside they went to Cassandra's sitting room in which there was now a card table and two chairs. Cassandra opened the case with the combination only she knew. On the top of the case was an envelope which she could tell was addressed to her in her father's handwriting. She read it and put it back in the envelope. There was another and it was from Chas. her father's Secretary of State. She read the note. She looked at Stan, "You'd better have Bob come up."

Cassandra sat thinking. This changed everything and it was not something she wanted and it would create all kinds of problems. She kept turning the situation over in her mind and finally came to the conclusion the upsides outweighed the downsides for both her and the country. It made a certain kind of sense.

Greg came back with Stan. Cassandra said, "I need to tell you what has happened. It seems my friend the president called my father the president. The Mexican president now considers me the unofficial ambassador and he wants me to be appointed the official ambassador. He didn't drop a hint, but came right out and asked if that would be possible and did it formally."

Bob said, "I suppose that is unusual?"

"Yes and it presents some unusual political problems for my father. I did not see this one coming."

"Ambassador to Mexico will look good on your curriculum vitae."

Cassandra shook her head in disbelief and asked, "Where do you come up with this stuff, Bob?"

"I'm just a natural I guess."

Cassandra said, "Well, if I'm Ambassador that will make you Military Attaché."

Bob said, "Crap. I hate hob knobbing."

"Careful Bob, you are an officer and a gentleman."

"Yes, Madame Ambassador," Bob said with just a hint of sarcasm.

Cassandra said, "It is only that simple in the short term, Bob. My appointment requires confirmation by the Senate. As the Senate is in recess I have been appointed, but I will have to be confirmed by the Senate before the end of the next session of Congress. The president had to scramble and apparently has gathered commitment of enough votes to make that happen. Bob, as of now you are the military attaché. Your orders came in the diplomatic pouch. You were on the promotions list and that made it easier. As you say, this will look good on your curriculum vitae, Colonel."

Bob smiled, "Yes, ma'am, and thank you. Under normal circumstances I would not have made promotion this time around. I guess I will now really have to clean up my act."

Cassandra ignored the remark and said, "The Secretary of State is arranging for me to interview several career foreign-service officers as possible candidates for a Deputy Chief of Mission. I will need an encrypted link for the video calls."

Bob said, "Consider it done ma'am. When will you need it up?"

"I'll need a connection starting at two in the afternoon the day after tomorrow for about two hours. We have a lot to do. Is there anything else?"

Greg said, "What are your plans for the morning?"

"We'll be going shopping, so I will need a security detail. Tomorrow evening I will be attending a social function at the president's home, but I will be accompanied by Alejandro who I am sure will provide security."

Greg nodded, "What time do you want to leave in the morning?"

"Eight forty five. The advance team should leave about fifteen minutes earlier."

Amanda knocked on the door frame. Cassandra said, "Come in Amanda," and then, "If there is nothing else gentlemen, Amanda and I have business."

The men smiled and left and Amanda took a seat. Cassandra asked, "How did you make out?"

"As in any major city, money talks and so does a high profile. Several well known designers agreed to bring over creations for you to view. I gave them your sizes."

Cassandra said, "Good work. You make a good personal assistant."

Amanda said with a grin, "And in a pinch I can use a gun."

By nine that evening Cassandra had purchased a gown, a purse, and shoes. The designer's staff would make the slight alterations required overnight and deliver the goods by mid-morning. Jewelry would have to wait until the morning.

Cassandra slept well that night. No longer could gunfire be heard in the distance as the rebels had been pushed further south. Cassandra rose early and exercised as best she could, then showered and got ready. She made a list of furnishings she needed for her small suite which consisted of a bedroom, bath and sitting room. She described in point form what she wanted and the colors as well as the exercise equipment she'd need. The incline treadmill and weight training machine would fit in her very large bedroom.

Cassandra went downstairs to get breakfast and when she took a seat in the dining room Bob came over to talk to her.

She greeted him, "Good morning, Colonel."

"Good morning, Ambassador."

Cassandra noted Bob was already wearing the insignia of his new rank. She said, "Would you care to join me for breakfast."

Bob sat down and Cassandra said with a smile, "You might want to have your men's dress uniforms shipped here in a couple of weeks. Hopefully, we will soon be attending formal functions."

"Yes ma'am, but I think you may be overly optimistic."

They talked as they ate a light breakfast.

An advance team left at eight thirty to make sure there were no unpleasant surprises waiting for Cassandra at the jewelers. Cassandra's little convoy left at eight forty five and arrived at the jewelers at five after nine. Cassandra chose a stunning silver necklace inlaid with Mexican fire opals and matching bracelet. She left it to Stan to negotiate for her as she drank coffee. She knew this was how the game was played here.

Stan was able to strike a very good purchase because the transaction was paid for in U.S. currency with small bills. At this time when people were still leery of the peso, the dollar was king. That gave Cassandra an idea.

They returned to the embassy and Cassandra called Washington to make personal arrangements. She then made a call to her bank in New York. It took some doing, but her personal packet would arrive on a flight the next morning.

Cassandra went out to the garden to drink a cup of coffee. A sergeant came to tell her Diego was on his way. Cassandra nodded and said, "Thank you, Sergeant."

Diego came and said, "Good morning, Cassandra."

Cassandra got up and greeted him, "Yes it is, Diego."

Diego took her hand gently and bowed his head ever so slightly.

Diego said, "I am amazed that I'm allowed to wander around here freely, Your Excellency."

Cassandra smiled broadly and said with exaggerated drama, "Why not? You are an ally and a friend of the ambassador after all."

Diego laughed.

Cassandra became serious, "How is the war going?"

"Things are going very well in the south. I am still worried that there are still some traitors in hiding here in the city. They might yet cause trouble."

"And if they do, we are likely to be a target."

Diego nodded, "I am afraid so. Your security assigned by the president will be substantial. Is that acceptable?"

"Of course it is acceptable, Diego. Are you to accompany me?"

Diego said, "I have been entrusted with your security by the interior minister."

"Then I am in good hands. Please ride with me in one of our embassy cars.

"It will be as you wish."

Cassandra changed the subject, "Diego, I have a personal request."

"How may I be of service?"

Cassandra said, "Do you know a realtor you can recommend? I would like to purchase a home here in Mexico."

Diego smiled, "Yes. I know of a man who can be trusted with such business on a confidential basis. I will have him come to meet you at your convenience."

Cassandra said, "Thank you Diego. Perhaps he could come tomorrow afternoon."

Mike Moore came to the roof top. Cassandra greeted him, "Hello, Mike."

Mike said, "Madame Ambassador. Captain Sanchez."

Cassandra smiled, "What do you have for me, Mike?"

Mike handed her some papers which she read and commented, "It seems to be a good price, Mike."

"Some people are still afraid. Fear is a strong motivator, but I am not sure what the real market value is under the circumstances."

Diego looked at Cassandra and she said, "The estate next door is for sale. We are considering purchasing it to expand the embassy, if I can talk Enrique into agreeing."

Diego smiled, "How could he refuse such a request? In fact, I will ask the president on your behalf. Why not let my friend purchase it for you so he can share in the commission? You will probably also get a better deal that way. He is very knowledgeable about such things. I'll have him come to meet you if that is acceptable."

Cassandra nodded, "Mike, I'll leave that up to you." Cassandra looked at Diego, "Thank you, Diego."

Diego nodded, "I'll go with Mike to make arrangements." The two men got up and left.

Chapter 5 – The Saving Social Event

Stan came onto the rooftop, "It seems your gown for this evening has arrived. Your personal assistant suggests you come and try it on to make sure it is to your liking before the seamstress leaves."

Cassandra got up, "Thank you, Stan." She went and tried the gown on and it fit perfectly. Cassandra was very pleased with the way she looked in the dress. She considered it to be very chic.

At six o'clock, Cassandra was waiting on the sofa for her escort to arrive. Sergeant Kelsey came to tell her the escort had arrived. Cassandra went to the door to find Alejandro was there with Diego.

Alejandro said, "You are beautiful, Cassandra."

Diego added, "I would say stunning is an appropriate description."

Cassandra said, "You gentlemen look quite handsome this evening. I would say we all clean up nicely."

Alejandro offered his arm and Cassandra took it and they walked to Alejandro's vehicle. Cassandra thought she liked being on Alejandro's arm. He held the door open and she slipped in the back seat. Diego took the front passenger's seat and Alejandro went around and got in the other side. One of the embassy armored SUVs with Cassandra's personal security slipped into line behind them. They were also escorted by three vehicles filled with Mexican security men as they left for the president's residence.

Cassandra said, "I am looking forward to this evening."

Alejandro said, "We have to get back to some semblance of normality."

Cassandra said, "I understand. Perception affects how one views reality."

Diego smiled, "That is something that someone in my profession would say."

Cassandra returned the smile, "I think I read that in a manual you wrote, Diego."

Diego smiled, "I will not ask how you came to read my manual."

"Thank you for that, Diego."

Alejandro interjected, "I am jealous that you two have so much in common."

Cassandra smiled, "I am flattered that you are jealous."

Diego laughed, "She has your measure, Alejandro."

Cassandra noticed that Alejandro blushed ever so slightly. Perhaps his interest was mostly personal and genuine. She hoped so, but time would tell. She certainly found him attractive and he was good company, but she did not know enough about him yet.

They arrived at their destination without incident and were passed into the building. Alejandro, with Cassandra on his arm, entered the room where cocktails were being served. Diego followed. The president saw them coming in and nodded to Alejandro who led them to the president who was surrounded by army officers and ministers and their wives.

Alejandro and Cassandra entered the group and Enrique said in Spanish, "*Good evening, Ambassador.*"

Cassandra smiled broadly and answered in Spanish, "*Mr. President thank you for your kind invitation.*"

The President said, "*This is my wife Maria. Maria this is Cassandra Crossing.*"

Maria said, "*My husband has told me much about you, Cassandra. Please, as you and my husband are friends, call me Maria.*"

Cassandra said, "*Thank you and it is an honor, Dona Maria. It would also be an honor if you would call me Cassandra.*"

The President said, "*Alejandro, why don't you do the introductions?*"

Alejandro said, "*Certainly, Mr. President.*"

Cassandra's trained ear told her much about the background of those she was being introduced to just by their accents. It seemed they were impressed by her command of Spanish. Cassandra could tell the wives, of the men she was being introduced to, were relieved she had attached herself to Alejandro. More than once she noticed them giving him the once over the way the men were sneaking glances at her.

Alejandro asked, *"Cassandra, may I get you a drink?"*

"Yes, please."

Alejandro motioned to a server who brought a tray and Alejandro took two crystal goblets and handed one to Cassandra who said, *"Thank you, dear."*

The women noticed the term of affection and several looked at each other. It occurred to Cassandra that her slip might lead the Latin females to assume she and Alejandro were lovers. It would serve to put them at ease.

Maria said, *"Your necklace and bracelet are beautiful Cassandra. Did you get them here in Mexico City?"*

"Oh, yes. I could not resist the beauty of the stones and the workmanship. I doubt they will be my last purchase. I can't wait until my duties allow me to do some serious shopping."

Maria smiled at the remark and said, *"When things settle down, perhaps I may show you around."*

Cassandra said, *"That would be delightful."*

The generals and ministers as on signal started to drift away. Enrique and Alejandro drifted away with one of the generals and Maria took Cassandra's arm and led her to a corner where they could talk in private.

"Diego told my husband that you intend to buy a home here. Is that a private decision?"

"Yes."

Maria asked, *"Are you and Alejandro lovers?"*

Cassandra answered calmly, *"No. I will not share my bed with a man until I am married. I must admit, just between us, I find him not altogether unattractive and he is a great temptation."*

Maria laughed and said, *"I see. Your morals are very unusual in these times; especially for a woman as beautiful as you."*

Cassandra said, *"Thank you for the compliment. Unfortunately it is unusual to be chaste, but it shouldn't be. You are quite direct, Maria."*

"I am just a girl from the country whose husband has risen to high office. Life is too short to waste time making friends. Enrique is the only man I have been with, so I understand your position."

Cassandra changed the subject, *"I imagine it is hard for you surrounded by people whose motives you do not know. Are they merely courting favor or are they truly friends to trust?"*

Maria smiled, *"It is not hard to sort them out. I have but a few true friends and many enemies I keep close."*

Cassandra said, *"Understandable. I hope eventually to be in the former group."*

"Given what you did for Carlos that is a possibility."

Cassandra responded simply, *"Good."*

Enrique and Alejandro returned and Enrique said, *"I see you two are getting to know each other."*

Maria said, *"Yes, my dear."*

The bell was rung announcing dinner and the guests went to the dining room. Cassandra calculated there were just over fifty guests at the dinner. All, but her, were high ranking officials of the Mexican government. Cassandra and Alejandro sat next to the President and Maria. The conversation was pleasant and the food was delicious. Cassandra was thoroughly enjoying herself and Alejandro's company.

After the meal, the men retired for a cigar and the woman gathered for coffee. It was before they were seated that a woman approached Cassandra.

"Ambassador Crossing, I am Adelina Mendez. My husband is Colonel Carlos Mendez."

Cassandra said enthusiastically, *"I am so pleased to meet you, Dona Adelina."*

Adelina was an attractive woman and probably ten or twelve years younger than her husband. Adelina said, *"Thank you for what you did for my husband. I would be lost without him. If there is anything I or my family can do for you, please call on us."*

"Thank you, Adelina. Perhaps we can be friends."

Adelina smiled broadly, *"I would be more comfortable with that if you were married, unattractive, or fat, or perhaps some combination of those."*

Cassandra laughed, *"Thank you for the compliment, Dona Adelina."*

Adelina said smiling broadly, *"You have a good sense of humor for an Americano del nord."* Cassandra just smiled broadly and Adelina continued, *"I expected you would look like a female Russian weight lifter; big and manly."*

"Then it must have been a shock to meet me."

Adelina smiled and said, *"Indeed."* Adelina took Cassandra by the arm, *"Come sit by me."*

The women took a seat on a sofa and servants came to serve coffee and light pastries. Cassandra accepted coffee but passed on the pastry.

Maria came and sat by them, *"I suppose in your country, Cassandra, you would be with the men."*

Cassandra smiled, *"Yes, but here I am with the people who really hold the power."*

Maria and Adelina both laughed lightly. Cassandra was no fool and knew she was being tested. She wasn't afraid, which was not to say she took the situation lightly. It was just that she was confident she could hold her own.

She added, *"Besides this is a social gathering not a formal one."*

Maria said, *"That is true."* She abruptly changed the subject, *"I was told you used to by a spy."*

Cassandra was taking a sip of her coffee and finished it calmly. *"It is true I was employed as an intelligence operative, but my duties now are quite different."* She looked at Maria smiling, *"I now have others to do the kind of work Diego does."*

Maria laughed again and Adelina added, *"Maria, I think we may have met our match."*

Cassandra added, *"I must admit, I like my present work better."*

Adelina asked, *"How is it different?"*

Cassandra said, *"It is now my job to make friends rather than keep track of enemies. I interact with people I like rather than those who I might have to, well, treat with extreme prejudice."*

Adelina asked, *"The way you treated Major Reyes with extreme prejudice?"*

Cassandra looked at Adelina and nodded seriously, *"It is necessary sometimes to protect one's friends and allies."*

Maria said, *"Adelina, I think we should make her our friend. She is much too dangerous to have as an enemy."*

Adelina answered, *"Certainly. Cassandra did my family a great favor treating Reyes with extreme prejudice. I now feel I must warn her about a danger."*

Cassandra asked, *"What danger is that?"*

Adelina answered, *"Alejandro. He seems to be quite taken with you."*

Cassandra smiled, *"I have been warned and I recognize the danger. It is indeed great."*

Maria interjected, *"Ah yes, but you seem to like adventure, Cassandra."*

Cassandra simply said, *"True, but only with calculated risk and when things are in my favor."*

Maria shook her head and said, *"Don't underestimate the danger Alejandro poses. Even honorable men sometimes give in to their passions."*

"I understand. I will not tempt him beyond what he can bear."

The women smiled at the remark. Maria and Adelina spent some time discussing the shops that Cassandra must see and the places they would visit when circumstances allowed, which Cassandra took to mean when the conflict had ended.

A servant came and whispered in Cassandra's ear and she said to her new friends, "*Excuse me please. Duty calls.*"

Cassandra got up and gave Maria a serious look. Cassandra knew something wasn't right and the hairs on the back of her neck felt like they were standing on end, but she followed the servant. If there was to be unpleasantness, it would be better if it took place elsewhere away from the wives of dignitaries. She had no sooner followed the man into the hall then she just walked out of her shoes preparing for a fight as she followed barefoot. The man turned on her with a knife and thrust it toward her.

Cassandra moved like lightening and diverted the knife thrust. The man screamed as his wrist was broken. He backed up and swung wildly with his good left hand, but Cassandra blocked the blow and struck the man under the rib cage forcing his diaphragm up and the air out of his lungs. He collapsed. Cassandra heard footsteps and reached under her gown and removed her small pistol from the holster on her thigh. She used the, butt to render her attacker unconscious. She held her weapon against her side as she backed toward the drawing room door.

Cassandra looked over her shoulder, saw Maria, and said, "Go back inside and lock the door." Maria immediately hustled the women inside and Cassandra heard the door closed and the lock set.

Three men came around the corner to face Cassandra's weapon pointed at them. The man in charge had his weapon by his side, "Ambassador Crossing, we are security."

Cassandra said, "Gentlemen, please drop your weapons. We'll wait until one of your colleagues whom I know comes to confirm your identity."

The man raised his weapon and Cassandra shot him in the forehead and he fell backward into the two men slightly behind him. Cassandra wasn't about to take chances and before the men could recover she shot them both. Cassandra heard more footsteps and raced forward moving her weapon to her left hand. She picked up a fully loaded weapon one of the men had dropped and moved into a side room the weapons she held at the ready.

Diego's voice came, "Cassandra, it is I Diego. It is all right to come out."

Cassandra stuck her head around the door.

Diego asked, "Are the wives all right?"

Cassandra moved into the hall both weapons at her side, "They are locked in the drawing room."

Diego looked at the men on the floor.

Cassandra said, "The one closest to the drawing room is still alive."

Diego motioned to men who went to the man a removed him roughly. Diego examined the three men Cassandra had shot and looked at her and shook his head. Cassandra already knew they were dead.

Cassandra sensed Maria beside her who asked, "How many?"

Cassandra said, "Four. Three are dead."

Maria almost spat the word, "Traitors."

Cassandra simply said, "Yes. These are dangerous times."

Enrique came to his wife, "Are you all right, dear?"

She answered, "Yes."

Cassandra looked at Maria who had a pistol in her hand. She had prepared to repel any attack on the wives. Cassandra expected she might not be the only one of the women who had been armed. She looked at Diego and handed him the pistol she had in her right hand. "I took this from one of the attackers."

Diego turned and gave it to one of his men. The halls were now filled with men with weapons. Diego gave some orders then turned to his president, "I suggest, Mr. President, we get the wives into the drawing room where my men can protect them until we sort out this mess."

Cassandra noticed Alejandro leaning against the wall. He had been taking everything in. It was then that Cassandra realized that the warning about him might have been more than just about his affect on the ladies. He realized Cassandra had noticed him and his demeanor changed. A charming smile came across his face.

Cassandra picked up her shoes and noticed Enrique looking at her.

She said, "It is better not to have high heels on if one is anticipating a fight."

Enrique nodded understanding.

The women were ushered back into the drawing room and Enrique said, "Cassandra would you accompany us. The president looked at her weapon.

Cassandra said, "Please, may I have a minute Mr. President."

He nodded and Cassandra slipped into a side room closed the door and put her pistol in its holster and slipped her shoes back on. She went back into the hall and Enrique said, "We'll go to my library."

They started walking and Enrique motioned for Cassandra to walk next to him. He leaned his head to toward Cassandra and said so no one else could hear, "Maria also keeps hers in a holster on her thigh."

Cassandra just nodded, "Your wife is a wise woman."

Enrique said, "I think my friend Alejandro does not know quite what to make of you. If he was wise, he would embrace the possibilities of having a strong partner, but unfortunately he has only known weak women."

Cassandra did not respond, but made note of the comment. The President obviously did not approve of Alejandro's usual choice of women. Cassandra decided she needed to learn more about that. The group marched in lockstep to the president's library. At the destination, several of the men following the president took up positions at the door. Alejandro, Diego, a General, and Cassandra followed Enrique into the room and the doors were closed.

The president said, "Cassandra, I don't think you've been formally introduced to General Cruz-Guzman. General this is our friend Ambassador Crossing."

Cassandra said, "General," and offered her hand which the general shook gently. Cassandra did not know why, but she did not like this man. Her instincts were usually right.

The General said, "Ambassador Crossing, I would be honored if you would call me by my given name Ramone."

Cassandra replied, "Thank you, General."

The general smiled and the president motioned to chairs so they all sat down at a small round table. Cassandra sat between Enrique and Alejandro facing Ramone.

Enrique said, "Cassandra, on behalf of the nation and on a personal level, I offer my apology for the lapse of security. That such a thing should happen here is unthinkable."

Cassandra smiled, "No apology is necessary, Mr. President. I came here knowing these are dangerous times for you and we anticipated we would share in the danger. My government has decided we are not to be just fair weather friends."

Enrique sighed and looked at Diego, "Still, we should have realized the danger you are in and took special precautions. It seems there are parties who desire to cut the new bond we are forging between our countries."

Cassandra said, "So it appears, Enrique." Cassandra began to speak again, but the sound of gunfire could be clearly heard. Diego got up and looked at the Enrique who nodded and Diego left.

Enrique looked at Alejandro, "It appears we have not rooted out all the traitors."

Alejandro simply said, "Yes, my President."

Cassandra didn't know why, but she sensed danger and under the table slipped her pistol out and onto her lap. In the process her dress rode high and Alejandro noticed and was distracted. The hairs on the back of Cassandra's neck were again screaming danger and Cassandra knew she only had two shots left. The thought had hardly burst into her mind when Ramone raised a weapon and was tracking it toward the President. Cassandra moved so quickly the general was not able to bring his weapon to bear on the president before Cassandra shot him in the forehead.

Alejandro's face registered shock and Enrique jumped up. Ramone slumped in his chair and the weapon dropped from his hand onto the table as armed men came bursting into the room. The president said, "It is all right. Take up defensive positions."

The men did as they were ordered and went back into the hall. Alejandro got up calmly and looked at Ramone. There was a small hole in his forehead.

Alejandro pronounced, "He is dead."

Enrique went to his desk and took out two weapons and came back to the table. He handed one to Cassandra. She made sure a round was chambered and put the weapon in her lap. Enrique put the other on the table in front of him.

Enrique said, "Will this never end?"

Diego came rushing into the room. He looked at the weapon in front of the President and then at the General's body then looked at Cassandra. Cassandra just nodded in the affirmative.

Diego said, "The plan was to kill the Ambassador and ambush you, my President, as you went to ensure your wife's safety."

Enrique said, "It could have worked. The traitor security detail would have been waiting and assisted by the general, they probably would have been successful." Enrique looked at Cassandra. "I suspect we would have been ambushed in the hall as we discovered your body."

Cassandra nodded agreement.

Enrique said to no one in particular, "It is getting harder to know who to trust."

Diego said, "Colonel Mendez has taken charge. He has ordered all but his own troops out of the residence."

Enrique said, "Good."

Cassandra looked at Enrique seriously and said, "Our lives are now all in his hands. Does he have enough men to ensure your safety?"

Enrique said, "Alejandro?"

Alejandro said, "No, because we can't rely on the general's men now."

Cassandra said, "Since there was an attempt on my life, will you allow me to have my embassy security come here to protect me?"

Enrique knew exactly what Cassandra was suggesting. He smiled and said, "I think it is the least we can do under the circumstances. Diego inform Colonel Mendez of the arrangement while the ambassador makes a call, and give orders for her security team to be allowed to come here."

Cassandra called her security team and asked them to come to her and then phoned the embassy to have everyone put on alert. Cassandra's security detail came literally on the run having unloaded their heavier weapons, body armor and ammunition from their vehicle trunks. They waited in the hall while Stan was led to the president's library.

Cassandra said, "Please assist the president's security detail in forming a perimeter around this room."

Stan said, "Yes ma'am," and rushed back into the hall. In the meantime, Alejandro had made some calls. He finished and said, "It is being circulated that you and the ambassador have been assassinated. The rebels have started a counter attack and some military units have deserted and joined them. We have had calls from the media."

"Tell them that we are having a pleasant evening with the ambassador and the reports of my death are greatly exaggerated. Invite a few major reporters to come and meet with me and the ambassador."

Diego scurried out.

The President looked at Alejandro, "We do not have a large force here since we cannot now rely on the General's men. We are vulnerable."

Alejandro said, "Yes, my President."

Cassandra said, "It would be a nice way to end the evening to do an inspection of the airport operations and have coffee and refreshments there. You could even invite the press to the airport to cover the event."

Enrique looked at Cassandra, "If they attack there, your military will have no choice but to defend the airport."

Cassandra said, "Yes. That is what they have been ordered to do." She paused to let her statement sink in then went on, "The rebels will know that and if they go there they will face a formidable fighting force. The airport may be the safest place in Mexico City at the moment until the Colonel can muster the necessary forces."

Colonel Mendez had come into the room and overheard the conversation, "Mr. President, I recommend a social call to the airport. I will stay here with my troops and I will lead a counterattack."

Diego said, "We had better act quickly. It will be dangerous travel to the airport."

Cassandra said, "Our small party could travel by helicopter. It would be good public relations."

Alejandro said, "I will have a reporter and cameraman come directly."

The President said, "Let's do it."

Alejandro and Colonel Mendez hurried away to make an arrangements. Cassandra made the call.

Matt answered, "Good evening, Ambassador. I hear you are having an evening with the president."

"Yes I am, General. I have invited the president and some dignitaries to inspect the airport operations this evening and we will have some media people with us. Would you please arrange a show for our guests and the media? Given the president will be visiting a high state of alert is in order."

"I would be pleased to make arrangements. We are good at making the impossible happen."

Cassandra laughed, "Thank you, general. How soon can we have air transport arrive at the presidential residence?"

Matt asked, "How many will be coming?"

Cassandra said, "Just a minute, Matt," and turned to the President, "How many guests will we be entertaining?"

Enrique looked at Alejandro who did a head count in his mind, "Fifteen for us: four men and nine women, two media people. Then add the Ambassador and her security team."

Cassandra turned to Alejandro and said, "Could my security team be of assistance here?"

Alejandro said, "Please. We can use all the help we can get."

Cassandra spoke into the phone, "Sixteen Matt."

"They are ready for takeoff now and will be there directly. I am sending two Cobra gunships as the President will be visiting."

Cassandra said, "Thank you, Matt." She ended the call and turned to Alejandro, "I have my security at the Embassy if you need them."

The President said, "Only if you come under attack here Alejandro."

"Yes, my President." Alejandro turned to Cassandra, "Thank you."

"You are welcome." She made another call to the embassy.

Enrique said, "Diego, tell the wives we are making a social call and they are going to have an adventure. Please explain the situation and that we will have reporters with us."

Diego scurried off.

Twenty minutes later the president with the first lady of Mexico on his right arm and the ambassador to his left came out to waiting TV cameras broadcasting live.

The president said, "Good evening ladies and gentlemen. Tonight I and my wife and a small party are pleased to exchange visits with my good friend the U.S. Ambassador to Mexico, Her Excellency Cassandra Crossing. We had dinner here at Los Pinos and we are now going on an inspection tour of our friends' operations at the airport where we will have more opportunity to socialize. We have invited one of the TV crews to accompany us and they will make their recording available to all of you. Thank you."

The three of them strolled to the waiting helicopters as the TV cameras recorded the small party climb into the aircraft and take off.

In the air Enrique said, "That went well."

Maria said, "Some of the TV people really seemed to be shocked that the reports of your deaths were unfounded."

Enrique said, "Yes. I noticed. I'm sure Diego's people will figure out who had knowledge of the assassination attempts before they occurred."

At the airport, the cameraman and reporter were first out of the helicopters when they landed. They were to record their president and his wife being greeted by General Brite and his senior staff with an honor guard. Even from a distance it was obvious introductions were being made. The party was taken by vehicle to the terminal building where a reception awaited.

There they drank wine and ate finger foods while sitting in comfortable chairs watching large transport planes take off and land as well as seeing some unloaded under spotlights. They also mingled and talked with a few of the senior U.S. officers. The TV crew was recording the entire event.

The reporter came to Cassandra with her cameraman, and introduced herself, "Good evening, Excellency. I am Maria Aleta Ortega Hernandez."

Cassandra said, "I am pleased to meet you."

The reporter asked, "What is the purpose of tonight's gathering, Excellency."

Cassandra smiled, "It is about friends getting to know each other better. It is about having a pleasant time with our friends and allies."

The reporter said, "It was reported earlier tonight that you and the president were assassinated."

Cassandra laughed, "Where did you hear such a ridiculous thing? As you can see we are both very much alive and enjoying a pleasant evening."

Maria came over to Cassandra, "I see Cassandra that you have met one of our country's foremost reporters."

"Yes Maria and she is such a delight."

The reporter asked, "Are you friends?"

Maria said, "Yes, of course. My husband and her father are good friends as are we."

Cassandra added, "We have many things in common."

The reporter asked, "Such as?"

Cassandra smiled, "Good friends, good wine, good food, a love of Mexico and of democracy."

Maria said, "Well spoken."

Adelina came to Maria, "General Brite has offered us rides in the armored military vehicles. You really have to give it a try, Maria."

Maria said, "Excuse us," and Adelina led the way and the reporter followed.

One of the general's officers came to Cassandra, "You are needed, Ambassador."

He led Cassandra in another direction. Maria watched her go then turned and went with Adelina to be photographed riding in the military vehicle.

Cassandra was led into a room where Enrique and Matt were waiting. Matt spoke, "It seems the coup attempt has collapsed. The troops which had been advancing on the City turned and ran when Colonel Mendez leading the Presidential Guard brigade and the two mechanized brigades stationed in the city moved to engage them. The broadcast of the little party and the fact the president was here at the airport surrounded by several thousand American troops seemed to cause them to lose heart. They are fleeing south to seek refuge with the other rebels."

Cassandra said, "It is unfortunate we don't know where their leader Eduardo Castillo is at the moment. It would be to our advantage if something were to fall out of the sky and crush him."

Enrique said, "Or a ton of bombs were to fall on his head. He will no doubt take his men to the jungles and mountains. He is not going to make it easy for us to root him out."

Cassandra asked, "Then why do it?"

Enrique said, "I can't just leave him there. How else do we attack him?"

Cassandra smiled, "Small scout teams to target concentrations, camps, supply dumps, and command centers, then use air strikes. Bomb them into the stone-age when you locate a target. Refuse to fight them on their terms. Destroy their supply lines and starve them of food and munitions while at the same time giving help and protection to the local people."

Enrique said, "Where did you learn such things, Cassandra? You sound like a military officer."

Cassandra looked at Matt, "I had a good teacher."

Enrique became serious, "It seems you did."

Chapter 6 – Getting Feet on the Ground

It was almost three in the morning when Cassandra and her security team arrived back at the embassy grounds. Cassandra did not go to bed, but instead changed and called Stan and Greg to a meeting.

Stan and Greg arrived and Stan said, "It was an interesting night."

Cassandra said, "Yes it was. How many have gotten in."

Stan said, "Thirty seven came in by way of the airport. Another nineteen came by sea and eleven by ground across the border. We still have four in the area of the airport."

Cassandra said, "Priority is to get feet on the ground in Castillo's area of operation to find out what we can about what he is up to. Secondly, I want to know everything there is about Alejandro. I want to know about his family and his mistresses and past romantic entanglements. I also want to know about Carlos and his wife Adelina. We know next to nothing about the new inner circle. I especially want to know about their families. We need to know a lot."

Greg asked, "What about use of resources?"

Cassandra answered, "I'll leave the how up to you Stan; you're now the Station Chief. I'm no longer a field person; I'm an end user. Fund C is to pay for your operations."

Stan said, "Understood."

Cassandra said, "That's all for now. I'm going to file my report and get some sleep."

The men left and Cassandra wrote her report. She took it to the communication specialist and transmitted it and left copies for Bob and Stan before turning in. She did not set the alarm. Cassandra woke at eleven in the morning and after showering went downstairs for lunch.

Bob was there and greeted her, "Good morning."

Cassandra smiled, "Good morning, Bob, though it's almost afternoon. "

Bob said, "I have a diplomatic bag for you that came in early this morning. The communication link for your afternoon interviews has been arranged. I have a question about the men I have here."

Cassandra nodded, "Do you want to keep the team you have here?"

"Yes."

Cassandra said, "That will not be a problem. I'll see to it. I was promised whatever I needed within reason."

Bob said, "Thank you. I saw from your report you had an eventful evening."

"Yes."

Bob said, "I was impressed by the way you handled the situation. It is no wonder the Mexican President wanted you to stay."

Cassandra just nodded, "It seemed my experience and skills outside the normal diplomatic routine have proved very useful."

Bob said, "After the incident with Colonel Mendez, the men have started calling you Ambassador Death. Mind you, it is a term of respect coming from those men and they will never say it within your hearing."

Cassandra said smiling, "I consider it an honor coming from such a fine group of warriors."

Mike came into the dining room with another man and came to where Cassandra was sitting.

She said, "Hello, Mike."

Mike responded, "Madame Ambassador." He introduced Diego's friend, "This is Adolpho Perez. Adolpho is a lawyer who acts for prominent citizens to facilitate real estate transactions."

Cassandra offered her hand which Adolpho shook as Cassandra said, "I am pleased to meet you. Please join us."

The man said, "It would be my honor, Excellency."

He and Mike took seats and food was brought to them.

Mike said, "He got us a good deal on the house next door. I have a contract I recommend you sign." He took the document out of his briefcase and Cassandra read it as she ate. When she finished she said, "That is a good price."

Mike smiled as did Adolpho.

Mike added, "The fact we specified the purchase was to be paid for in U.S. dollars in cash sealed the deal."

Cassandra asked, "Do you have a pen?"

Mike handed one to her and she signed the document and Adolpho witnessed the signature.

Bob had finished eating and said, "If you will excuse me Ambassador, I have other duties."

Cassandra nodded and Bob left. Cassandra said to Adolpho in Spanish, "*Did Diego tell you I wished to make a personal purchase.*"

"*Yes he did, Excellency. I would be pleased to be of assistance if you will tell me what you want.*"

Cassandra said, "*I would like a retreat outside of the city. I understand the current circumstances have reduced the price of real estate and that cash in U.S. dollars may give an agent a negotiating advantage.*"

Adolpho said, "*That is the situation.*"

Cassandra said, "*I would like to purchase a nice estancia if the price is right. It would however be important to be near neighbors with whom I would have common interests. It would also be desirable if the estancia could generate an income.*"

Adolpho smiled and said, "*I understand perfectly. I may be able to find you what you are looking for among neighbors with whom you would have common interests. If you would allow me to act as your agent for a commission I'm sure I could arrange a beneficial arrangement.*"

Cassandra and Adolpho came to an agreement on a commission and Adolpho took his leave.

That afternoon, Cassandra interviewed several career diplomats and none of them impressed her. She was in fact quite disappointed. They were obviously not the kind of people she needed given the present situation.

Cassandra went to the communication room and made a call to Washington. Chas Elliot happened to be available and took her call, "Hello, Ambassador."

Cassandra said, "Mr. Secretary, I hope you are well."

Chas said, "Yes I am, thank you, Cassandra. It seems my newest ambassador has been involved in some very dangerous circumstances."

"All's well that ends well, Chas."

Chas laughed lightly, "It seems though your ways are unconventional your results are outstanding. The newly appointed Mexican Ambassador came to pay me a social visit. He is apparently under instructions from his president to develop and I quote, 'intimate friendly relationships with his U.S. contacts similar to those his president enjoys with our Ambassador.' That is the highest of praise Cassandra."

Cassandra said, "Thank you, sir."

Chas added, "The ambassador is having an intimate dinner with your father and a few of his cabinet tonight."

Cassandra said, "That is a good development. I assume you will be there."

Chas said, "Of course. What can I do for you?"

"As you know, I interviewed candidates to be my Deputy Chief of Mission and basically run the day to day operations here. The situation here is far from normal and I do not think the people I interviewed are suitable for this location though I have no doubt they will do well elsewhere. Do you know of someone that speaks fluent Spanish, knows the country and its politics, and could whip this place into shape without worrying about cracking a few eggs?"

Chas said, "I suppose you want someone who thinks outside the box."

"Yes."

"I know such a person, but he has had some problems with his superiors and is not always, well, sensitive to the feelings of others within the service, although he does well with those outside the diplomatic corps. He seems to think most of his colleagues are dull of mind. He is very bright, but all his superiors have found him difficult to control. He knows Mexico and has family there."

Cassandra asked, "Where is he now?"

"Here in Washington while the bureaucrats try to figure out what to do with him. It seems he is not a favored person amongst the U.S. diplomatic community in South America. He has been very outspoken. Your predecessor sent him away."

Cassandra asked, "Could you send him here to meet with me."

Chas said, "That will not be a problem. I can have him on a military plane tonight."

"Thank you, Chas. Give my best to your wife."

Chas said, "I will. God be with you."

The call ended and Cassandra went to the room that had been set up to serve as her office. She sat thinking. It seemed Chas was happy to have her here taking one major headache off his worry list.

Cassandra knew with the events happening in the Middle East that Chas had his hands full. That was his area of specialty and her father and the country needed Chas concentrating on that region.

The upside here was that with the arrangements in place, her father's administration, with a minimal military force, had helped avert a Mexican crisis. The only question was if she could keep enough pressure released from the boiler so it did not blow up.

Cassandra's thoughts were interrupted by Bob and Mike knocking on the door frame to what was now her office.

She said, "Come in and have a seat."

Mike and Bob came in and sat down. Mike started, "Some military engineers are arriving on tonight's aircraft to oversee the security and other renovations. I have arranged contractors and Bob has arranged security. Diego will advise us concerning the workers."

Bob said, "Some of them will be Diego's agents, but that is to be expected and since we have nothing to hide that will not pose a problem."

Cassandra sat waiting for the men to say more. Bob unrolled plans on Cassandra's desk so she could see them. Bob pointed as he spoke, "We are turning the outbuildings into guard posts slash quarters. We will also build guard posts and entry barriers at the main and secondary gates. We are installing emplacements as indicated. We will make two gates in the wall between this property and the new one. With your approval, we will use the basement here and at the other mansion for troop housing. Here we will add two more entrances to the basement. "

Cassandra said, "These plans look good. Has Washington reviewed them?"

Bob nodded, "The brass had them reviewed by specialists who suggested a few minor revisions which are included. It seems you have the final say."

Cassandra said, "In that case, I think you should alter the parapet walls on the roof. We do use the roof as a deck and I wouldn't want anyone falling off."

Bob smiled, "I'll make sure it's solid enough to stop bullets."

Cassandra smiled and said, "That would be good, Colonel. By the way, I'm expecting a guest will arrive this evening on one of the military flights. He is coming to meet with me about a job. His name is Juan Alvarez." Cassandra said with a smile, "Please see he has VIP accommodation."

Mike smiled and Bob laughed, "Big room and a bed."

Cassandra smiled.

It was the next morning before Cassandra met with Juan Alvarez. She had finished a very early breakfast and was in her office when he showed up and knocked on her door frame, "Ambassador Crossing."

Cassandra said, "You must be Juan."

"Yes ma'am."

"Please come in and have a seat."

Juan Alvarez came in and took a seat. Cassandra looked him over with a trained eye. He was about five nine and had the build of an athlete and his hair was cut military short. He was well groomed. She guessed he was in his early thirties and he was dressed casually in a sport shirt and slacks with brown walking shoes.

He said, "This does not look like any embassy I've ever seen."

Cassandra said in Spanish, "*Nonetheless it is. Did you bring a copy of your personnel file?*"

He replied in Spanish, "*I did, Ambassador,*" and he pulled it out of a briefcase and handed her a large brown sealed envelope which she opened.

Cassandra continued in Spanish, "*I understand you have family here in Mexico.*"

Juan replied, "*Yes, two aunts and three uncles. They are here in Mexico City. I talked to one of them last night after I landed. I hope to visit them all while I'm here.*"

Cassandra said, "*I take it they weathered the recent unpleasantness well.*"

Juan said, "*Yes, they came through the civil war without being harmed. One of my uncles is a loyal officer of the republic. He told me of your exploits. You are not the typical diplomat.*"

Cassandra said in an even voice, "*I am not or else you wouldn't be here.*"

"*I understand that. I'm afraid I do not fit in the usual diplomatic mold either. I thought my career might be over until I was sent here. Because of what I have learned about you, I hope I might be useful here. I would like a chance.*"

Cassandra asked in an even tone, "*A chance to do what?*"

Juan shrugged, "*Redeem myself and show there are circumstances where I can be useful to my government.*"

Cassandra looked at him, "*Why did you dress so casually?*"

"*I knew what I was coming into and this dress seemed appropriate to the circumstances. I do have clothes suitable for formal occasions, but not with me. I can send for them if you decide to keep me.*"

Cassandra said in English, "Give me a half hour to review your file and then return."

"Yes, Madame Ambassador." He got up and left.

Cassandra read through Juan's file. It contained both personnel records and intelligence reviews of his status. She was good at reading between the lines. Juan's biggest problem was probably that he was smarter than a lot of the people he had served under. She read the unsolicited reports he had submitted.

It was obvious those reports had got him into trouble with the bureaucrats because he had been right so often. If he'd had a mentor and a back channel to go through he'd probably be a rising star instead of an outcast. She leaned back and thought about the man. He had served one tour in the military out of high school then got out and went to university. From there he had joined the Department of State where he had been promoted to a level where he was visible enough to be a threat to the career ambitions of more conformist employees. He'd been allowed to languish in a meaningless position for some months. Chas had done her and this man a favor.

Cassandra was brought back from her thoughts by a knock on her door frame. It was Juan. She said, "Come in and have a seat."

Juan came in and sat down. He waited patiently while Cassandra just sat there. She waited five minutes without saying anything waiting to see what he would do and thinking. He waited patiently not fidgeting. She looked at the clock and then at Juan. "How would you like to come to work for me?"

Juan said, "I would like that. What would I be doing?"

Cassandra got up and went to the window and looked out and then turned and looked at him, "You would be my Deputy Chief of Mission."

For the first time she saw emotion on Juan's face; it was shock.

Juan said, "That is well above my current rank."

Cassandra said, "Nonetheless that is what I am offering. I need someone to get this place up and running and to get it staffed to function as an embassy. I also need you to help me get a feel for what is happening here. Can you do that?"

"Yes I can, Ambassador."

Cassandra said, "Then I'll give you a try. You start immediately. What will be your order of business?"

"With your permission, I will develop a staffing table and fill the positions. I will introduce myself around and then get this place organized. Who is presently working on that?"

"Mike Moore, my Administrative Attaché."

Juan said, "A spook, I presume. I take it the intelligence function is already in place, Ambassador."

"Yes."

Juan said, "Then with your permission, Ambassador, I'll get started."

Cassandra nodded and said, "Very well. I'll want daily briefings, but keep them short and sweet."

"Yes Ambassador."

Juan hurried off with what Cassandra assumed was a sense of purpose. Cassandra hoped she was right about this guy and figured she was. He was probably one of those that just needed to be given a big task and lots of responsibility to keep him grounded. She had seen that type before and she figured she was one. She sat thinking about what her next move would be.

Stan came to her office and Cassandra waved him in. He said, "I take it Juan is staying."

"Yes. He has an uncle in the Mexican military. His personnel file is on the desk. Find out about his family here. There is not much in the file about them."

Stan said, "I will see to it. The covert communications have been set up. I am keeping them separate from the military. Do you think that will create a problem for Bob?"

"No. Be sure to tell him what you are doing and that's its necessary because of the number of operatives we have in the field. Tell him if there's anything he wants to know to ask you or me."

"That sounds good. Do you expect Diego to stay here now?"

Cassandra shook her head no, "No, but he'll have men on the construction crews and among the civilian workers. I suggest you tell Juan to ask Diego for recommendations for people we could hire without worrying about what they see getting to the rebels. Also ask Diego yourself to have a one of his staff posted here as a liaison officer."

Stan smiled, "Then we'll know which camel has its nose under the tent and which are nearby."

Cassandra nodded, "We'll keep the third floor off limits to anyone who does not stay there."

Stan said, "For security reasons."

"Yes. Bob, me, my personal staff, my Deputy Chief of Mission and you will stay here. More junior staff will stay below or at the other house until it is converted to the working embassy. This will be the official residence. Keep an eye on my new protégé and he is to have security and use an embassy vehicle when he does go visiting his family. Discuss with him the needs you and I have regarding the compound."

Stan nodded, "Understood. Is there anything else?"

"I'd like you to do me a personal favor. I'd like you to purchase a personal vehicle for me while prices are depressed."

"I'd be happy to. What do you have in mind?"

Cassandra sighed, "I want a four wheel drive; rugged, but comfortable, some sort of SUV."

Stan asked, "Do you expect to be going into the country?"

Cassandra looked at Stan, "I plan to buy an estancia. See what you can find out about our lawyer friend."

Stan said, "I take it this is all part of your grand plan."

"Yes. If it doesn't work out I'm going to be out a lot of money from my personal accounts."

Stan smiled, "But if it does work out you will make a lot of money and a lot of friends here."

Cassandra said, "Yes." She handed Stan a key, "That is for my personal box in the safe. Take what you need for the car purchase and then bring me back the key."

Stan nodded and left. Cassandra's cell went off and startled her. She looked at it. It was Alejandro and she answered in Spanish, "*Hello, Alejandro.*"

"*Hello, Cassandra. I am calling on official business. May I drop by?*"

"*Of course you may. When are you coming?*"

"*Would half an hour be acceptable?*"

Cassandra said, "*Yes, I'll see you then.*"

It seemed every time she was to have contact with Alejandro her heart started to race. She realized she was unable to control the reaction. She called the front gate post and advised Alejandro would be coming. Twenty minutes later, two cars came to the Embassy and were allowed to enter the compound. They came up the drive and stopped at the house entrance. Alejandro got out and his men waited while he came into the house. The guard greeted him and led him upstairs to Cassandra's office.

Cassandra was at work sitting at her steel desk when Alejandro's escort announced him, "Madame Ambassador, the Interior Secretary has arrived."

Cassandra looked up, "Alejandro. Come in."

Cassandra got up and gave him a hug. In spite of her resolve, she knew her face was slightly flushed. She noticed he was struggling to control his breathing.

She said, "Please have a seat. How are you?"

Alejandro smiled and sat down, "I am well. The president sends his regards."

"Please thank him. He is too kind. What can I do for you?"

Alejandro said, "We have been approached by one of your airlines to resume limited commercial flights now that the airport is secured by U.S. troops. The president would like to do that, but the military flights are of course of the higher priority. Still, if regular commercial flights are established then when things are normalized it will be much easier for other airlines to feel safe in coming here."

Cassandra nodded, "I will see how soon we can arrange that. I expect the sea shipments to start soon. What will you want to do about General Brite and his troops?"

Alejandro asked, "When the time comes would your government be willing to have him secure the port as he is the airport, for a few months?"

"I will ask for approval. How are things going in the south?"

"As expected, now that we have sufficient munitions we are making steady progress and the rebels are withdrawing into less populated and more difficult terrain. We have intelligence that many are deserting from the rebel forces. It seems these troubles have resulted in the less, ah, reliable soldiers being removed from the ranks. It has also had the effect of destroying the power of the drug lords. The government and the army are determined not to let that get out of control again. We have seen the true danger they present."

Cassandra asked, "What about police?"

Alejandro sighed, "We are rehiring, but very carefully. Anyone with the least hint of past corruption is being bypassed and we are training new recruits, but it goes slowly. We do not have many who are capable of instructing in proper policing. We are planning to import contract instructors. Our ambassador to your country will be asking for the advice and assistance of your government in the matter."

Cassandra nodded, "I think he will meet with success."

Alejandro said, "Especially if the way is made easy?"

Cassandra smiled, "I will do what I can."

Alejandro smiled and said playfully, "In spite of your humble surroundings and furnishings, I have heard you may have some influence in Washington."

Cassandra laughed lightly, "Yes, some."

Alejandro said, "I thank you for taking time to see me on these important matters. I would also like to extend a personal invitation for you to come to my home for dinner on Friday at seven in the evening. It will be a small gathering and you may of course bring a chaperone. Maria has warned me to guard your reputation or she will exact revenge."

Cassandra smiled, "It is good to have friends like Maria who are concerned with my reputation. I accept your kind invitation."

Alejandro said, "Well, then my visit having been successful on both a business and personal level, I will ask your permission to take my leave."

Cassandra smiled, "Of course."

She got up and Alejandro took her hand and kissed it. Cassandra's pulse rate went up again. The man had that effect on her.

She watched him leave. She thought he certainly was a charmer and very handsome. She imagined he'd had many women swooning over him through the years. She really wanted to know his story, but now she had work to do. She prepared a communication to send to Washington then had it transmitted. An hour later she got a reply.

The return message said in part, "Advise no problem in establishing airline schedule. Military will coordinate schedules and handle air traffic control. General Brite will be assigned to port security when sea delivery ready to start. We will coordinate timetables and details with Mexican Ambassador. Police instruction assistance will be arranged. Please advise your friends of approvals. Your father likes the newly appointed Mexican Ambassador." It was simply signed "Chas."

Cassandra called Alejandro after supper and a female answered, "Good evening."

Cassandra said, "Good evening. This is Doña Cassandra Crossing Santiago, may I speak to Alejandro?"

The woman said, "One moment please."

Alejandro took the phone, "Good evening, Cassandra."

"It is. I called to tell you that you may tell the president that my government has approved in principle all the things we discussed today."

Alejandro said, "I will tell the president. Thank you, Cassandra."

"You are welcome. I look forward to seeing you Friday evening."

Cassandra hung up. Cassandra made a phone call back to the U.S. and made arrangements for some of her things to be sent on the next military flight.

The next morning, Cassandra rose very early to the sound of construction downstairs. She rolled out of bed and looked out the window. The sun was barely rising. Cassandra showered and went downstairs to the second floor which was the source of the construction noise. She found men putting up a doorway in the hall of one wing. Juan was there talking with a man who was obviously a contractor.

As Cassandra approached, Juan saw her and excused himself and came to Cassandra, "Good morning, Ambassador."

Cassandra smiled, "You are at it early. What do we have going on?"

"They are configuring your suite. In the interim it will serve as your office, but eventually be your residence suite. Your bedroom slash interim office overlooks the garden. There will be an outer office in the living room for your secretary and another room will serve as the office for your Assistant. My office will be down the hall. Would you like to see?"

"Yes please."

As Juan led her to the construction work the men all stopped working and took off their hard hats.

Cassandra said in Spanish with a large smile, *"Good morning and thank you for the courtesy. You are all very gallant."*

This seemed to please the men and they all smiled.

Juan showed Cassandra the space, "We are taking down a wall between two rooms to make a room suitable in size for the Ambassador's master bedroom slash temporary office. The Assistant's office will be there in a smaller room," and Juan pointed to an area being framed. He continued, "This area where we are standing, which was formerly part of the hall, and the room across the hall will be your living room to be used temporarily for your secretary's office. The bathroom is being renovated and will be accessible from your bedroom. The rest of the rooms on this floor will just be painted as they are suitable for use as temporary offices as they are. Later, they can be converted to other uses."

Cassandra went to the window and looked out. The view over the garden was very nice. She turned and looked at Juan, "It will be very nice. Please have the men continue."

The workmen had all heard her remark and they all put their hard hats back on and went back to work as she left. Cassandra went to the stairwell and walked downstairs. She found workmen were constructing a wall with a steel doorframe on the large landing leading to the second story. She assumed the door would limit access to the floors above. She passed the large main floor living room to find men busy painting the walls.

Cassandra walked into the dining hall to find the tables used for the mess were gone. She went into the kitchen and found a man in a chef's uniform reading the newspaper.

He saw Cassandra and jumped up saying in English, "Good morning, Excellency. May I prepare breakfast for you?"

Cassandra smiled and asked in Spanish, *"What do they call you?"*

Pedro smiled and said in Spanish *"I am called Pedro Tonio Moreno Rios. I am the new chef."*

Cassandra smiled, *"I am Cassandra Adora Crossing Santiago. I am pleased to meet you Pedro."* She held out her hand and Pedro somewhat shyly shook it gently. Cassandra said, *"Please, prepare me a cheese omelet, Pedro."*

"It will be my pleasure, Excellency."

Cassandra went to the cupboard and got a cup and poured coffee and then went and sat outside in the garden and sipped her coffee. Stan came out of the embassy and toward Cassandra, "Good morning, Ambassador."

Cassandra said, "Good morning, Stan."

"It seems your new fellow doesn't lose any time. He sure has things hopping. The military mess hall has been moved to the newly acquired building and the beds will be moved there for quartering except for the beds that will be moved to the basement here. The military guys like the pool next door and have already been using it."

Cassandra said, "It's progress."

Stan changed the subject, "We found out quite a bit about your friends." Stan stopped as a man came out of the embassy carrying a tray. He came to their table and put down three covered plates and a carafe of what, from the odor, was coffee.

He said in accented English, "I will wait nearby in case you need anything else."

Cassandra asked, "What is your name?"

"Luis Sancho Reyes Vargas, Excellency."

"Thank you, Luis."

Luis went and took a chair near the door to the Embassy. Stan had his back to Luis and said, "I wonder if he can read lips at sixty feet?"

Cassandra laughed and said, "Not through your back." She took the cover off her plate and Stan did the same to his. The third plate when uncovered revealed slices of fruit. Cassandra said the blessing then they started eating. Stan said between bites and sips of coffee, "This is very good."

Cassandra said, "It is. I'd keep Pedro on even if he was a spy for the Russians."

Chapter 7 – The Unexpected

Stan started with his report, "It seems your friend Alejandro's reputation with the ladies is somewhat justified, but not in the way you would think. He is often pursued, but not snared. He is seen accompanied by beautiful women, but he has been careful not to become involved with any of them sexually, as far as we can determine. He has had one mistress and she came into the picture after his wife died when he was very vulnerable and lonely. He is reportedly a devout Catholic and had great guilt over the affair and broke it off after a short time as he did not want to marry the woman. He comes from a middle class family and was a very successful military officer before becoming involved in politics. His father was a doctor; a surgeon."

Cassandra said, "So Alejandro has cultivated a playboy façade to add to his image, but it is mostly window dressing."

"Correct. His friend Carlos is from a working class family and very ambitious. Alejandro and Carlos met at the military academy and became friends. Carlos' wife Adelina on the other hand comes from a very wealthy family. Her family was originally opposed to the marriage, but now they are happy with Adelina's husband since he can protect them. Alejandro was responsible for Carlos and Adelina meeting. A word of caution is in order as Alejandro is a cunning man and has a reputation for uncovering treachery."

Cassandra said, "I expected under his charming exterior was a formidable man."

Stan nodded, "I wonder if his failure to uncover the recent coup attempt has created resentment toward you."

Cassandra said, "I don't think so. I am invited to a social dinner at his home Friday evening."

Stan raised an eyebrow and said, "One thing we uncovered; he has never had any of his women friends to his home." Stan paused and continued, "Adelina is a close confident of the First Lady. Adelina has a younger sister

Josefina and a brother Lonzo. She received a large inheritance from her maternal grandparents when they passed and as a result is quite wealthy. Her parents are very wealthy industrialists. Carlos married into the privileged class; estates and factories privileged."

Cassandra nodded in acknowledgement as she finished the last bite of her breakfast. She said, "This was all very good." She looked at Stan and he knew she meant the report as well as the breakfast. Cassandra added, "I want more."

Stan said, "We'll keep digging."

Cassandra sat back, "I need to talk to Amanda. Please tell her to come see me."

Luis came and retrieved their plates.

Cassandra said, "Thank you, Luis."

Luis bowed his head slightly and hurried away with the plates on a tray.

Stan asked, "Do you think he's one of Diego's?"

"Of course he is. As a server most people will say things in his presence that they shouldn't without realizing it. I haven't seen the new building yet. Would you care to join me?"

Stan nodded agreement and they got up and walked next door. As she toured the building, Cassandra realized it would serve them well and would need little change in the short term. The kitchen was large and the open living and dining room would make a good dining hall. The indoor squash court had already been converted to a barracks room for troops as had the large open spaces in the basement. Cassandra went upstairs and inspected the bedrooms and she made a decision.

Cassandra returned to the embassy. She looked for Bob and found him in the front yard talking to Juan. She overheard Juan say, "I see your point. We'll leave that for the military crew to work on."

Cassandra approached the men and said, "Good morning, gentlemen."

The two men said almost in unison, "Good morning."

"I have visited the new house. I would like that to become the man cave. The senior male staff may take up residence in the bedrooms there. I want the female staff on the third floor here. I don't want any problems resulting from females sharing accommodations with testosterone charged males."

Bob said, "I suppose we will have more female staff arriving."

Juan said, "Yes, Colonel. They will start to arrive shortly. I think the Ambassador makes a good point. Some of the junior women staff can double up until the situation in the city becomes more normal and they can live off the grounds."

Cassandra said, "In the meantime, we can manage."

Juan said, "Indeed. I imagine eventually we will have to build on to the new structure. The operation here will be quite large."

Cassandra nodded agreement and changed the subject, "Colonel, do you have any female military personnel here who could serve as guardians of the third floor?"

Bob smiled, "Oh do I. I have three real ball busters."

Cassandra faked shock, "Colonel!"

Bob said with a grin, "Sorry Ambassador. I guess I have not adjusted fully to my new position."

Cassandra smiled then said, "That makes two of us. I will leave you men to finish your business."

Cassandra walked back into the embassy and saw Amanda coming to meet her.

"You wanted to see me, Ambassador?"

Cassandra said, "Yes. Let's go to my suite."

Amanda followed Cassandra to her sitting room. Cassandra closed the door to her suite and sat down. "I have been invited to dinner at the interior secretary's home. I may bring a guest as chaperone and you are the designated person. It will be semi-formal and you'll need a thigh holster and a handbag with another weapon. Do you have those?"

"Yes ma'am."

Cassandra said, "Good. What about clothes?"

"That will be a problem. I have no evening wear here."

Cassandra said, "Go into the city and acquire something appropriate and really nice as we are representing our country. At the same time, choose something that will tastefully appeal to the males and see if you get any response and information in conversation. Tell Stan to give you money for shopping from the special fund."

Amanda said, "I understand."

"Good."

Amanda got up and left the room. Cassandra sat thinking about how quickly events were moving. There was a knock on the door.

Cassandra said, "Come."

A female staff sergeant came into the room with two other females in uniform. She came to attention and said, "Sergeant Coyne reporting, ma'am, with detail as ordered."

Cassandra said, "At ease sergeant. Please have a seat, ladies." The women all took a chair. Cassandra asked, "Did the Colonel tell you the nature of the assignment?"

"No ma'am. He just told me to report to you."

Cassandra looked at the three women, "You three are to be guardians of the third floor. You are charged with maintaining the sanctuary of the female floor. You will take up residence in two rooms by the stairs and allow only authorized personnel on this floor. You will eat here in the kitchen. You will keep your weapons close at all times and ensure the security of this floor. Two of you must always be here; one on guard duty and one off until I can get other Amazons assigned."

The women smiled at the reference.

Cassandra became serious, "Take this detail seriously. There have already been two attempts on my life since I arrived. There may be others. Be under no misconception, this is a potentially dangerous post."

Cassandra looked at each of the women and they all looked her in the eye.

Cassandra continued, "The only males to be allowed on this floor without my prior express permission communicated directly to you are the Colonel and Stan. Is that clear?"

Sergeant Coyne said, "Yes, ma'am. Do you have a preference as to how we arm ourselves?"

Cassandra smiled and said, "Effectively."

The sergeant returned the smile. "We will requisition special weapons. It may take some time to get them."

Cassandra said, "Talk to Stan and he'll get you what you want straight off."

"Yes ma'am. May I speak freely?"

"Yes."

"Three Amazons isn't enough. There should be at least three more so we can have a guard at the secondary stair well."

Cassandra said, "Understood. I'll talk to the Colonel. Is there anything else you need now?"

"No ma'am."

Cassandra said, "Then you are dismissed."

The three women got up and left. Cassandra decided to call Bob and realized she still had his cell phone. In an off chance he'd replaced it, she called his number. He answered, "Yes, Ambassador."

Cassandra asked, "Bob do you have time to come up to the roof and talk with me?"

"Can we make it in fifteen? I'm in the middle of something."

"Fifteen will do."

Cassandra went up to the roof and sat thinking. Bob showed up as promised. He had a small box with him. She explained to him about the Amazons.

Bob smiled, "The sergeant caught me as soon as she left here and gave me the scoop. Someone overheard our conversation and now the men are already talking about Ambassador Death and her Amazons."

Cassandra smiled and said, "That's a good one. What do you think?"

"The sergeant was right about the need. I'll get six more females who have combat experience here on a flight tomorrow. With nine the rotations there will be no seven day weeks, even if it is short term."

Cassandra asked, "How are things on your end?"

"No problem; we are organized and can defend the embassy. In the case of an attack everyone takes positions here and we abandon the building next door."

Cassandra said, "Please forgive me, Colonel."

"Why?"

"I stole your cell phone."

Bob laughed and Cassandra handed him a one hundred dollar bill, "It was used so that should cover it."

Bob took the bill and pocketed it and said, "Thanks. It was a fifty dollar phone."

Cassandra shook her head, "I think we should have a senior staff meeting after supper."

"That would be a good idea." Bob slipped a small box across the table, "That's for you."

Cassandra opened it. She knew what it was, "Thanks Bob. I've been so preoccupied I didn't think to ask."

Bob said, "Your call sign is Eagle One. Mine is Tiger One and Sergeant Coyne is Amazon One."

Cassandra shook her head and said, "You have a sick sense of humor, Bob."

"What does that say about you, Ambassador, that you understand it?"

Cassandra was about to say something unladylike when Stan came onto the roof and she bit the retort off. Stan said, "Would you like to see your new ride, Ambassador?"

"It's here already?"

"Oh yes. At the moment Yankee greenbacks are king. Follow me."

Cassandra shrugged and got up and followed Stan downstairs and outside with Bob trailing along. She looked at the vehicle. She went and opened it and said, "This sure is a beauty." She looked at the odometer and it had just over ten thousand miles on it. She asked, "How much did I pay for this?" Stan handed her the invoice and she said, "Get out of here. You stole the thing; these sell for sixty grand new back home. Thank you, Stan."

"You are welcome. Do you want diplomatic plates on it?"

Cassandra said, "Not on this one. It is for my private use."

Stan said, "We'll put it in the garage next door."

Cassandra nodded, "Thanks. Do you think you can get me another SUV at a good price?"

"That would be no problem. I'll see to it."

Stan got in the SUV and drove it next door.

After supper, the senior staff compared notes as to their progress. Things seem to be going smoothly. The final item for discussion was that from all reports the war in the south was going well. Castillo's forces were being relentlessly driven back and were seeking refuge in the rugged terrain of the Sierra Madre del Sur. They had been reduced to a large guerilla force without major armor or air support.

On Friday evening, Cassandra and Amanda arrived at the Alejandro's home at ten to seven. One of the security team opened the door for her and Amanda. They were met at the door by a matronly woman whose voice she recognized from the phone when she said, "Good evening and welcome. Please come in."

Cassandra and Amanda followed her into the house. Cassandra said, "I am Cassandra Crossing and this is my friend Amanda Hopkins."

The woman smiled, "I am Alejandro's aunt Adriana. Alejandro is in the living room with the other guests."

Cassandra and Amanda followed Adrianna into the living room. Alejandro rose and said, "There is the guest of honor."

He came to Cassandra and took her hand and kissed it. Cassandra's physical reaction was involuntary and her pulse quickened. Alejandro turned to Amanda, "And who is this lovely lady?"

Cassandra said, "Alejandro, this is my friend Amanda Hopkins."

Amanda offered her hand and Alejandro shook it lightly.

Cassandra saw Diego and said, "Good evening, Diego."

Diego said, "Excellency, may I present my wife Clarisa."

Cassandra said, "I am very pleased to meet you," and the two women shook hands.

Alejandro introduced Diego and his wife to Amanda then he introduced a cleric, "Cassandra this is my good friend Vicente. Do not hold it against him that he is a priest."

Cassandra said, "I am pleased to meet you, Reverend."

Alejandro next introduced a young colleague Tomas. Tomas was a about Amanda's age and not altogether hard to look at and he seemed very attracted to Amanda. Cassandra noted that Alejandro's intelligence gathering had been good.

Alejandro said, "May I offer you a glass of wine, ladies."

Cassandra said, "Yes, please."

Amanda said, "No thank you."

A server brought Cassandra a glass of wine. Cassandra asked, "Vicente are you Alejandro's parish priest?"

Vicente smiled, "No. We were childhood friends and from time to time he invites me to social gatherings so I do not lose all my social graces."

Cassandra smiled, "I have the feeling you are toying with me, Vicente."

Vicente said, "I never disagree with a beautiful woman."

Alejandro interrupted, "Behave yourself Vicente and remember you are a priest." Alejandro looked at Cassandra, "He is such a flirt."

Adrianna said, "Alejandro, behave yourself. Vicente is a priest."

"Yes, but he is no saint," Alejandro teased.

Vicente laughed then said, "I can always depend on my friend to ensure I remain humble."

Cassandra said, "Even if he doesn't?"

It was Vicente's turn to laugh and he said, "She has your measure, my friend."

Cassandra noticed on the edge of her peripheral vision that Tomas and Amanda were talking. Diego interjected, "These two are like little schoolboys when they get together."

Cassandra smiled, "It is good friends who are able to be at ease in each other's company."

Diego said, "True."

Adrianna asked, "Have you always been a diplomat, Ambassador?"

Cassandra said, "Please call me Cassandra. No, I used to be in the same business as Diego."

Adrianna blurted, "Oh my."

Cassandra said, "Yes, quite."

Diego laughed and his wife looked at him strangely. She asked Cassandra, "Do you know what it is my husband does?"

"Yes. He is a master spy, an intelligence operative, a national security operator. He wears many hats."

Diego said, "True."

Clarisa was sitting opened mouth and apparently shocked.

Cassandra said, "Everyone here knows what your husband does Clarisa and his job is important and necessary. We all know that too."

Clarisa smiled, "I did not realize so many people know."

Cassandra said, "There are secrets and there are public secrets. Your husband has been so successful that everyone who is anyone knows his work. He is respected by his friends and feared by the enemies of the republic."

Clarisa looked at her husband as if she had not realized before how important he was.

Vicente said, "Are you a Catholic, Cassandra?"

"As a baby I was baptized in a Catholic church, but no, Reverend. I do not attend a Catholic church. I'm a Christian and a disciple of Jesus by faith and a Methodist by choice."

Vicente said, "Then you are opposed to Catholicism?"

"On the contrary, Vicente, rather I am for Jesus since there is only one name under heaven by which a person can be saved and we are all saved by the one Jesus."

Vicente said, "That is true."

Adrianna said, "I thought Vicente that all Protestants were damned to hell?"

Vicente said, "Many errors in teaching have occurred, my dear Adrianna. Don't tell the Pope I said that."

Alejandro said, "The next thing you know we'll be talking politics."

Diego said, "If you insist."

Cassandra chuckled, "Yes, the two things avoided by cowards are conversations about politics and religion."

Clarisa said, "That has been my observation."

Cassandra said, "When the men are alone they dive into such conversations with vigor. It is only because they think the female character is too fragile for such controversy that they avoid it in women's presence."

Clarisa said, "You mean the same men who are frightened to death to be in the labor room when the weak wife delivers them a son or daughter?"

All the women and Vicente broke into laughter. Diego had a stunned look on his face and that caused the rest to break into laughter. When they settled down, Adrianna said, "I have never heard such a conversation in polite company."

Clarisa said, "What makes you think this is polite company?"

Everyone started laughing again. A servant was standing waiting and Alejandro said, "It seems dinner is ready."

The group got up and went into the dining room. Alejandro seated Cassandra next to him. Before the serving started, Vicente gave thanks.

Cassandra said to Alejandro, "You have a beautiful home."

Alejandro said, "My uncle owned it before he passed. I bought it from Aunt Adrianna on the understanding she would live here for the rest of her life."

Cassandra said, "That is a good way to protect your reputation."

Adrianna was sitting next to Cassandra and said, "She is a wise woman, Alejandro."

Diego asked, "How is your real estate shopping coming Cassandra."

"My agent has not turned up anything yet, Diego, but it has been only a short time since he agreed to be my agent."

Diego said, "It is strange under the circumstances that he has not found anything yet."

Cassandra said, "My desires were very specific."

Adrianna said, "Does not the Ambassador live at the Embassy?"

Cassandra said, "Yes, but someday I will no longer be Ambassador and I'd like to own property here."

Vicente added, "Now is a good time to buy."

Clarisa asked Amanda, "What do you do at the embassy, Amanda?"

"I am the ambassador's assistant."

Adrianna asked, "What does an assistant do?"

Amanda laughed and said with dramatic flair, "Well for example, arrange for an evening gown for the ambassador at the last minute so she can attend a dinner with the President of Mexico. I had to arrange for designers to come to the embassy and make sure they aren't there at the same time so there was no hair pulling or eye scratching." Amanda looked around the table, "Women can be so competitive." That brought light chuckles. She continued, "I had to arrange fittings and rush alterations. Luckily the ambassador is of athletic build so that made the job easier."

Vicente asked, "How is it you have no gowns at the Embassy?"

Amanda answered, "We have no dress clothes at the embassy because we came on a military airplane that does not have room for personal baggage, but if you can believe it brought lots of guns and armored vehicles and such. I would have thought they could fit a few garment boxes on board."

The way she said it resulted in some laughter. Amanda continued, "I will tell you those military planes are not as comfortable as commercial planes. You have no idea what a good assistant has to put up with." Amanda looked at Cassandra and said with a big smile, "I do however sometimes get to go to really enjoyable social functions with my boss."

Adrianna looked at Amanda and said, "I still don't understand what you do?"

"I take care of all the small things so the ambassador can concentrate on the big things."

Clarisa said, "Like a wife does for her husband."

Amanda said, "Exactly."

The men were all smiling. Diego was looking at Amanda who smiled at him. He shook his head in what Cassandra thought might be disbelief. Whether it was at her explanation or at her claim Cassandra did not know, and she thought it didn't really matter.

After dinner the group went into the sitting room for coffee. Diego whispered to Cassandra, "What does Amanda really do?"

Cassandra leaned toward Diego and whispered back, "Bodyguard and she is very good and very few suspect. She is also secondarily, my assistant."

Diego nodded understanding.

The group took seats and Alejandro sat next to Cassandra. A server brought more wine for the guests.

Cassandra said, "That was a delicious meal and I enjoyed it thoroughly."

Vicente said, "I agree."

Alejandro said, "A toast to good wine, good food, good friends and our good God."

Cassandra said, "And may He bless us one and all."

Vicente said, "Amen," and they all raised their glasses.

Alejandro asked, "Vicente, how is your church doing?"

"I am an undertaker and I am overseeing the death of a congregation. The young people have abandoned the church and the old people are dying off. It won't be long at this rate until there is no congregation."

Cassandra said, "Then change things to bring the young people to hear the word."

Vicente said tongue in cheek, "And how do I do that?"

Cassandra said, "Young singers with guitars and sermons geared to young people telling them why they need what Jesus offers."

Vicente looked at Cassandra. He sat obviously considering what she'd said. The group was aghast that she had presumed to tell Vicente how to minister and there was a deafening silence.

Vicente said, "I'll try it on Saturday evenings. Thank you, Cassandra."

"You are welcome, Reverend."

The tension disappeared and Diego said, "I must make my excuses Alejandro for I have duties to attend to in the morning. I thank you for a most enjoyable evening."

Cassandra said, "I think we should be going as well."

Alejandro walked his guests to the door. Diego and his wife followed.

Cassandra said, "Thank you for an entirely enjoyable time, Alejandro."

She leaned over and kissed him on the cheek. He seemed taken aback and blushed. Amanda had taken a position between Cassandra and the vehicle that had pulled up. She opened the door for Cassandra and Cassandra got in noticing Diego had observed Amanda's action. Amanda went around to the other side and another of the security team opened the door for Amanda.

Diego said to Alejandro, "It was an enjoyable evening. I think she likes you Alejandro."

Clarisa said, "Do not be afraid of a strong woman."

Diego looked at his wife. He was not used to such comments from her. Their car pulled up and they left. Alejandro went back inside and sat own.

His aunt said, "She might be too much for you to handle, nephew. She is not like the women you usually date and she's not just a pretty thing to be worn on your arm to one social event and discarded."

Vicente said, "Be careful, Alejandro. She is a serious woman for a serious man."

Alejandro said, "I know. She makes me want to be a serious man."

On the drive back to the embassy Amanda said, "Tomas works for Diego and he tried to pump me for information. He's pretty good for a newbie."

Cassandra said, "Diego asked me what you really did. I told him you were my bodyguard."

Amanda said, "That's true, at least in part."

"What did you think of the group?"

Amanda smiled, "I found the people he chose to invite an interesting collection. They seemed quite comfortable with us which means you have earned a certain level of trust."

"Yes and that is good."

Amanda paused and then said, "I think Diego and Tomas were intended to keep you off guard. Instead you kept Diego off balance and his wife thinking. Vicente and Adrianna were the chaperones and Tomas served the added function of keeping me occupied. Of course Alejandro's aunt had to be there since she lives with him. I find that arrangement interesting and I will ask to have her looked into. I expect she is a woman of impeccable reputation and thus there would be no rumors of Alejandro having sleepovers there with the women he escorts."

Cassandra smiled, "You are probably right."

Cassandra slept well that night, but was awakened early. It seemed the construction workers were working on Saturday. Cassandra got ready to go down for breakfast. She was hungry this morning. She grabbed her Bible and headed for the kitchen.

On her way Cassandra found one of the Amazons was keeping guard at the top of the stairs. She greeted the woman, "Good morning, Corporal."

"Good morning, ma'am."

Cassandra went downstairs. She had not noticed when she came home last night that the downstairs painting had been completed. The place looked grand. She went into the kitchen to get a cup of coffee. Luis and Pedro were sitting at the kitchen table and they both jumped up as though they had been caught doing something they shouldn't.

Pedro said, "Good morning, Excellency. May I prepare you something for breakfast?"

Cassandra said, "Please; something simple, Pedro. Good morning, Luis."

Luis said, "Good morning, Excellency."

"I'll eat in the garden."

Cassandra took her cup outside and sat at the table under the gazebo. It was a beautiful warm morning and in spite of the sounds of construction and the presence of soldiers on the grounds, Cassandra found it peaceful. She sat just having a quite time sipping her coffee and reading her Bible.

Luis interrupted her thoughts when he brought her plate and a carafe of coffee on a tray.

She said, "Thank you, Luis."

Luis retreated to a chair near the Embassy door. Cassandra lifted the lid over the plate. Pedro had prepared her a breakfast burrito surrounded by slices of fruit. She gave thanks and started eating and found it was very good. She read her Bible as she ate. When she finished, she poured herself another cup of coffee and Luis hurried over to clear away her plate.

Cassandra said, "It is a beautiful morning is it not, Luis?"

Luis smiled, "Si, Doña Cassandra."

Cassandra smiled at the semi informality and asked, "Where are you from, Luis?"

"I am from Celestun, do you know it?"

Cassandra smiled, "I do. It has become less a fishing village and a bit of a tourist place now. There are a lot of Americans there aren't there?"

Luis said, "Yes, Excellency."

Cassandra smiled and Luis left hurriedly. It seemed to her that she made him uncomfortable. She suspected it was because he was not invisible to her. The fact he had told her where he was from also probably made him uneasy. Cassandra went back to reading her Bible and sipping her coffee. Her concentration was interrupted by the sound of trucks. She decided to investigate.

When she got to the front of the house, she found Juan inspecting furniture as it was unloaded. There were three large trucks in front of the building. Her curiosity satisfied Cassandra went back through the embassy building and into the garden. She sat back down and sat listening to the construction noises mixed with the sounds of birds singing.

She saw Stan coming and he said, "Good morning, Ambassador."

"Good morning, Stan."

Stan took a seat, "I have found some interesting things about Juan's relatives."

Cassandra said, "What did you find out?"

"Juan's two aunts are married to businessmen. They are solid middle class with nothing that would cause us concern. Two of his uncles are professionals; an accountant and a dentist. His third uncle is a different animal. He is a Colonel and a decorated war hero. He is commanding forces that are fighting in the south against Castillo rebels. He is dedicated to the elected government and a devoted nationalist. He is a very influential man. He and Carlos are expected to be promoted soon."

Cassandra said, "What about Castillo?"

"His forces have disbanded as a cohesive fighting unit. He has sent his men to operate as semi independent units to redevelop his drug trade with which to finance further adventures. It will be difficult for him to do that now that the military sees the extreme threat that he presents after the incidents with the special cargo. The military is having difficulty finding the small units, but when they do they destroy them to the man. There is talk of an amnesty offer for any who desert Castillo and surrender to the authorities. It is not in place yet and we do not expect it will be approved." Stan paused for effect.

"Alejandro has authorized and Diego has sent agents to locate Castillo's units. They are having some success as the majority of people don't seem to want a resurgence of the drug lords. I don't think there will ever be a drug trade like there has been in the past."

Cassandra asked, "Do we have any idea where Castillo is?"

"No. He was reported to be in Venezuela two days ago, but he has dropped out of sight. The analysts think he is back in Mexico. The Agency is trying to figure out what is up."

Cassandra said, "Do we know who he met with in Venezuela?"

"Officials of the state intelligence agency and some very unsavory terrorist watch list types."

Stan handed her a list.

"Have any of our people located any of Castillo's units?"

Stan smiled, "We know of one that the government doesn't apparently know about."

Cassandra said, "Would it hurt our intelligence operation to give the location to our friends?"

"No."

"Then give me the coordinates and I'll invite Alejandro for lunch."

Stan nodded and said, "I'll go get them." He got up and left. Cassandra made a call.

Alejandro answered, "Good morning, Cassandra."

"Good morning, Alejandro. Thank you for an enjoyable evening. Would you like to come for a light lunch here at the embassy around twelve thirty? I have a gift for you."

"I'd be delighted."

"Good. I'll see you then."

Cassandra went to the kitchen and Pedro rose as she came in and said, "Pedro, I will have company for lunch in the garden. Please prepare something nice."

"Will there be just one other person, Doña Cassandra?"

"Yes, Pedro."

He bowed slightly. She went through the dining room and found men had brought in a large table and were placing other furniture. She thought this would be a place for semi-formal dinners. Out of curiosity, she went into the living room and found new furniture had been placed there.

She ran into Juan who said, "Good morning, Ambassador. We are setting up the other building's living and great rooms as business reception areas. The small main level rooms will be offices."

Cassandra said, "This place is looking up."

Juan smiled, "Yes. To change the subject, I have identified two qualified potential candidates to be your secretary. I can have them here Monday for you to meet if you'd like."

Cassandra smiled, "The afternoon would be best."

Juan said, "I will arrange it."

Cassandra called down to the front gate to tell them she expected Alejandro for lunch. She decided to stop on the second floor and see how the work was progressing. A soldier was on guard on the second floor landing.

He said, "Ma'am" and Cassandra replied, "Good morning."

Cassandra looked around. She noted the hall had been painted and the door to her new temporary office suite had been installed. She looked in both directions and went left. She looked in each room as she went down the hall. Each had been painted and was ready for furniture. Cassandra walked back toward her office.

There had been ten rooms on this floor, but now there were only six. What would eventually be her residence suite and for a while her temporary office suite took up most of one wing. She inspected the door to the suite and found it was in fact a steel door on a steel frame. She assumed the drywall covered an equally strong structure. She opened the door and four men were still at work finishing the trim. The men stopped working.

Cassandra said in Spanish, *"Good morning. Please don't let me disrupt your work."*

The men went back to work as Cassandra looked around. The room that would serve as her office and later her bedroom was large and the two other rooms would be temporary offices and main space was huge. It would be the outer office for the time being and could easily accommodate several desks. Eventually it would be her private living room. Cassandra went upstairs where she found the Corporal still on guard, but now she had a machine pistol slung over her shoulder.

Cassandra said, "I see you have been issued your new weapons; good choice."

The Corporal smiled and said, "Yes ma'am."

Cassandra went to her suite and found two men installing a new steel door frame and steel door. Cassandra could tell it would look like the wood doors on the floor when it was painted. A soldier was standing close by watching the men. The men stood aside and Cassandra entered and deposited her Bible then went back downstairs. She knew things had to change here. Cassandra took the service stairs down and found a soldier guarding the stairwell on the second floor landing.

She said, "Good morning"

He replied, "Ma'am."

Cassandra out of curiosity visited the other building and saw the work being done there. It was obvious this would be more of a public space. She returned to what she thought of as the main building and went to sit in the garden gazebo. The chair was comfortable and she drifted off.

A gentle voice woke her, "Ambassador, your guest has arrived."

Cassandra looked up and said to Amanda, "Thank you." Amanda passed her a slip of paper.

Cassandra walked to the front door where she greeted Alejandro when he got out of his vehicle, "Hello, Alejandro."

He smiled, "Hello."

"We are having lunch in the garden. Please come with me."

Cassandra put her arm through his and he smiled as she led him away. One of his security men followed.

Alejandro looked around, "It is a busy place."

"Indeed. There is much to do. While these men are working hard, I have been enjoying a relaxing morning and have done little."

Alejandro said, "It has been the same for me. My friend Vicente is much taken with you."

"He is delightful company. It is unfortunate Catholic priests don't marry. He would make some woman a good husband."

Alejandro laughed and said, "I'll tell him that. He will be delighted. He is after all still a man and compliments from an attractive woman are always welcome."

Cassandra smiled, "Yes, compliments are good for the disposition."

They arrived at the garden table and Alejandro pulled Cassandra's seat out for her. His man was nearby. Alejandro asked, "Do you not have security for your person?"

Cassandra said, "They are on the roof and elsewhere."

Alejandro glanced at the roof and saw two soldiers with rifles and another with field glasses. He said, "I see. I am glad you take precautions."

Luis came to the table and Cassandra said, "Luis, I believe you know Alejandro."

To Luis credit he was smart enough not to deny it.

Cassandra asked Alejandro, "Would you like coffee or perhaps a glass of wine?"

Alejandro asked, "What are you having."

"I think a nice glass of wine."

Alejandro looked at Luis, "I'll have the same."

Cassandra said, "I have something for you."

She handed him the slip of paper.

"What is it?"

"The coordinates for a unit of Castillo's men that we don't think you know about."

Alejandro nodded, "Thank you."

"You are welcome. The business being concluded let us now enjoy our lunch."

"Yes, of course."

Luis arrived with the wine.

Alejandro asked, "I have not had time to inquire. What kind of real estate are you looking for?"

"An estancia and I hope to have friendly neighbors."

"Adolpho is well connected and is trustworthy. His contacts bring him a lot of commissions. He will not suggest anything that is not worthwhile. This is a good time to buy with dollars as the recent troubles have created distress for many formerly prominent families."

"I know my U.S. dollars will go far at the moment. Unlike others, I am optimistic about the long term prospects in Mexico in spite of recent events."

Luis came with their lunch. He set the plates before them and took the covers off. It was baked fish on a bed of rice.

Cassandra said, "Thank you, Luis."

She turned to Alejandro, "Would you say the blessing?"

Alejandro smiled and said the prayer. Cassandra took a bite of the fish.

She said, "This is very good."

Her guest took a bite and smiled, "Indeed."

They ate and talked.

Alejandro asked, "Do you want to invest in an estancia just to resell it?"

"No. Someday I'd like to live on it. The prices are depressed right now and that may present a good opportunity to get what I want."

Alejandro said, "I will talk to Adolpho. I know of a property that has been in a family for a long time. The father and sons died in the recent unpleasantness. The widows need to sell the property and of course there are not many buyers at this time. I think you are wise to buy now."

Cassandra asked, "What have you been investing in?"

"I am part of a privately held company that is building a munitions and small arms manufacturing plant to replace ones that were destroyed. We will take precautions in the design so the business is not easy to sabotage. If we succeed, I'll be rich. If not, I'll be poor again."

Cassandra asked, "Are you accepting new investors?"

"Are you interested?"

"Perhaps, but I would need to know more."

Alejandro said, "Each investor must contribute at least two hundred thousand U.S. dollars."

Cassandra asked, "All the investors?"

"Yes. I have two shares. We needed a minimum of two million U.S. dollars to get the balance of the financing. At present, we have twelve investor shares. Our limit is fifteen. Many of the investors have mortgaged their homes and businesses to come up with the money. We have a royalty license for innovative small weapon designs."

Cassandra asked, "Israeli?"

"Yes."

Cassandra said, "I am definitely interested. Please ask the other investors and provide me with information," she paused and added, "for personal use."

"I understand and will see what I can do."

Alejandro said, "I know you are not a Catholic, but would you accompany me to church in the morning?"

Cassandra said, "Where do you plan to go?"

"Vicente's church."

"Well, if you don't think he will have a heart attack if a protestant attends, I am willing."

Alejandro was smiling, "I don't think that will happen. What are your plans for the afternoon?"

"I don't have any."

Alejandro smiled, "I am going to play golf. Do you play?"

Cassandra smiled, "Yes, but I don't have my clubs or shoes here."

"The Club will have extra clubs and you could get new shoes there."

Cassandra said, "I accept and entrust my person to your protection.

Alejandro smiled.

Cassandra asked, "Does your club have a dress code?"

"What you have on is acceptable."

Cassandra smiled, "Then I am ready."

She told her staff what was happening and Stan insisted Amanda accompany her. Cassandra relented, but held the line at Amanda's presence. Cassandra went back to Alejandro,

"My head of security insists Amanda go with us. Your men would not be allowed in the women's room."

Alejandro smiled, "I understand."

On the way to the club, Alejandro called in the coordinates Cassandra had given him. He ordered immediate action to be taken. Cassandra realized that her date was a powerful man second only to the President.

Cassandra knew how difficult it was to get on a golf course in Mexico City. She found that she would be part of a foursome which consisted of Enrique, Maria, Alejandro and her.

Enrique greeted her, "Good afternoon, Cassandra. I am glad you could make it."

Maria embraced her, "Now I know we will have an enjoyable afternoon?"

After Cassandra got equipped, they set out. They talked and played through the eighteen holes. Of course a large entourage followed. Cassandra was at best a respectable golfer and out of practice, but she held her own and played better than she had expected. She could just match Maria, but Alejandro and Enrique were much better than the women and they both finished seven or eight strokes lower.

After the round they went to have drinks. Enrique said, "Cassandra you are like Maria. You play consistent golf and score well enough to be good company on the course."

Maria said, "Enrique you should be a more gracious winner." Maria turned to Cassandra, "Men are so macho when they play sports."

Enrique said, "Cassandra, I see your assistant is following us everywhere."

Alejandro said, "In Cassandra's defense, it was pointed out to me that my security men could not enter women's sanctums."

Enrique laughed saying, "Quite so and we have no women in security."

Maria looked at her husband and said, "Perhaps we should."

Enrique nodded agreement and took his wife's hand, "Forgive me for being so careless."

Maria smiled and kissed her husband on the cheek.

Enrique looked at Cassandra and said playfully, "See, it is possible for an old dog to learn new tricks."

After finishing their drinks, the president and his party left and Alejandro took Cassandra back. They arrived at the embassy about six thirty. Alejandro opened Cassandra's vehicle door and walked her to the entrance to the building.

Cassandra said, "Thank you for an enjoyable afternoon."

She leaned over to kiss him on the cheek and he moved slightly and their lips touched. Electricity sparked between them and Cassandra thought she would combust. Alejandro was smiling and slightly flushed.

Cassandra said in a raspy voice, "You are a sneaky one, Alejandro."

He just smiled and said, "Good evening."

She watched him return to his car then went inside and sat in the living room. Amanda took a seat beside her.

Amanda said, "You know he's gorgeous."

"Not bad."

Amanda said, "No, gorgeous."

Cassandra said, "I'm hungry. Let's see if Pedro is still here."

They had just finished eating a small meal at the kitchen table when a sergeant came for Cassandra, "Ambassador, there is an encrypted call for you."

Cassandra went to the communications room and picked up the handset. The operator left the room.

Cassandra said, "This is Cassandra Crossing."

The voice said, "Good evening, Cassandra."

"Father, it is so good to hear from you."

He said, "Well I had to get the scoop on the guy you are dating. I hear he kissed you in public."

Cassandra said, "Your reports are premature daddy. It was a peck and we have not been on a date."

"What happened last night and today?"

Cassandra sighed, "Last night was a dinner party at the secretary's home which I attended with Amanda. There were other guests."

"I know. I have spies. Where did you go today?"

Cassandra caught her father off guard, "I played golf with the president, the first lady and the secretary of the interior."

"Now that I didn't know and it has to be a first for one of our ambassadors."

"Well, have you and mother played with the Mexican Ambassador and his wife?"

"I don't know if he even plays."

Cassandra couldn't help teasing her father, "Well, you said you had spies."

She heard her father's laugh.

She added, "So as you won't be shocked, I am going to a Catholic service in the morning at Vicente's church. Vicente is a nice man."

Her father said, "And also the youngest bishop ever in the Catholic Church."

Cassandra didn't let on she didn't know that. Craig asked, "How do you know him?"

"He is a friend of Alejandro's and we were introduced at the dinner last evening. We hit it off."

Her father said, "You seem to have a knack for being a diplomat. I received Stan's report about Castillo and the background files you asked him to prepare. It seems you are making progress. You are gathering as much intelligence as ambassador as you did as an agent."

Cassandra said, "I'd like to discuss why Castillo was in Venezuela with Alejandro. Do you know?"

"He met with some of the same people as last time. I see no harm in discussing it with your boyfriend."

Cassandra ignored the boyfriend remark and took a deep breath, "Do you think Castillo is trying to arrange more special cargo?"

"The intelligence community doubts he has that level of credibility now."

Cassandra said, "It is supposition without basis in fact. "

"Probably and I don't think you can be sure of anything when you're dealing with terrorists or drug dealers."

"I agree. These terrorists like big plans and action even when it doesn't quite work out. It was a very close thing and that may encourage them if Castillo comes up with another plan."

"Yes. Keep up the good work. Your mother sends her love. "

Cassandra said, "Good night daddy and you as well Mr. President."

Her father laughed and the call ended. Cassandra left the communications room and went back upstairs. Amanda was sitting in the sitting room talking with Mike.

Cassandra said, "I'm turning in. Amanda, we'll be leaving for church at seven thirty. Please let Stan know."

Cassandra headed upstairs. When she got to the top of the stairs, the Amazon was not there. Cassandra drew her weapon and quietly backed down the stairs. On the second floor landing, she sent out an alert on the small radio on her belt. In a minute, armed men were rushing up the stairs. She heard shots on the third floor and went down toward the first floor. She met Amanda and Mike coming up the stairs with their weapons drawn.

Cassandra said, "To the main floor."

When they reached the first floor, men were rushing toward her. The formed a cordon around her and took her outside to an armored vehicle and she and her two companions got in. Troops had taken up positions everywhere.

Cassandra's radio buzzed and she said, "Eagle One."

"Is your situation stable?"

Cassandra said, "Affirmative Tiger One."

She found out almost immediately her response had been a little premature. Small arms fire started pinging off the armored vehicle's skin. A soldier jumped in and drove the vehicle forward a few feet and stopped because now gunfire could be heard everywhere.

There was gunfire at the main gate and behind them. Cassandra went for the gun turret. There were men trying to come over the walls. Then there was a blast and a large hole was blown in the front wall. There were three more similar blasts at various places along the wall.

The standing order was to kill anyone attacking the compound once they were on embassy property. Suddenly the men who had come over the walls were being decimated by automatic fire. The breach in the wall was covered as a Mexican armored personnel vehicle trying to come through was met by chain gun fire and then one of the infantrymen fired an M136 shoulder fired rocket launcher. The Mexican armored vehicle exploded bursting into flame and blocking the gap in the wall.

The heavy machine guns made quick work of the men trying to enter the breaches in the wall. It was then that a helicopter made a strafing pass at the embassy. It made only one because as it passed over one of the men on the embassy roof fired a Stinger at the helicopter and it took only a second to catch the aircraft and reduce the helicopter to a falling ball of fire.

Cassandra had a front row seat in the gun turret. She saw several men dressed in civilian clothes running with charge satchels coming from the left. She charged the turret weapon and opened fire trying to fire downward at the attackers. She was inexperienced with this particular weapon, but she spent enough rounds to cut the attackers to ribbons first below the knees and then as they fell they were riddled with rounds. One of the satchel charges exploded. Suddenly the night was silent for a few moments.

The silence was broken by a loud explosion and some more small arms fire from behind the Embassy and then everything went silent again. Cassandra's radio buzzed and she answered, "Eagle One."

Bob said, "Where the hell are you Eagle One?"

"I'm in the gun turret of an armored vehicle at the north corner of the Embassy. Remember who you are addressing Tiger One. Over."

Amanda laughed nervously.

The soldier in the driver's seat said, "Man, the guys are going to rib me now."

Amanda said, "Yeah, you're nickname will be chauffeur."

Mike added, "For Ambassador Death."

The soldier's mouth dropped open. Amanda teased him, "Yeah, she heard."

Cassandra said, "Open up. The Colonel is coming." Cassandra got out of her position and climbed out of the vehicle.

Bob yelled, "Get down."

Cassandra ducked instinctively and Bob walked to her and handed her body armor, "Please put that on Ambassador. There may still be snipers around."

Cassandra didn't tell him she was wearing a custom fitted ballistic vest under her blouse, but just said, "Thank you, Colonel." She put the vest on.

Bob pointed to what was left of the men with the charge satchels, "Are you responsible for that carnage?"

Cassandra said, "Yes."

Bob said with a smile, "Beginner's luck."

Cassandra smiled and shrugged, "Maybe. There's a lot you don't know about me." She started walking toward the embassy and went in. Bob was right behind her.

Jake came running up, "Colonel, they destroyed one of the outbuildings. We have casualties. Two dead and eleven wounded so far."

Bob said, "Shit!"

They entered the Embassy and Cassandra's phone rang and she answered it. Alejandro said before she could say anything, "Are you all right?"

"Yes, but we have wounded and some seriously. Where is the nearest hospital?"

"Don't take them there. The hospital is overwhelmed. You should send your wounded men to the airport. Is your situation stable?"

Cassandra said, "We are stable. We'll air evacuate our wounded. Take care of yourself, Alejandro."

"You be careful as well." Alejandro ended the call.

Cassandra said, "The hospital can't take our wounded. Call General Brite and airlift our wounded to the airport."

The Colonel turned to Jake and Jake said, "I'm on it."

Bob rushed off. Cassandra heard the chairs in the dining room being moved. She assumed it would become a triage station. Amanda was standing against the wall her weapon at her side. Cassandra went and sat on the sofa.

Amanda joined her, "It's a hell of a way to end what was an enjoyable day."

The two women just sat there. At the moment, this was a military operation.

Helicopters started landing in the front yard within minutes as the wounded were evacuated by air. Cassandra sat in the front room watching the copters land and take off. Replacements came on the inbound flights.

Finally Bob came into the room and sat beside Cassandra. "Two workmen were still on the floor when you got home.

They killed the soldier with them and the Amazon. Both were shot in the back of the head with a silenced pistol."

Cassandra said, "When she wasn't at the top of the stairs, I knew something was wrong."

Stan came and sat beside Cassandra, "There were five coordinated terrorist attacks; the subway, the light rail system, a bus station, the main Cathedral and here. The attack at the Cathedral resulted in the most casualties as Saturday evening mass was in progress."

Bob showed up, "Our injured are all evacuated. Only one wound is life threatening. We killed thirty nine attackers and wounded another twenty two not counting the helicopter we shot down. The fireball didn't hit any houses, but went down in a wooded ravine. Fire fighters are on the scene now."

Stan said, "I sent people to the airport for the interrogations."

Bob said, "The attack was on U.S. soil so technically they are our prisoners."

Cassandra said, "It is a moot point and not practical for us to hold them. We'll turn them over eventually. In the meantime, Bob get what you can. I'm going to call Washington. Have someone start photographing and searching the dead attackers."

Cassandra's call was put directly through. Her father came on the line, "How bad is it, Cassandra?"

"Bad. Here we lost two dead and eleven were wounded. We killed thirty nine attackers and wounded twenty two. The wounded are now being airlifted to the airport for treatment. Stan's team will interrogate the wounded attackers. We lost an outbuilding and shot down a helicopter. The initial reports were that there were five simultaneous terrorist attacks."

Cassandra told her father what they knew. She concluded her report with, "There must be mass casualties because we were advised not to bring our wounded to the local hospital because it was overwhelmed."

Her father said, "Please keep us informed. Are you secure there?"

"I believe so. We easily repelled the attack. I don't think they could mount another attack if they wanted to. I believe it was a last ditch effort."

Her father said, "When you get the lowdown on what happened, let us know."

"I will. Now about the prisoners we took."

They discussed how to proceed with the prisoners. It was agreed they would be turned over at Cassandra's discretion. Her father was in a serious mood.

While Cassandra was on the communication link, a helicopter came and took Stan to the airport. When she came upstairs from the basement, she found fresh coffee had been made. Cassandra was drinking coffee in the kitchen when Alejandro called back three hours later. She answered, "Crossing."

Alejandro said, "I can't talk long. Are you all right?"

"Yes and we have things in hand. We do have a lot of bodies and body parts to dispose of though. Do you have any ideas?"

"I'll send a refrigerated meat truck for the attackers."

Cassandra said, "That will work. Is Vicente all right?"

"Yes, but a lot of people died in the attack on the cathedral. The death toll is over three hundred and climbing. I will not be coming to take you to church."

"Of course not; you have a lot to do."

Alejandro said, "I must go now." He hung up.

Cassandra put the phone back in her pocket. She went to the communications center and sent the report, "Initial reports on the Cathedral attack are that civilian casualties are over three hundred and climbing." She went back to the kitchen and poured another coffee and radioed Bob.

He answered, "I'll be there in a minute."

He came through the kitchen door and said, "Oh that coffee smells good." He got a cup and was pouring himself one.

Cassandra said, "Alejandro is sending a refrigerated meat truck for the bodies and body parts of the attackers."

Bob looked at Cassandra, “There wasn’t a lot left of that group you mowed down. Your body count was eleven of the thirty nine killed and four of the wounded.”

Cassandra looked in her coffee, “Beginners luck.”

Bob started laughing and it was contagious. A sergeant came into the room and gave them a strange look as he passed through.

Cassandra said, “So what happened?”

“Two of the workmen stayed over to finish a task. They must have had a pistol in a tool box. The soldiers never knew what happened. The assassins did not have a radio so the attack must have been set for a specific time or event. I think when you came back it started some kind of count down.”

Cassandra asked, “Why did they risk so much here?”

Bob said, “You might want to put a bug in the secretary’s ear. We paid cash for the place next door. There was only one place where that kind of money would be kept safe. They weren’t military or if they were, they were not very good. I doubt they knew what they would be facing.”

Cassandra said, “That makes sense, but they would have had to know about the terrorist attacks ahead of time.”

Cassandra thought that she had let it be known she was looking to buy a ranch with American green backs. That wasn’t smart, but who was the leak?

Cassandra added, “It would indicate these guys had a link to Castillo. What was Castillo trying to accomplish? That part doesn’t make sense. We could start with the contractor who hired the assassins. I suppose they are both dead.”

“No. One of them is wounded, but alive and was taken to the airport. He will be the first focus of Stan’s interrogations.”

“Ah, I see. I hope Stan is successful.”

Bob said, “Stan was pissed so I expect he’ll get what he wants even if he has to take the guy away from the airport.”

Cassandra said, “Bob watch the language.”

“As stressed as I am, I consider that diplomatic.”

Cassandra nodded, “Fair enough.”

Bob said, “You should try and get some sleep.”

"Yeah, like that's going to happen. Sometimes this ambassador's job sucks."

Bob smiled, "Well, if you ever want a job we could use you as a turret gunner."

Cassandra gave him the look and then smiled. They both laughed. Cassandra knew it was nerves. She was sitting drinking her second cup of coffee when she overheard the radio chatter.

"Tiger are you expecting a meat truck?"

Bob said, "Is it empty?"

"Yes sir."

"Then I'm expecting it. Send it to where we laid out the body bags."

"Yes sir."

Cassandra smiled. Alejandro had not been kidding. A strange thought hit her. She wondered if the dead would end up as dog food. She shuddered and questioned where that thought had come from. She thought, I need to pray, and she did. Afterward she felt better. At three in the morning she went to her suite and fell asleep on top of the bed.

She woke to sun streaming through the window. She looked at her clock. It was eight o'clock and she had slept for five hours. She took off her clothes, showered, brushed her teeth and dressed in fresh clothes. When she went into the hall, she found several female soldiers in the hall.

Cassandra said, "Good morning, ladies. What is happening?"

The closest woman, a sergeant answered, "Good morning, ma'am. We are your night time floor guard. We are just being relieved."

Cassandra said, "Very well. Would the night shift like to join me for breakfast?"

"Yes ma'am. It would be a privilege."

They went downstairs and Cassandra noticed the dining room table was gone as she went through on her way to the kitchen. Pedro and Luis were there.

She said, "Good morning. Are your families well?"

The men looked at each other and Pedro said, “Yes, Excellency.”

Cassandra sighed, “Thank God.” She paused and then said, “I am ready for coffee and breakfast.” Cassandra said to Pedro and Luis, “Please bring breakfast for four to the garden.”

She walked into the garden and took a seat at the table in the gazebo and the sergeant and the other two soldiers took a seat after her. Cassandra noticed some damage from small arms fire. The sergeant saw it too.

Cassandra said, “That will need a little repair.”

The sergeant said, “Yes ma’am. I think a lot of things will need repair.”

Cassandra smiled, “Where are you from, Sergeant?”

“I’m from Delaware, ma’am.”

Cassandra asked, “How long have you been in?”

“Seven years, ma’am.”

Cassandra said, “I can see getting you into a conversation is going to be like pulling teeth.”

The two women at the table smiled and the sergeant said, “Actually, it’s my older brother who is the dentist. I have two brothers. The youngest is in the navy.”

Cassandra said, “What does your father do?”

“He’s a dentist. What does yours do, ma’am?”

Cassandra smiled, “He’s your Commander In Chief.”

The sergeant was stunned. She asked, “He’s your father?”

“Yes.”

The Sergeant smiled, “And he couldn’t get you a better gig than this?”

Cassandra laughed. Cassandra had never been to Delaware and asked the sergeant about it. She asked the other two about their backgrounds and where they were from. Luis brought breakfast and Cassandra said the blessing. She enjoyed talking with the women and the time passed quickly.

When they finished eating, Cassandra said, "I suppose you all could use some sack time. Thank you for the company ladies. "

The sergeant smiled, "I enjoyed it, ma'am. Thank you for breakfast."

The other two women thanked her and the three left.

They had been gone a matter of a couple of minutes and Cassandra was sipping her coffee when Bob showed up,

"Good morning, Ambassador."

"Good morning, Bob."

Bob sat down and Luis hurried over, "Coffee, Colonel?"

"Please, Luis."

Cassandra asked Bob, "What's the damage?"

"The walls will need to be rebuilt, but the new ones should be blast resistant. The one outbuilding damaged in the explosion will have to be torn down. We have a lot of broken windows and some minor damage to buildings; mostly from small arms fire. We need to install cameras all over and especially on the new walls so charges can't be placed without our knowing."

Cassandra sat back, "This is certainly not your normal diplomatic posting."

"It's been more like a forward fire base. My people have started calling it Forward Fire Base Embassy."

Cassandra said, "I like that."

Bob asked, "Are you all right?"

"Yes. I'm not new to this sort of thing."

Bob just nodded and asked, "You really were a field spook?'

"Yes."

Bob asked, "Where?"

Cassandra smiled, "If I told you, I'd have to kill you."

Bob said, "Well you know Matt so you were definitely in the Middle East and your Spanish is excellent so you've been to South America. Do you speak other languages?"

Cassandra said, "I studied languages at University. I have a knack for that sort of thing."

Bob changed the topic of conversation, "Have you heard from Stan yet?"

"Not yet."

Bob said, "I'd better get back to work." He got up and left.

Stan returned before lunch and came to see Cassandra. She was sitting in the garden, but she had her laptop and was making notes. She said without looking up, "Just a second while I finish this thought." After a moment she closed the cover and asked, "What did you find out."

"The contractor's family was held hostage to gain his cooperation in switching out two workers. Diego's people found him and his family murdered in their home. Castillo was behind the attacks, but the guy didn't know why. His group had been told we had a lot of U.S. dollars here. They didn't know our strength and had assumed a regular embassy guard. The guy gave us what he had. I gave some information to Diego about where others from his unit might be found."

Cassandra said, "Good. I think Castillo had two purposes. Bob and I had already figured the money thing out. Perhaps Diego can find the leak. I think Castillo staged the terrorist attacks to appease his foreign backers. In the process, he used the money here to entice some criminals on the periphery to undertake what he knew would be a suicide mission. I don't think those men he baited with our cash knew it was a suicide mission. Castillo used them to make a bigger bang knowing they'd be slaughtered. Who were the other attackers?"

Stan sighed, "The Mexican intelligence service has not found the bombers. The bombs were remotely detonated and probably placed some hours before they were detonated."

Cassandra said, "That fits the theory."

Stan said, "I'll prepare and transmit a report with our theory to Washington."

"Please do."

Stan left to file their report. Cassandra was sitting in the Gazebo thinking when Bob returned. He said, "You'll hurt yourself thinking that hard."

She said, "Castillo has to be stopped. We need to find him, so he can be neutralized."

Bob said, "I have some shooters in my group."

"I know and I'd use them if I could."

"You can take the liberty of ticking the Commander-In-Chief off and not have it ruin your life entirely, but I can't."

Cassandra looked at Bob and said in jest, "Then I'll do it myself."

Bob said, "You can't. You no longer have a license to kill; you're an ambassador now."

Cassandra said with a smile, "You're taking all the fun out of this, Bob."

Bob said, "Be nice or I won't let you play with my toys anymore."

Cassandra smiled, "I did like that turret gun. By the way, where did all the Amazons come from?"

"The general sent them. He said your daddy insisted and he's the boss. Besides the Mexican government isn't doing a head count."

Cassandra said, "The women on the third floor should sleep better."

The rest of the day was busy on the embassy grounds. Juan had arranged dumpsters and the troops cleaned up a lot of the rubble from the damage. In the evening, Alejandro called.

Cassandra answered, "Good evening, Alejandro."

"Good evening, Cassandra. Would it be convenient for me to drop by?"

Cassandra said, "You are always welcome."

Alejandro said, "Good. I'll be there shortly."

He was at the gates within a half hour. Cassandra got a call from the front gate and met him in the front yard as he exited his vehicle.

She said, "Good evening, Alejandro."

He said, “Good evening, Cassandra,” and kissed her on the cheek.

She thought even a peck on the cheek from him set her blood to racing.

She smiled, “Please, come in.”

She led him to the small main floor library and they sat at a reading table. Luis came in and waited by the door.

Cassandra asked, “Would you like something to drink, Alejandro?”

Alejandro said, “Cognac, please.”

Cassandra looked at Luis, “Coffee for me please, Luis.”

Luis left.

Alejandro said, “I want to thank you for the information on one of Castillo’s units. We were able to capture a few rebels and it has been an intelligence gold mine.”

Cassandra restrained herself from asking for details and just said, “Good.”

Alejandro said, “So far it was just locations on other possible sites. We have raided them and interrogations are ongoing as we speak. I’ll send you copies of what we find.”

Cassandra said, “Thank you. We have formulated a working theory about the attacks.”

She told him what she had concluded. She also told him about Castillo’s visit to Venezuela.

Alejandro said, “We did not know all of this.”

Cassandra handed him the list Stan had given her, “These are the people with whom he had contact there.”

Alejandro read the list and then looked at Cassandra, “Thank you for this information.”

“You are welcome.”

Luis brought their beverages and Cassandra said, “Thank you, Luis.”

Luis left.

Alejandro said, “Now I have something for you.” He passed her a card.

Cassandra opened it. It was very formal and impressive. She said, “I’d love to go. Good for Carlos.”

Alejandro asked, "May I accompany you?"

"I would like that."

Alejandro handed her another card and said, "This one is for Juan. His uncle is being promoted as well."

Cassandra smiled, "I'll pass it along."

Alejandro asked, "Did you choose him to be your deputy chief of mission because of his uncle."

Cassandra said, "Not really. It was because I thought he would be good in this situation and understood what was happening because he has family here. He understands how things work in Mexico." Cassandra smiled and added, "His uncle's position is just a happy bonus."

Alejandro laughed, "You my dear are an entirely dangerous woman. Is it true that you killed eleven of the attackers and wounded four others?"

Cassandra looked Alejandro directly in the eyes and nodded yes.

He said, "Four in the attack when you saved Carlos, four at the President's residence, and eleven here, not counting the four wounded and one captured. That is quite a record not to mention you saved the president as well as Carlos."

Cassandra sighed, "I never really looked at it like that. I just reacted as I have been trained."

Alejandro said, "I know. Now I have distressed you."

"Perhaps just a little, but it is of little consequence. It is something I had not thought about and should have." Cassandra said in a normal voice, "Luis." He came in the door, "I would like two fingers of whiskey with a little ice."

Luis said, "Yes, Excellency."

Alejandro raised an eyebrow, "You don't mind that he listens."

"It is professional courtesy, Alejandro. He knows that I know, but it goes unsaid. Besides, I have nothing to hide from my friends and it helps to develop trust."

Alejandro said, "As when you let me know you had agents in the field by passing me intelligence."

"Yes."

Luis brought Cassandra her drink and she said, "Thank you." He went back into the hall and Cassandra took a sip of the drink, "That is good."

Alejandro asked, "May I speak directly?"

"Yes, of course you may."

"I find you irresistible and I intend to pursue you. To that end, I ask that you accompany me to a formal dinner the president is hosting next Saturday evening. You will be there as my escort and not as ambassador."

Cassandra smiled, "I accept."

Cassandra thought her heart must have skipped a beat.

"I will come for you at six." Alejandro took a drink of his cognac, "Now to personal business."

He took a thumb drive from his pocket and handed to Cassandra. She took it and waited for an explanation.

Alejandro gave it, "The partners involved in the new munitions plant have approved your participation and up to two shares to be sold to you."

Cassandra took another sip of her drink, "Who are the partners?"

"The partners are Maria, Adelina, Adrianna, Clarisa, Josefina and me. The contracts on which the financing is being arranged are with South American countries which are friendly to the U.S. and several distributors in the U.S. The latter will require normalization of trade which I believe will occur. Perhaps after production starts the company will bid on Mexican military contracts. It is all on the drive."

Cassandra said, "I will review the material. Thank you."

"You are welcome. Call Adelina if you decide to participate, which I believe you will. Her private number is on the drive."

Cassandra asked, "Do you think there will be more terrorist attacks?"

"Unfortunately, I do. Castillo, I think, has badly misjudged the Mexican people. The outrage at the attacks is fevered and Castillo has become the most hated man in Mexico. I think his days are numbered here and he may move his base to another country. I did not see any televisions here. You should get some and follow what is being reported."

Cassandra nodded, "I'll do that."

Alejandro had finished his cognac.

"I should take my leave. I will see you at the ceremonies on Wednesday."

He rose and Cassandra put her empty glass down and got up. Alejandro offered his arm and Cassandra took it and walked him to his car.

On the way she said, "When we are settled here, I will have to have a reception."

At the front door, Alejandro kissed Cassandra on the cheek. Cassandra smiled and watched him go to his vehicle. He drove away with Cassandra watching the car leave. Amanda came to her side.

"He is smitten with you, Ambassador."

Cassandra looked at Amanda, "It is not the ambassador he is smitten with."

Chapter 8 - Settling In

Monday, Cassandra reviewed the information Alejandro had provided. She decided she wanted to invest. The drive contained the phone numbers of the partners and Cassandra programmed them into her cell then called Adelina.

Adelina answered her phone, "Hello."

"Adelina, this is Cassandra."

Adelina said, "Good morning, Cassandra. We were all happy to hear you are all right. It was such a tragedy that we lost so many people. I was told two of your military lost their lives. Please accept my condolence."

Cassandra said, "Thank you."

"Have you decided on the investment?"

"Yes. I want to invest and I need to meet with you and arrange to finalize the contract and give you my money." The women made arrangements.

Cassandra then went to work preparing for the afternoon interviews. The secretarial candidates had arrived on a morning flight and Cassandra prepared to interview them. Their personnel folders were impressive.

Cassandra ate a late lunch and arranged to interview the candidates in the library. The first interview went very well and Cassandra decided the woman would do a good job. The second interview was with Carol Walters who had twenty five years experience serving in embassies in countries around the world. Her performance reports were outstanding and Cassandra wondered why she was here.

Carol came into the library at the appointed time. She was about five six and a slightly built woman. She was very well groomed and wore casual clothes unlike the previous candidate who had worn a business suit.

Cassandra stood and offered her hand, "You must be Carol?"

"Yes, Ambassador, and I am pleased to see you again."

Cassandra said, "Please have a seat." Cassandra could not place the woman though she looked familiar and Cassandra asked, "Where did we meet?"

"It was in the Green Zone in Iraq."

Cassandra thought that explained the clothes. Carol had learned about the situation here and that she would be coming in a military aircraft. Cassandra said, "I don't remember you."

"It doesn't surprise me. You were in the military hospital when the ambassador came to see you. I was with him taking notes."

Cassandra said, "I see."

Carol changed the subject and said, "It seems this place is more dangerous than it was there."

Cassandra smiled, "I suppose it has been, though hopefully that is over."

Carol smiled, "The emphasis is on hopefully, Ambassador. I understand the staff is staying on the grounds."

"Yes."

Carol said, "Then Ambassador, I suggest things are anything but normal."

Cassandra smiled and said, "True. Why are you here Carol? You should have your choice of posts given your experience."

Carol nodded, "I did and I asked to be considered for this job."

Cassandra sat back in her chair, "Why is that?"

"May I speak candidly?"

"Please."

Carol paused, "You need me. You are new and you'll need experienced people around you who won't run for the hills if there is trouble and there probably will be. I also owe your father and I can repay that debt by helping you. It will also again allow me to prove my worth."

Cassandra was curious, "How did my father help you?"

"It is personal, but I will say he saved my career and most certainly my dignity."

Cassandra smiled, "When can you start, Carol?"

"I can stay. I brought two bags just in case. I will send for the rest later."

Cassandra said, "All right then. Welcome aboard. The room next to my suite on the third floor is vacant and it has its own bath. You may want to move in there before someone else claims squatter's rights."

Carol said, "I will. Thank you."

Cassandra said, "You've met Juan. Do you know him?"

"I know of him and he has the reputation of being a maverick and too bright for his own good, so he'll probably fit in here."

Cassandra laughed lightly then got up saying, "Get settled and then you may join me for supper. Our temporary offices should be ready this week. You know what is needed, so I'll leave you to get things organized so we'll be ready when normal operations start."

Carol rose and the women shook hands again.

On Tuesday, furniture for the offices was delivered. Juan and Carol were busy getting things organized. Cassandra went to the morning appointment to finalize her investment in the munitions company. The lawyer did not want to take the cash Cassandra had brought so she kept the cash and gave him a check which he was happy to accept.

She was back at the Embassy in time for lunch and the cash went back into the safe room lockbox. Cassandra had sold her big city condo prior to coming to Mexico and a portion of those proceeds were now invested here.

Cassandra had just finished eating lunch when her cell phone went off. She answered, "Ambassador Crossing."

"Excellency, this is Adolpho. With the assistance of Don Alejandro, I have found just what I think you are looking for. I would like to show you pictures of the property and a map. When would it be convenient for me to come to see you?"

Cassandra thought and then said, "Can you come about three this afternoon?"

"I will be there, Excellency. Thank you."

Cassandra said, "Then three o'clock it is." The call ended and Cassandra went upstairs to see the progress on the offices.

Cassandra arrived to find Carol at work at a beautiful desk and the renovations finished. The only workman in the office was a military technician installing the phone system.

Cassandra said, "Good afternoon, Carol."

Carol smiled, "Good afternoon, Ambassador. We are almost up and running. Amanda is in her temporary office working on some kind of report."

Cassandra asked, "Do we have computers?"

"We have the office computers and printers up. We have a local area network that for security reasons is only connected within this suite. If you want to go on the internet, you can't use any of the computers in here."

Cassandra said, "Good. I have a three o'clock business appointment with Adolpho Perez."

Carol said, "Thank you. I will keep your calendar and provide you with a weekly schedule and a daily updated agenda each morning."

Cassandra smiled, "I will be attending a promotion ceremony tomorrow afternoon and it will be necessary to book all afternoon. I also will be attending a Dinner Friday evening at the president's residence as a guest of the secretary of the interior."

Carol looked at her, "Not as ambassador?"

"No. It was a personal invitation."

Carol smiled, "I usually keep track of all commitments of the ambassador's time."

Cassandra walked into what was her temporary office and would eventually be her master bedroom. It was huge. A very large desk was placed near the windows overlooking the garden. Cassandra went and sat in her chair. It was luxurious. She pivoted in the chair. In front of the desk were two wing chairs. Further back in front of the desk the room contained a meeting table at which there were ten chairs. There was also to her right a seating area with a sofa and arm chairs as well as coffee and end tables. To her left was a beautiful view of the gardens. Cassandra noticed something about the glass and went to check and verified it was bullet resistant glass.

She noticed one wall area was covered with framed photos. Cassandra went and looked at them. There were photos of her receiving The Presidential Medal of Freedom with Distinction from the former President. There were pictures of her in uniform and with a myriad of influential people.

There was also a very nice photograph of her with Enrique and Maria on the steps of the President's residence. Cassandra recognized it must have been taken by one of the Mexican press corps the night they went for the "inspection" at the airport. Carol had arranged them to impress. Among the most prominent photos were those of her at her father's inauguration events. Cassandra looked around and realized that Carol had set this up so visitors could not help but see the photos and the display was meant to impress.

Cassandra went to the far end of the room and opened some sliding doors to reveal a wet bar. She went behind the counter and looked at the microwave. She also looked in the refrigerator and cupboards. She closed the sliding doors and opened a door on the same wall. It led to a private full bath with a tiled shower. The third door contained a large walk in closet.

Cassandra went back to her desk and noted there was a pull out keyboard, but no monitor. She noticed a, button next to the keyboard and pushed it and a monitor slowly rose from the desk's top. She opened a door under the large desk and pushed the on, button for the computer tower. She was exploring the programs when the phone on her desk rang.

Cassandra answered, "Yes."

"Mr. Perez has arrived, Ambassador."

"Please show him in."

Carol opened the door and Adolpho came in as Cassandra rose from her desk and the monitor disappeared. She said, "Good afternoon, Adolpho."

"Good afternoon, Excellency."

Cassandra smiled and gesturing to the sitting area said, "Please have a seat."

Adolpho said, "Thank you," and sat down putting his briefcase on the floor.

Cassandra asked, "Would you like a beverage, Adolpho?"

"Yes, please. I would like a beer, if you have one."

Cassandra went to the refrigerator and found bottles of Corona and took one out and grabbed a glass and took it back to the table. Adolpho was looking strangely at her and Cassandra knew why so said, "I am very informal when I deal with people I trust."

Adolpho said with a broad smile, "Gracias. You pay me a great compliment, Dona Cassandra."

Cassandra put the beer on the table and Adolpho opened the bottle and poured it. He took a sip. He then opened his briefcase and took out a file which he put on the coffee table.

He continued, "This is a very nice property. It consists of five hundred and ninety six hectares plus a residence. One family has owned it for several generations, but the family has experienced tragedy and the widow of the patriarch is forced to sell it. The family has been breeding fine horses there for many years, but the operation no longer makes a profit as the widow has had to sell off much of the breeding stock. She is in a desperate situation."

Cassandra started looking at the photos in the file. She did the land conversion in her head; five hundred and ninety six hectares was in the area of fourteen hundred and fifty acres. The house looked old and run down, but the photos of the lush land of what appeared to be mountain foothills were intriguing. She saw one photo of a small waterfall which fell into a glistening pond.

Cassandra said, "The house looks to be run down."

"It is Doña Cassandra. It would be best to renovate it for use by and estancia manager and build a new house. The barns are still in good condition and there is a good road on the property. There is a good size town close by." Adolpho put a map on the table, "The property is about here."

Cassandra said, "It is about one hundred and fifty miles from here."

Adolpho nodded, "Yes. It is paved road for all but about ten kilometers of gravel road."

"Why is the operation doing so badly?"

Adolpho shrugged, "The locals say the family let the men who knew about horses go because of money problems and then the money problems just got worse because the family did not know horses. I think if you hired the right people you could make enough money to keep the estancia up and perhaps have a small income. Do you know horses?"

"Not enough to breed them, but I can hire someone to do that."

Adolpho sipped his beer, "The men the family let go are still around. They know horses, but they are not good at estancia management."

Cassandra thought for a minute, "What are the neighbors like?"

Adolpho smiled, "Adelina's family owns about two thousand hectares to the south and Adelina owns the estancia immediately to the west. She and Carlos spent a lot of time there before all the recent unpleasantness."

Cassandra asked, "How much are they asking for the property?"

"They were asking the equivalent of seven hundred and fifty thousand U.S. dollars. They will take five hundred for a quick sale."

Cassandra asked, "Was the family aligned with Castillo?"

Adolpho sighed, "They became involved with one of the other anti-government groups."

Cassandra said, "I see. The family men were purged." Cassandra knew it was a polite way of saying they were executed without trial or killed by the military in a battle where no quarter was given.

Adolpho said, "It was necessary. The women will leave the country. They plan to go to Venezuela. I have a contract signed by the widow which is irrevocable for seven days."

Cassandra said, "You have done well, Adolpho. I am very interested and I will go see the property before I sign the contract to purchase it. I will have to arrange security and transportation. Will you be available on short notice?"

"For you, I will of course make myself available, Doña Cassandra."

"Thank you, Adolpho. I'll review the file and be in touch." She stood and offered him her hand and he shook it gently. He took his briefcase and left.

Cassandra took the file to her desk and examined the contract and the financial statements. She looked over the pictures, the survey, and the topographical map. Adolpho had been thorough. She was quite sure she would buy the property. It would eat up a large portion of what was left from the sale of her condo, but it was an excellent exchange.

On Wednesday, Ambassador Cassandra Crossing arrived in a navy business suit in an embassy vehicle with her assistant as well as her security detail. At their destination, her security team stayed with the vehicles and she and Amanda were led in. They were taken to a room where Maria greeted Cassandra with an embrace.

"Cassandra, it is so good to see you. Adelina will be here in a moment. It is a grand day for her and Carlos. Enrique will be making a special presentation." Maria turned to Amanda and said, "I am glad you are taking good care of my friend."

Amanda said, "Yes ma'am."

Cassandra smiled, "Maria, your enthusiasm is contagious."

Adelina came into the room, "What is contagious?"

Cassandra said, "Maria's enthusiasm."

Adelina smiled and hugged Cassandra. "I heard you will be escorting a certain prominent man to dinner on Saturday evening."

Cassandra smiled, "The walls have ears."

Adelina said, "No, my friend Maria approves the guest list."

Cassandra smiled broadly and Maria said, "His intentions seem to be clear. You do realize he is pursuing you seriously?"

Cassandra said, "So he proclaimed to me?"

Adelina said, "Then he is very serious."

Maria said, "We had better be going." She saw Amanda and said, "You'd better come along and guard your ambassador, Amanda."

Amanda smiled and said, "Yes ma'am."

Cassandra found the pomp and circumstance of the ceremony quite impressive. She enjoyed watching it and was surprised that near the end of the ceremony the President called on her and awarded her the Order of the Aztec Eagle Sash for her contribution to the Mexican Government. He recounted her heroism in taking up arms to repel terrorists during an attack on a military convoy she was travelling in. The President stated the ambassador had in the process saved the lives of Mexican soldiers. The President did not mention she had saved him and Carlos. He also cited Cassandra's work to effect normalization of diplomatic and trade relations between the U.S. and Mexico.

He asked her to say a few words which she did eloquently in fluent Spanish to the enjoyment of the crowd gathered there. After her remarks, the President embraced her and she returned to her seat.

As the ceremony ended, Cassandra leaned over to Maria, "That was unexpected."

Maria smiled and replied, "And the lack of notice was a well deserved warning. You should have called and told Adelina and me about Alejandro asking you to accompany him."

Cassandra said, "It didn't occur to me."

Adelina interrupted, "It should have." Adelina smiled and said, "If you will excuse me, I have to go find my husband the general and congratulate him with a kiss." Adelina hurried off.

Maria said with a smile, "Let us retire for refreshments."

They ended up in a small sitting room and a server brought them a small cognac. Maria took a seat and so Cassandra sat down as well. Maria started the conversation,

"I hear you are considering buying property in the mountains."

"Yes. I intend to ask Alejandro's advice about travelling to inspect it."

Maria said, "You should charter a helicopter and get one or two of your military aircraft to accompany you. There are still pockets of bandits here and there."

"I expected that. Thank you for the advice. I do believe that things will settle down eventually."

Maria said, "It is now inevitable. The military, the wealthy, and the politicians will not let the drug criminals get out of control again."

Cassandra said, "I believe the military now has a different view of the threat the drug cartels represent."

Maria nodded. She changed the subject, "My husband and I hold Alejandro in high esteem. I think his intentions toward you are honorable because, in spite of his reputation, he is not frivolous about his relationships."

Cassandra nodded, "So I have been told."

"I suppose with your government's resources you know more about us than we know about you."

Cassandra replied, "Whatever you want to know about me personally, you have but to ask. Friendships demand trust."

Maria sipped her drink, "Are you serious about considering Alejandro's courting?"

Cassandra sighed, "Serious enough that I risk my position. My father loves me, but he will not let me put our country in a compromised position."

"So, if you were to marry a Mexican national you would have to resign as ambassador."

Cassandra said, "Perhaps or perhaps not depending on the circumstances. It is the combination of Alejandro's current position and mine that complicates matters. My father wants his children to be happy, but he has a duty."

Maria asked, "You do know Alejandro is not a wealthy man. He is middle class as my husband and I are. It was difficult for me to raise my share of the investment. We risk a lot of what we have in this venture as does Alejandro."

Cassandra said, "I know. Alejandro told me he has risked everything on this."

Cassandra noted Maria seemed surprised to learn Alejandro had confided this to her.

Maria said, "Is your family as wealthy as it is said?"

"Yes."

"Are you wealthy in your own right?"

"Yes. My grandparents on both sides of the family left me and each of my siblings, substantial inheritances."

Maria said, "Then your family is like Adelina's?"

"Yes. In my country many Presidents are successful in business and wealthy before being elected but not all of them are. It does help though."

Maria said, "And if wealth does not come before election, it comes afterwards."

"True."

Maria took another sip and said it as a matter of fact, "You are a trained killer."

"I prefer warrior. I am not an assassin. I have only killed as a law enforcement officer, a government agent, or to protect my friends or allies."

"Yes, Enrique told me about the general you shot. How do you reconcile that with your faith?"

"The Bible says the state may wield the sword to keep the peace. As a warrior of the state, some actions are thus justifiable."

"But not all are?"

Cassandra shook her head from side to side, "No, not all."

Adelina came into the room. She took a seat, "Enrique is with Carlos who is enjoying the congratulations of the officers in his command."

Maria said, "It seems you and Cassandra may become neighbors."

Adelina said, "I heard Adolpho had talked to the widow. How much is the agreement for?"

Cassandra said, "Five hundred thousand American dollars."

Adelina said, "Adolpho has negotiated a very good price. If you decide not to buy the property, I will."

Cassandra said, "I plan to see it before signing the contract."

Adelina smile, "I would like to have you for a neighbor. My home is only about three miles from the house on the estancia."

Cassandra asked, "Do you ride?"

Adelina smiled, "Of course I ride. Do you?"

"Yes, but I'm afraid I know little about breeding horses for profit."

Adelina smiled, "You can learn." Adelina looked at Cassandra and said mischievously, "Owning the estancia will only make Alejandro pursue you harder. He loves to ride horses."

Cassandra said, "Perhaps I shouldn't tell him about my plans; I don't want him pursuing me for my land."

Maria said, "It is probably too late for that. Adolpho is very close to our husbands and Alejandro."

Cassandra took a sip of her drink and then said, "Ah well, then I am undone."

Adelina said, "Speak of our absent men."

Enrique entered the room with Carlos and Alejandro in tow. Cassandra and Adelina stood up. Enrique went to his wife and sat beside her and the others took seats. Alejandro came and sat beside Cassandra. His nearness brought out emotions she had not known she was capable of feeling.

A server came and took drink orders from the men. Enrique asked, "What have you women been plotting?"

Maria said, "How Cassandra is going to travel to see the property she is probably going to purchase."

Enrique said, "She should go by helicopter."

Maria said, "That is what I told her."

Enrique looked at Alejandro and said with a sly grin, "You should go with her to provide security and advise her."

Alejandro looked at Cassandra, "It would be my pleasure to arrange it."

Cassandra said, "Since the president has assured your good behavior by suggesting you accompany me, I accept."

The people in the room broke into laughter including Enrique. Alejandro just shook his head in disbelief.

Adelina said, "I'd like to go along. We can take a small side trip so I can visit my parents and you can meet them."

Cassandra said, "I'd love to meet your family."

Enrique said, "Then it is settled."

So it was the next morning Cassandra found herself on a helicopter with Alejandro, Adelina, and Adolpho heading for the estancia. Along the way Alejandro and Adelina acted as tour guides pointing out places of interest. They were accompanied by two Mexican military helicopters that were actually on loan from the U.S. Government and specifically the embassy. The group arrived at the estancia at mid-morning. They were greeted by soldiers and several military vehicles as well as two civilian four-wheel drive SUVs.

They deplaned and Alejandro led the ladies to one of the civilian vehicles. He held the rear door open for Cassandra and Adelina, and then once they were in he climbed into the passenger's seat. Adolpho got behind the wheel.

They went to the main house and from what Cassandra could see it needed repair, but was structurally sound. They went to the horse barns and found them in good condition, but almost all of the stalls were empty. They then inspected the three workers' houses on the property. They were small, but sound and functional but in need of repair and updating. Adolpho took them on a driving tour of the property. The land was beyond what Cassandra had imagined and she fell in love with the place.

They returned to the main house about noon and tables had been set up outside under a covered patio. They ate a cold lunch of freshly baked bread, cheese, fruit and wine. All in all it was an enjoyable time.

As lunch finished, Adolpho asked, "What do you think Dona Cassandra?"

Cassandra said, "I like it very much."

Adelina said, "Good. Next let's go visit my house and then go to my parent's home."

They boarded the helicopters and flew over Adelina's home. They landed and went on a tour of the main house. It was very nice. It was not a working estancia and two servants lived on the site. Cassandra noted there were two armed men at the estancia. After the tour, they flew to meet Adelina's parents.

The helicopters landed near the Hacienda. It was obvious this was the home of very wealthy people. There were several armed guards who came to meet the aircraft. Adelina greeted them by name, but did not introduce her company.

At the hacienda, Adelina was met by a servant who led the small party to a patio area where an older couple was sitting. Cassandra assessed that these were people who came from privilege and were aware of class distinction. The man was slender with graying hair. Cassandra could only describe the woman as voluptuous and she was remarkably attractive for her age. The man and woman rose to meet the visitors.

Adelina did the introductions, "Father, mother, this is Ambassador Cassandra Crossing. Dona Cassandra this is my father Don Manuel Carlos Flores Diaz and my mother Dona Ana Catharina Nunez Vega de Diaz."

Cassandra said, "I am pleased to meet you Don Manuel and Dona Ana."

Cassandra shook hands politely with the two parents. The introductions put Cassandra on notice that Adelina's parents were traditionalists.

Don Manuel turned to Alejandro, "It is good to see you again, Alejandro."

Alejandro smiled, "And to be here, Don Manuel."

Manuel said, "Welcome, Adolpho."

Adolpho bowed his head, "Thank you, Don Manuel."

Don Manuel said, "Come and sit, everyone. Let us have wine."

Cassandra saw one of the servants hurry off to bring wine. They all took a seat.

Don Manuel smiled at Cassandra, "I take it by your Spanish accent your mother is of Mexican heritage, Dona Cassandra?"

"Yes, Don Manuel. My full name is Cassandra Adora Crossing Santiago. My mother is from Veracruz and she met my father there. He was a marine attached to the embassy in Mexico City and was on vacation. They married and my brother and I were born here in Mexico. My father and the family returned to the U.S. after my grandfather took ill as father had to leave the military and return to run all the family businesses."

Don Manuel said, "I see. I take it your mother taught you Spanish."

"Yes, Don Manuel, though my father is fluent in the language."

Don Manuel said, "I take it you are a dual citizen of the U.S. and Mexico?"

Cassandra answered, "Yes. I am fortunate in that."

Cassandra noticed that Alejandro's interest perked up at that news. He now knew that she probably had two passports and the Mexican one had aided her in her intelligence work.

The wine arrived and everyone took a glass and went through the rituals of enjoying the fine wine.

Cassandra took a sip of the wine and said, "This is very good."

Don Manuel said, "Dona Cassandra, I understand we may be neighbors."

"That is my wish and hope."

Don Manuel asked, "Have you signed a contract yet?"

Cassandra said, "Not yet, Don Manuel. I thought it best to visit and meet the neighbors first."

Don Manuel said with a smile, "I think you will like it here."

Cassandra recognized that Don Manuel was giving his approval to her buying the property and moving here. Apparently that was expected and she thanked God silently she had not blundered but unknowingly had done the correct thing. In spite of her training, she sometimes forgot cultural differences and local traditions. Don Manuel was obviously very influential here.

Cassandra said, "Your advice means a lot to me, Don Manuel."

Her remark seemed to please Adelina's father and Adelina and her mother were smiling.

Don Manuel said, "If you need any advice, Dona Cassandra, please do not hesitate to call on me."

"Thank you, Don Manuel. I will most certainly do that."

Dona Ana asked, "Have you made a decision on the purchase?"

Cassandra said, "I now feel comfortable about making a decision and will sign the contract when I return to the city."

Adelina seemed delighted, "It is good I will have a friend my age nearby. I will finally have someone to ride with regularly." Adelina looked at Cassandra, "Carlos can ride well, but he does not enjoy it like I do."

Don Manuel asked, "Do you intend to breed horses, Dona Cassandra?"

"I am seriously considering it. It would help to keep down the costs of keeping up the estancia. What do you think?"

Don Manuel said, "That would be a wise decision. The parents of former owners had a good reputation for breeding good horses, though their politics were suspect. People from all over used to come here for the horses. It was good business for the local inns and shops and was very profitable in the past when the operation was well managed. Your intentions will be appreciated by the town's folk."

Dona Ana said, "The men who used to work the estancia are currently unemployed. You would gain much good will by hiring them back. We know them and they are loyal and good workers, but you will need a good manager."

Cassandra said, "Thank you. I will do as you advise."

The Don smiled, "Will your father and mother come to visit here?"

Cassandra said, "I expect so, but it may not be for some time. The duties of his office are heavy on my father at this time."

Don Manuel said, "I understand. Things in the Middle East are very tense at the moment, not to mention the recent problems elsewhere."

Cassandra looked at the mountains and changed the subject gently, "I think my mother will especially love it here."

Don Manuel asked, "What do your mother's family do?"

Cassandra said, "They mostly grow sugar cane and coffee and have plantations in the State of Veracruz though they have other interests. I have some part ownership in the family businesses here and in Spain that I inherited from my maternal grandparents. My grandparents immigrated to Mexico from Spain after the Second World War, though some of the family stayed in Spain. That is why the family has interests here and in Spain."

Don Manuel said, "It is good to be diversified."

Cassandra said, "Yes, it is."

The Don asked, "Have you visited Mexico often?"

"Oh yes. I have visited my mother's side of the family at least once a year all of my life and often more frequently. I have not been to Veracruz recently because of the press of business, but I keep in touch by phone or using the internet. While I was in school, I spent my summers with my grandparents or great aunts and uncles either here or in Spain. My mother's extended family is much larger than my father's. I will have to visit Veracruz when my duties allow."

Dona Ana said, "Family is important."

Cassandra added, "As are loyal friends."

Don Manuel smiled. Cassandra noted that Alejandro was not saying much. If it was out of deference to persons of perceived higher status or to let her interact with Don Manuel more she could not be sure. She suspected it was the latter because he was learning a lot about her.

Dona Ana said, "I hear the president gave you an award."

Cassandra said, "It was unexpected. Enrique is very generous."

Cassandra noticed Don Manuel's right eyebrow lift.

Don Manuel asked, "Does the president allow you to call him by his given name?"

Cassandra nodded and said, "Yes, but I do it only in certain social settings and would not do in formal situations or where it might be inappropriate."

Adelina added, "Dona Maria is also a friend of Dona Cassandra."

Cassandra noted this seemed to impress Don Manuel. He said, "You keep good company, Dona Cassandra."

"Thank you, Don Manuel."

The Don said, "I need a moment with Alejandro. Adolpho you may come along."

The men got up and left the women sitting alone.

Dona Ana said, "Cassandra, I see Alejandro does not take his eyes off of you. Are his intentions honorable and serious?"

Cassandra noted the informality now that Don Manuel was not present and said, "So he proclaims, Ana."

Ana said, "Good. He has grieved too long. It is time for him to become serious." Ana turned to Adelina, "Congratulations on Carlos' promotion."

Adelina smiled, "Thank you, mother."

Ana added looking at Cassandra, "And in your choice of a new friend."

Cassandra nodded slightly in acknowledgement of the compliment and sipped her wine.

Ana asked a question that Cassandra had not expected, "Are you sharing your bed with Alejandro?"

Cassandra looked directly at Ana. She paused slightly and decided to answer directly rather than be offended. She shook her head no and said quietly and firmly, "No man who is not my husband will share my bed."

The answer seemed to disarm Ana, "Really? That is a very traditional view."

Cassandra said, "My family is very traditional in the important things, as I am. Besides, it would be a sin against God."

Ana laughed, "Good for you." She looked at Adelina and said, "She loved Carlos so much she didn't wait, but it turned out all right, though it took her father a long time to forgive Carlos."

Adelina protested weakly, "Mother."

Ana said, "Dear, everyone knows. I doubt this will destroy the friendship between two women."

Cassandra said, "True," and sipped her wine.

Ana not to be outdone said, "Your traditional values are driving Alejandro crazy."

Cassandra smiled, "Good. He should learn patience and that some things you must wait for."

Ana laughed and Adelina giggled.

The men came back into the room and Alejandro said, "Ladies, it is getting late and we should start our return trip to the city."

The group said their goodbyes and returned in vehicles to the aircraft. All in all, it had been an enjoyable day. On the return trip they talked about the estancia. Alejandro dropped Cassandra back at the embassy before dark and walked her to the door where he kissed her on the cheek causing her to flush ever so slightly.

He said, "Until I come to pursue my beautiful escort, I will be thinking of her."

Cassandra smiled and looked into Alejandro's eyes, "Now you speak in the third person?"

Alejandro shrugged and smiled. Cassandra watched him turn and walk back to the vehicle then went inside.

Chapter 9 – Plans and Changes

Cassandra had not eaten since lunch at the estancia so went directly to the kitchen and asked to have a meal prepared. In the meantime, she went to her office and wrote a report and had it transmitted to Washington. She scanned in some photos of the estancia and sent them with an email to her mother. She then called her father.

Craig came on the phone, "Good evening, Cassandra, and congratulations on the award."

Cassandra signified this was a personal call by saying, "Thank you father. I wanted to let you know that I am buying some property here. I have sent information and photos to mother."

She told her father about the estancia and he asked a few questions.

Craig said, "It sounds interesting."

"It is beautiful and you and mother will have to come visit it sometime. I also want you to know that Alejandro has advised me that he intends to court me."

Craig said, "I know. He called to ask my permission. I had not expected that; it is so old world. I told him I had no objections and I don't. He seems a nice enough fellow and I'm told he is very bright, ambitious, and a man of honor. Do you think it will work out between you?"

Cassandra said, "I am inclined to say yes."

Craig said, "Given his position this may become an issue in the future."

"I know father. I will just have to wait and see. I will do whatever you think is appropriate."

There was a knock at the office door and Cassandra said, "Excuse me for a minute, father." She muted the speaker, "Come."

Luis brought in her dinner and put it on her desk with a smile. Cassandra said, "Thank you, Luis."

She reactivated the phone, "Sorry, Luis just brought me a meal."

"I'll leave you to eat in peace. May God bless you, daughter."

Cassandra said, "Thank you, father."

She had just about finished eating her food when there was a knock on the door. She said, "Come."

Stan came in.

Cassandra said, "Have a seat Stan and tell me what's on your mind."

Stan asked, "Do you want the details or the short version?"

"I would like the short version please."

Stan started, "Well, Castillo is hard pressed. We think he has left the country again and went back to Venezuela, but we have conflicting reports. He is definitely up to no good and we're working hard to figure out what it is. It is difficult because as you know we have few feet on the ground in Venezuela. The rebel resistance here will probably collapse within the next week. The news that the back of the rebels has been broken will have a great impact on the economy, especially given that the economic infrastructure is generally not damaged and Mexico's institutions are working."

Cassandra thought to herself she would have to work fast to consolidate her personal business affairs.

Stan continued, "Juan's ties here are similar to yours. I do not think there is any reason for concern under the circumstances. Adelina's family is loyal to the democratically elected government and her father is a very powerful and influential man. Her mother is also from a family of fine reputation. As for Alejandro, we have to be very careful because he is very crafty. He knows we have been looking into his background. Today we received information CISN agents started looking into your mother's family. As you know, they are all above board so I expect it has more to do with his personal interest in you than any suspicion your family is a threat to the nation."

Cassandra nodded agreement.

Stan said, "We located another unit we don't think Alejandro knows about. I have taken the liberty of having a note with the coordinates prepared and I can have it delivered."

Stan slipped the note across the desk. It contained only printed coordinates. Cassandra just signed her first name and put it in an envelope and sealed it. She handed it to Stan who just nodded.

Cassandra said, "Thanks, Stan. I will be going out on personal business in the morning and will need transportation and security."

"I'll let our people know."

At eight o'clock in the morning, Cassandra was in her office dressed in a very expensive navy blue business suit and wearing expensive jewelry. Adolpho was present and Cassandra executed the contract for the estancia. She gave Adolpho notarized copies of certain documents and two envelopes; one containing a deposit and the other a partial commission for him. He gave her receipts for the cash.

Directly upon his leaving a small convoy of Embassy vehicles took Cassandra to the bank with which her maternal family did business. There she converted most of her U.S. cash into a pesos account at a very favorable exchange rate. She anticipated she would do well when the value of the peso rose on news the rebellion was over. The peso's value had already started to recover. Normally conversion was difficult, but given the international nature of the family business the bank was used to facilitating such transactions for Dona Cassandra Adora Crossing Santiago and her family. Her connections had served her well as an intelligence operative as had her Mexican passport.

After conducting her business at the bank, Cassandra went shopping and purchased a new evening dress, new shoes, and some very expensive new jewelry. She returned to the embassy in time for lunch.

Cassandra found the outer walls had been torn down and the embassy building was now surrounded by several armored vehicles that were manned and ready for action. Men using heavy equipment were dismantling and trucking away the wall debris. They were busy and paid little attention to the wary soldiers keeping an eye on them and the street from the gun turrets and the embassy roof.

After eating a light lunch, Cassandra returned to her office to find Carol talking on the phone and so went directly into her office. A moment later Carol knocked on the door frame and Cassandra motioned her in.

"Ambassador, there is a message for you in the communications room. Do you want me to have them bring it up?"

Cassandra said, "That would set a bad security precedent. I'll go down."

Cassandra walked down the stairs and decided she had been wise to wear only a low heel. Once in the communication room, she took a seat and the operator passed her the message. Cassandra read it and knew this was a turning point. She went back to her office and called Bob to come up. Bob arrived five minutes after she'd called.

"Good afternoon, Ambassador."

Cassandra smiled, "Colonel. I see things are busy outside."

"Yes. Your man Juan lost no time in getting things organized. I hear he has more staff coming tomorrow."

Cassandra motioned to the door and Bob shut it, took his cover off, and sat down.

Cassandra asked, "How often are we sweeping?"

"Every two hours while there are workmen on site."

Cassandra said, "Good. Matt is moving his people to the port starting Monday. The airport is going to reopen to limited commercial flights the following week. If there is anything you need from the General now would be the time to arrange for it."

Bob asked, "Does the General know yet?"

"Yes. He has received orders. Anything he gives to you is less for him to transport and he'll have a whole shipload to take from if he needs anything."

Bob said, "Thank you. We could use a couple more vehicles. I'll talk to my officers and find out what we can use. On another note, we think we should put in a helipad between the two properties."

"I take it we have room?"

"Yes. We are burying all the over-head electrical and communication wires."

Cassandra said, "It sounds like a winner to me."

"It will cost relatively little to develop compared to some of the other things we are doing. If that's all, I'll get back to my other duties."

Cassandra said, "Thanks, Bob. Tell the men I appreciate their efforts."

Bob smiled, "They seem to know that, but I'll pass it on."

Bob left and Cassandra went to her room and relaxed for a while. At five o'clock, she went to the kitchen and ate a salad then went back to her suite.

On Saturday, Cassandra was in her office early. She studied material and that had been prepared for her on the general duties of an ambassador. She decided that she would fulfill the public ones and delegate the rest. She had no intention of being a long term career diplomat.

In the evening, she went to her suite to get ready for her date. When she was dressed, she looked at herself in the mirror and liked what she saw. The dress was sexy yet classy. Her new jewelry was just the right touch and she thought she looked like a trophy wife and laughed at the thought.

Alejandro arrived at the appointed time and Cassandra went downstairs to meet him in the living room. As she passed the Amazon guarding the third floor the woman said, "You will certainly turn heads, ma'am."

Cassandra said, "Thank you," and went downstairs.

Alejandro's eyes seemed to light up when he saw her. Cassandra thought that the way she looked had the desired effect. A woman could tell when a man had a burning desire for her just by the way he looked at her.

Alejandro said, "You look stunning, Dona Cassandra."

Cassandra smiled, "Thank you, Alejandro."

She took Alejandro's arm and he walked her to their waiting car. A security man opened the door for her and she got in while Alejandro went around to the other side and got in.

In the car, Alejandro said, "You my dear are a very sly woman."

"How is that Alejandro?"

"Until our little trip, I did not realize you were a citizen of Mexico. Now I know how you travelled so freely here. You made a lot of trips from Spain to here and vice versa, but none to the United States on your Mexican passport."

Cassandra smiled, "It was all quite legal."

Alejandro laughed, "And I thought I was the sneaky one. Did you finalize your contract?"

"Yes. I will have to hire a manager when it closes and I must go to hire men for the estancia and arrange to have renovations to the existing houses done and a new home built."

Alejandro said, "I will volunteer to help you in your endeavors as I expect to soon be able to take some time for myself and to look after my personal affairs."

Cassandra asked, "Is the building of the plant on schedule?"

"Yes. Site worked started today. It seems the officials of the bank are impressed that you and Adelina are investors."

"Good."

Alejandro said, "I am having my people look into your family's background."

"I know, but thank you for telling me."

"You are not offended?"

Cassandra smiled, "Of course not for I did the same thing and I think that is just prudent."

Alejandro said, "Where is the romance in that?"

Cassandra smiled, "I thought the male was responsible for the romancing."

Alejandro laughed and said, "Si. I will have to work at the romance part."

"I should hope so."

Alejandro said, "Thank you for the little note. It was accurate."

"You are welcome."

Alejandro smiled, "The men at the dinner will take one look at you and be envious of me because you are on my arm."

Cassandra teased, "Ah, so it is a trophy wife you seek?"

She found she was enjoying the flirting and teasing.

Alejandro said, "Well Cassandra, you would be that and much more."

They sat in silence for the rest of the drive. It was a comfortable silence for Cassandra had her arm through Alejandro's and from time to time he would just look at her and smile. She was very comfortable and just enjoyed his silent attention.

When they arrived at their destination, they were escorted by a security detail right to the doors of the reception hall. Cassandra had her arm through Alejandro's as he led her directly to the president. Enrique was holding court. He saw them coming.

"Alejandro, Cassandra, come join us."

Alejandro walked into the group and positioned Cassandra so she was standing beside Maria who was dressed in a black dress with pearls. Cassandra had to admit Maria looked stunning. Maria leaned over and said to Cassandra, "You will drive many husbands to lust and their wives to jealousy in that tight red dress."

Cassandra smiled, "Perhaps, but the way you look you have nothing to be concerned about."

Maria laughed lightly and said, "Oh, I like you."

Carlos came over with Adelina on his arm. He said to Cassandra, "I hear we are to be neighbors Dona Cassandra."

Cassandra smiled, "So it seems, General. I am looking forward to it."

A man standing next to the president asked, "Who is this vision of beauty on your arm, Alejandro?"

Alejandro said, "Felipe Castro Rodriguez, may I present Dona Cassandra Adora Crossing Santiago."

Felipe said, "It is a pleasure Dona Cassandra. How did you come to know Alejandro?"

Cassandra smiled, "We met at a state dinner."

Felipe said, "I see," although it was obvious he didn't, but he was too polite to ask further.

Alejandro asked, "Would you like Champagne, Dona Cassandra?"

"Please, Señor Secretary," Cassandra said playfully.

Alejandro smiled and waved for a waiter. Alejandro took two flutes off a tray and handed one to Cassandra.

Maria took Cassandra by the arm, "Alejandro, I am going to steal Cassandra away." Maria looked at Adelina who let go of her husband to join Maria and Cassandra.

Alejandro bowed slightly, "Your wish is my command."

Maria smiled and walked off with Cassandra and Adelina. She said, "Enrique has been trying to corner Felipe between him and Alejandro for some time. He finally succeeded."

Cassandra smiled, but said nothing. Maria led them to a corner seating area with four chairs and the women sat down.

Maria said, "I hate these formal events. They are so stuffy. Just four more years and we can retire to the country."

Cassandra said, "Perhaps by then our business venture will be successful and you can buy property near our places."

Maria said, "We own about ten hectares near your estancia on the road to town. We hope to eventually build a house there."

Cassandra said, "Wonderful. We can all go riding on the horses I will breed at my new estancia."

Maria looked at Adelina, "She is already planning my retirement for me."

Adelina looked at Cassandra, "And we will have such wonderful parties."

Cassandra sipped her wine, "Of course, but first Maria's husband and my father have to get trade back to normal."

A man approached Maria and whispered in her ear and she said, "Please excuse me. I have a minor matter I must resolve."

Carlos came over and said, "Dona Cassandra, I must borrow my wife to make some introductions."

Cassandra nodded and remained seated. A young woman came over and sat next to Cassandra. She said, "I see you came with Alejandro Garcia Ramirez."

Cassandra said, "Yes."

The young woman said, "Don't waste your time on him. I hear rumors he likes boys. He escorts pretty things like you once and then poof they are gone."

Cassandra looked at the woman, "Do you speak from experience?"

The woman looked blankly at Cassandra which Cassandra took to be a negative answer.

Cassandra paused and said, "No, I suppose you are not pretty enough."

Cassandra regretted saying it as soon as it was out of her mouth for it was not a Christian thing to say. It would not be her only failing of the night.

The young woman became angry and said, "Be careful pretty one or I may claw your eyes out."

Cassandra's face turned threatening and she said, "I rather doubt it," and looked at the woman. Cassandra leaned toward her, "I am Dona Cassandra Adora Crossing Santiago. You had best be careful who you threaten lest you end up in an early grave señorita for I will not tolerate slander of my fine gentleman suitor or threats to my person."

Cassandra leaned back. Her little monologue had the desired affect and the woman was ashen. Cassandra said, "On the other hand, I am a forgiving person and good to my friends."

The woman said, “Forgive me, Dona Cassandra. I did not know.”

Cassandra said, “You are forgiven. What is your name?”

“Ivette Jacintha Rodriguez Flores, Dona Cassandra Adora.”

Cassandra asked, “How is it you come to be here, Ivette?”

“My brother is in the congress.” Ivette paused, “I do not wish to cause him embarrassment.”

Cassandra said, “You are young and inexperienced in such matters, so I will keep your secret, but you must promise to behave. This is not a girl’s school, but a place full of serious people many of whom could cause great trouble for your brother. Sharing wild rumors is not the way to gain acceptance.”

Ivette said, “I promise to behave and thank you.”

Adelina came back and took a seat, “And who is this young woman.”

Cassandra said, “Dona Adelina Maria Diaz Vega de Mendez this is Ivette Jacintha Rodriguez Flores.”

Ivette said, “I am pleased to meet you, Dona Adelina. Your husband the General is a hero of the nation.”

Adelina smiled and said, “Thank you. What do you do, Ivette?”

“I am a student at the university. My brother is in the congress and this is his first time here and I begged him to bring me.”

Adelina said, “It is good experience, Ivette.”

Ivette nodded, “Yes, Dona Adelina.”

Adelina asked, “What are you studying Ivette?”

“I study veterinary medicine.”

Cassandra said, “It is a good profession. When do you graduate?”

“Next year. May I be excused?”

Adelina said, “Yes, Ivette.”

The young woman got up and hurried away. Cassandra asked, “Do you know her family?”

“No.”

Cassandra decided she would find out about the family. If her brother was in congress this was a connection that might be useful to Stan.

Alejandro came and sat beside Cassandra, "Forgive me for leaving you."

Cassandra smiled, "All is forgiven. It is a business dinner and you have responsibilities."

Alejandro smiled, "You are very gracious."

"I am a realist. I understand to some degree who and what you are."

Alejandro said, "That is what frightens me about you. I do not understand you at all. You are not like other women I have known."

Cassandra said, "I think we need to circulate."

Alejandro got up as did Cassandra. She took his offered arm and they went to mingle. That evening Cassandra met a lot of influential people and to Alejandro's surprise knew a lot of the guests.

At dinner, as fitting Alejandro's position, he and Cassandra sat near the president. The food and wine was excellent. The stated purpose of the dinner was to celebrate the president's first two years in power. In fact it had been a way to entice representatives from other countries to come to Mexico. Now that the U.S. Embassy had re-opened, Enrique and his cabinet hoped others would follow.

The Ambassador of Spain was seated next to Cassandra and the Canadian Ambassador was next to him.

The Spanish Ambassador said to Cassandra, "It has been some time since I last saw you, Dona Cassandra."

Cassandra said, "I am pleased to see you again, Don Carlo. When did you arrive?"

"I came on a commercial flight earlier today."

Cassandra said, "I am sorry your wife was not able to accompany you. It has been some time since I've seen Dona Maria."

Don Carlo replied, "My government did not think it was wise for her to make the journey at this time."

Cassandra turned to Alejandro, "Have you met the Spanish Ambassador, Alejandro?"

Alejandro said, "I have not had the pleasure."

Cassandra introduced the two men.

Alejandro asked the Ambassador, "How do you know Dona Cassandra, Don Carlo?"

"Her family and mine are friends. I have known her since she was a little girl. She spent parts of every summer in Spain and sometimes other holidays. Since I have been appointed here, I look forward to visiting some of her family I have not seen in years."

Alejandro said, "I see."

Don Carlo changed the subject, "Cassandra, I hear the American Embassy had some trouble."

Cassandra replied, "Yes, Carlo. It was the last gasp of a lost cause and it lasted only a few minutes. The military has broken the back of the rebel forces and it just a matter of time before the international community realizes that. The side effect is that the country has been rid of the drug cartels and Mexico will now be able to fulfill its full economic promise."

The Ambassador said, "You really believe that?"

Cassandra said, "So much so that I have transferred funds from the U.S. to make substantial new personal investments here in real estate and business."

Cassandra was aware that Alejandro was listening intently as was the Canadian Ambassador.

Don Carlo nodded, "I see. Do you think it is safe to reestablish our embassy?"

Cassandra said, "There is still some terrorist threat, but I believe it is now minimal and less than you face in other parts of the world. I think normal security precautions would be adequate and I am hoping those countries that are first to return will be seen as the closest friends and allies of the Mexican people."

The ambassador nodded understanding of what she implied. Carlo asked her about her real estate investment and she told him about the estancia and her plan to breed horses.

The Ambassador was a lover of horses and he was willing to spend some time discussing breeding with her. He offered to give her written introductions to some people he knew in the breeding business in Spain.

After dinner, the group adjourned to another room for wine. Some of the men drifted off to smoke cigars and talk away from their women. Alejandro did not leave.

He took two wine glasses from a waiter and handed one to Cassandra and said, "I was not aware you knew so many influential people in Europe and here."

Cassandra said, "My family does business in North and South America and in Spain. Over the years I have met a lot of people."

Alejandro said, "And in your previous profession you were thus able to move freely between continents."

Cassandra looked at Alejandro and smiled, "I gave up that profession some time ago."

"Our relationship will be complicated."

Cassandra said, "Just in the beginning. We are fortunate that our countries' interests coincide at this time."

"Most certainly, but your dual citizenship creates divided loyalty."

Cassandra said seriously, "Not necessarily. When I am just a citizen, I will have much more latitude. I expect to be just another international businesswoman."

"I doubt the word 'just' will ever be applied to you, my dear."

Cassandra smiled, "Perhaps God has gifted us both with special talents."

Alejandro asked with a smile, "Speaking of God, would you accompany me to mass at Vicente's church in the morning."

Cassandra smiled, "If you would agree to attend the Methodist Church with me the next Sunday."

Alejandro was horrified and said, "Vicente would excommunicate me."

Cassandra smiled, "Where does it say in the Bible that going to one place of Christian worship or the other sentences one to hell?"

Alejandro shrugged, "I do not know? The priests have said it is so."

Cassandra said, "I will accompany you tomorrow without condition."

"Thank you."

Alejandro seemed relieved. Cassandra hoped that Alejandro's curiosity would cause him to question his friend Vicente about what she had said. Then she realized given that Alejandro was brought up in the Roman church, he was probably blinded to its faults. The rest of the evening was pleasant and Cassandra enjoyed Alejandro's company. They arrived back at the U.S. Embassy compound at a little after eleven.

Before they exited the car, Alejandro leaned over and kissed Cassandra. It caught her off guard and she did not immediately withdraw. She lingered a moment and realized the contact had taken her breath away and set her body on fire.

She moved away just a few inches and whispered, "Alejandro, behave."

He smiled and teased her, "Perhaps you really are the virgin princess."

Cassandra said a little more forcefully, "Alejandro, please behave."

"Si cielito lindo."

Cassandra smiled at being called Alejandro's lovely sweet one. He had started the romancing. He got out of the car and came around to the other side and opened Cassandra's door. She took his arm and he walked her to the door where he said, "I will come for you at eight thirty."

Cassandra said, "Come at eight and we will have a light breakfast here."

"That is agreeable."

Alejandro took her hand and kissed it. He turned and went to his car and drove away as Cassandra entered the building. The guards were smiling.

She looked at them and said, "Watch and learn. That is how a gentleman treats a lady."

She went inside and after closing the door heard the soldiers laughing. She smiled and enjoyed the humor of the situation.

Sunday morning Cassandra was at the dining table when Alejandro was brought in. Cassandra rose and said, "Good morning, Alejandro."

"Good morning, Dona Cassandra."

Cassandra kissed him on the cheek, "Pedro has been good enough to prepare us a light breakfast.

Alejandro held the chair for Cassandra then took a seat. Luis came into the room carrying a tray with the meals. He served and left.

Alejandro said, "It seems the Spanish ambassador told the president last night over cigars and drinks that he is going to recommend his country reopen their embassy."

Cassandra said, "That is good."

"Enrique knows of your relationship and conversation with Don Carlo."

Cassandra looked at Alejandro who added, "Maria was listening to your conversation."

They had an enjoyable breakfast discussing the people they had encountered the previous evening and sharing what they knew and their impressions. After finishing breakfast, they set out for church with both of their security teams. The little cavalcade stopped in front of the church and Alejandro did not get to open the door for Cassandra as a security man had gotten to her door first.

As they entered the church, Cassandra pulled the lace shawl over her head out of respect for Alejandro and Vicente. Her thought was "when in Rome". As they entered Cassandra noticed some areas were roped off and there were scaffolds and other construction materials where pews must have at one time been located. There were scorch and pock marks on some pillars and walls. There was plywood where before there had been stained glass windows.

Alejandro led Cassandra to the front row. Cassandra had attended mass when she visited her family in Spain and here. She knew what to expect. Vicente officiated at the service. When the time came, Cassandra did not get up and go to participate in the Lord's Supper which the Catholics referred to as Communion and neither did Alejandro.

As they left, they encountered a priest who said, "You have been invited to meet with the bishop, Don Alejandro."

Alejandro looked at Cassandra who nodded agreement. They were led to the rectory with their security scrambling to keep up to the changing events. As they left the church proper, Cassandra removed the lace from her head. They entered the living room of the rectory and were greeted by Vicente.

He greeted Cassandra first, "Welcome your, Excellency."

"Thank you, Most Reverend."

Vicente held out his hand and Cassandra did not kiss the ring, but took his hand and shook it respectfully.

Vicente turned to Alejandro, "Welcome, Alejandro. I am glad you both could come."

Alejandro asked, "Do we stand on formality today, Vicente?"

The bishop laughed, "I suppose not."

Cassandra said, "Thank you for your kind invitation, Vicente."

Vicente said, "Please have a seat." They all sat down and a servant brought coffee and they all took a cup. Vicente said, "I was surprised to see you at mass Cassandra. I understood you were a Protestant."

Cassandra said, "In spite of our differences in our understanding of God, I have many family members who are Catholic and it is not my first time to attend a Catholic church."

Vicente said, "I suppose not." He said with a smile, "How is it then that you do not respect the priesthood?"

Cassandra smiled, "I think you are baiting me Vicente." Vicente's smile grew wider and Cassandra continued with a wry smile, "I respect all those who pastor the followers of Jesus Christ."

"But you don't have a priest."

Cassandra said, "Oh, but I do. My high priest is the Lord Jesus himself who sits at the right hand of God the Father. It is he who paid the price for my sins and he through whom I am forgiven."

Vicente said, "Then you do not believe in mother church as the original and only true church?"

Cassandra said, "Vicente, between friends, I tell you that Romans chapter ten, verses nine and ten, tell us how a person is saved from condemnation for offenses against God. I believe the Catholic Church is like all the other denominations in that it has truly born again believers, but it is also a human institution full of error and sin because it is run by sinners."

Vicente smiled and asked, "Why do you say the Mother Church is run by sinners?"

Cassandra smiled, "It is written, 'All have sinned and fall short of the glory of God', is it not?"

Vicente smiled, "So you tolerate the Catholic Church's faults as you do your denominations?"

"Exactly. I have just assessed that which I believe has the lesser fault differently than you have. I do not think we can reconcile my views of the Bible and the Roman church's view of it. I believe in my personal responsibility to know and understand it and the Catholic Church believes it has the sole right through the priesthood to interpret and add to or take away from its fundamental principles."

Alejandro said, "These things are of no consequence?"

Vicente said with a smile, "I think Dona Cassandra would disagree. She has quite strong thoughts on matters of theology."

Cassandra said, "And it seems my view is more forgiving than the Catholic Church's."

Vicente laughed, "Perhaps."

They were saved when a young priest came in to say, "The meal is ready," and led them into the dining room. It was a light meal and after Vicente said the blessing they ate.

Vicente asked as they started eating, "What are your long-term plans Cassandra?"

Cassandra told him about the estancia and that she had other business investments. They talked at some length about the estancia and Vicente asked, "So you plan to live permanently in Mexico?"

"It seems likely."

Vicente asked, "How will that work legally? You are a U.S. citizen?"

Cassandra said, "My mother was born here as was I. My father was of course born in the U.S. I am a dual citizen."

Vicente said, "So you have family here?"

Alejandro interjected, "Here and in Spain."

Cassandra said, "I have a very large family on my mother's side."

Vicente asked, "If you live on the estancia where will you worship."

Cassandra said, "I suppose I will have no other choice but to worship at home or the local church where I will keep a low profile."

Vicente smiled, "So you propose a theological truce for the sake of God and the locals."

Cassandra nodded, "It seems the only practical solution." Cassandra looked at Alejandro who was very uncomfortable with the conversation. She said, "I think our talk is troubling Alejandro."

Alejandro simply said, "Indeed."

Vicente asked, "So you would not convert to Catholicism?"

Cassandra said, "I am a follower of Christ so I do not need to convert to anything. I will be true to my God and His word and try not to be disruptive of the unity of the local church."

Vicente said with a smile, "That is very open-minded of you. I see no problem if you do not disrupt the church." Vicente paused, "Besides you were first baptized as a Catholic, so I see no barrier." Vicente shrugged, "Perhaps you will even change your mind about Catholicism."

Cassandra said, "I doubt it."

Vicente smiled, "Perhaps you will be a good influence on Alejandro. He is angry at God since his wife died."

Cassandra said, "That is unfortunate."

Vicente said, "I agree." Vicente turned to Alejandro and said, "My friend you have your hands full with this one."

Alejandro said with a smile, "Yes and she frightens me, but I am absolutely under her spell."

When they finished their meal, Vicente said, "Let us go into the living room and have coffee."

They moved into the living room and coffee was brought. The conversation was pleasant and after twenty minutes Alejandro suggested it was time to leave and after saying their goodbyes and thanking Vicente for his hospitality they left.

In the car Cassandra said, "I am surprised you and Vicente are friends. You are so different."

Alejandro said, "Perhaps that is why we became friends. Vicente can afford to have his head in the clouds, but I must have my eyes focused around me."

Cassandra said, "It may be possible to do both." Alejandro acted like he had been shot and Cassandra asked, "What is wrong?"

"My wife said that very thing once and the memory came shooting into my mind."

Cassandra smiled, "Perhaps God is trying to tell you something."

They rode in silence for the rest of the return journey. Cassandra was not uncomfortable with the silence and Alejandro seemed lost in his thoughts. They arrived at the embassy and Alejandro was brought out of his thoughts. He looked around and said, "Forgive me, Cassandra. I was lost in my thoughts."

Cassandra smiled and caressed his face with her right hand, "I know. You are troubled. God is convicting you."

Before he could say or do anything, she opened the car door and, accompanied by security, went into the building. Alejandro tapped on the glass and his driver put the car in gear.

Chapter 10 - Normalization

Monday morning first thing, Cassandra met with Stan for updates on the military's advances on the rebels and general updates. She then met with Bob for an update and then with Juan about the progress on staffing the embassy and the renovations. They discussed the problems they would have in getting things done if they were taken off of emergency status. Cassandra saw the problems that would create. They also discussed Juan's role. After Juan left, she went to the secure communications room and called Chas Elliot.

Chas answered the phone, "Hello, Cassandra."

"Mr. Secretary."

Chas said, "I am very pleased with the advances you are making. It is beyond anything I could have hoped for."

Cassandra said, "Thank you, sir."

"What can I do for you?"

Cassandra said, "First of all, please have us left on emergency status as we have a lot of repair and renovations to do as a result of the attack and the growing need here. The work on the embassy is urgent and I don't want government bureaucrats getting in the way."

Chas said, "It is done. What else?"

"I talked with Juan today. He is very good at getting things done, but we are agreed he is not the one to be the public face of embassy routine. Do you have someone you can send us who can manage the more routine and mundane things and yet stay out of our way on the important behind the scene things."

Chas laughed lightly and said, "Yes, I can send you someone that fits the bill. I just want you to continue, as you have, to develop the relationships and manage the big picture."

Cassandra said, "Thank you, sir."

Chas said, "The president there is very pleased with your work to help him get other embassy's to return to Mexico City and sent a note of appreciation through the Mexican Ambassador here. Apparently Spain and Canada are going to reopen their embassies there. I expect that will soon lead to a chain reaction."

Cassandra said, "Thank you for telling me."

"You are welcome. Is there anything else I can help you with?"

"No sir. I thank you for taking this time with me."

Chas said, "So long, Cassandra."

The call ended and Cassandra went back upstairs to the kitchen. It was past lunchtime and she was hungry. Pedro was cleaning up the kitchen. When he saw Cassandra, he stopped what he was doing and said, "Would you like lunch, Excellency?"

Cassandra said, "Yes please, in the garden. Something light would be nice."

Pedro nodded understanding and said, "Yes, Excellency."

Cassandra went into the garden and sat at the table. Stan came and sat down and Cassandra said, "Have you had lunch?"

"Yes, thank you."

Stan slipped an invoice across the table and Cassandra looked at it. It was a very good deal and she said, "Thank you, Stan."

Stan asked, "Why do you need two SUVs?"

"They are for the estancia." Stan nodded understanding and Cassandra added, "Please check out a young woman by the name Ivette Jacintha Rodriguez Flores. Her brother is reportedly in the congress and she is supposedly a veterinary student. I'd like to know about that family. I want to know if there is a connection there we could use."

Stan said, "Will do."

Cassandra asked, "What's wrong?" Cassandra had known Stan a long time and she knew something was troubling him.

"It's not what is wrong, but rather a matter of adjustment. Being Station Chief in practice is much different than knowing what is involved. I spend a lot of time reviewing reports and analyzing them for connections and clues and then using agents to verify or discount conclusions or suspicions. It is interesting, but much different than being a handler. The scale is so much broader. I have been thinking about when I am doing this in an embassy run by someone else; someone who doesn't have your background or clearance to be in the know. I don't know if I want to deal with that."

Cassandra nodded and said, "I understand, but be open to the possibilities, Stan. A year ago I would not have seem myself as an ambassador, not even in my nightmares. It seems I am of some use here now, but that probably won't last. The difference is you will get to decide if you want to continue in your present role or do something else. I won't have that luxury."

Stan said, "I see your point. I can go back to doing what I used to do somewhere else and you can't."

"That's it in a nutshell."

Luis brought the food and Cassandra said the blessing and started eating.

Stan said, "I have been working with Diego to find out how the attackers found out about the money here. It seems the man we bought the place next door from has a cousin who works for Castillo. Diego thinks the fact that we paid cash and did not go to a bank got someone to thinking and it was reported to Castillo. Diego was able to round up some servants who worked next door. He established we were being watched from there. The short ending is the family has fled the country and is now on the Mexican government's terrorist watch list."

"Do you think that is what happened?"

Stan said, "Probably."

Cassandra said, "You did well, Stan."

Stan said, "Thanks, boss. I'll leave you to eat in peace." He got up and left.

Cassandra finished lunch and Luis cleared away the plates. She sat sipping the last of her coffee. The truth was she did not know what she should do next. She finished the coffee and headed for her office and took the service stairs. Carol greeted her as she went in, "Good afternoon, Ambassador."

"Good afternoon, Carol. Is anything happening?"

"Yes we had another survivor show up about five minutes ago. A military nurse is checking her out in the library. Stan has been notified. Mike also would like a few minutes."

Cassandra said, "What is the survivors name and what did she do?"

"Her name is Connie Mallin and she was a Visa Clerk."

"I'm going to see her and then I'll meet with Mike."

Cassandra went downstairs. She entered the room where Connie was and Stan was talking to her.

Cassandra walked over and Stan said, "Ambassador, this is Connie Mallin. Connie this is Ambassador Crossing."

Cassandra held out her hand and Connie shook it.

Cassandra said, "You seem to be in good condition."

Connie said, "I am. I was on vacation in the State of Vera Cruz visiting friends. Their place is out in the boonies and I was on a five week vacation. I did not realize there had been a rebellion until I was ready to come back and was told the bus in the remote area where I was had been cancelled due to fighting. I tried to phone the embassy, but there were no phone connections. I was able to call stateside and learned what had happened. They told me to stay in place until they called back. They called me yesterday and told me to come here."

Stan asked, "How long had you worked here?"

Connie said, "Just a couple of months, sir. I had vacation and time off I'd accumulated and I was told I had to use it or I'd lose it."

Stan looked at her, "I'll need the names of your friends you were staying with."

"No problem, sir."

Cassandra asked, "Did you have friends at the embassy?"

"Not really. I hadn't been here long enough."

Cassandra asked, "Do you want to stay and work here or be released to go home?"

Connie said, "I came back to go to work."

Cassandra said, "We can use you."

Connie said, "I'll need some help. I dropped by my apartment on the way here and all my things are gone, even my motor scooter. Everything I own is in the little luggage I took with me."

"No problem. We'll get you set up here in a room and put you to work. We'll help you get re-established later."

Connie said, "Thank you, Ambassador."

Cassandra looked at Stan and he nodded. Cassandra knew his suspicious nature meant he had or would check out everything she had told him. The way he had introduced Connie meant he had already confirmed she was who she said she was.

Cassandra went back upstairs and said to Carol, "Connie Mallin is ready to go back to work. Please advise Juan and arrange accommodation on the third floor for her. I can see Mike now."

Five minutes later Mike was at her office door and she said, "Come in, Mike. What's on your mind?"

Mike took a seat, "Well, I have the initial accounting almost ready to go to Washington. I think the bulk of the embassy money should be deposited in the local banks before I file the reports. If it was me, I'd convert to Mexican Pesos, but I fear the bean counters in Washington would not know how to handle our making a profit."

Cassandra thought, "Do it anyway and let's make them sweat a bit. Keep some U.S. dollars in small bills in the lock box in case of emergency; say a couple hundred thousand. Don't touch the Special Fund the Agency uses. The Secretary of State doesn't account for that."

Mike nodded and said, "I'll get a security detail and go this afternoon. I'll have the report for your review tomorrow morning."

Cassandra said, "Good. How are we doing with the repairs and renovations?"

"We have done very well. By paying in U.S. dollars we got some real bargains in the beginning. That won't last because the fear is diminishing because people are getting the idea the government is in control. Things in the city are returning to normal. The criminals were mostly eliminated or bailed when the shooting got serious and the military was not taking prisoners."

Cassandra said, "We can use some normal. Thanks for stepping up to the plate to handle the financial aspect. How has it been going with Juan?"

Mike smiled, "He's a 'get it done' kind of guy. We meet every morning to figure out where we are financially. He's kept a spread sheet of contracts and that helped a lot in preparing the reports and records to send to Washington. If there's nothing else, I'll have to hurry to make it to the bank before it closes."

"All right, Mike."

Mike left and Cassandra went to her suite and fired up her laptop. She got on the net and pulled up information on currency exchange. Sure enough the Peso had started to climb in value. She had exchanged her personal funds at just barely above five cents per peso and it was now closing in on six. Cassandra figured it would climb back to at least eight in no time now that it was becoming known the big drug gangs and the rebels were eliminated. Cassandra figured some would "lose their shirts" because they panicked and exchanged the Peso for U.S. dollars when the peso was at its lowest.

Tuesday morning, the financial report went to Washington in a diplomatic pouch. Two days passed and Cassandra did not hear from Alejandro. She found she did not like it when he didn't call.

The embassy grounds were a flurry of construction and other activity. It was quickly being transformed into a working embassy and ambassador's residence. It didn't look like it, but it was also becoming something of a fortress.

Cassandra did not have much to do at the embassy as others were doing all the real work. She spent much of her mornings talking with her senior people. The rest of the time she researched and organized what she would need to do to get her estancia up and running properly. She was working on this research when Alejandro called her cell.

Cassandra answered, "Hello, Alejandro."

She could hear Alejandro's deep sigh, "It is good to hear your voice. I am sorry I have not contacted you before now, but the burdens of my position have demanded all of my time. I know it is short notice, but would you accompany me to lunch?"

Cassandra said, "It would please me."

"If it is acceptable, I will come in half an hour."

"Agreed."

Alejandro said, "I will see you then, cielito lindo," and the call ended.

Cassandra went to her suite and put on her going out attire. Alejandro arrived promptly at the appointed time and was led into the living room where he greeted Cassandra with a smile and said, "Your Excellency."

Cassandra smiled, "I thought this was a social call, Alejandro?"

He smiled, "So it is, Cassandra. I am tired and this is a welcome change. Forgive me?"

Cassandra said, "You are forgiven."

He offered her his arm as she stood. They walked to Alejandro's car and he opened the door for her. After he was sitting beside her and their security had loaded into other vehicles they set out.

Alejandro said, "After many months of turmoil, the country is returning to normal. I am thankful that I will now have time for personal concerns." He looked at Cassandra and smiled. He asked, "What has been keeping you busy?"

"We have a lot of work to do to get the embassy staffed as well as renovated and repaired. I have also been doing some preparation for initiating work on the estancia. After the sale is complete, I will go and visit. I will need to arrange hiring the people I will need to work there."

Alejandro said, "I would be pleased to go with you."

"I would like that."

"Is there anything else I can do?"

Cassandra said, "Well you could help me get a concealed carry permit and a collector's permit. "

Alejandro chuckled, "It will not be difficult given your recent defense of certain members of the government. I will of course be happy to do that. "

It was unspoken that they both knew most wealthy and politically connected Mexican citizens had such permits. The collectors permit allowed a person to own military style weapons that would in reality serve in the defense of their homes and family. They also knew that if Cassandra was to remain here when she was no longer ambassador, her security needs would change, but still be important. She could have only small caliber handguns, long shotguns, and certain kinds of rifles at the estancia if she did not have the collector's permit.

Alejandro said, "I suppose you already have a transportation permit for firearms from the Secretaria de la Defensa Nacional?"

Cassandra laughed, "I suspect you already know the answer to that and that my family members have various permits."

Alejandro said, "Yes. You should join the shooting club near the estancia. It is a very select group. "

Cassandra smiled, "I will do that and I will appreciate your assistance."

After arriving at the restaurant, the couple had a long and leisurely lunch which Cassandra enjoyed immensely. She and Alejandro had much in common. Cassandra asked, "Have you ever considered spending time abroad when you are no longer in government?"

Alejandro answered, "Yes. I enjoy travelling and unlike you, I have seen so little of the world. Someday I would hope to broaden my horizons."

Cassandra didn't see the man until the last minute when he dropped the tray with the coffee cups on it. She reacted quickly to his drawing a handgun. She grabbed the table and threw it over so the table top formed a barrier between the gunman and her and Alejandro. She knew Alejandro was drawing his weapon. All the things on the table went tumbling across the floor. Cassandra felt the painful impact that punched her. The breath was forced from her lungs and she went down hard then her world went black.

Cassandra had to fight to open her eyes and the light was blinding. She closed them and tried again. She saw only white and realized she was looking at a stark white ceiling. She tried to sit up and felt pain shoot through her left side and her head. She grabbed for her weapon, but it was not there. Cassandra felt a moment of panic.

She turned her head and realized from her surroundings she was in a hospital room. She felt with her hand realizing she was in a hospital gown. There was a tube connected to her left arm. She heard a slight buzzing and realized it was some kind of signal. A nurse came into the room and smiled at Cassandra.

The nurse spoke in Spanish, *"It is good you are awake. The doctor will be here shortly."*

The nurse looked at the monitoring equipment.

Cassandra tried to move her left arm and this resulted in agonizing pain on her left side. She sucked in a shallow breath and the nurse looked at her, *"It will hurt less if you lay still and take slow shallow breaths."*

Cassandra realized her rib cage hurt more when she moved. Her mouth and throat were dry and she said with difficulty and in a hoarse voice, "Water."

The nurse brought a cup with a straw close to her head so she could sip some water. Cassandra took a little and laid her head down and slipped back into the blackness.

The next time she woke she was in a tunnel. She moaned than went back to sleep. The third time she came awake a doctor was standing over her. He smiled and said in Spanish, "*Good. You are awake.*" He took out a small light and looked into her eyes.

Cassandra managed to say in a hoarse voice, "How long?"

The doctor said, "Two days."

Cassandra croaked out, "Where am I?"

"This is the American British Cowdray Hospital. You had us worried for a while."

Cassandra said, "Water." A nurse brought some and Cassandra sucked on the straw. Cassandra asked, "Injuries?"

The doctor smiled, "You have three broken ribs where your vest stopped four bullets at close range. You also suffered a severe concussion. The last had us concerned at first. I believe you will make a full recovery."

Cassandra sighed and went back to sleep. When she woke, she heard gentle snoring. She turned her head and saw she had company. Alejandro was asleep in the chair beside her bed. She smiled and sighed before going back to sleep. The next time she woke, Stan was sitting beside her bed reading a newspaper.

Cassandra said, "Hi."

Stan looked up, "Well our hero is back to the land of the living."

Cassandra said, "Water please."

Stan brought the cup to her so she could reach the straw and she took a long sip and then said, "Good."

"Do you want more?"

"Please."

Stan put the cup back so she could take more. She finished and Stan put the cup on her tray. She saw her book on the tray and asked Stan, "Did you bring my Bible?"

He nodded yes and then said, "Your father has been climbing the walls. He was worried about you getting the best treatment even though this is a world class hospital. It took a lot of people to persuade him not to have you airlifted home."

Cassandra asked, "What happened?"

"A long time waiter at the restaurant tried to assassinate you or Alejandro but probably both of you. You saved Alejandro's life and distracted the shooter who was a rank amateur. The stainless steel table top stopped some of the slugs. The shooter hit you and knocked you down and you hit your head hard. The shooter was killed. It turns out he had connections to Castillo. Alejandro wasn't hit. You got it all."

Cassandra smiled, "All things work together for the good of those who believe."

"Yeah, but your guardian angel surely was on overtime. The attack was reported in all the papers and on TV, so now you are a national hero again."

Cassandra found she was very tired and she tried unsuccessfully to stay awake. She was later woken by a nurse who said, "It's time for you to start eating." The nurse took the needle out of Cassandra's arm. The nurse then said, "I'm going to raise your bed and it will hurt." It did, but finally Cassandra was in a sitting position.

A worker brought in a tray and Cassandra ate the soft food that was on it. Stan was still there and read get well cards to her as she was eating. Cassandra knew the soft food was necessary to ease her body back to work. Her stomach had not digested food for some time. Still, it felt good to eat.

Stan stayed for an hour before he was asked to leave while they got Cassandra up. She found she was very weak. It took a lot out of her and it hurt just to walk for a short time with help. Still it was good to be up, even if it was painful to move about.

Alejandro came after lunch as Cassandra was sitting up in her bed reading her Bible. He came into the room, "There is my heroine. It is good to see you are recovering cielito lindo."

He came to Cassandra and kissed her on the forehead. "I was very worried about you."

Cassandra's heart soared and she said, "Thank you for being here. I woke to find you snoring gently."

"Ah now you know my deepest secret."

Cassandra smiled and whispered, "I doubt that."

Alejandro returned the smile, "Now I know you are feeling better. When you are released and up to it, I invite you to dinner."

Cassandra said, "In spite of the fact being with you can be dangerous to one's health, I accept the invitation."

Alejandro got serious, "You saved my life." Alejandro smiled, "My life is now yours."

Cassandra just smiled, "You are a silver tongued rogue, Alejandro, and it won't be that easy."

Alejandro added, "I did not see him in time. I would have surely been shot if not for your actions."

Cassandra said, "I'm sure you would do the same for me. You were obviously very tired. You need to get more sleep."

"Most assuredly I would, but it seems you have quicker reflexes in any event. I did however send him to hell."

Cassandra said, "He made his choice."

Alejandro brought Cassandra up to date on what had been happening during her recovery. They spent some time talking until Alejandro had to excuse himself to attend a cabinet meeting. He said, "Enrique will want to know how your recovery is proceeding."

"Tell him I am doing well and give him my regards."

A half hour after Alejandro left, Maria and Adelina came to see Cassandra. Their entourage of security lined the hall.

Maria said as she came into the room, "We came to see our friend and the woman who has Alejandro completely smitten."

Maria came to Cassandra and kissed her on the cheek and Adelina followed Maria's example. The two women claimed the two chairs in the room.

Adelina said, "Alejandro has a bad case of love sickness. He spent a lot of time by your bedside."

Cassandra teased her friends, "He just feels guilty because I was shot and he was not."

Maria smiled broadly and made a dramatic gesture of waving off the remark, "Nonsense."

Adelina giggled like a school girl, "You didn't see the state he was in when you were first brought here."

Maria said, "The news reported how Alejandro's, how did they put it, oh yes, romantic interest saved his life."

Cassandra said, "They didn't!"

Adelina said, "Oh yes they did. There was a feeding frenzy when they found out it was Ambassador Death who saved Alejandro."

Cassandra said, "Where did they come up with that name?"

Adelina said, "Apparently the Mexican military refers to you that way and they got it from them. It seems the story about how you saved Carlos is now public as well."

Cassandra said, "That may be a political problem."

Maria said, "Not here. The women love it and the men find it amusing. Alejandro has taken some good natured ribbing from his friends over being saved by a woman. Carlos men already knew about the attack on the convoy as some of them were there. The whole world now knows about you saving Adelina's husband. We know you have Alejandro's heart because when he is teased he just responds they should be so lucky."

Cassandra said with exaggerated gesture with her right arm, "It seems I may be stuck with him." She grimaced at the pain the movement caused.

Maria said, "It seems you are, whether you like it or not."

Adelina added, "He is like the homeless hungry puppy which shows up at your door and after you feed him and show a little affection, he refuses to leave."

The ladies had a good visit and the ladies told her about the progress on the construction of the factory. They spent some time talking and Cassandra's friends left before supper was served.

After supper, Vicente came to visit. He came into the room with a large smile on his face and said, "Good evening, Excellency."

Cassandra smiled, "Good evening, Most Reverend."

Vicente laughed lightly and came and laid his hand on Cassandra's good shoulder. "I prayed for you."

"Thank you, Vicente."

Vicente saw the Bible on Cassandra's tray and said, "I see you read a lot."

Cassandra said, "I never tire of God's love letters."

Vicente chuckled and sat down, "It seems you are winning the hearts and minds of your fellow citizens. It seems your celebrity has revealed your dual citizenship to the world."

Cassandra said, "I'm afraid my celebrity may end my career as a diplomat."

"Would that be so bad? You could always get married and raise a family and run an estancia and look to your business interests."

Cassandra replied, "Vicente, Vicente, you must let Alejandro do his own courting. You are a poor matchmaker."

Vicente bowed his head in mock respect, "As you say, Dona Cassandra. Do you know that reporters even came to see me about you?"

Cassandra said, "That is indeed interesting."

"It seems the people are curious about the Ambassador of the United States who is also a Mexican citizen. You seem to have caught the imagination of the people. Your mother's family is also well known as devout Catholics and strong supporters of mother church."

Cassandra smiled at Vicente, "Oh you are a sly man, Vicente."

He smiled at Cassandra, "It is sometimes necessary to be that way in order to safeguard the spiritual well being of the flock."

Cassandra enjoyed fifteen minutes with Vicente before her doctor came into the room. After giving deference to Vicente, he most politely asked him if he could have some time to examine his patient. Vicente politely agreed and came and kissed Cassandra on the forehead saying, "God bless you my child and my friend. I will look forward to our next meeting."

The exchange seemed to impress Cassandra's doctor more than any of the other things that had happened.

The next morning, Stan came to the hospital early to find Cassandra was sitting in a chair. Stan said, "Good morning, Ambassador."

"It is indeed. I am starting to feel human, though I'm still sore. They give me some magic little pills that make the pain go away for the most part."

Stan handed Cassandra a satellite phone and said, "Your father wants you to call him."

Cassandra knew the phone was encrypted. Stan went and told the security team they were not to be disturbed and then closed the door.

Cassandra dialed and her father answered, "How are you, Cassandra? Your mother and I are worried sick."

"I'm a little sore, but fine. They have been taking very good care of me here. I will fully recover."

There was a pause at the other end and Dorothy came on the line, "I just needed to hear your voice."

"I'm good, mother. The people here have been good to me and I've had friends come to visit. I am recovering nicely."

"Your father wants to talk to you. I wish I could come, but under the circumstances your father has forbid it."

Cassandra said, "He is wise, mother. Listen to him."

Craig came back on the line, "I love you daughter, but you sure know how to make my life difficult. Your celebrity there has endeared you to the Mexican people, but the opposition here was having a field day with the potential conflicts of interest with your being romantically linked to Alejandro."

Cassandra said, "I figured that might happen when this latest incident went public."

"Well the fact that your mother, you and your brother have dual citizenship has been talked up in the media. The work you did on border protection has stopped criticism of your heritage for the time being. The opposition got quite a backlash when they attacked us on that and are leaving it alone now. They don't want to alienate the Hispanic voters and they are now afraid they may have hurt themselves with the criticism."

Cassandra said, "The solution is simple. In the next year or so I will just retire once relations are stable with the government here."

Craig said, "I think you have already accomplished that. We just need to build on it."

"I will do that."

"Your mother can arrange a trusted family friend to come and help you; Teodoro. He would be a good estancia manager and he knows horses and has a lot of contacts. He is eager, if you want his help."

Cassandra said without hesitation, "I'd appreciate that."

Craig said, "I have to go."

Cassandra said, "I will talk to you later, father."

The call ended and Cassandra handed the phone back to Stan, "Thanks, Stan."

"You're welcome."

Cassandra looked at Stan, "You know we have to get Castillo. There will be no relative peace until he is removed."

Stan smiled, "Great minds think alike. I have all but three of our people on it; Castillo is priority one. My bosses in Washington have been uncharacteristically hands off and I am thankful for that."

Cassandra sighed, "They have been told I'm in charge and as long as I am, I can probably keep the bureaucrats out of the operations here. I would really like to be able to tell Enrique where Castillo is. If he is not in Mexico, it may get messy."

"I understand. If you don't have anything else I'll get back to the embassy. Oh, I almost forgot; I have a present for you." Stan handed her a small gift wrapped box and she opened it.

She smiled and took the pistol out of the box and made sure it was loaded before hiding it, "Thank you, Stan."

"You are most welcome."

Stan left and Cassandra sat thinking about Teo, as the family affectionately called him, coming to help her. Teodoro Sosimo Nunez Ortega's family had worked for the Santiago family since they had emigrated from Spain. The mutual affection and loyalty between the families was strong. Teo was a year older than Cassandra and they had played together as children. Though she had not seen Teo in several years, she knew he would be helpful in many ways and absolutely trustworthy. Teo had made many influential friends and contacts during his employment with the Santiago family and during his time in the army. Teo was also exceptionally bright and had a good head for business. His wife and two sons would be a welcome addition to the estancia.

Two days later, Cassandra was getting around quite well and was back to eating solid food. The doctor's decided to release her which turned out to be quite a production given the concerns about Cassandra's security. The U.S. military had arranged for a female duty nurse to stay at the embassy until she was completely healed. Cassandra figured the nurse would have little to do and it was probably more for the sake of those worrying about her than for her real need.

Cassandra arrived at the embassy grounds in mid afternoon. She was amazed at the progress that had been made in the short time she had been gone. There was now a guard house at the front gate to the residence and fancy steel gates through a partially complete concrete wall that had been made to look as if it were constructed of stone. The wall had been moved back so that the embassy grounds could include some grass between the street and the walls which were still under construction. Vehicles once allowed on the grounds had to maneuver through concrete barriers that slowed the vehicles progress.

Cassandra's little convoy stopped at the front door to the residence building and she got out. She was wearing a loose fitting vest over her street clothes. Her security had insisted and she had readily agreed. Juan, Stan, Carol and Bob met her at the front door and greeted her. Once inside, she was introduced to Carl Samson, the new Management Counselor for Administration candidate who had been invited to the luncheon.

Bob said as they walked into the living room, "Welcome back, Ambassador. We have a small luncheon prepared to be served in the dining room."

Cassandra said, "That is thoughtful."

She took off her vest and handed to one of her agents and nodded appreciation.

The little group enjoyed a light lunch and everyone brought Cassandra up to date on what had been happening. The new building had been successfully converted into the working part of the embassy and three new concrete buildings were almost finished. They would serve as quarters for some of the security force. The staffing was at a level that they had started to function and fulfill the normal duties of an embassy. They had started to process visas now that trade was increasing between the U.S. and Mexico.

After lunch, Cassandra asked Carl to come to her office. Once there Cassandra said, "Have a seat, Carl."

Carl said, "Thank you, Ambassador."

Carl waited for Cassandra to sit and then took the wing chair opposite her. Cassandra had been sizing Carl up during lunch. Cassandra guessed he was probably in his late fifties or early sixties, well groomed, though a little paunchy, dressed very well, and had thinning hair and an infectious smile. She was inclined to like the man.

Cassandra asked, "Why did Chas send you, Carl?"

Carl smiled, "The Secretary told me he was sending me because I can be trusted and this situation is both complex and sensitive." Carl paused, "And you sometimes work outside the box which I can cope with; I know when not to be curious."

Cassandra nodded and said, "Continue, please."

"You are accomplishing a level of cooperation with the Mexican government that may be unprecedented. I was told you needed and requested a career person to organize, plan and direct the routine work. I am very good at that. I will probably never advance beyond what I do now in reality and I'm all right with that because I love what I do and have had a rewarding career."

Cassandra said, "Fair enough. What is your assessment so far?"

"The people you have here are highly motivated and are getting the place in shape very quickly. Your key people trust each other and I think the trials you encountered here have created a bond between them and you, but I'm still an outsider. They get the job done though sometimes in, ah, unconventional ways. Some things need to be done conventionally so that the paperwork does not create a problem with those stateside and that is where I help."

Cassandra asked, "How well do you know the Secretary."

"I met him for the first time just before I was sent here."

"Then why did he select you?"

"He said it was because I'm nearing the point where I can voluntarily retire so I am not subject to the same pressures as others may be subject to within the bureaucracy."

Cassandra smiled, "In other words you don't have to be concerned about ruffling feathers to get things done or someone pressuring you for information they don't have a real need to know."

"That's right, Ambassador. The Secretary also promised me a reward of sorts if I work out for you."

Cassandra said, "Let me guess. You will be promoted just before you retire."

Carl replied, "Yes, Ambassador."

Cassandra said, "Good. I am glad we had this talk." She rose and offered her hand, "Welcome aboard, Carl."

Carl smiled, "Thank you, Ambassador."

Cassandra sat down as Carl left. Carol came in with some files and took one look at Cassandra and asked, "Are you all right?"

"No. I forgot to take my pain medicine. Would you please call the duty nurse?"

Carol hurried out and came back shortly with a glass of water and Cassandra's medicine. Cassandra took it and said, "I won't forget that again." Cassandra remained in the chair and said, "Please have a seat Carol." Carol sat down in a wing chair and Cassandra asked, "What do you have for me?"

Carol placed a file folder on the coffee table, "I have some routine documents that need your signature. I have kept your public agenda clear for the next week while you recuperate. I hope that is all right."

Cassandra smiled, "Thank you. Do you know what happened to my personal weapons that I had when we were attacked at the restaurant?"

"They are in your suite. They were returned this morning."

Cassandra said, "Just put the file folder on my desk. I'll sign the papers later. Please keep people out for a bit as I'm going to lie down on the sofa and cat nap."

Carol got up, "I will see to it." She put the file on the desk and went out the door closing it after her. It occurred to Cassandra that she was past her prime. She did not rebound from injuries as she had in the past.

Cassandra woke to a gentle buzzing and realized her cell was going off. She took it out and looked at it. She had been asleep for only five minutes. She noted the caller ID and answered, "Good afternoon, Alejandro."

"Good afternoon, cielito lindo. Would you have dinner with me?"

Cassandra said, "I would like that, but please, may we dine here? I am afraid I'm still sore and I would prefer to eat in. I'll have Pedro prepare something nice for just the two of us."

"Most certainly, as your wish is my command. Would seven o'clock be acceptable?"

"Yes, Alejandro. I will see you then."

There was a knock on the door and Cassandra said, "Come."

Carol opened the door, "Are you all right I heard you talking."

"I had a cell call. Please ask Pedro to prepare a meal for two for seven o'clock. I'm going to go upstairs and have my nap."

Cassandra went to her suite and slept for forty minutes. When she woke she did deep breathing exercises which caused her pain. After the pain subsided, Cassandra showered. She had just finished dressing when there was a knock at her suite's door. Cassandra answered it and it was the duty nurse.

"Good evening, ma'am."

Cassandra invited her in and they went and sat in the sitting room. The nurse checked Cassandra's vitals and listened to her breathing. She asked, "Have you had any pain?"

"I did when I forgot to take my medication. I took it about an hour ago. I also had some when went through my breathing exercises, but I think that is normal."

"It is, ma'am. Everything seems normal and your lungs are clear. I'll check back in the morning. Please remember to take your medicine before you turn in. Starting tomorrow, we'll start easing off your pain medication."

Cassandra asked, "Can you make that decision?"

"Yes ma'am. I'm a nurse practitioner and that's why they sent me."

Cassandra asked, "What is your name?"

The woman answered, "Colleen McGuire, ma'am."

Cassandra smiled, "Thank you, Lieutenant."

"You're welcome, ma'am."

The nurse left and Cassandra sat down and started reading. At a quarter of seven, she went downstairs. She was sitting in the living room when Alejandro arrived. Luis let Alejandro in and he came to greet Cassandra.

He said, "It is good to see you up and about."

She stood and paid the price of feeling the pain in her side. Her reward was that Alejandro kissed her on the cheek. She sat and Alejandro sat opposite her.

Cassandra asked, "Would you like a drink?"

"Some wine would be nice." Luis hurried off and came back with a glass. He handed it to Alejandro and left.

Alejandro asked Cassandra, "Aren't you having any?"

"I am not supposed to have alcohol with the medication I'm taking."

Alejandro nodded and sipped the wine. "This is very good."

Cassandra smiled and asked, "Did you put Vicente up to acting as matchmaker?"

Alejandro smiled, "I did not know he had. I simply asked him some questions."

Cassandra asked, "Such as?"

"What he sees as the barriers to a mixed marriage."

"And what did he say."

Alejandro looked into his wine, "He told me as bishop what the church teaching on such matters is and that it is discouraged. He told me as a man and friend if I was talking about you specifically, I'd be a fool not to pursue you for my wife."

Cassandra said, "I see. What do you think?"

Alejandro looked up and smiled then said, "I think I am no fool and I am no slave to the church."

Cassandra said, "I should hope not."

Alejandro asked, "When is the sale of the estancia to be completed?"

"I don't know. I have not been in contact with Adolpho."

Alejandro nodded and reached into his pocket and took out two folded sheets and handed them to Cassandra, "Don

Manuel sent this for you. The first contains the name of a trusted local contractor who could build you a new house and the names of the men who used to be employed at the estancia." Alejandro smiled and said, "The second is a membership bill for the local gun club; your application with references was completed for you and you can sign it on your first visit. The contractor will treat you fairly and has the right connections to ensure things go smoothly."

Cassandra smiled, "Thank you."

"You are welcome. What about someone to manage the estancia?"

Cassandra smiled, "My mother's family has helped with that. He is enthusiastic about managing the estancia and his wife will be a welcome addition."

Alejandro asked, "What is his name?"

"Teodoro Sosimo Nunez Ortega. You don't have to do a background on him. I have known him since I was a child and his family has worked with my family from the beginning."

Alejandro nodded and Cassandra knew because he had not agreed verbally he would check Teo out. It occurred to her that she was having insights about him that usually only married couples had about each other. She supposed it was her training and experience; it then occurred to her there might be another reason.

Alejandro said, "It seems the coverage of the attack and our personal relationship has caused your father some little difficulty."

"It has passed, but it may start up again as the next election nears."

Luis came into the room and announced, "Dinner is ready, Excellency."

Cassandra said to Alejandro, "Shall we."

She got up and Luis led them into the small sun room where a small table had been set with fine china and silverware. There were only two chairs and Alejandro pulled one out for Cassandra. When they were seated, Luis served them. Alejandro said the blessing and they started eating.

Alejandro said, "This is very nice. Thank you."

Cassandra smiled and answered, "You are welcome. The big formal dining room seemed much too big for two people."

They enjoyed the meal which was delicious. They talked about the local economy, the progress on the embassy, and discussed what the estancia home should be like. Cassandra said she would like to build a day cabin on the estancia property next to the pool at the bottom of the waterfalls. Alejandro thought that was a grand idea. Cassandra realized they were perfectly at ease with each other. It was another story when they were in physical contact.

After dinner, they went back into the living room and drank coffee and talked. Alejandro told Cassandra about his family and Cassandra told him about the Crossings and the Santiago families. There was a lot to tell.

About eleven o'clock Alejandro said, "I had best leave now as I have duties in the morning."

Cassandra said, "I understand."

She rose and walked Alejandro to the door where he took her by surprise and kissed her. It was not a polite kiss and she felt she would melt. She did not resist.

Alejandro said, "Please let me take you to dinner at one of the best restaurants in Mexico City on Friday evening. I beg you to accept."

Cassandra said with a smile, "I accept."

She noticed Alejandro was just a little flushed. She thought she must be as well for she felt like she was on fire.

Alejandro said, "Gracias, cielito lindo. I will come for you at six thirty."

He opened the door, smiled at her and then walked to his car. Cassandra watched him go until he was in the car. She closed the door and went to the sofa and sat down. She had never felt like this. Well perhaps close once in university, but Cassandra had broken that off early because his character became apparent when he had tried to pressure her into having a sexual encounter. This was different and though he had left, she still had a burning desire and that was new. She also realized the effect Alejandro had on her was dangerous to her virginity. She had kept it for over thirty years and it was a precious gift she would only give to her husband.

Cassandra of course understood the physical responses and how it all worked. In practice it was quite a different thing. It occurred to her in spite of her experience in other areas, this was one where she was a novice and would have to be very careful. Cassandra was troubled when she went up to her suite and had some difficulty going to sleep.

Chapter 11 – Recovery and Discovery

Cassandra woke at a little after five in the morning. She was sore and realized she had not taken her medication before bed. She took the anti-inflammatory pill and took only half of the pain pill. She showered and got ready because did not feel up to her regular exercise. She called the nurse who came and took her vitals and listened to her lungs. Cassandra found she could breathe quite deeply now without a lot of pain.

The lieutenant said, "Your lungs are still clear. How is the pain?"

"It is decreasing. I find a half a pain pill is enough"

The nurse said, "Good. You are mending well. I still advise you to continue to take it easy while you heal."

Cassandra said, "Thank you, Lieutenant. I will take your advice."

The lieutenant left and Cassandra decided to walk the grounds and went downstairs and into the kitchen.

She greeted Pedro, "Good morning. I compliment you on the meal last evening. It was delicious."

Pedro smiled, "Thank you Excellency."

Cassandra said to Luis, "And the service was good and I appreciated your discretion."

Luis smiled, "Thank you."

Cassandra said, "I am going for a walk around the grounds. Perhaps when I come back, you will prepare something light for breakfast."

Pedro said, "I will, Excellency."

Cassandra went out the back door and was aware that two soldiers were trailing behind her; they were her "on the grounds" security. One rushed forward and Cassandra said, "Good morning."

He responded, "Good morning, ma'am," and handed her a vest with, "Please."

She put it on.

Cassandra went around inspecting the work underway and saying hello to the workers and military guards. She walked beside the newly poured concrete road going to what was now the actual working embassy. The foundation for a large addition to the new building was being poured. She walked into the working embassy and was surprised by the fact that a number of people she did not recognize were at work. They were all dressed in business attire.

None of the staff paid her much attention as she was dressed in casual attire even though she was wearing a ballistic vest. It finally occurred to someone that since she was accompanied by two military guards she might be someone of importance. A man approached her, "Good morning. I'm Frank Albright."

Cassandra smiled, "Good morning Frank. I am Ambassador Crossing."

Frank said, "I am pleased to meet you, Ambassador."

Cassandra asked, "Is my deputy around?"

"I believe he is on the second floor inspecting the renovations for your office."

"Thank you Frank, please carry on."

"Yes Ambassador."

Cassandra went to the second story. This building only had two stories, but it was as large as the three story building next door and so it was spread out over a larger area with a front wing and two wings on either end that went back perpendicular to the front wing. Cassandra found Juan and he greeted her.

"Good morning, Ambassador."

"Good morning, Juan. How is it going?"

Juan smiled, "Very well. Your new offices are finished and we will be moving the office furniture over here in the next day or two and then we can furnish and move you into your new quarters."

Cassandra said, "Well then, let's have a look."

Juan led her to her new offices which were quite impressive. The office was in the corner of the building, but this time at the front and overlooked the front garden. There was an outer office for Carol and five other offices within the closed off area. Cassandra was impressed with the lay out.

Juan said, "I anticipated one of the offices would be mine and the others would be for the Colonel, Carl, Amanda, and Stan." Juan looked at Cassandra and she knew he was awaiting her approval.

"Very good. I am impressed by the progress. Perhaps this afternoon we can have a staff meeting and you can introduce me to everyone."

Juan asked, "Would four fifteen be acceptable? We close the offices at four."

Cassandra said, "That will work."

The rest of the day was very quiet except for a call from Adolpho about the closing of the estancia sale. He came by and she gave him a check and signed some more papers. At four fifteen, Cassandra was introduced to the staff. After the meeting, she went back to her small suite and was sitting reading when her cell sounded. She looked at the phone and noted it was Alejandro.

She answered, "Good evening, Alejandro."

"It is indeed now that I have heard your voice."

Cassandra's heart started to speed up and the thought struck her it was something she had seldom experienced outside of combat situations. She noticed some other reactions as well. She figured she had a bad case of raging hormones. No man had ever had this effect on her.

She said, "That is a sweet thing to say."

Alejandro said, "I will have to work late, but I was hoping I could call on you and we could have coffee."

Cassandra said, "I would like that. You are invited."

"I will look forward to visiting you."

The call ended and Cassandra felt like a schoolgirl. Why did he have such an effect on her? She knew the answer was obvious and she had not known him very long. In fact, she decided that this was not logical. She finally really understood the term 'matters of the heart'.

She called down to Pedro to tell him she would be having company over and would need freshly brewed coffee and some small pastries. Pedro asked how many persons he should prepare for and she said two. Because of the way Pedro responded with "Yes, Excellency," it seemed she could hear a smile in his voice. Latinos were such romantics. It occurred to her she was half Latina.

Cassandra ate a very light meal in her suite and was reading in the library. She was dressed in loose casual slacks and a flowing blouse and had her legs under her when Alejandro was announced at eight thirty. He came into the room and came over to where Cassandra was sitting and kissed her on the cheek and handed her a bouquet of flowers.

Cassandra knew she was blushing slightly when she said, "Thank you, Alejandro." She said, "Luis, would you put these in water for me please?"

Luis came and took the flowers and left as Alejandro took a seat.

Alejandro asked, "How are you feeling?"

"I am feeling better thank you, but it will be a little while until I'm a hundred percent." Cassandra paused, "I am well enough however to go to dinner with my handsome suitor."

Alejandro smiled and chuckled, "I feel blessed that you would say such a kind thing to your humble servant."

It was Cassandra's turn to be amused and she smiled broadly.

Luis returned with a tray on which was a pot of fresh coffee and small pastries as well as the vase containing the flowers. Luis put the tray on the coffee table and poured two cups of coffee before leaving.

Cassandra said, "Thank you, Luis," and Luis bowed his head slightly then left the room. Cassandra leaned over and took a cup from the table and sipped it.

Alejandro picked his up and said, "Thank you for receiving me. I find when I spend time with you that the worries of my office flee. I cannot explain how much I enjoy our time together."

Cassandra said, “I too, enjoy your company.”

Alejandro asked, “How is the estancia purchase progressing?”

“Adolpho came by today and told me I will soon have the deed to the estancia.”

Alejandro said, “Have you decided on a house plan yet?”

“No, but I will do some research and come up with a layout and design I like. I was thinking a four bedroom, four and a half bathrooms with a large open living area, modern kitchen, a large patio and a nice swimming pool.”

Alejandro smiled and said playfully, “Why so many bedrooms?”

“I expect to entertain prominent visitors.” After the slightest pause Cassandra added, “Besides, someday I may marry and have a family.”

Alejandro smiled knowing she was toying with him and flirting. He said, “Any man would be fortunate to claim you for a wife.”

“True.”

Cassandra realized she had much experience flirting, but this was the first time it was with serious intent.

Alejandro laughed and sputtered through the laughter. “You have no humility, cielito lindo.”

Cassandra smiled, “It does not have to do with pride or humility Alejandro. I was just stating the obvious.”

That caused Alejandro to bend over in laughter and it was contagious and Cassandra started giggling like a school girl. She had not ever done that before and it hurt.

When they finished laughing, Alejandro raised his head and said, “It has been much too long since I laughed. You are a good influence on me, Cassandra.”

Cassandra smiled and said, “Good.” She picked up her coffee and took another sip.

Alejandro said, “I see the work on the embassy compound is progressing quickly.”

"It is. I am fortunate to have good staff. I wonder if I can persuade Luis and Pedro to come to work for me at the estancia."

Alejandro said, "Perhaps."

"Diego would miss them, but perhaps I can persuade them."

The shocked look on Alejandro's face was priceless and it made Cassandra smile.

Alejandro asked, "How long have you known?"

The response was direct, "Since day one, of course."

"How did you know?"

Cassandra smiled, "It is what I would have done. Those who serve are often invisible to most people."

"Ah, but it is obvious to the trained operative."

Cassandra smiled, "Of course, my dear Alejandro."

Alejandro had noted the use of "dear" and it had an obvious effect on him. He had tilted his head and was looking at her strangely. He said, "You never cease to amaze me. Are you serious about hiring them?"

"Of course, they are very good at their jobs and I suspect in a pinch they know how to use a weapon. Diego is a friend to both of us so I foresee no problem. I would want them to of course stay here for the time being."

Alejandro seemed to gloss over the implications of Cassandra's use of "us" and said, "They have families."

"There are three houses on the estancia. I intend to improve them and build more."

Alejandro said, "They might be persuaded."

Cassandra asked in a normal voice, "What do you think, Luis?"

Luis did not insult her by pretending he did not hear and came into the room, "I would be honored to serve you, Dona Cassandra, and estancia life has a certain appeal. Captain Ramos Sanchez would release us if his superior authorized it."

Luis looked at Alejandro.

Cassandra said, "Thank you, Luis."

Luis asked, "May I discuss this with Pedro. We have worked together for a long time."

Cassandra looked at Alejandro who nodded agreement.

"Yes. Let me know what your salary requirements would be if I provide suitable housing."

Luis said, "I will do that, Dona Cassandra."

Alejandro said, "You are dangerous woman. You maneuvered me into that very well."

"You did not go where you were not willing to."

Alejandro smiled, "True. I must go now before you maneuver me out of everything I have."

Cassandra got up and Alejandro was in front of her moving like a tiger and had his right hand on her cheek. He looked into her eyes and kissed her and it was passionate. Though their bodies were not touching Cassandra felt the heat.

Alejandro moved away and said passionately, "You have trapped my heart."

Cassandra smiled and took his arm, "I look forward to our rendezvous Friday evening."

She walked him to the door where he kissed her on the cheek and left. She closed the door thinking Friday could not come soon enough.

Each morning, Cassandra spent time in her new office learning about the people working in the embassy and very generally what each of them did. In the afternoons, she spent time reviewing intelligence and other reports and researching designs for her new house.

Thursday morning, Cassandra emailed Teo photos of the existing home at the estancia. In the afternoon she called Teo and talked with him. They discussed salary and she offered him less fixed salary than he asked for, but offered him a share of the breeding profits, which if he made the estancia profitable would result in a higher income than the salary he requested. He agreed because he knew she was putting him a very good position.

Friday morning was moving day and her office furniture was moved to the new building. The furniture for the second floor suite was delivered in the afternoon and Cassandra supervised the move of her few possessions to the second floor and the arranging of the furniture. The Amazons now took up guard duty on the second floor to prevent any unwanted visitors on both top floors of the residence.

The Amazons would be housed on the second floor and they considered it a prime billet as they were only two to a room and each room had a private bath. Cassandra let Carol take over her small suite on the third floor which left one room vacant there and two vacant on the second floor next to Cassandra's suite. All of the rooms on the third floor were now occupied and they had two junior female employees sharing a room.

The women did not complain about the housing arrangements because by not having to pay rent they kept more of their paycheck and it was safe here. All of the women were single as the carnage at the previous embassy was still fresh in the minds of the diplomatic corps. The security of living in the heavily guarded compound was enough to allow Juan to staff certain positions, but so far only unattached women and men had volunteered to come.

Alejandro came promptly at the appointed time and Luis let him in and brought him to Cassandra who was waiting in the living room. She wore a navy dress with a pearl necklace and matching earrings.

Alejandro came to where she was sitting and she got up. He bowed slightly, "You are beautiful, Cassandra."

"And you are handsome, Alejandro."

He offered his arm and she picked up her evening bag and took his arm. He led her to the car and opened the door and she glided in gracefully. Their car was part of a small convoy of other vehicles filled with security people.

Alejandro said, "We make quite a spectacle just going out for dinner."

Cassandra said, “Yes, but at least we don’t have paparazzi following us around.”

She was to find out her assessment was wrong. When they arrived at the restaurant there was a lineup of expensive cars dropping off customers. A photographer was taking pictures of prominent people who were entering. Alejandro got out of their vehicle and personally opened the door for Cassandra. She took his arm and they went into the restaurant surrounded by security. The photographer was obviously capturing their images.

Alejandro and Cassandra were greeted by the manager, bypassed those waiting to be seated, and were led to a private booth where they were seated.

Alejandro asked, “Have you been here before?”

“No, I haven’t. What do you suggest?”

“They serve a wonderful steak with green poblano rice. The marinade they use is superb. I suggest the house soup to start. Will you have wine this evening?”

Cassandra said, “Yes. I am no longer taking the pain medicine.”

Alejandro ordered and the waiter hurried away. Alejandro asked, “Have you finalized a contract with Teo?”

“Yes. My hope is the estancia will pay for its own upkeep and perhaps provide a small income. I expect my main income will come from other business interests and investments. Are you satisfied with the reports on Teo?”

Alejandro smiled, “Most certainly. They were informal, but I am told he is a man of fine reputation and comes from a fine family.”

Cassandra said, “Thank you for caring enough to check up on him.”

Cassandra could tell Alejandro was a little surprised by her attitude.

He said, “You never cease to surprise me.”

Their wine was brought and then their soup. Alejandro said the blessing and they began to eat. Alejandro asked, “What is your father really like?”

Cassandra said, "He is a devoted and fiercely loyal patriot and family man. He loves my mother passionately. They still act like teenagers when they think we are not looking. He is ambitious, but not a workaholic. He is one of the most intelligent people I have met. He has embraced my mother's family with a fierce loyalty and it is mutual. He is also a combat veteran and hero; he was awarded a silver star. He has a natural aptitude for business and managing." She looked at Alejandro, "He is not afraid of the hard decisions and is very ethical. What he says is what he means."

Alejandro nodded, "What about your siblings?"

"My brother is my twin though I was first out of the womb so technically I am the older sister. He endures my teasing him about it with good humor. He is like my father in many ways. He is a thoughtful man and perhaps slower to act and less demonstrative than the rest of the family. He is very intelligent and ambitious, but not so as to lead an unbalanced life. He is happily married and happy with his life. My sisters are smart and I think they will live their lives as middle class professionals married to middle class professionals and be happy because they have good judgment about men."

Alejandro said, "You are fortunate to have such broad family ties."

"I am indeed blessed."

They had finished their soup and the table was cleared and the main course was brought to the table. They started eating and Cassandra found Alejandro had been right; the food was excellent. She said so. The waiter came and asked if everything was to their liking. Alejandro expressed his appreciation and the waiter left.

Cassandra said, "It is a good thing he didn't ask me?"

Alejandro suddenly seemed concerned and asked, "What is the problem? I will see it is resolved."

Cassandra smiled and said, "Your steak is bigger than mine."

Alejandro smiled, "It is the nature of things that men get the bigger portion."

Cassandra said, "The next time you bring me here you had better tell them I expect an equal portion because the food is very good."

Alejandro smiled and said teasingly, "Of course I will tell him you eat like a man."

Cassandra kicked Alejandro gently under the table and he smiled. She asked Alejandro about his time in the military and he was pleased to tell her. She asked about his wife and he was candid.

"She was different than you in many ways. She was a very quiet and reserved woman; almost shy. She was very fragile and petite, but highly intelligent and well educated. She was a medical doctor. In spite of the fact we seemed to be opposites in so many ways, I loved her deeply and I suffered her loss for a long time."

Cassandra said, "I apologize if my question made you sad."

"Not at all, she is now with God and I finished grieving some time ago."

Cassandra said, "Tell me about your parents."

"My father was a surgeon and my mother a home maker. I am an only child. My mother had difficulty in childbirth and could have no more children. I think it must run in my mother's family because she was an only child for the same reason. My father had two brothers. You have met my aunt who married one of my father's brothers. Her husband was a lawyer; a prosecutor who was assassinated on the orders of a drug lord and at the time he was with my parents. They died with him. My other uncle is a shopkeeper. My family is middle class." Alejandro paused.

Cassandra said, "I take it the drug lord you referred to is no longer of this world."

"He is not."

"Did you have a hand in it?"

Alejandro sighed, "Yes I did. He was killed by the military during the recent unpleasantness."

Cassandra said, "That was good. The drug lords were a cancer on the society."

Alejandro said, "You are certainly a remarkable woman to understand such a thing."

"You must remember my background."

Alejandro said, "Yes, I sometimes forget that. You have had an effect on me I cannot explain."

Cassandra responded, "Oh, I think you know why."

Alejandro nodded. When they had finished eating the waiter came and took their plates away. They did not want desert, but asked for coffee.

Cassandra said, "That was a very good meal."

The waiter poured coffee and they sat sipping it.

Alejandro said, "I'd like to ask you a personal question."

Cassandra said, "What?"

"Will you marry me?" He took out a small box and slid it onto the table and opened it.

Cassandra was speechless for a moment then asked, "Why do you ask?"

"I ask because I love you, cielito lindo."

Cassandra reacted from the heart and not with her brain and said, "In that case, I accept."

Alejandro took the ring out of the box, "I have one condition."

Cassandra was taken aback, "Condition?"

"You must agree to a pre-nuptial agreement to protect your property because I do not want it said I married you for your money and land. Everyone knows I am not a wealthy man and I will not have your reputation as a serious woman questioned."

Cassandra smiled, "But of course we will enjoy my blessings together."

Alejandro smiled and said, "I'm not a fool."

Cassandra held out her hand and Alejandro put the ring on her finger. It was an exquisite ring and Cassandra said so.

Alejandro said, "I am glad you like it."

Cassandra said, “I must tell my father before this becomes public. It may cause him political problems.”

“You need not worry for I asked your father’s permission to ask you and I told him my plan for the pre-nuptial agreement. He gave me his blessing. He said it was likely to cause some reaction, but no one can guess how much. He wants you to be happy.”

Cassandra said, “What about the marriage ceremony?”

“I am not opposed to a secular marriage.”

Cassandra said, “It would keep our good friend Vicente from having to deal with what he knows about your future wife’s religious beliefs.”

“Of course and it seems like a good solution.”

“Yes, but my parents may want to come here and if they do it will be a security nightmare.”

“It will be a nightmare if Enrique and Maria insist on coming. Your neighbors of course cannot be left out. Then there is your mother’s family here.”

Cassandra said, “Oh my!”

“Exactly.”

Cassandra said, “Perhaps under the circumstances we can talk the presidents and my family out of coming.”

“I doubt we could talk your father out of being at the wedding.”

Cassandra said, “We had better get the new main house and staff houses built.”

Alejandro smiled, “I love the problems we have.”

Cassandra smiled, “Yes.”

Alejandro leaned over the table and kissed her. She felt the heat and decided she didn’t want to wait too long for the marriage ceremony. They talked and drank coffee for a very long time and finally Alejandro called for the check and he paid it and they left the restaurant arm in arm.

In the car, they discussed the issues that would arise related to the wedding. They decided they would need someone to organize everything. When they arrived at the embassy, Alejandro walked Cassandra to the door and inside he kissed her on the cheek because Luis was there.

Cassandra went up to her suite and pulled out her cell phone and made a call. Maria answered, "Do you know what time it is. This had better be good."

Cassandra teased, "Well if you want to wait until tomorrow to hear the news of the century then so be it."

Maria said, "I'm awake now so tell me now."

Cassandra said casually, "Alejandro proposed marriage and I accepted."

Maria said, "He did what?"

Cassandra said, "What part of marriage don't you understand?"

Maria said, "You are serious?"

"Yes. I have to go now. I have to wake Adelina up."

Cassandra felt just a little mischievous hanging up on Maria.

She quickly dialed Adelina who answered, "Hello Cassandra. What's the matter?"

"Maria didn't seem to believe my news."

"What news?"

"Alejandro proposed marriage this evening and I accepted."

Adelina said, "He did what?"

"It seems no one wants to believe me. I have to call my mother. Bye." Cassandra was now feeling really mischievous.

She called her mother who answered, "Hello dear. What's the matter that you are calling at this time of the morning?"

Cassandra said, "Why does everyone assume I'm calling about bad news?"

"Most people assume middle of the night calls are bad, especially when the calls wake them up."

Cassandra said, "Well I'll let you go. I just wanted to tell you Alejandro proposed marriage tonight. I'll talk to you later mother."

Dorothy said sternly, "Don't you dare hang up! Give me the details."

Cassandra spent fifteen minutes talking with her mother. It was time well spent. When the call ended her phone rang immediately.

Maria said, "How could you do that to me?"

Cassandra teased Maria, "Do what?"

"You hung up on me!"

"Well it's your own fault. You obviously didn't believe me."

Maria said, "Give me all the details."

It was another fifteen minute call and Maria decided she and Adelina would just have to have lunch with Cassandra tomorrow. The call no sooner ended than the phone rang again.

Cassandra took the call and before she could say anything Adelina said, "You hung up on me!"

"Well you apparently didn't believe me and I hadn't yet told my mother, so what do you expect?"

"All the details," and it was another long call.

Cassandra told Adelina about Maria's luncheon idea and thus the date was on.

Cassandra's next call was to Alejandro's Aunt Adriana. Adriana answered the phone after Cassandra let it ring for some time, "Hello. Who is calling at this time of night?"

Cassandra said, "I beg your pardon, Dona Adriana. It is I Cassandra. I wanted to share my news with you. Alejandro proposed marriage to me and I have accepted. My father has given his blessing."

Adriana said, "This is good news and I am happy for you. My nephew has good sense after all."

Cassandra said, "I would like to meet with you early in the week. I will call you to arrange a time, if that is agreeable."

"Oh, most certainly, as we have much to discuss. I forgive you for calling so late."

"Thank you. I was bursting to tell you."

"Well I know Alejandro came in, but he did not have the courtesy to come and tell me. He will pay for that. Goodnight Cassandra."

"Good night, Adriana."

It was very late when Cassandra finally turned in after calling all her family women to tell them the good news. She thought she would have trouble sleeping, but she didn't. She slept like a baby and slept late. She woke to a gentle knocking at her door. She opened it a crack, weapon in hand and found it was the nurse.

Cassandra said, "Good morning, Lieutenant."

"Good morning, ma'am. I was worried about you."

"I had a late night. Please come in."

The lieutenant examined Cassandra and proclaimed, "Everything is fine. I think they will soon be pulling me out of this cushy billet."

Cassandra asked, "You ever serve in a combat hospital Lieutenant?"

"Yes ma'am, in Afghanistan and Iraq."

Cassandra nodded. The lieutenant left and Cassandra got ready. She dressed in casual attire and walked to the other building with two soldiers following her. She went up to her office and the soldiers took positions in the hall with the floor guard who had a permanent station at the stair landing.

Carol was in the office even though it was Saturday and said as Cassandra entered, "Good morning, Ambassador."

"Good morning, Carol. Is anything happening?"

Carol got up and followed Cassandra into her office, "Mr. Perez would like you to call him on Monday. He has the deed for your property. Other than that, it has been quiet."

Cassandra said, "Close the door," and Carol did. Cassandra asked, "Do you know the role an embassy plays if the president visits a foreign country on a state visit?"

Carol said, "Our president?"

"Yes."

"That is a big deal."

Cassandra said, "I thought you might say that. Would you research that for me on Monday please and prepare a synopsis of the major issues. This is strictly confidential."

Carol blurted it out, "Oh my, you are getting married to the secretary of the interior." Cassandra looked at Carol who said, "The ring gave it away. Who else could it be? It all makes sense. When will you the public announcement be made?"

Cassandra said, "That is a topic for discussion today. In the meantime it is not to come out of this office."

"Yes, of course, Ambassador."

"Please close the door as I have some important calls to make."

Carol left and Cassandra called Alejandro first.

He answered, "Good morning, Cassandra."

"Indeed it is, dear. We have a problem. A public announcement needs to go out and soon. You have the senior position so I would assume your office will make the announcement."

Alejandro paused, "No. I think we should make an announcement together. I can arrange a meeting with the society reporters for later this afternoon. You are right; we have to make the announcement soon. I will talk to Enrique and get back to you."

"I'll look forward to your call."

Cassandra made a call to Washington, but her father was in a meeting. She left a message for him to call her on an important personal matter. She sat thinking and it was fifteen minutes later when her father called.

Cassandra said, "Hello, father."

Craig asked, "Hello. Your mother filled me in. When are you making the announcement?"

"Probably we'll do it this afternoon. I suppose it would be good form for you and mother to make an announcement to the society page reporters there about the same time."

"Yes. I'll get my people on it. Let me know the time of the announcement there."

"I will father, as soon as Alejandro discusses it with Enrique."

Craig asked, "Do you love him?"

"Yes and he is head over heels for me."

"That's good enough for me. You will both have to come visit us before the wedding. I suggest the Coral Gables location. I suppose you will get married in a Catholic church. How will that work?"

"I don't think it will. We will probably have a secular marriage."

Craig laughed and then said, "Unfortunate, but perhaps necessary. I will talk to you later, daughter dear. I have to go to a meeting."

Cassandra sat at her desk thinking. There was a knock on her door and she said, "Come."

Carol opened the door, "I was thinking of calling it a day unless you have something you want me to do."

"You deserve time off. How do you like the suite?"

"I love it. Will it be permanent?"

Cassandra smiled, "As long as I am here, you can stay there."

Carol smiled, "Thank you," and then left.

Cassandra was waiting for a return call and thinking when there was a knock at her door. Cassandra said, "Come in."

Stan opened the door and entered, "Good morning."

"Hi Stan, what's up?"

Stan put a file on her desk, "That's what we found out about Ivette Jacinta Rodriguez Flores and her brother. They are on the up and up; well sort of. Her brother is a supporter of the current president. He is what they call an up and comer. The young woman is an average student and not a good girl; apparently she likes women. In this country that is frowned upon and it will get her into trouble eventually. Her brother is taking steps to distance himself from her because of a recent indiscretion she was involved in."

Cassandra asked, "Do you think she could be useful?"

"Nah, she wouldn't be worth the effort to get her out of a jam."

Cassandra said, "Thank you, Stan." Stan left and Cassandra's cell phone went off. She looked at the caller ID and answered, "Hi, dear."

"I talked to Enrique and we can set up a three o'clock press meeting at the presidential residence with the society reporters. Enrique talked to your father and your father, ever the statesman, asked Enrique to make the announcement here on his behalf. Your father will make a similar announcement in Washington. Is that agreeable?"

Cassandra said, "It is brilliant."

"I do have the occasional good idea."

"I will be there about two thirty if that is agreeable."

Alejandro said, "It is. Enjoy your luncheon with Maria and Adelina."

Cassandra called her friend Matt Brite and gave him the news. She also talked to him about the lieutenant nurse. Given past events and the presence of so many females in the compound, she made the case for having a combat experienced nurse in residence in case of another attack. Technically she could have ordered Matt to do it, but he was a friend and friends did not treat people they respect like that. He thought the idea was a good one and agreed to pass on the "request."

Cassandra returned to her residence and got ready for lunch realizing she would have to go directly from lunch to the press conference so dressed appropriately. At twelve thirty, she arrived with her security detail at the agreed upon restaurant. Maria and Adelina were already there drinking wine when Cassandra went in. She found them and after hugging her friends took a seat.

Maria said, "We were so pleased with your good news we have decided to forgive you."

"Forgive me for what?"

A waiter brought wine for Cassandra which she accepted and sipped.

Adelina said, "Forgive you for teasing us so in the middle of the night."

Cassandra smiled, "Guilty, but you both deserved it."

Maria said playfully and with a big smile, "You will pay for that."

Adelina said, "When will the wedding be?"

Cassandra said, "I don't know. That will be complicated as I am not Catholic and we don't want to put Vicente in the middle of a controversy. It will probably be a secular wedding and will take some planning. It also depends upon what Maria's husband and my father decide about attending. If they both go, can you imagine just providing for the security and press alone would be daunting."

Adelina said, "I know an outstanding wedding planner who could handle this. It will be my wedding present to you."

Cassandra said, "That is very generous."

Adelina said, "She'd probably pay you to do this as it will make her name a household word. I'll get a big discount."

Cassandra said with mock seriousness, "How much do you think we can get for the TV rights?"

Her friends laughed.

The waiter came and took their order and when he left Cassandra said, "I think our wedding may cause a lot of complications."

Maria said, "I agree, but love will prevail."

Cassandra said, "Alejandro and I have a lot to work out."

Adelina said, "You have a lot of work to do. You should get someone local to help you."

Maria said, "Oh sure, that works for you as you are local. I am inviting myself to be involved."

Cassandra said, "Of course my best friends will be involved. It would probably be inappropriate for the nation's first lady to be the maid of honor."

Maria said, "True."

Cassandra sighed, "I guess that just leaves Adelina."

Adelina said gleefully, "I accept. What about bridesmaids?"

Cassandra said, "Perhaps my sisters and Josefina."

The food arrived and was served and when the waiter left, Maria announced, "There will be a social for the media and then an engagement dinner at our residence.

They continued to discuss the wedding through lunch. After lunch, the three women started out for the presidential residence. They all rode in separate vehicles to make the security people happy. They arrived just after two o'clock. They went to a small room where they continued their conversation over a glass of wine.

Ten minutes before the announcement, Enrique, Alejandro, and Carlos came to the little room to accompany their women. There was a small number of media people seated there when the couples came into the room arm in arm. Cassandra counted fourteen reporters not including camera people. The president went to the front with his wife.

"Ladies and gentlemen I thank you for coming. This is a happy occasion. I am honored on behalf of my friend, President Crossing, to announce the engagement of his daughter Ambassador Cassandra Adora Crossing Santiago to Secretary of the Interior Alejandro Carlos Garcia Ramirez. My friend President Crossing is at this time making a similar announcement in Washington. I cannot tell you how pleased I am to make this announcement of the engagement of my friends. You are all invited to join us for champagne in celebration where you will have a chance to talk to the happy couple. Cameras and recorders will not be allowed. Thank you."

The group moved to the hall and the media members were allowed into the hall after surrendering their cameras and recorders. The first reporter into the hall was not a society reporter, but the one who had accompanied the president's dinner guests to the airport inspection.

She said, "Good evening and congratulations."

Alejandro spoke first, "It is good to see you again, Maria Aleta."

"Thank you, Señor Secretary."

Maria Aleta turned to Cassandra, "Excellency, how did you meet the Secretary?"

Cassandra was aware others were now gathering to listen to the conversation. Cassandra smiled, "We met in Washington at a formal function when Alejandro was the Mexican Ambassador. We saw each other socially after that."

Maria Aleta asked, "Does your father approve?"

Cassandra smiled and said, "Alejandro is very traditional and he first asked my father for permission to court me and later for permission to ask me to marry him. My father gave him his blessing both times."

Maria Aleta seemed surprised, "Are you serious? Did he really do that?"

Cassandra smiled and put her arm through Alejandro's, "Oh yes. It was quite romantic of him to do that. My father was pleased with the display of respect."

Another reporter asked, "Excellency, is it true you are wealthy?"

Cassandra said, "I am comfortable." Cassandra decided to make a statement that would cut off further questions about wealth, "I thought it was both gallant and romantic of Alejandro to insist on a pre-nuptial to protect my finances and demonstrate he was interested in the woman and not the wealth. He made that a condition of his proposal."

Someone said, "That is quite unusual."

Alejandro smiled and said, "I think it is appropriate, even if unusual."

A reporter holding a glass of champagne asked, "When and where will the wedding be held?"

Alejandro said, "It has not been decided yet. Obviously, there are many things to take into consideration under the circumstances."

A waiter came and offered champagne and Alejandro took two flutes then handed one to Cassandra.

Someone Cassandra did not know asked, "Did your father really ask our president to make the announcement?"

Cassandra laughed, "Oh yes and I was told of it after the fact, but we think it is marvelous."

Alejandro said, "We are very honored and pleased."

A question was asked that Cassandra was prepared for, "Excellency will your engagement cause political problems for your father?"

Cassandra said, "Why should it? Mexico and the United States are close friends and neighbors. I have relatives both here and in the U.S., as do many American citizens. It might be different if the two countries were adversaries."

Enrique and Maria came into the circle and the reporters started asking the president questions about how he came to be the one making the announcement. Enrique made it a humorous story about how he and Cassandra's father had conspired to surprise the couple with the announcement meetings and made them an offer they couldn't refuse. There was much laughter and light hearted questions. Cassandra hoped that her father and Enrique had coordinated what they would say.

After the social gathering, Cassandra and Alejandro agreed to pose for photographs. They had some taken of them alone and some with the president and first lady. Some of the media people wanted their photographs taken with the couple and they stayed for the better part of a half hour posing with people before they finally took their leave.

They were escorted to another room where the president and a number of his cabinet members and their wives were having drinks. Alejandro and Cassandra were again receiving congratulations. Soon the room was filled. There was polite conversation and then they went to dine.

After the meal, they adjourned for coffee and the women congregated in a room and gave Cassandra all kinds of advice from where to get a wedding dress to the best caterers. All in all it was an enjoyable evening.

When the festivities were over, Alejandro accompanied Cassandra back to the embassy residence. As they walked to the door Alejandro asked, "Would you let me accompany you to church in the morning?"

"I would like that."

Alejandro kissed her lightly and even that set her blood to racing. Alejandro said, "I find it is very difficult to restrain myself."

Cassandra smiled and said, "I appreciate that you do."

She left it unsaid that for the first time in her life she was increasingly finding it difficult to exercise self control.

Alejandro said, "Good night, my love."

Cassandra went in the residence and up to her suite where she prayed for God to give her strength to resist the temptation that Alejandro presented. She then gave thanks that he was in her life. She found it humorous that God's blessing, the devil turned into her greatest temptation. She felt thankful God would not let her be tempted beyond what she could handle.

Chapter 12 – Plans

Alejandro arrived in the morning and had coffee with Cassandra before they left for church. They drew much attention at the church because they were surrounded by security. When they came out, several photographers moved to where they could take pictures of the couple.

Alejandro leaned toward Cassandra and said in a low voice, "I hate paparazzi."

Cassandra answered, "They are just trying to make a living. I will show you how to minimize the intrusion."

She led Alejandro toward them and the security people moved to keep some semblance of order. Cassandra said, "Good morning gentlemen. If you would like we will pose for you before we leave." She turned to Alejandro and said, "Smile dear." She turned to the security, "Please move enough so these nice men can get the church in the background."

They posed for a short time then Cassandra said, "Thank you gentlemen. Have a blessed day." They left as the photographers gave shouts of appreciation.

In the car Cassandra said, "Would you care to have lunch at my residence. I would like to show you some ideas I have for a home at the estancia."

Alejandro said, "I would like that."

Pedro prepared a light lunch which they ate in the sun room. Afterward, Cassandra fetched her laptop and showed Alejandro the designs she liked and the floor plan she had designed. He had a few suggestions which Cassandra liked. They altered the floor plan slightly. The home would have about twenty five hundred square feet of interior space, a large covered patio and a swimming pool. It would be a comfortable and attractive sprawling single story home similar to ones that might be found in upscale California neighborhoods.

Cassandra showed Alejandro how the design would create shade and keep the interior rooms cool. The windows were large and deep set. The overhangs would allow winter sun in, but keep the summer sun out. It was a type of passive solar. The high ceilings would allow cool breezes to flow through the open concept home and fans would be hung on the ceilings. The walls would be thick and heavy; made of concrete to keep out the heat. The outside would be covered with colorful stucco and the patio would be made of stone work. In the living spaces the floors would be of materials that provide cool surfaces like ceramic tiles and stone slabs.

Alejandro looked at the photos of the homes with the rooms that Cassandra had based her design on and said, "It will be a beautiful home. Where will Aunt Adriana live?"

Cassandra said, "Will she want to live there?"

Alejandro said, "I don't know. I will ask her?"

Cassandra said, "I think we should ask her together."

Alejandro asked, "Where will she stay if she wants to come live there?"

Cassandra said, "We can add a small one bedroom suite on the other side of the swimming pool. It would be joined by the patio roof to the main house. Adriana could have her privacy as could we, but she would be still be part of the household."

Alejandro nodded, "If she agrees, perhaps I could sell the house and we could take a small apartment in the city when we are not here."

Cassandra nodded agreement. "We had best go ask her."

Alejandro said, "I agree."

They packed up Cassandra's laptop and her file on the new house and went to Alejandro's home. On the way to the house, Alejandro called Adriana to let her know they were coming. When the cavalcade of security vehicles pulled up at the door, Adriana opened it and when the couple went to the door Adriana gave Cassandra a long, but light hug. Then they all went in.

Adriana said, “I have coffee ready and sweet empanditas. We will sit in the kitchen.”

She led the way and they all sat at a kitchen table at which three cups and the plate of pastries was set. They all sat and Adriana poured coffee for each of them.

Cassandra started the conversation, “Has Alejandro told you I have bought and estancia on which I intend to breed horses.”

“Yes, he told me but not about the details. How big is it?”

Cassandra answered, “Almost fifteen hundred acres; sorry almost six hundred hectares. It has a main house and three smaller houses for workers. I plan to move the manager into what is now the main house and build a new home and two smaller homes. Would you like to see the plans for the home?”

Adriana said, “Yes please.”

Cassandra showed her what she had on her laptop and the file with the maps and photographs of the property.

Adriana said, “It is a beautiful spot and the home you plan is beautiful.”

Cassandra said, “We just have one problem with the plans that we cannot resolve yet.”

Adriana asked, “What is that?”

Cassandra said, “See here by the pool. We don’t know if we should build a suite there for you? We would be delighted to have you live there with us if you’d like to.”

Alejandro added, “If you’d like you can of course stay here.”

Adriana looked at Cassandra and smiled, “I never really liked the city. I think country life would agree with me. What would you expect of me?”

Cassandra smiled, “Be part of the family.”

Adriana sipped her coffee and smiled. After a slight pause, she said, “I would like to live there as I love to ride. I haven’t been able to in a very long time.” She turned to Alejandro, “I will have to buy a horse.”

Alejandro said, “Of course, Adriana. We all will.”

"How big will my suite be?"

Cassandra said, "We were thinking a nice large bedroom, a bath and sitting area. The family could eat together so you wouldn't need a kitchen. If you do want a kitchen, we can put one in the suite. The suite would be at least seven hundred and fifty square feet; more if you want a kitchen."

Adriana said, "I would prefer to eat with you."

Cassandra said, "Good. We plan to hire a cook and house man."

Adriana asked, "Will you have children?"

Cassandra said, "That is up to God."

Adriana smiled, "That is a good answer. I would like to help with children." Adriana looked at her nephew, "You might as well sell this house and furniture. I will buy new modern furniture."

Alejandro said, "Whatever you wish. Do you like the design of the house?"

Adriana smiled, "It is much nicer than this old thing. It is modern and bright. I never really liked this house since the day your uncle and I moved in. Cassandra has good taste and I trust her judgment."

Cassandra said, "Then it is settled. Our family will live together.

Adriana said, "I have a suggestion."

Alejandro asked, "What is it?"

"If you can afford it, Cassandra, you may want to build another suite on the other side for when your side of the family visits."

Cassandra said, "Good point. We will get a cost on everything."

Alejandro said, "I can see to that as I know a good architect who will draw the plans at a reasonable cost. After you approve them, we can get a price from the contractor. I will talk with Don Manuel."

Cassandra said, "Thank you, dear."

They finished their coffee and Alejandro proposed to take the women out to dinner. They ate at a local restaurant and talked about the wedding and their plans. Alejandro and Adriana dropped Cassandra at her residence about nine o'clock.

Cassandra came to her office early Monday, but Carol was already there. She said, "Good morning, Ambassador. "

Cassandra said, "Indeed it is, thank you."

Carol added, "Lieutenant McGuire is waiting to see you. I left the early morning papers on your desk. You may want to watch the local TV news later."

"Please send the Lieutenant in."

Cassandra was no sooner seated at her desk than Lieutenant McGuire knocked on the door frame and Cassandra said, "Come in, Lieutenant."

The Lieutenant came in with her cap under her arm, "Lieutenant Colleen McGuire reporting for duty, Your Excellency."

Colleen was at attention.

Cassandra said, "At ease, Lieutenant. Have a seat."

Colleen gave Cassandra a copy of her orders and sat down. Cassandra reviewed the orders which had been electronically sent to the embassy.

Colleen said, "Permission to speak freely, ma'am."

Cassandra sat back in her chair, "Granted."

Colleen looked at Cassandra, "Thank you for arranging for me to stay here."

"You are welcome, Lieutenant. The Amazons are on the second floor of the residence. Carol has just vacated her room so you may want to talk to her and move in there. It is a large room."

Colleen said, "Yes ma'am. What are my orders?"

"Set up an infirmary for the women and be there to take sick call for at least one hour every weekday morning or until you treat all those who show up. You will of course be on call for emergency treatment. You can set up office in one of the vacant rooms on the second floor. Ask the Colonel if he can use your assistance to help the medics for a couple of hours each weekday. In the unlikely event we have another attack, you will report immediately to the Colonel to help treat the wounded. The rest of the time you are free to do what you want, just stay on the grounds and in radio contact. At this time we are keeping everyone on the grounds until we are sure things are safe. Do you have any questions?"

Colleen said, "No, ma'am."

Cassandra smiled, "Then you are dismissed, Lieutenant."

"Yes ma'am." Colleen got up and started to leave.

Cassandra said, "Colleen," and the lieutenant turned around, "Welcome to your new station. I'm glad you are here."

Colleen smiled, "Thank you, ma'am. I'm overjoyed to be here."

Cassandra called Carol on the intercom, "Please see Bob gets a copy of Colleen's orders."

"Yes Ambassador. I have something for you. May I bring it in?"

"Please do."

Carol came into the office carrying newspaper page clippings, "I thought you should see the write ups of your engagement announcement reporting. There are also a lot of photos of you and your fiancé." Carol put the papers on the coffee table. "Would you like coffee while you review these?"

"Yes, please."

Cassandra went through the morning papers and the clippings. She read the local papers and looked at the photos. There was nothing adverse in any of them. She then looked at copies of U.S. paper clippings that had been electronically transmitted. About a quarter of them had negative comments about the possible conflicts of interest and negative predictions of the impact of the engagement. Some of the photos taken of her and Alejandro had obviously made it to the wire services and ended up in U.S. papers. Cassandra shrugged off the negative reports as just part of the reality of the U.S. media which traded on negativity.

Cassandra called Adolpho and arranged to have the paperwork on the estancia delivered. She thanked him for his work and told him that Alejandro might have some work for him in the future.

She called Teo who answered, "Hello."

"Hello, Teo. I now officially own the estancia."

"When do you want me to come?"

Cassandra answered, "I will need you to come as soon as you can. The houses need repair and we need to hire the men to work the estancia. You have the list of men who used to work there. Interview them first and hire them only if you like them. You have the name of the contractor to use for any repairs you cannot do. I have prepared a budget for repairs. My fiancé Alejandro is arranging for the architect for the new home. You can see what you can work out for four more workers homes as we will need to house others. Go ahead and contract if the workers' homes can be built within the budget."

Teo said, "I will see about a local bank when I get there. How long do you think it will take to repair the present main house? Maria asked when I can send for her. We are not used to being apart."

"The work required is mostly cosmetic. Perhaps two weeks to a month at most."

"I will leave tomorrow morning."

"I pray you have safe travel, Teo. Give my love to Maria and the family. I will see you when you get here."

Cassandra hung up and discovered she was hungry. She walked over to the residence to have a light meal. Afterwards, she went back to her office and called for Juan.

He came to her office and walked in the open door, "You called for me, Ambassador?"

"Yes, Juan, please have a seat." Juan did and Cassandra continued, "How is your family?"

"They are all doing well. I went to church with an aunt yesterday."

"What is your assessment of what is happening in the city?"

Juan thought for a moment, "The murder rate is way down and during the day the city functions normally and there is little crime. It is a different story at night. There are not enough police on the streets and though the military is patrolling there is a lot of petty crime. There are muggings, purse snatching, burglaries, rapes, and robberies each night and that is not unusual in a big city. The problem is the number of such crimes exceeds the ability of the military police to investigate. I'm told most respectable people who can, stay in their homes at night. I only go to see my family during daylight hours and because I have security I am safe as the petty criminals are looking for easier targets."

Cassandra said, "I see. Have the employees been warned about this?"

"Yes. They have been told to stay in the compound for the time being and why. I arrange for security to go with them when they are approved to go out during daylight."

Cassandra said, "Thank you, Juan." He left and Cassandra called Stan. Stan was able to come and did.

His first words were, "Good morning, boss. What's up?"

Cassandra said, "Good morning, Stan. I want you to make an assessment for me."

She told him about Juan's observations and they needed to confirm what was really happening. After some discussion concerning the use of resources, they called Bob in. It was agreed some of the Spanish speaking military would go out "on the town" in teams of three. They had diplomatic status in the event anything went wrong and they would only defend themselves if attacked. They were not to intervene.

On Tuesday morning just before lunch, Teo showed up at the embassy in a cab which had brought him from the bus terminal. He had taken a bus into the city knowing he had to pick up one of Cassandra's two SUV's to drive to the estancia. He was brought to Cassandra's office.

She got up and went to greet him as he came into the office. She hugged him and said, "Teo, it is so good to see you."

Teo was smiling and said, "Cassie, you are looking very good."

Cassie was Teo's pet name for Cassandra that he only used when they were alone or with the family.

Cassandra said, "We have so much to talk about. We'll go over to the residence for lunch."

Over lunch, they discussed the news of the Santiago family and Teo showed her photos he had brought for her. After lunch, he set out for the estancia.

At midafternoon Alejandro called, "Good afternoon my lovely wife to be."

Cassandra said, "Hello, handsome." She sat back in her chair.

Alejandro said, "I have already arranged for an architect to draw plans for the new home. The cost he quoted was very reasonable, so I told him to proceed. He promised to have the plans and drawings ready by the end of the week. I also made inquiries about the electric service to the estancia. It seems the lines to the estancia are not heavy enough to service the new homes and what is already there. New wire will have to be strung and since it is a private service we will have to pay for it. The good news is the poles are in good condition. I also think we should include an emergency generator in our plans."

Cassandra leaned forward, "You have been a busy man. Thank you, my dear. Teo arrived this morning and is on his way to the estancia. He will interview the workers Don Manuel recommended and see the renovations are started."

"Have you talked to Pedro and Luis about coming to work for us?"

"Not yet. Would you join me for dinner here?"

"I look forward to it. I missed not seeing you yesterday."

Cassandra said, "Then come at seven."

It was about five o'clock and Cassandra was headed back to the residence when she was asked to come and make a communication link. In the communications room, she was told the president had called. The link was established and she was left alone. Her father came on the line.

"Hello, Cassandra."

"It is good to hear from you, father."

Craig paused, "This is a business call, Cassandra. I need you to come to Washington as soon as possible. There is an executive jet coming to get you. I need you to be on it. It should be arriving about now. It will leave as soon as it refuels and you can get there."

"I will pack and leave right away."

"There will be people to meet you when you arrive here and they will bring you directly here. I will talk with you when you arrive. Please be careful, daughter."

"Yes, father." The call ended.

Cassandra went upstairs and called Bob, Stan and Juan to come to the communication room immediately. She called Alejandro, but he did not answer and she left him a voice mail. When Bob, Stan and Juan assembled she told them she was going to Washington and did not know when she'd be back, but her absence was not to be public knowledge. They asked her what was up and she told them she assumed it was in relation to her upcoming nuptials. She then went upstairs and changed for travel and packed an overnight bag. Alejandro called before she finished.

Alejandro said, "What is happening, love?"

Cassandra answered, "Hello, dear. I have to make a trip to Washington. I'll let you know what is up when I know. It must be important because father called. I will not be able to have dinner with you."

Alejandro said, "Please call me when you can."

"I will. I should not be gone long. This is to remain between you and me. I think it may have to do with our engagement."

Alejandro said, "I understand."

Cassandra arrived at the airport before dark. She was able to bypass customs and was led directly to the waiting aircraft. She was greeted at the door of the plane and led to a seat. The aircraft was airborne within five minutes of her arrival. Cassandra was asked if she had eaten and she said she had not. She was served a light meal of chicken Alfredo with a glass of wine. She had a lot of time to think.

Cassandra fell asleep on the flight and was woken just before the aircraft landed. After the aircraft taxied to its hanger a motorized stair was brought to the plane and Cassandra got off. A limousine and two SUVs were waiting for her. She got into the limousine and was driven into Washington and to the white house. On the drive, she called Alejandro and told him she had arrived safely. They talked briefly and she said she'd talk to him tomorrow.

At her destination, an Agent took her bag and she was led to her father's office. Roger and Chas and General Ed Cook the Director of National Intelligence were already there waiting. Cassandra greeted them, "Good evening, gentlemen."

Cassandra figured she knew what was happening given the people in the room.

Roger came to Cassandra and she hugged him, "It is good to see you, Roger." Chas rose and Cassandra surprised him by hugging him. She said, "I know that isn't protocol. " She turned to General Cook and smiled, "Good evening, General. I haven't seen you since the inauguration. Congratulations on your appointment." She offered him her hand and they shook.

They all sat down and Roger said, "We are waiting for the president."

Cassandra nodded. The door opened and Craig came in and everyone stood. Craig went to his daughter and embraced her saying, "It is so good to see you, dear." He then said, "Please everyone, be seated." They waited for the president to sit and then they did.

Craig said, "Cassandra, your recent engagement has been the subject of some controversy by short sighted people. The negative press backfired and your exploits in Mexico which were widely reported here have made your confirmation by the Senate a sure thing. Those who were opposing your confirmation have taken heat from their constituents. "

Cassandra said, "I thought you were going to ask me to resign."

Chas said, "Not a chance, my dear."

Cassandra looked at her father.

He sighed, "With the problems in the Middle East I have to choose our battles. We have credible information that several terrorist organizations have banded together and will attempt attacks on both Mexico and the U.S. in order to distract us from the real problem." He looked at Cassandra.

Cassandra said, "I did not expect that. Tell me what you want me to do."

Craig nodded to Chas and said, "Tell her."

Chas said, "We do not want to do anything that will endanger our losing the amazing relationships you have established or the connection with the Mexican President and his people."

Ed added, "Or your extraordinary understanding of the situation there. The only thing that might bring criticism is if when you marry Alejandro, you are living in the embassy residence."

Cassandra nodded understanding.

Craig looked at his daughter, "Given what we are hearing you may be the target of terrorists as you have become a symbol of the close ties being established between our countries."

Cassandra said, "How credible is the threat?"

Ed said, "It is very credible."

She could read between the lines and answered without being asked the obvious question. "I will agree to stay and I'll find my own place in the city. When we are married, Alejandro and I will move between the city and the estancia."

Her father said, "Then it's settled and we'll provide a security team for you."

Ed added, "We will soon have more information for you. We are monitoring three ships that have transited some very suspicious ports of call with very suspicious cargo being loaded."

Cassandra asked, "What type of cargo."

Ed said, "It is military small arms, explosives, and jihadists. We still don't know their destination other than they are headed for South America. They are from the same groups that support Castillo."

Cassandra said, "It seems Castillo is not yet out of the picture."

Ed said, "So it would seem."

Her father said, "So daughter, though we are aware you are going to be targeted by terrorists, here we are for political reasons, asking you to move out of the safest place for you to be in Mexico."

Cassandra smiled, "Do you know the military call me Ambassador Death because of the number of men I've killed since going to Mexico?"

Ed nodded, "We heard."

Cassandra said, "I am going to do everything I can to make sure the nickname doesn't change to Ambassador Dead."

The men in the room chuckled at the unexpected remark and Cassandra's father smiled though Cassandra could tell the remark worried him. She changed the subject, "I will have to share this with Alejandro. He is no fool and will know something is wrong. I will also not lie to my future husband."

Craig smiled, "I assumed as much. Tell him what you think is appropriate. We will be concentrating on finding persons subversive to both the U.S. and Mexico who are harboring there or using it as a base or transit point so it is in both our interests to cooperate. We will give you a report on the present threat to pass to Alejandro who will in turn tell Enrique. It will be a summary of what we have discovered but not including how we got it."

Cassandra said, "I think they will understand."

Ed asked, "Do you think we could cooperate directly?"

Cassandra said, "I do not."

Her father asked, "Why not?"

"Enrique is a proud man and a patriot. It was difficult to smooth over our actions in Mexico with respect to the special cargo."

Ed asked, "Even though we saved the lives of at least hundreds of thousands of his citizens?"

Cassandra said, "Yes. He is president and was offended he was not informed of the actions against the nuclear bombs brought into Mexico until after the fact. If you ask him to let us operate our intelligence openly in Mexico, he will not agree. He will be offended and everything we worked for will go down the drain."

Ed said, "But he must know as ambassador, you ran intelligence operations."

Cassandra said, "General, he suspects because of my background, but it is a case of don't ask don't tell. Under the present circumstances, he considers me a user of intelligence not a spy and it is also the way all countries play the game, so it is acceptable. What we would be asking would be different and taken as an insult to Mexican sovereignty and their intelligence ability. "

Her father smiled at her, "How certain are you that he would refuse."

Cassandra looked at the floor and said, "Certain enough to walk away to protect you if you insist on it."

It was apparent she was troubled by the way the conversation was going.

There was silence in the room for some time. Craig said, "If that won't work what will?"

Cassandra looked at her father and said, "I will continue to provide informal information to Alejandro who will tell Enrique. It will be don't ask don't tell situation where everyone knows I am passing on intelligence, but there is nothing formal or embarrassing that can result. I assume our communications could be two way and Alejandro will provide me with helpful information I can pass on."

General Cook said, “So we achieve the same thing, but very informally, but perhaps less effectively in order not to offend sensibilities.”

Cassandra said, “Yes, sir. That sums it up nicely.”

The three men in the room exchanged glances. Both Ed and Chas nodded agreement when Craig looked at them.

Craig said, “Then that is the way we will play it.”

Cassandra said, “Thank you. What about the team I have in place at the embassy?”

Craig looked at General Cook who said, “The military team will remain in place. Also, any information that will be helpful to our friends, I’ll send along.”

Cassandra looked at Chas, “What about Juan and the rest of the diplomatic team in place.”

Chas said, “I see no reason they should not stay in place.”

Cassandra asked, “Then we continue as we have in the past?”

Craig said, “Yes, the same as you have in the past.”

Cassandra nodded, “I will need some additional security staff. How many may I have?”

Craig looked at Chas and Ed. It was the General who asked, “Would twelve be sufficient?”

Cassandra looked at Ed, “Yes, General.”

Ed smiled, “Just give me your list and I’ll see you get them.”

Ed said, “We will increase the special fund for your operations. Keeping Mexico stable is crucial because of the troubles we are having with the terrorists elsewhere.”

Cassandra nodded understanding.

Craig said, “Then it is all settled. Thank you gentlemen, I will now escort my daughter to the residence.”

As they walked, Cassandra said, “This is a most unusual circumstance, don’t you think?”

Craig said, “Your friends already know you had access to intelligence as ambassador because of the information you gave them. This is really no different and Enrique will be once removed so insulated from any political criticism.”

"I think it will continue to work."

Cassandra spent a half hour talking with her mother and father before going to bed. In the morning, she ate breakfast with her parents and they talked about the problems the wedding would create if both heads of state attended. Her father said under the circumstances it would be irresponsible for him or Dorothy or any of the family to attend. Cassandra agreed. Craig said he hoped Enrique would agree to stay away as well. Her father also asked Cassandra to see if she could arrange for Alejandro to come and visit soon. They all retired.

Cassandra ate breakfast with her father and mother. After breakfast, she was taken to a plane and flown back to Mexico. When she arrived, the first thing Cassandra did once she was in the embassy car was phone Alejandro.

He answered, "Hello, love."

Cassandra said, "Hello, handsome. I am back and on my way to the embassy. We need to meet and talk. Can you meet me at the embassy residence?"

"I will."

Alejandro was waiting when Cassandra arrived. When she went to the door, Luis opened it and Cassandra said, "Thank you, Luis."

She found Alejandro in the living room and embraced him. She simply said, "I missed you."

"You make my heart happy."

"Have you eaten?"

Alejandro said, "Not since lunch."

Cassandra said, "Luis, would you please ask Pedro to prepare a light meal. We will take it in the atrium."

Luis said, "Of course, Excellency."

Alejandro offered his arm and Cassandra took it and they walked to the atrium. Cassandra closed the door as they entered. Alejandro pulled out a chair for Cassandra and she sat and waited for him to do the same.

Cassandra said, "I had a very interesting trip. The long and the short of it is the senate will be confirming my appointment. However, for political reasons related to our engagement, I will have to move out of the embassy residence."

Alejandro said, "It is because they can't have me roaming the embassy."

Cassandra nodded and continued, "I will have to find a residence in the city for when we are here."

Alejandro said, "That should be easy."

"Not as easy as you think, my dear." Cassandra paused and slipped the report to Alejandro. "It seems that terrorists aligned with Castillo have painted a target on our backs as we are now a symbol of the close relationship between our countries. There is also a greater threat to Mexico."

Alejandro said, "I take it these papers you gave me are about the threat."

"Yes. It also means my parents and family will not attend our wedding for practical reasons nor should our friends in high places here. It will have to be a quiet affair."

Alejandro nodded, "I suppose then we can have it anywhere."

"Yes."

Alejandro said, "Then we can set a date without regard for affairs of state."

Cassandra smiled, "Exactly. I just need to find a defensible residence close to here."

Alejandro said, "I will not be secretary of the interior forever and when I am not, we will have much more flexibility." He paused, "In the meantime I suppose from time to time you will slip me notes with important information as you have in the past."

Cassandra said coyly, "Except soon I will leave the notes under your pillow rather than put them in a card that is delivered."

Alejandro smiled, "Our life will not be boring."

After her fiancé left the embassy, Cassandra called Stan and met with him. She explained what was to transpire, but for the time being it was to stay between them.

Chapter 13 – New Ways

It was three weeks later when Alejandro and Cassandra accompanied by Adriana caught the early afternoon direct flight from Mexico City to Fort Lauderdale Florida. Adriana had never been outside of Mexico or flown on an airplane and she had been eager to go to the United States. She sat at the window and joyously watched as the ground faded away.

As they rose into the clouds she exclaimed, "It is like being an angel."

They were met at the airport by Secret Service Agents who drove them to Coral Gables. As they approached the Crossing homes Adriana asked, "Do you own all this?"

Cassandra said, "My brother and I own the house on the right and my parents own the one to the left of it. This is a family compound. The plan is that Alejandro will stay in my parents' home and you will stay in mine with me and my brother and his wife, if that suits."

Adriana smiled and said, "That is proper if I am to be guardian of your virtue."

They were immediately passed through security at the compound because all of the Secret Service Agents knew Cassandra and Alejandro by sight and they had seen a photo of Adriana. When their bags were taken from the car, Cassandra directed where they should go and then they all went into main house. Cassandra's parents were in the great room and rose to greet them.

Cassandra's mother embraced her daughter and said, "It is good to see you, dear." She turned to Adriana and said in Spanish, *"You must be Adriana. I am so pleased,"* and hugged her as well. Alejandro was beaming as Dorothy hugged him and continued in Spanish, *"Welcome, Alejandro. It is good to see you again."*

Alejandro said, *"Thank you, Dona Crossing."*

Dorothy said, *"Such formality is not necessary as we will soon be family. Please call me, Dorothy."*

Alejandro bowed slightly, *"As you wish, Dorothy."*

Cassandra's father followed suit embracing the visitors.

Cassandra said in Spanish, *"Adriana this is my father Craig Crossing and my mother Dorotea Elicia Santiago de Crossing whose American name is Dorothy Crossing. Mother and father this is Adriana Maria Alvarez Rivera de Ramirez."*

Dorothy said, *"Please sit and let us have coffee and get to know each other. "*

They had been speaking Spanish and Adriana said in English, "We in America, so we speak English. I understand but speaking is weak. I need practice."

Dorothy said in Spanish, *"Then we will speak in English, but only if you ask in Spanish if there is something you don't understand. We are to be family and there is no need to be embarrassed."*

Adriana smiled and said, "Yes. Some day babies will come and I will speak in dos languages."

Dorothy said, "Yes the babies will learn two languages. I want grandchildren."

Craig asked, "How was your flight, Alejandro?"

"It went quickly and without delay, Mr. President. I had good company so that made it pleasant."

Craig said, "The family calls me by my given name unless we are in a formal situation so you may do it also."

Alejandro said, "Thank you, Craig."

Craig asked, "Do you like to fish or golf, Alejandro?"

"Yes, both."

"Good then we will do both while you are here. We must get to know each other better since you are to be my son-in-law."

The next day Cassandra's younger brother Cal and his wife Maggie arrived as did younger sisters Molly and Katie. Everyone was introduced and the family had a good time. Adriana was pleased to find that all of the family spoke Spanish. On the second evening in Coral Gables, Cassandra showed the family the photos of the estancia and the drawings of the new home that was being built for her and

Alejandro. She told them when the work was done they would have to come and visit.

The family visited together for five days during which Craig, Cal, and Alejandro spent a lot of time together fishing, golfing, swimming, and talking. The women talked about many things and spent some time talking about Cassandra and Alejandro's upcoming wedding. On the last evening, Craig got his daughter alone as they were sitting by the pool.

Craig simply said, "I like Alejandro and he will be a good addition to the family."

Cassandra said it without thinking, "And a good addition to my bed." It was no sooner out of her mouth than she realized what she'd said to her father. He surprised her by laughing heartily.

When he finished laughing, he leaned over and said to Cassandra, "Your mother was a virgin when we wed, but she was a wildcat in bed. Still is."

Cassandra said, "Father!"

Craig smiled and shrugged. Cassandra did not know what to think. This was her father and the President of the United States.

After a slight pause she said, "I will try to live up to my mother's example."

Craig smiled and said, "Good. If Alejandro is half as happy with you as I am with your mother, you will have a good marriage."

On the flight back to Mexico, Alejandro and Adriana talked with Cassandra about the good time they had enjoyed. During the conversation, Adriana said, "Dorotea is a joyful soul. I like your father and your sisters are delightful. Your brother is very nice, but a little stiff necked."

Cassandra said, "If you think he is stiff necked now, you should have seen him before he married Maggie. She has loosened him up and that will continue."

Adriana asked, "Will I meet many of the Santiago family at the wedding."

Cassandra said, "I don't think so."

Alejandro said, "I will explain it when we are at home."

It was early evening when Cassandra arrived at the embassy residence. She said goodbye to Adriana as Alejandro got out of the car and opened Cassandra's door. One of the staff was already getting her luggage out of the trunk. She exited and Alejandro walked her to the residence door. He kissed her lightly and Cassandra ran her hand over his cheek.

Alejandro whispered, "You are driving me crazy, woman."

Cassandra smiled, "I am worth waiting for."

Alejandro said, "Indeed. I will call you."

Cassandra opened the door and Luis met her at the door, "Good evening, Excellency."

"Good evening, Luis. How have you been?"

Luis smiled, "With you gone, Pedro and I have had a chance to catch up on our reading."

Cassandra smiled, "I understand. I don't want Pedro's cooking skills to go unpracticed. Please ask him to prepare a light meal for me. After I eat, I'd like to talk with you both."

"Yes Excellency."

Cassandra went to the library and called her mother to let her know she had arrived. They had a brief conversation. Cassandra was sitting staring off into space and thinking when Luis brought her meal. She thanked him then prayed before eating her meal. After Luis had cleared and taken away the dinnerware, he came back with Pedro.

Cassandra said, "Please have a seat." The two men took chairs. Cassandra continued, "Have you come to a decision about coming to work for us?"

Pedro said, "We have discussed it and we have some questions before we give our answer, Excellency."

Luis said, "We understand you will provide housing for us and our families. "

Cassandra said, "That is correct. The staff houses have two bedrooms and are currently being renovated. They each have one bath and a modern kitchen."

Pedro asked, "What will my duties be?"

Cassandra said, "I need meals prepared regularly for the three family members and the security staff. Of course you will cook for more when we have guests. Your only responsibility will be the kitchen and shopping. In the event we are attacked by bandits," and at this point Cassandra paused, "you would be expected to protect the families."

Luis asked, "What would be my duties?"

"I would like you to serve when we have guests and keep your ears open." Cassandra paused for effect, "I will need you sometimes to drive me, to run errands, ensure the vehicles are maintained, and do the light maintenance on the house such as keeping the pool clean and the windows washed and such. That will take little of your time and your underlying duties will be to help with security."

Luis asked, "Do you have a housekeeper?"

"Not yet."

Luis said, "We propose to do all that you have asked and also with our wives will ensure the main house is cleaned and the laundry and such is done." Luis took out a sheet, "We propose you pay each of our families a salary as outlined."

Cassandra opened the folded sheet. She looked at it and was surprised by how modest the request was.

She said, "This is agreeable."

Pedro said, "We would like to have Sundays off unless you have guests, but even then we would like time off for church."

"That is agreeable. I suspect from time to time you will have some other down time and you will be close enough to spend it with your family."

Pedro said, "Then it is agreed, Excellency."

Cassandra smiled, "Good. I am very pleased and I think this will be good for us all."

Pedro asked, "When will we start?"

Cassandra said, "I do not know exactly, but soon. You will have the first week to get your family moved in and settled in your new homes. I will give you money for moving expenses."

The men said, "Thank you, Excellency."

After they left, it occurred to Cassandra the men had been working seven days a week. She was ashamed it had not occurred to her. Cassandra retired.

On Sunday, Cassandra accompanied Alejandro and Adriana to church. Afterwards, they had lunch in a local restaurant. Cassandra arrived back at the residence about three in the afternoon. The truth was they were all tired from their vacation and needed rest.

On Monday morning, Cassandra exercised then went to her office about eight. As she entered the office, Carol said, "Welcome back, Ambassador. How was your vacation?"

Cassandra said, "Thank you. It was a totally enjoyable time with the family. Has the office been cleaned this morning?"

The question was code for being swept for electronic listening devices.

"Yes Ambassador."

"Do I have anything pressing today?"

Carol said, "Your schedule is clear today."

Cassandra was signing routine documents at midmorning when she received a call from her father. She went and took it in the communication room.

She answered, "This is Ambassador Crossing."

The White House switchboard operator said, "This is the White House switchboard, one moment please for POTUS."

Her father came on the line, "Good morning, Ambassador."

"Good morning, Mr. President."

Her father asked, "Why do we play this game?"

"I don't know, father."

"Your confirmation hearing is coming up. It needs to be circulated that you are moving from the embassy residence prior to your marriage to Alejandro. You had better work on your arrangements."

"Thank you. I'll get on it."

Her father said, "I would like to talk longer, but I have a cabinet meeting to attend. God bless, dear."

"Thank you and peace and blessings."

The call ended and Cassandra went back to her office. She said as she came through Carol's office, "I'd like to talk to Stan and Bob first then Colleen when she finishes at the infirmary."

Carol said, "I will arrange it.'

Ten minutes later Stan and Bob showed up and found Cassandra sitting on her office sofa sipping coffee. Bob closed the door.

Cassandra said, "Good morning, gentlemen."

Stan said, "Did you have a good vacation?"

"Oh yes. Help yourself to coffee," and she pointed to the cups and carafe on the table. The men sat and poured a cup and Bob asked, "What's up?"

"My confirmation will be voted on and is expected to pass. There is one little complication." She proceeded to tell them what the plans were regarding her residence. Stan sipped coffee and listened closely.

When she finished Stan said, "That seems like a very workable arrangement if you can find the right place."

Cassandra said, "I think so. We have a real problem though."

Cassandra talked about the threat and the threat assessment.

Bob said, "So we should be on alert."

Cassandra said, "As best you can arrange it without telling anyone why."

Bob smiled, "At least this time I'm not one of those totally in the dark."

Cassandra said, "Look at the bright side, Bob. Alejandro and I are the targets and soon I'll only be here during work hours and those will be sporadic as my main role is to schmooze. That will make your job easier."

Bob smiled, "Oh yeah, firebase embassy has been a cakewalk."

They all found that amusing.

Stan asked, "What about your security outside of the grounds?"

Cassandra said, "I will have additional security coming for that. The present staff will stay here with the exception of Amanda because my friends are used to her being around. Luis and Pedro will be going on my private payroll. I will let you both know who is going to be on the security detail. They are going to be visible, so I am using military people I've worked with before."

Stan nodded, "I assume you will have a communication center at the estancia?"

"No, we will use satellite phones. I can't have the place looking like a C.I.A. operation. With the horse breeding business, there will be a lot of people coming and going through the town. The town is quite large and my new enterprise will make strangers even less an object of local curiosity. I have enough family business interests in Mexico that I should have lots of reasons to travel around, so who knows what I might pick up."

Stan asked, "When will you move out of here?"

"As soon as I can find a place, I'll move. I don't have a lot to move; just personal belongings."

Stan asked, "How many will you bring in?"

"Over time, I'll bring in as many as twelve to be on the security detail off-premises. Now to change the subject, are things still the same in the city at night?"

Stan said, "Yes and I have a generic report for you to pass on." He handed Cassandra a letter sized envelope that was unsealed. He said, "It seems there is no central place for citizens to call if a crime is in progress. There is no 911 type of service up and running."

Cassandra said, "Thanks, Stan."

Stan said, "Good coffee here. I guess we'll talk to you later, boss." He and Bob left.

Cassandra told Carol she wanted to speak with Juan and Carl and her at eleven. At the meeting, she broke the news about her moving residence. She simply said that her pending marriage made her staying on site problematic. They were all bright people and she didn't have to explain.

It was late in the morning when Cassandra phoned Alejandro who answered his cell, "Hello, my love."

Cassandra answered, "I have a love note for you. Can you get away and come for lunch here?"

Alejandro said, "Yes. We have things we should discuss. I will leave directly."

Cassandra called down and gave Pedro notice. When Alejandro arrived, he was led to the sun room where Cassandra was waiting for him. He came and kissed her lightly and lingered just a moment. Cassandra sighed deeply.

Alejandro withdrew and sat down, "I know."

Luis came with wine, "May I pour some wine."

Alejandro said, "Please."

Luis poured and Cassandra said, "Luis and Pedro have agreed to come to work for us."

Alejandro said, "That is very good news."

Luis said, "Thank you, Don Alejandro," and left the room.

Cassandra said, "My confirmation will be voted on soon. It will also be made known I will be taking a private residence away from the embassy. I will of course have to move out of here as soon as possible."

Alejandro asked, "What is your plan?"

Cassandra said, "I intend to find a place to rent here in the city. I have a lot to do."

Alejandro said, "What about the estancia?"

Cassandra said, "I thought we'd stay there on the weekends and have a place here during the work week as long as we hold our current positions."

Alejandro said, "I will ask Carlos if I can stay at his and Adelina's estancia on weekends so I can visit until we are married."

Cassandra said, "Adriana can stay with me in the worker's house until the new house is finished."

Alejandro nodded agreement, "Yes, I think she would like that."

Cassandra looked at Alejandro and smiled. She thought about how handsome he was. She added, “We will need a place in the city even after we are married. Do you think we should keep your house?”

Alejandro said, “I think after what Adriana said, I should sell the big house. The estancia should be our main residence. It is not an unmanageable commute from the estancia, but I need to be able to get back to the city quickly in an emergency and we need a place to stay when we are here in the city.”

Cassandra said, “We could always buy a small plane and fly back and forth.”

Alejandro said, “Yes, a small aircraft would be easy to operate out of the estancia. Do you know how to fly?”

“I do not.”

Alejandro said, “I will arrange instruction. I suggest you rent a place in the city for the time being. If it is agreeable, I will arrange the purchase of a small aircraft out of my own funds.”

Cassandra said, “Agreed. I’ll have Theo arrange to have a pole building erected to store it in.”

Alejandro asked, “Pole building?”

“It’s a basic pole structure building that is steel sided and roofed and generally used for storing equipment. I will need to know how big it needs to be to cover the plane.”

Alejandro nodded, “When I find a suitable aircraft, I will let you know. In the meantime, the government can send a helicopter for me in an emergency.”

Cassandra asked, “What do your people say about how safe the city is?”

“They tell me it is very safe now.”

Cassandra slipped him the envelope. He took it, but before he could open it, Luis brought the meal, so it went into his jacket. They discussed the size and location of the place to be rented. It could serve them after they married. When they finished lunch, Alejandro gave Cassandra a paper and she looked at it.

“Alejandro do you think this is really necessary?”

"Yes for two reasons. First is that I want everyone to know I married you for love. Second, I don't want your wealth to become a political issue."

Cassandra nodded, signed, and put the pre-nuptial agreement Alejandro had executed aside.

Alejandro continued, "Now we should discuss a date for the wedding."

"Agreed."

"Enrique has agreed under the circumstances that our wedding should be very small and private. He and Maria will stay away, but Carlos will be my best man and Adelina your maid of honor. As a matter of practicality, I propose we be married at the estancia."

Cassandra said, "It is a good plan."

Alejandro shrugged and said, "It seems we have little choice in the matter. I wish it could be otherwise."

Cassandra asked, "We just need to set a date?"

Alejandro took a slip of paper out of his pocket and slipped it to Cassandra. She looked at it and said, "It doesn't give us enough time to complete the new house?"

Alejandro said, "No it doesn't, but I have no problem staying the small house on weekends if I can be with you."

Cassandra said, "Because I will be living outside the embassy, the U.S. Government will provide me with a security team."

Alejandro asked, "Will they be C.I.A.?"

"No. They will be military. Will that be a problem?"

Alejandro smiled, "No. I will see they get accredited and get the necessary paperwork to enable them to guard you properly. Some of my men will be there as well."

Cassandra nodded, "Thank you, dear. I think when we are no longer in our official capacities we will hire our own security."

Alejandro nodded agreement. He sighed, "I regret, but I have to get back to my duties."

Cassandra walked him to the door and saw him off. She went to the communications center and made a call. The code she used put her through.

The voice said, "Personnel."

"This is Eagle One. I want Anita, Carmen, Miguel, Pete and Novio immediately. Please send Shaun, Seve, and Antonio when they are available."

The voice said, "Confirm Anita, Carmen, Miguel, Pete and Novio will be in transit within twenty four hours. Shaun, Seve and Antonio are to arrive at an unspecified date."

Cassandra said, "Confirmed." She hung up. Cassandra went to her residence suite and called Alphonso. He answered almost immediately.

"Hello, Excellency."

"Hello, Alphonso. I have a challenging request for you."

"What is it Excellency."

Cassandra told him what she was looking for and Alphonso said, "I will call you back soon, Excellency." Cassandra ended the call and decided what she needed to do next. She called Teo.

"Hello, Cassandra."

"Hello, Teo. How are things progressing?"

"The workers' homes are renovated and my home is done. The contractor is working on your new home and so far the architect and I are satisfied with the quality of work. The three men are good workers. We have been busy and soon we will be ready to buy breeding horses."

Cassandra said, "I may come up on the weekend to visit. I will stay in one of the vacant worker's homes. Pedro and Luis will be taking up residence in the other two week after next. I am bringing in security people and will need a place to house them. Perhaps you can come up with a plan?"

Teo said, "There is a good solid workshop building we could convert into rooms. How many will you bring here?"

"I will initially have three women and four men. Later I may have six more."

Teo said, "We can have eight rooms by the weekend, but they will only have ceiling fans and a window. The occupants will have to go out to another building for the toilets. I will get beds in town."

Cassandra said, "That is acceptable. Do you need anything?"

"No, we are all right and under budget. I will look forward to seeing you."

It was mid-afternoon when Alejandro called and Cassandra answered, "Hi, handsome."

"Thank you, cielito lindo. The love notes you gave me are very motivating."

"You are welcome."

Alejandro said, "I have a love note for you when I see you."

Cassandra said, "When will that be?"

"I invite you and Amanda to dinner at our home tomorrow evening. There will be other guests."

"I accept."

Alejandro said, "Please come at six for drinks. I have a meeting and I have to go. I will be working late. It seems coincidental that every time you give me a love note, I get very busy at work. Adios."

After the call, Cassandra sat thinking. Carol rang through, "Señor Adolpho Perez is downstairs Madame Ambassador. He asked to see you."

"Send him along, please."

Adolpho appeared a couple of minutes later at her door and knocked on the door frame asking politely, "May I come in, Excellency?"

"Please." Cassandra got up and greeted him and they sat around the coffee table. Cassandra said, "I did not expect to hear from you so soon."

Adolpho smiled, "It is good fortune." He opened a file and showed the photos to Cassandra and said, "It is for rent for seven thousand American dollars per month furnished and the owner will give an option to purchase."

Cassandra nodded and looked at the photos and floor plan. She read the listing material. It was close to the embassy and was the right size and it was beautiful. It also had a wall around it and a four car garage. She asked, "When may I see it?"

Adolpho said, "Whenever you wish Excellency. It is vacant."

Cassandra asked, "What do you think of the purchase price?"

"It is neither too low nor high; it is in the right price range for comparables in the neighborhood for unfurnished houses. This one is well furnished and that is a bonus."

Cassandra said, "Well, there is no time like the present." She called Carol, "Please have my car brought around."

Carol said, "Yes, Madame Ambassador."

Twenty minutes later the security detail had cleared them for entrance to the house and they went inside. It impressed Cassandra. It was a large two story modern home with a pool. The house was on a corner lot and the pool could not be seen from the neighbors' homes. Cassandra was very impressed.

Adolpho asked, "What do you think?"

"I will take it providing the owner will agree if I exercise the option the lease payments will be applied to the purchase price and Alejandro likes it."

Adolpho answered, "With your permission, I will call Alejandro and ask him to come to see it."

Cassandra, "Wait just a minute." She dialed Alejandro's number.

He answered, "Just a minute." She heard him moving and a door closed. He said, "What is it, love?" Cassandra told him and he said, "I trust your judgment and I don't need to see it. Can we afford it?"

"Yes."

Alejandro said, "That is wonderful. I have to get back to the meeting."

She said, "I understand." The call ended and she turned to Adolpho, "Prepare the papers. I want to move in within a week if the owner accepts."

Adolpho smiled, "Yes, Excellency."

On the way back to the Embassy, Cassandra was calculating in her head how much she had in the bank account here. She had enough left out of the money from the sale of her condo that as a result of her currency speculation would pay for her present commitments at the estancia and here, even if she exercised the option today. She would have to transfer money from her U.S. or Vera Cruz accounts eventually. Her train of thought was interrupted by Adolpho.

"I have added the clause to the lease option agreement." He handed it to Cassandra and she read it.

"That looks acceptable." She took out her checkbook and wrote a check.

Adolpho said, "I will be surprised if we do not have a deal."

The home was close to the embassy. They arrived at the embassy and Adolpho took his leave and went to talk to the owner of the house. Cassandra went in and to her suite. She called Amanda and told her about the dinner the next evening. She then called Carol and asked her to share dinner with her and Carol agreed.

The next day Cassandra was sitting in the garden eating her lunch when a lieutenant came to see her, "Your people have arrived from stateside, ma'am. They hadn't eaten so I took them to the mess."

"Good. Bring them here when they are finished but don't rush them."

The lieutenant said, "Yes ma'am."

Cassandra had finished eating her lunch when Luis came to her, "Señor Perez is here Excellency."

"Please bring him, Luis."

Adolpho was brought into the garden. He said, "Good afternoon, Excellency."

Cassandra said, "Hello. Would you like coffee?"

"Please."

Luis came and poured coffee without being asked. Cassandra said, "Do we have a deal?"

Adolpho sipped his coffee and said, "They owners asked if you would buy the property outright now? They will give you a substantial discount for cash."

Cassandra sipped her coffee then said, "This is unexpected. How much of a discount did they offer?"

Adolpho finished a sip and said, "They offered five, but I got them to ten percent."

Cassandra said, "How did you manage that?"

"I had made some inquiries prior to negotiations and found their new home went over budget. They are by no means broke, but it has left them pressed for cash. Perhaps more pressed than I had perceived."

Cassandra sipped more of her beverage, "What about occupancy?"

"They will rent the house to you for one dollar until the transaction is completed. You are, after all, a woman of fine reputation."

Cassandra smiled, "Have they signed papers?"

"Yes." Adolpho drank the remainder of his small cup of coffee.

"Very well and I will leave the details to you. You deserve a little extra on this Adolpho."

Cassandra would ensure he got it. It was a nice piece of work.

Adolpho said, "You are too kind, Excellency."

He gave her the papers. She read them and called Carol to witness her signatures. Adolpho notarized the papers and Cassandra took back the lease check and wrote a check for the deposit.

Adolpho gave her a copy of the papers and handed her keys. He said, "Your reputation and status persuaded the owners to give these to me to give to you when you signed."

Cassandra smiled, "Thank you, Adolpho." She stood and offered her hand.

Adolpho took it and shook it gently and bowed slightly, "The pleasure is all mine, Excellency."

He left and Cassandra sat and Luis came and poured more coffee. She was finishing her coffee when she saw her security team coming across the lawn. She had worked with them before under much different circumstances and knew they were not only good, but trustworthy.

As they approached, she said, "Well you got here quickly."

Captain Novio Vega was the leader of the group and answered, "When Ambassador Death calls, we come running."

Cassandra shook her head in disbelief and said, "Please everyone, have a seat." The group pulled a couple of chairs from the surrounding tables and when they were all seated, Cassandra turned to Anita and Carmen, "You ladies are looking as fine as ever."

Anita answered with a smile, "Thank you, Excellency."

Carmen said, "I never thought we'd be calling you that."

Cassandra replied, "Life is full of surprises."

Miguel, who everyone called Mike, said, "It has been a long time, boss."

Cassandra smiled, "It has."

Pete said, "What is the assignment?"

Cassandra said, "Well it seems my body count as ambassador has risen to the level that some terrorists want me dead. I have the added benefit as a target of having a high profile father." Cassandra spread her arms, "To complicate matters I must move from here which is probably the safest place for me in Mexico."

Novio asked, "Why?"

Cassandra smiled, "I am engaged to the Mexican secretary of the interior and politically it would not go over well back home if he was living here once we are married."

Carmen said, "Wow. I can see why that would present a problem."

Cassandra motioned to her cup and did a circle with her hand and Luis headed for the kitchen. "My fiancé and I will need a lot of security given our positions. It will be the same as in past operations where you will operate outside the military chain of command. I have an estancia about one hundred and fifty miles from here and I just bought a home about five minutes from here. My fiancé will provide you with the documentation to allow you to go around armed to the teeth. He knows you are military and some of his people will be guarding him, so I needed not only heavy hitters, but people who speak Spanish."

Pete asked, "Why am I here?"

"We'll need surveillance and proximity alarm systems and such at the estancia and the house. Shaun, Seve, and Antonio will follow. Amanda from here will join us and I may bring in a couple more. Two will stay at the house and two at the estancia at all times. The rest will travel with me."

Novio asked, "When you said Amanda, did you mean Amanda Hopkins?"

"She is my personal assistant."

The group looked at each other and then they knew. Cassandra, even as ambassador, was involved in intelligence operations. They said nothing.

Luis came out with a tray and poured coffee for the group. Cassandra introduced him, "This is Luis Sancho Reyes Vargas. He will be working at the estancia." Cassandra then introduced her security team and finished with, "They are all military, Luis, so you will all have something in common. Please introduce Pedro to them when you have a chance."

Luis said with a smile, "Yes Excellency."

Cassandra said in front of Luis, "I suspect if in the unlikely event trouble starts at the estancia you will find Luis is good with a weapon. Pedro as well, so make sure they have something effective."

Luis nodded and left.

Novio asked, "Does he work for Mexican intelligence?"

"Of course, but remember my fiancé is in charge of all interior matters."

Carmen said, "Life around here will be interesting."

Cassandra laughed, "My fiancé and I are allies in our official capacities as well as in our personal lives, but to a certain degree it is don't ask, don't tell. Do you understand?"

She looked around at each of the group and they all nodded understanding.

Novio asked, "How will assignments be determined?"

Cassandra said, "That will be up to you, Novio."

Novio said, "Understood."

Cassandra said, "The only caveat is that either Anita or Carmen is with me and Amanda at all times when I'm not on the embassy grounds. There are some places gentlemen can't go."

Novio said, "Understood ma'am."

Cassandra said, "The first order of business is to scout out my new home. See Colonel Sharp about side arms. He will also provide you with the good stuff as soon as my fiancé gets us the right paperwork, so we'll be able to take them off the grounds." She handed the keys to Novio and gave him the address then said, "See my Deputy Chief of Mission Juan Perez for temporary quarters. We'll be moving to the house as soon as you have special consideration. In the meantime, the people here will continue to provide my security. This weekend I intend to go to the estancia, so I'll be in your hands. We'll take my personal vehicle and two of the embassy vehicles."

Novio said, "Yes ma'am. I'll let you know as soon as we figure out what security needs we have at the house."

Cassandra nodded and the group left. Luis came to collect the cups and Cassandra went to her office. She called for Stan to come to her office and he came with a cup of coffee in his hand.

He closed the door and said, "Good afternoon, boss."

Cassandra said, "It is. Thank you." She noticed Stan had dark circles under his eyes. She asked, "Did you have a late night last night?"

"Yeah, we have an operation under way to track Castillo. He is a sly one. He seems to be one step ahead of us. I don't like that he is apparently in the city."

Cassandra said, "Are you sure?"

"Ninety nine percent certain, but we just can't figure out his exact location. We have been able to expand our eyes on the ground and have a lot of locals feeding us information. It was a fluke he was spotted at a town to the south last night, but we weren't sure it was him. We have locals keeping eyes open for him and keeping watch at the main transit points. We didn't expect him to show up here, but he did and at a major bus depot. We spread a little cash and got a surveillance tape from the bus depot copied and confirmed it was him about five minutes ago."

Cassandra said, "When did he arrive? Was he alone?"

"He arrived alone about eleven this morning. He took a cab and was dropped in a very busy and public place and just disappeared. I think you should tell Alejandro so his people can be on the alert. We are working to back trace his steps."

Cassandra nodded and called Alejandro on the speaker phone. He answered, "Hello, love."

"Good morning, handsome. I wanted to let you know the man we would least like to see at our wedding is in the city."

Alejandro said, "Are you certain?"

"Yes. I was told it has been confirmed. I was asked to pass the information on to you."

"I take it you do not know where our uninvited guest is?"

"No, otherwise they would have told me."

Alejandro said, "Thank you. I will put out an alert."

Cassandra asked, "My security people have arrived. When will you have my paperwork ready?"

"I will give it to you this evening at the dinner party."

"Thank you, dear."

The call ended and Cassandra looked at Stan. He said, "He didn't ask for details."

"We have an unstated understanding. I tell him everything I can up front and he doesn't ask further."

Stan said, "You will have an interesting marriage."

Cassandra smiled, "You have no idea, Stan."

Stan smiled and got up, "If you have no further need of me, I will get some shut eye."

"It sounds like a good idea."

Stan left and Carol called in, "There is a Novio Vega to see you, Ambassador."

"Send him in Carol. He is in charge of my off site security."

Carol said, "Yes, Ambassador."

Novio came into her office and shut the door.

Cassandra said, "Take a seat and tell me what you think."

"In the event of attack with the right weapons we could successfully defend the house against multiple attackers. There are good lines of sight from the upper floor and with it being a corner lot there are multiple routes away from the house. The wall around the grounds is only seven feet tall, but it is substantial. We'll need surveillance cameras and sensors installed and we can put a communications dishes in two places on the roof where they are not visible from the street. It is not ideal, but no urban site is."

Cassandra sat back and said, "What else?"

"We can stay in the pool house when we are not on duty, but I'd want someone monitoring and two on patrol whenever you are there, so I suggest we add the manpower for that to be twenty four seven. I'll need another three man shift."

Cassandra said, "Let me know who you want. I'll arrange it."

Novio asked, "What about the estancia?"

"It is in the middle of open grazing pastures. Unless the shooter can hit us from more than two miles, he would have little cover. If an attack comes there, we will have some warning. There are trees close in around the houses for shade, but they would provide no cover for an approach. I expect we can manage for the time being. Once Alejandro and I are married, we'll have reinforcements from his security people. Once we are no longer in our current positions, we will be able to get by with private security."

Novio looked at Cassandra, "That would be nice work."

She smiled, "Yes." The rest was left unsaid.

Chapter 14 – The Calm and the Storm

Cassandra and Amanda arrived at Alejandro's five minutes early. Adriana greeted them first with hugs and warm words of welcome. Alejandro came and hugged his fiancé and kissed her. It caused them both to flush ever so slightly. Adriana and Amanda exchanged knowing smiles at observing the effect the little kiss had on the couple.

They walked to the living room where Vicente was already sitting. Adelina and her father Manuel and mother Ana were already there. Cassandra and Amanda greeted everyone and took seats. Cassandra sat next to her fiancé.

Vicente said, "I understand you have set a date."

Alejandro said, "Yes."

Manuel said, "It is good that you are to be married here. " He looked at Cassandra, "I understand your man Teo has made much progress on the estancia."

Cassandra nodded, "Yes, Don Manuel. I am going up this weekend to visit and see for myself the progress."

Alejandro added, "And Adelina has graciously agreed to allow me to stay with her. Adriana will be staying with Cassandra."

Manuel said, "But the new house is not completed."

Adriana said, "We are staying in one of the houses that were renovated for the workers."

Ana said, "Oh."

Cassandra realized the Ana was a bit of a snob. Cassandra liked Ana and would not hold that against her. Besides, she had learned a long time ago if you looked for friends who had no faults, you would never have friends.

Adriana changed the subject, "I recently got to travel to Florida and meet Cassandra's parents. It was wonderful. I flew on one of those big airplanes for the first time. It was amazing. I must tell you all about it and about Cassandra's family and their beautiful vacation compound."

Vicente said, "I would like that."

Ana asked, "How big is the home."

Adriana raised three fingers, "They have three on the ocean and each is bigger than anything any of us live in. I have pictures I will show you after dinner. It is lovely there."

Manuel looked at Cassandra. She pretended not to see the expression on his face. It occurred to her that Manuel was used to being top dog in the region where he lived and might feel a little threatened by what was being said. She decided only time would tell and she knew just how to smooth the waters with him.

The dinner was served and they went into the dining room. Vicente said the blessing and the food was served. During the meal, Adriana told the story of her marvelous vacation. She told about all the things she'd seen and all the people she met including Cassandra's family. Her enthusiasm and humor were contagious and she answered many questions and caused much laughter. Cassandra watched and noted even Manuel was enjoying Adriana's story.

Ana said, "Surely you exaggerate, Adriana."

"Oh no Dona Ana, it is as I have said. America surely is a land of opportunity and beauty."

Cassandra said, "Don Manuel, I invite you and your wife to come with us the next time we visit Coral Gables for vacation. We usually go there in the winter."

Alejandro said, "The fishing and golfing are good. You would enjoy it, Don Manuel."

Adriana said, "And the shops are wonderful."

Ana looked at her husband with a look that Cassandra imagined was both a pleading and promise. Don Manuel capitulated.

"I would enjoy that, Dona Cassandra, and I accept."

Cassandra smiled, "Good."

Talk turned to the wedding. Adelina explained about the festivities as she had arranged the wedding planner.

Cassandra said, "Of course everyone here will receive a formal invitation, but you must all mark it on your calendars.

My family and some of my friends cannot be there for reasons of security, but those who are local we hope will attend."

Manuel asked, "Will you be attending, Vicente?"

"I'm afraid not. I will be one of those friends who cannot attend. To draw too much attention would be to invite trouble."

Manuel nodded, "I understand. The threat to my friends is still real."

After dinner, the women retired to drink coffee while the men went away to smoke cigars and talk about manly things. Cassandra was able to get Josefina aside and asked, "Would you be a bridesmaid?"

Josefina was stunned and then clapped her hands and said, "Oh yes." She turned to the group and announced, "I am going to be a bridesmaid."

Adelina said, "Oh that is grand."

The women discussed the wedding and later the men returned. Unnoticed, Cassandra got Alejandro aside and whispered something to him. He nodded agreement. A few minutes later, she was able to get close to Don Manuel.

She walked up beside him and said, "Don Manuel, I have a great favor to ask of you."

Don Manuel looked at Cassandra, "What is it, Dona Cassandra?"

"Would you do me the honor of standing in for my father and giving me away?"

A broad smile appeared on Don Manuel's face. He said, "It is I who would be honored."

Cassandra said, "Thank you, Don Manuel. You are altogether kind."

Adriana called out, "Cassandra come sit by me. I am going to show everyone my pictures."

The showing lasted about ten minutes and everyone drank coffee as they passed the photographs around. Adriana explained the photos. Manuel was asking Alejandro about his thoughts on the place.

When the gathering ended the guests started to drift away. Cassandra cornered Alejandro and said, “We have a place here in the city. Can you come for breakfast in the morning and I’ll take you to see it.”

Alejandro said, “I would like that. May I bring Adriana?”

Cassandra said, “Oh yes, most certainly. She will be spending time there too.”

Cassandra and Amanda were the last to leave and Alejandro kissed his fiancé. They had the “effect” on each other and Cassandra knew she was flushed and wondered if others noticed. The broad smiles on Adriana and Amanda’s faces told her they had.

Alejandro stepped away and said, “I will see you in the morning. Would nine be acceptable?”

Cassandra said, “Yes.”

Alejandro opened the door and the women left.

Once they were in the vehicle, Amanda said, “Josefina is really nice. She invited me to go horseback riding at Adelina’s when I have a day off.”

Cassandra said, “I like Josefina. I think you will enjoy her company. We will have to arrange when we are at the estancia for you two to have time together.”

The next morning, Cassandra was up and ready early. She called Pedro just before she left her suite to let him know she was having company for breakfast. She then went to her office and found Carol was already there.

Cassandra said, “Good morning.”

Carol got up and followed Cassandra into her office. “Was your dinner pleasant last evening?”

“Yes, very. Did you have a pleasant evening?”

Carol smiled, “Yes. We now have TV here and I enjoyed watching a movie.”

Cassandra said, “I have made an appointment which will take up most of the morning. Do you have anything for me?”

Carol said, “It seems your deputy and management counselor are handling everything. I don’t have any appointments for you. I have been helping Juan with routine correspondence. Some of it will need your signature. Juan would like to talk to you about having an official function to celebrate the reopening of the embassy."

Cassandra said, "See if he can meet with me later this afternoon. I want you there as well."

"Very well, I will see to it." Carol left.

Cassandra checked her emails of which there was exactly zero. She read and signed certain routine documents that had been prepared. She read through each one before signing it. Cassandra knew being a regular ambassador would not be for her. Fifteen minutes before Alejandro and Adriana were due to arrive Cassandra went downstairs to the sun room. Her guests arrived a few minutes late. Luis met them at the door and brought them to Cassandra.

Cassandra rose from her chair as they entered, "Good morning and welcome."

Adriana said, "This is a beautiful building."

Cassandra kissed her fiancé on the cheek and hugged Adriana, "Yes, it is. Please have a seat."

Luis came in and served coffee. Cassandra said, "Adriana this is Luis Sancho Ruez Varga. He will be working at the estancia. Luis this is Dona Adriana Maria Alvarez Rivera de Ramirez, Alejandro's aunt."

Luis said, "I am pleased, Dona Adriana."

Adriana smiled, "I am also pleased as we will all be at the estancia."

Luis announced the menu for breakfast and took their orders and then left.

Adriana asked, "Why did you buy a house when we already have one in the city?"

Cassandra smiled, "First you said you never liked the house you live in now."

Adriana said, "True."

Cassandra continued, "Second, it is much too big for the time we will spend here in the city. After we are no longer in our current positions, I expect to spend most of my time at the estancia with my husband."

Adriana smiled, "Yes, that makes perfect sense."

Cassandra was on a roll, "Thirdly, it is close to the embassy and just as close to Alejandro's office as your present home."

Alejandro added, "And you can always go to the embassy if there is ever trouble."

Cassandra said, "It will also be easier to defend if the need arises. Fourthly, I need a place to live now and Alejandro and I are not yet married. Besides, it will also be less costly to run and it is much more modern. It will also allow Alejandro to put the current house up for sale."

Adriana said, "I see you have thought this through."

Cassandra said, "Yes and I had to act quickly. Alejandro has not even seen the house."

Adriana looked at Alejandro, "You did not tell me that."

Alejandro was wearing an expression like the child who has just had his hand caught in the cookie jar. He just shrugged.

Adriana laughed, "And here I thought Alejandro was keeping me in the dark."

Alejandro said with a shocked expression, "Never."

Cassandra said, "Men. They don't always tell the women in their lives the important things."

Adriana said, "So true."

Alejandro was wise enough to let go of the matter and said nothing.

Cassandra said, "I had intended just to rent the house, but the owners made me an offer I couldn't refuse."

Luis came in with their breakfast and served them. When he left, Alejandro said the blessing.

After prayer, Adriana said, "I am looking forward to seeing the home. When can I stay there?"

Cassandra said, "Anytime you want. We are all to be family. You will have your own room there."

Adriana said, "He did not mention that either."

Cassandra said, "I assumed it was just implied, so the fault is mine because I did not ask him to tell you that."

Adriana was in a teasing mood, "Yes, unfortunately you have to be very specific with men."

Cassandra smiled because Alejandro was squirming and so Cassandra added, "So true." She looked at Alejandro, "But some of them are so adorable."

Adriana said, "Yes there is that," then put a fork full of food in her mouth and looked at Alejandro.

He said, "I don't stand a chance with you two."

Cassandra said, "I think we have poor Alejandro on the defensive. I think we should show mercy."

Adriana looked at Alejandro, "All is forgiven, nephew."

Alejandro sighed deeply. Cassandra was amazed that such a strong and powerful man could be so confused by two women who obviously loved him.

After the meal, Cassandra said, "Well, what do you say we go see the new house?"

It was a short drive with the little convoy of security people. They toured the house and Adriana made a lot of positive observations as did Alejandro.

When they had finished the tour, Adriana said, "It is much brighter than the big house we have now and so seems so spacious, though it is much smaller. I love it."

Cassandra said, "My male security people will stay in the guest cottage. Alejandro's live in the city, so I assume they will just work shifts when we are here. Two of my people will always be here to guard the house."

Adriana just nodded.

Alejandro asked, "When will you move in?"

Cassandra said, "As soon as certain necessary paperwork is available."

Alejandro said, "I apologize." He smiled, "Circumstances distracted me and I forgot to give them to you last evening. I brought them with me. They are in the car."

Cassandra smiled, "Thank you, handsome."

Adriana said, "My nephew is not bad looking, but handsome?"

Cassandra said, "Beauty is in the eyes of the beholder."

Adriana said, "True."

Alejandro said, "It is time to stop teasing me before you two drive me to drink."

The women each took one of his arms and walked him to the vehicle. In the car Cassandra asked, "Is there any word on our uninvited guest?"

Alejandro shook his head in the negative, "No, but it is not for lack of trying."

Adriana said, "I suppose you two are talking in code about things that are official?"

Alejandro said, "Yes."

Cassandra was dropped at the embassy and after saying their goodbyes, Adriana and Alejandro left. Cassandra went to her office and called for Novio. He came quickly to her office.

Cassandra said, "I have good news Novio. I have the necessary papers and permits. I also have a letter saying the Mexican Government recognizes the diplomatic status of those on my security team."

Novio said, "We have made a list of needed equipment. Stan has provided most of it and the rest he will purchase locally. Shaun, Steve and Antonio will arrive tomorrow. I also have Jace, Jordon and Ricardo coming."

Cassandra said, "Good."

Novio said, "I know we will have down time while you are at work here because of embassy security. In spite of that, I would like to always have one of us shadow you at all times, even here."

Cassandra said, "That is agreeable."

Novio said, "I will send two of our people from here to the new house immediately. I take it we can use embassy vehicles?"

"Yes, we have a Mercedes and BMW available. The SUVs are for ambassadorial use."

Novio said, "Then I'll get to it if you have nothing else."

Cassandra nodded and Novio left.

On Friday morning, Alejandro and Adriana arrived just before eight o'clock. Cassandra's vehicles were lined up in the driveway; two embassy SUVs, Cassandra's Jeep, and a pickup with a tarp covered load in the bed. Alejandro got out of his vehicle which was one of four in his little convoy and headed for the door. Cassandra came out with Novio and met him. She kissed Alejandro on the cheek and asked, "Are you already to set out on our little adventure?"

Alejandro smiled, "I am my love."

Cassandra said, "This is Captain Novio Vega my head of off-site security." Novio snapped to attention as Cassandra said, "Novio this is my fiancé Secretary of the Interior Alejandro Carlos Garcia Ramirez,."

Alejandro said, "At ease Novio. It is a pleasure to meet you." Alejandro offered his hand.

Novio relaxed, "Thank you, sir." The two men shook hands

Alejandro asked, "What branch of the service are you in Novio?"

"Army sir."

Alejandro asked, "Special forces?"

"Yes sir."

Alejandro nodded and then said, "I suppose we should be on our way."

Alejandro offered his arm and led Cassandra to his SUV and they got in. Adriana was waiting and said, "Good morning, Cassandra."

Cassandra said, "It is indeed Adriana. I am looking forward to our first road trip."

The trip was very interesting and took about three hours as they had some time in morning rush hour traffic. The drivers were experienced and the little convoy never really got separated though a couple of times cars did try unsuccessfully to merge into the line.

Once in the country, Cassandra was making note of points of interest and discussed the scenery and the places they passed by. It was an enjoyable trip. When they arrived at the little town near the estancia, Cassandra discovered it was not that small. It was a bustling place of several thousand. They decided to stop there for lunch and Alejandro knew of a good restaurant on the main street. The convoy drew quite a bit of attention when it stopped and so many armed men got out. There were two vacant parking spaces in front of the restaurant. Some of the security people took up positions by the door of the restaurant and two others stayed with the vehicles. The other vehicles went around back and took up positions.

Alejandro opened the door for Cassandra and Adriana and they exited. Amanda was suddenly beside Adriana in front of Alejandro and Cassandra.

She said, "Good morning, Dona Adriana."

Adriana said, "Hello, Amanda."

Cassandra noticed Carmen was following along behind arm in arm with Pete. They did not look like part of the security team. At the door, they were met by the manager who greeted Alejandro, "Good day Don Alejandro and welcome."

Alejandro said, "Hello, Juan. This is my fiancé, her Excellency Cassandra Adora Crossing Santiago."

Juan bowed slightly, "Your reputation is known far and wide, Your Excellency." Juan said, "Good day, Dona Adriana."

Cassandra said, "These are my associates Carmen Pena and Pete Townsend."

Juan said, "Right this way please," and led them to a small private room. One of Cassandra's and one of Alejandro's people took up station at the door. Two female servers came rushing in and took their orders.

Cassandra asked, "How long have you owned this restaurant, Juan?"

He responded, "All my life, Excellency. My father ran it before me and his father before him. My family has been blessed to serve this town for almost a hundred years."

Cassandra said, "Then indeed you are blessed."

Juan asked, "Pardon my curiosity, but it is rumored you are going to breed horses again at the estancia. Is that true?"

Cassandra smiled, "Oh yes and I look forward to living here." She motioned to Juan to come closer and he did. She said quietly, "Please arrange for food our people can eat in the vehicles as we drive to the estancia."

Juan smiled, "Yes, Excellency."

The meal was good and the conversation pleasant. Cassandra said, "We will have to come back to visit the shops."

Adriana said, "Oh, I would like that."

After lunch, Alejandro paid the large bill and Cassandra left a very substantial gratuity. Cassandra also had Amanda drive their vehicle, so their driver could eat lunch as they travelled the last few miles. The gravel road to the estancia was in very good shape, but the vehicles left a cloud of dust so the drivers left a large spacing between each vehicle. As they went through the gates the drive was paved and they drove up to what was now Teo's home. Teo had seen the dust and was waiting for them.

The security teams were already dispersing to take up positions before Alejandro got out of the vehicle. He opened the doors for the ladies.

They got out and Teo came and Cassandra embraced him, "Hello, Teo."

Teo said, "Dona Cassandra it is good to see you. Have you eaten?"

"Yes thank you, Teo. We ate in town."

Cassandra did the introductions and Teo invited them for beverages. They went inside and Adriana said, "Oh, it is so much nicer than the pictures."

Teo said, "Thank you. We did the repairs and painting the first week."

Teo's wife came into the room and Cassandra immediately went to her and hugged her firmly, "Maria, it is so good to see you!"

Maria was crying and smiling, "It has been too long, Cassandra."

Teo introduced his wife to the others informally just as Maria. The party sat in the large open living space and Maria brought them cool beverages then took a seat. Cassandra sat next to Alejandro on a small sofa.

Teo asked, “How was the journey?”

Alejandro said, “It was uneventful and I think enjoyable. I see you are making a lot of progress. The place looks so different from when we were last here.”

Teo related all the work that had been accomplished while the group finished their drinks. Teo said, “Would you like to see our progress?”

Cassandra said, “Please,” and everyone stood. Cassandra took Alejandro’s arm.

Maria said, “I think I will stay here.”

Teo offered his arm to Adriana and said, “Dona Adriana?” She took his arm and they went off on the tour.

They went to the workers’ homes first and as they looked around inside the first one Teo said, “As you can see we have repaired and renovated the houses. They are now modernized.”

After they toured the three renovated houses, Teo took them to see the barns, the shop that had been converted to house the security people, and the new workers’ houses that were under construction. They were built on a concrete pad and were being constructed of concrete block to help keep them cool. They would have high ceilings. Each of the houses had two bedrooms, a galley kitchen, a bathroom,

and a small living and dining area. They would be nice, but basic. They then walked up the hill to where the new house was being built. The concrete walls were in place with openings for the doors and windows that would be installed later. The roof trusses were already up and the workmen were putting sheathing on them. The building was one level, but there were two roofs; one to cover the main house which was higher and another to cover the wrap-around porch and extend over the patio.

Adriana looked around and said, "The views from here are magnificent. I will enjoy living here."

Cassandra said to Teo, "You have done a wonderful job Teo. Tonight Adriana and I will stay in the worker's house nearest the main house. Please set it aside for when we are here until the main house is finished. Pedro and Luis will be coming soon and they will take the other two. In the meantime, my security people may use them."

Teo said, "Of course Dona Cassandra. Perhaps your party would like to freshen up and explore the surroundings. You are invited to share the evening meal with my family."

Cassandra said, "That will be delightful."

Alejandro said, "I think I will go explore," and sauntered off with a security man.

Cassandra and Adriana walked toward the house where they would be staying. Their bags were brought and the women unpacked. Cassandra was sitting in a wooden chair on the small covered porch when Alejandro returned.

He sat in the chair next to her and said, "It is a beautiful spot."

"Yes, it is."

Adriana came out of the house and took a seat.

Alejandro asked, "I noticed Teo's wife Maria called you by your first name. Why was she so familiar with you?"

Cassandra said, "She is my cousin; uncle Vicente's daughter."

Alejandro asked, "And your uncle approved of her marriage to Teo?"

Cassandra smiled at Alejandro, "Are you a snob, my dear?"

Alejandro looked shocked before realizing his fiancé was half teasing and relaxed. He said, "I half deserved that. I must remember where my family started out."

Cassandra continued, "My uncle gave his blessing to the marriage because Maria loved Teo and he her. Teo is a man of fine character and from a good hard working family."

Alejandro said, "I think being married to you will help me be more grounded. The security men thanked me for the lunch. I did not consider their needs."

Cassandra nodded.

Adriana asked, "What are they going to do about the evening meal?"

Alejandro said, "I suppose I should send someone to town to get them food that can be heated."

Adriana said, "That would be wise."

Alejandro waved to a security guard to come closer and Alejandro gave him orders to make arrangements to have food brought from town.

Amanda came to the porch and took a seat. The group sat in silence for a while enjoying the light mountain breeze rolling into the valley and the surroundings.

Amanda said, "This is a lovely place and it's so peaceful."

Alejandro said, "It will be a nice place to raise a family," and looked at Cassandra who smiled.

Adriana said, "I'd like to go for a walk."

Cassandra looked at Amanda then looked at Alejandro's security and Amanda nodded and said, "I'll go with you Adriana." The two women got up and walked off.

Cassandra said, "If I were Castillo I would visit the town."

Alejandro said, "I have some agents carefully asking around about strangers. So far, we have found nothing, but the search is not over."

Cassandra said, "You know he is eventually going to have a go at us either here or at the house in the city. If I were him, I would try in town because it is where we have the least control. He knows security here and at the wedding will be heightened."

"What are you thinking?"

Cassandra said, "If we know he is here, but can't locate him, it might be possible to trap him with the right bait."

Alejandro looked at her.

"You could arrange to have some of your people in town undercover when Amanda, Carmen and I go to town with what is supposedly one security guard."

Alejandro asked, "How good are the women?"

"They are deadly good. When we know your undercover people are close we could arrange for the security man to be distracted."

Alejandro said, "It is a dangerous plan."

"Yes, but I'd rather we ambush him rather than the other way around."

"It makes sense. I'd feel better if you wore body armor."

Cassandra smiled, "I have body armor on now under my blouse. It is a custom fitted and made vest. It is very expensive, but it does not show. All my team members are wearing these vests."

Alejandro said, "I never would have known. "

"That's the idea."

Alejandro looked at her, "Aren't they hot?"

"I have worn one for so long I'm used to it. We will often wear the outer body armor when we want a show of force and protection against heavier weapons."

Alejandro just nodded, "I need to go and relieve myself and it would be improper to go into the house where you are staying. I'll be back shortly."

Cassandra said, "I'll be in the big stable."

They both left in different directions. It was a mild day and Cassandra enjoyed the short walk to the stable. It was a large building and the entrance was large enough to drive a tractor through. The building had twenty stalls, a horse shower, a tack room and a feed room. The building had been completely cleaned and sanitized so it did not smell like a horse barn.

Cassandra's training kicked in immediately when she perceived movement in her peripheral vision. The attacker was quick, but Cassandra was faster. She blocked the knife thrust and as it sliced her arm she struck a killing blow. It was instinctive and the man dropped heavily to the floor his head making a loud noise as it struck the floor. Cassandra drew her weapon in one swift motion and looked for a secondary attack. She slipped into the nearest stall, but no attack came.

She realized the slice on her arm was significant and bleeding more than was healthy. She slipped out of the barn and headed toward the main house. Novio was coming toward her on the run his weapon trained to cover behind her. Suddenly the security men and women were around those they were protecting.

Alejandro came running to Cassandra and said, "Come. We need to get that looked after." He picked her up like she weighed nothing and ran with her to the house. She had not realized how strong or fit he was. The running carrying her weight did not seem to strain him in the least. At the main house, Alejandro put her in a chair on the patio behind a wall.

Maria came out muttering a prayer in Spanish. She carried a first aid kit. She wiped the arm and said, "It will need stitches." She bandaged the arm to stop the bleeding and said, "You had better get her to a doctor."

Cassandra said to Alejandro, "It could be a way to draw us into an ambush."

Alejandro said, "It would be good planning."

Novio and Alejandro's head of security were standing there. They both looked at each other.

Cassandra said, "If the assassin gets me then they have succeeded, but if I am just wounded and am rushed off for medical attention, they ambush us both for you would surely be with me."

Novio said, 'Then let us ambush the ambushers and have it over with."

Alejandro said, "Cassandra's embassy vehicles are armored so we race them down the road with just drivers in them. When the attack comes the drivers go to ground. The rest of us split into two groups and drive off road to either side. When the attack comes we attack the ambushers."

Alejandro's head of security started giving orders.

Cassandra looked at Teo, "Get all those not going into the house and we will make a stand here if others come."

Teo nodded.

Cassandra said, "Do not bring the other two workers here. Tell them to stay in the barn. It was one of the workers who attacked me."

Amanda came into the house with Carmen and Adriana. The women were carrying assault rifles and had two duffle bags that would have spare ammo and lighter equipment. Amanda said, "Carmen, Teo, and I can hold down the fort here."

Alejandro remembered what Cassandra had said about the women warriors. He said, "Then we have a plan." He hurried outside.

Adriana said, "I know how to shoot."

Amanda handed her a rifle and some extra clips. She pulled out vests from one of the duffle bags and passed them out saying, "Put these on."

Everyone hurried to do it.

The first vehicles were leaving and Teo ran back in the house. He said, "I gave the workers shotguns and told them to stay in the barn and defend it, but under no circumstances to come near the house as they might be mistaken for attackers."

Amanda handed him a vest and an assault rifle. Teo knew what to do.

Cassandra smiled and looked at her arm. It had stopped bleeding. She said, "Amanda give me a HK53."

Amanda complied and as well handed Cassandra extra clips. The shorter automatic weapon would be easier for Cassandra to operate with her injured arm and in Cassandra's skilled hands it would be deadly at close range. They all took up positions. Anyone rushing the house would have to cover a lot of open ground. It seemed they waited a long time and then they heard gunfire far off.

Cassandra started praying out loud and the others joined her. It was a short, but earnest prayer.

The gunfire seemed to last but a short time and then there was an explosion. This was followed by very heavy gunfire. Amanda looked at Cassandra. They both knew a serious firefight was under way. Everyone in the house was on edge.

Teo looked at Maria, "I didn't think we would have this much excitement."

Maria laughed almost hysterically. Cassandra knew it was the stress of the situation. The distant gunfire had settled into a sporadic pattern. Carmen said, "I think I am happier being here than there."

Cassandra said, "The gunfire has died down." Her cell phone rang and she answered, 'Yes."

Alejandro said, "You were right. Two got away and are headed through the woods your way. Be on guard."

Cassandra said, "All right." She hung up and said, "Carmen we have a sniper assignment. Two got away and are headed this way through the woods. If they come out of the woods drop them when they are in range."

Carmen smiled, "Yes ma'am."

She slipped outside crouching low. They waited some minutes in silence. In the far distance they heard the occasional shot. The tension in the room grew as time passed. Suddenly, after what seemed an eternity, there were two shots in rapid succession and they were much closer. Adriana looked at Cassandra.

Cassandra said, "It seems Carmen has two more notches."

Adriana stifled a laugh.

They heard vehicles approaching and Carmen came in crouching low, "I got them."

Cassandra's phone rang.

She answered, "Yes."

Alejandro asked, "Is everyone all right?"

"Yes, but there are two attackers out there in the field and they are down, but their status is unknown."

"Understood."

The call ended.

Cassandra looked at the road and saw the convoy coming. The vehicles pulled up in front of the house. Alejandro and the rest of the men got out. One of the drivers got out wearing a field dressing on his arm and one of Alejandro's men was helped out a field dressing on his thigh.

Cassandra asked, "Did we lose anyone?"

Alejandro shook his head no, "A few minor wounds. The attackers were undisciplined and poorly trained. Your embassy is unfortunately less one pretty SUV; RPG got it after the drivers escaped. "

Two men were pulled out of the back of one of the vehicles and forced to kneel on the ground. They both were slightly wounded and their minor wounds had not been treated. Their hands were bound behind their backs. One of them was crying in pain. The pickup pulled up and it was heaped with bodies. Another vehicle came in from the field and the two bodies of the men taken down by Carmen were transferred to the pickup bed.

Cassandra still had the HK slung over her shoulder and she went to the men and took off her shoe and hit them both with it. She knew it was a great insult.

One of the men spat at her and one of Alejandro's men, a captain, kicked him in the face and he went over.

Cassandra squatted in front of the other man her weapons barrel casually pointed in his direction. She said in Farsi, "What you fail to understand is that your allies tried to topple the government here and the country is still under a state of emergency. No one will care if one of Castillo's thugs ends up in the pickup truck or not."

The man looked at the bodies heaped in the bed of the pickup truck and pissed his pants and that's when Cassandra knew they had him and knew his origin.

Alejandro turned to the Captain who was head of his security, "Take them to the barn and question them."

The man snapped to attention and said, "Yes sir."

He ordered one of his men to get a battery and jumper cable from one of the vehicles.

Cassandra could tell the men were now anticipating the worst. The one man was defiant, but the other who had pissed himself said something to him and he looked up and the slightest hint of fear came over him before he regained his composure.

The two kneeling men were yanked to their feet by Alejandro's men. Four of the soldiers virtually carried the captives under their armpits toward the barn.

Alejandro asked, "What language was that?"

"Farsi which means they come from Iran or Western Afghanistan."

Cassandra and Alejandro followed the group into the barn and sat on hay bales. The body of the man Cassandra had killed was laying face first in a pool of blood. The stench was nauseating and Cassandra could tell it was having an effect on the men. They were forced kneel on the floor.

Alejandro's man picked up a hay bale with one hand and threw it in front of the men. He sat on the bale in front of the two men and started, "I am short on patience and I'm in a foul mood, but that does not mean I can't keep you alive for a long time if you make this hard. All I want to know is where Castillo is. Tell me that and you will be released in another country. "

The one who had urinated on himself looked at the other man who said, "I will tell you nothing."

The captain turned to two of his men, "Take this one outside. I'm tired of this pig's insolence."

The two soldiers lifted him roughly and took him out the back screaming and shouting curses. There was a shot and the screaming stopped.

The remaining man was now shaking uncontrollably. The captain said, "I want to know where Castillo is. Tell us what we want to know and I'll spare you and you will taken to another country and freed."

The man said, "How do I know I can trust you?"

"Because I give my word and you have no other choice."

The man blurted an address.

The captain said, "Now wasn't that easy. I will keep my word if he is at that address. Why did Castillo want you to attack the Secretary and the Ambassador?"

The man was hanging his head, he was broken. "It was part of the price for the next shipment of weapons."

The Captain ordered his two soldiers, "Blindfold him and see he gets first aid and is fed but keep him under close guard. No one is to harm him."

They blindfolded the man and led him away. The other man was brought into the barn still alive, but groggy. The captain said, "Your friend gave me an address in Mexico City where we can find Castillo. If you can confirm it I will let you live."

He told the man the street name.

The man confirmed the specific address and was blindfolded and led from the barn.

Alejandro pulled out his phone and made a call, "I have an address. It will be time sensitive. Castillo may be there." He gave the address.

Cassandra got up and Alejandro walked with her to the porch of the house where she was staying and they sat down. She took a moment to pray silently. Her arm was throbbing and trying to bleed again. Amanda brought her two pills and a bottle of water. Cassandra looked at Amanda.

Amanda said, "They are just aspirin."

Cassandra took the pills.

Alejandro said, "We need to get you and a couple of my men medical attention."

Cassandra nodded agreement. Alejandro, Cassandra, and half the security force left for town. It was a short drive to the clinic and on the way Alejandro recounted what had happened at the ambush site.

When they arrived at the clinic, the medical staff treated Cassandra and Alejandro's men first. Cassandra was getting stitches when Alejandro received a call. He went out to take it. He was gone a very short time and did not look happy when he returned.

When Cassandra came out of the treatment room, the wounded attackers were being treated. They were kept well apart and blindfolded.

Alejandro said, "We just missed Castillo by minutes. My agents were told he took a small plane to Belize."

"When did he get airborne?"

Alejandro said, "Perhaps fifteen minutes ago."

"Do you have a tail number?"

Alejandro told her and she smiled, "Give me a minute alone please. I want to pass this information along." Cassandra found a private spot and called Stan.

Stan answered, "What's up, boss?"

Cassandra said, "I have a gift for you. It seems Castillo went wheels up fifteen minutes ago in a small plane headed for Belize. Do you think you can have a welcome party pick him up?"

Stan said, "Oh yeah!"

Cassandra gave him the plane's tail number. She went to Alejandro smiling. She said, "I think our uninvited guest is going to get invited back for the wedding though I doubt he will be able to be at the service."

Alejandro said, "It would be a nice wedding present for your future husband, providing his plane doesn't have an accident en route."

Cassandra said, "Well, then what are you going to get me?"

Alejandro said, "It is a surprise."

Chapter 15 – The Unexpected

The little convoy arrived back at the estancia less one of Alejandro's security men who had been sent by ambulance to the city. It seemed his thigh wound was more serious than first assumed. They did get back in time for the evening meal which was running behind schedule due to the day's events.

When Alejandro and Cassandra entered the house, they found Maria was busy in the kitchen with Adriana. Some of the security people were on the patio eating. They had jackets on as the evening temperature was dropping.

Adriana said, "Oh good, you are back. The second meal serving will be ready shortly. It will be served in the dining room."

Maria looked up smiling and said, "These people sure have an appetite after a fight."

Cassandra went into the living room and found Teo and Novio sitting talking. Teo looked up and said, "Alejandro had to take a call. He is outside."

Teo had no sooner finished saying that when Alejandro came to the doorway and motioned to Cassandra. She went outside to join him.

Alejandro looked serious, "Jet fighters were sent to intercept Castillo's plane. The aircraft is not following the flight plan and has dropped off the radar. We have aircraft looking for Castillo's plane. I don't think he is going to Belize."

Cassandra said, "I was hoping we had gotten a break."

The thought ran through her mind that she should tell Stan, but then she just as quickly put it aside as in spite of being off the radar Castillo might still show up in Belize.

Alejandro said, "We might as well eat as there is nothing else we can do at the moment."

Cassandra took his arm and they went to the dining room. After dinner, Carmen and Amanda volunteered to clean up so the family went out onto the deck to drink coffee. They talked about everything, but what had happened that day. The emotions were too raw and most seemed to need some time to process it all. It was of course different for Cassandra and Alejandro who were used to processing traumatic events on the fly.

About eight o'clock Alejandro got a phone call and he went a little distance away to take it. He was told Castillo had not been located. He came back to the porch and Cassandra looked at him and he shook his head from side to side. Cassandra was disappointed they had not gotten Castillo.

By ten o'clock, everyone had gone to bed for the night except the security people on the first guard shift. Cassandra slept in a T-shirt and shorts with her pistol under her pillow and the HK on the night table. She had trouble sleeping and could hear Adriana snoring lightly. It was not the snoring or the repetitive noise of the ceiling fan turning nor the events of the day that were keeping Cassandra awake. It was the fact that Alejandro was in bed next door and she really wanted him with her. She prayed and finally fell asleep.

Cassandra awoke to the first rays of sunshine coming through the window. She gathered up her things and went to the bathroom to shower and got ready for the new day.

When Cassandra came out, she found Adriana in a housecoat waiting. Adriana said, "I thought you'd never finish," and rushed into the bathroom. Cassandra went to her room and packed her dirty clothes in a bag she had brought just for that purpose.

Cassandra went into the small kitchen, but there was nothing there to make coffee with. She took the HK, satellite phone and her laptop out onto the porch and sat down putting the weapon on the floor beside her chair. Her arm was now throbbing, but Cassandra just ignored the ache. She opened her laptop and wrote a report on the events of the previous day. She synched her laptop to her satellite phone and sent her encrypted document to Washington. She waited to receive a confirmation of transmission then shut down the laptop and phone.

Her thoughts turned to Castillo. She wanted him badly. It was not for personal revenge, but because of the potential harm he could do not only to her life, but to the two countries.

She took her laptop to her room and got her Bible then went back outside. She was sitting reading when Maria came from the main house carrying a tray. She came down the hill and joined Cassandra.

"Good morning. I made coffee and brought aspirin."

Cassandra said, "Thank you," and poured a cup. She took two aspirin out of the bottle and swallowed them with a sip of coffee.

Maria said, "Do you think we will be subject to another attack?"

"No I don't. The mastermind behind this has fled the country. He wants me and Alejandro. His people may try again, but I doubt very much it will be here."

Alejandro came out of the house where he was staying and came over. He came up on the porch and said, "Good morning, ladies," and he bent over and kissed Cassandra on the lips gently. It was unexpected and sparks flew.

Alejandro stood up and said, "Coffee is now unnecessary."

Maria teased, "All the more for me."

Alejandro said, "Ah I will take some anyway to be friendly." He bent over and poured a cup and sat down then asked, "Where is my dear aunt?"

Cassandra said, "I think she went back to bed."

Adriana chose that moment to appear dressed and ready for the day, "To hear you talk, Cassandra, I sound like a lazy lay-about. You promised me a shopping trip."

Cassandra smiled. Her special phone rang and Cassandra picked it up and said, "Excuse me, it is official business." She walked into the yard out of hearing and answered with, "Crossing."

Stan said, "Our friend did not arrive at his destination."

Cassandra said, "Too bad."

"The plane he was on did however land in Guatemala. He took a commercial flight from Guatemala City to Caracas."

Cassandra said, "Good work. The plot thickens if he is in Venezuela."

"We will probably be able to track him there, but it would be too dangerous and we don't have enough assets in place to grab or eliminate him."

Cassandra said, "Let me know when he leaves Venezuela and where he is headed."

Stan said, "Will do. There is a standing order and we will initiate action if we locate him in a place where we can act."

Cassandra said, "I understand."

Stan added, "The three ships we were tracking have docked in Venezuela and I doubt that is a coincidence. The passengers have not disembarked, so we don't think that is the final destination. We have documented that their leaders have met with high ranking Venezuelan officials. I'll contact you if there are any significant developments."

Cassandra said, "I will bet you Castillo ends up on one of those ships."

Stan said, "I think you may be right. We will keep eyes on the ships. I will let you know if anything significant happens."

"Agreed."

The call ended.

Cassandra went back to the porch. Adriana said, "That is an unusual phone."

Alejandro said, "It is a satellite phone. It will work just about anywhere."

Adriana said, "I'd like one like Cassandra's."

Alejandro said, "You can't get one like that because the U.S. government has its own satellites. A commercial satellite phone is very expensive."

Adriana said, "You have one."

Alejandro said, "It is for official business and I don't have to pay for it."

Cassandra said, "Alejandro, I'd like to go for a walk."

They got up and Cassandra slung the HK over her shoulder. They walked slowly away hand in hand. When they were out of hearing of the others Cassandra said, "I was just given information about Castillo and the ships." She told Alejandro what she had been told, but not who had told her. He didn't ask.

Alejandro said, "Those ships are up to no good and if they come into our territorial waters we will board or sink them if they resist."

Cassandra said, "It would be prudent."

Alejandro said, "I agree it is no coincidence Castillo is in Venezuela when the ships arrive."

"I wish I knew what they were up to."

They circled around and went back to the porch.

Maria was gone and Adriana said, "Maria went to get her purse. I want to go to town and visit the shops."

Cassandra said, "Let's."

Alejandro said, "I think I will stay here."

Cassandra said, "Of course, dear. This is after all a women's shopping trip."

Alejandro smiled.

The little convoy was soon on its way into town. The group decided they would first stop and eat. After brunch, they went shopping. The news of Dona Cassandra's upcoming move into the area had already spread throughout the business community and the party was welcomed wherever they went. The business people were very polite and respectful.

They went to the open market where Cassandra found colorful paintings by a local artist. She loved the work and bought five large paintings; four for the estancia house and one for her city house. They also found a local weaver selling her wares. The three women bought colorful hand woven wool jackets. They also found the town had a number of interesting shops. The women returned to the estancia about four o'clock. Life seemed normal again.

The women got out of the vehicles and with help unloaded their purchases and brought them to their homes. When Cassandra had stored the paintings in the closet of the little house and packed her purchases, she went out on the porch. Adriana was already walking up to Maria's house. Cassandra sat on the porch and Alejandro came from the stables to sit with her.

Alejandro said, "I have been thinking. Life is too short and we should be married. Why don't we get married in Coral Gables? It could be a family and very close friends' affair. Adriana, Adelina, Carlos, Josefina, Don Manuel and Dona Ana, Teo and Maria could come with us. This way we would avoid religious problems and not put poor Vicente in a compromising position and we could get married sooner."

Cassandra looked at her fiancé, "That is a stellar idea. Let's call my parents and run it by them."

Cassandra made the call. Her father answered, "Good evening, Cassandra."

"Hello, father. I have you on speaker and Alejandro is here. Is mother close by? We have something we want to run by you."

Craig said, "Just a minute."

A moment later they heard Dorothy say, "Hello. It is good to hear from you."

Alejandro said, "We want your opinion on our wedding." He proceeded to tell them.

Craig said, "That is an excellent solution. The family had planned to go for Christmas anyway and we could do it then between Christmas and New Years. Cassandra's brother Cal and his wife were married there during the Christmas holiday." They discussed the plans in detail and it was agreed that is what they would do.

After the call Alejandro said, "I am glad that is finally settled. "

Someone had noticed a cloud of dust on the road and security was running to take up positions. Cassandra went to her room and picked up the HK and came outside with it slung over her shoulder. The vehicles were stopped several hundred yards from the house by some of Alejandro's men who had blocked the road with two vehicles. The approaching vehicles were let through and came and parked in front of the main house.

Don Manuel and his wife got out of the first vehicle. Cassandra and Alejandro walked toward them. They met half way and Cassandra swung the HK to her back and embraced Ana and then Manuel saying, "Welcome. I am so glad to see you."

Alejandro hugged Ana and shook hands with Manuel.

Manuel seemed upset and Alejandro said, "What is wrong, Don Manuel."

Don Manuel looked at Cassandra's bandaged arm, "I ask your forgiveness, Dona Cassandra."

Cassandra said, "Whatever for, Don Manuel?"

Don Manuel took a deep breath, "I recommended the men Teo hired and one tried to murder you. I am to blame for if I had not recommended him, you would have surely investigated the ones you hired."

Cassandra said, "Don Manuel, of course you are forgiven. Think no further of it. These things happen." Cassandra did the unexpected and hugged him again as to reassure him. "Don't let such a thing come between us, please."

Cassandra let go of him and he said, "You are most gracious."

Alejandro said, "Now Cassandra must ask your forgiveness as our wedding plans have changed."

Cassandra said, "I ask you Don Manuel to release me from my invitation for you to give me away. Please come and sit down as we have plans to discuss with you."

They went to the porch of the little house and sat down. Adriana came from the big house with Maria and they had a pitcher and glasses. Maria and Adriana came onto the porch and Cassandra said, "Don Manuel and Dona Ana may I present my cousin Maria Adora Santiago de Ortega."

Maria shook hands with Manuel and Ana and they all sat down and Adriana started pouring lemonade.

Manuel asked, “Are you visiting, Maria?”

Maria smiled, “No, I live here. My husband Teo is managing the estancia for my cousin. He went to town with one of Alejandro’s men to purchase provisions for the security people.”

Alejandro said, “This is a good time to tell everyone about our plans.”

Alejandro told them about the plans to be married in Coral Gables and that they were all invited. Ana and Adriana were enthusiastic and Don Manuel said he and Ana would certainly go. It was agreed they would all travel together.

Cassandra said, “Now I just have to ask Carlos and Adelina, Josefina and my uncles.”

Ana asked, “May Lonzo come. It would be a good experience for him.”

Cassandra said, “Yes, of course.”

Manuel said with a broad smile, “Under the circumstances I am delighted if somewhat disappointed to not be giving the bride away.”

Maria said, “You must stay for dinner.”

Don Manuel looked at his wife and said, “We accept.”

The group drank lemonade and discussed the trip for a while.

Maria said, “If you will excuse me, I will go to see to dinner.”

Adriana said, “I will help you.”

The two women left. Alejandro and Cassandra offered to take Manuel and Ana on a tour of the work being done on the estancia. Ana was especially interested in the work on the new house.

Manuel said as they walked the grounds, “You will have a large number of workers houses.”

Cassandra said, “We will have security people and we will run our business interests from here.”

Manuel said, “So far from the city?”

Alejandro said, "We will have a small plane that can fly out of here."

Manuel said, "Yes that would make sense, but you can't fly to the city every day."

Cassandra said, "We have a home in the city as well. We will stay there three or four nights and here on weekends until our terms of office are completed."

Ana said, "Your cousin seems nice."

"She is and I love her and Teo." Cassandra saw the vehicles returning and said, "There is Teo now."

They walked over to Teo and Alejandro did the introductions. Teo suggested they all go to the house. They went to the patio and sat talking. It seemed to Cassandra that Don Manuel was more relaxed and informal when he was away from his estancia.

They ate dinner and spent a relaxing and enjoyable evening talking and getting to know each other. About nine o'clock, Manuel and Ana left for home.

Immediately Cassandra phoned Adelina who answered, "Hello Cassandra. I hear you had some excitement."

"A little. I have news about the wedding."

Adelina said, "So tell me."

"Is your passport up to date?"

Adelina asked, "What are you planning?"

Cassandra told her about the wedding plans and who was invited and Adelina was excited. She said, "I will somehow get my husband to agree to go. I imagine he will want to meet your father and I don't think he has ever been to Florida."

Cassandra and Alejandro then phoned Maria and shared their plans. Maria said, "I don't think Enrique can leave under the circumstances, but perhaps he will agree to let me go."

Cassandra said, "Just let me know. I am now getting excited as we have a plan and date."

Cassandra next called her mother and they discussed the invitation list. It was after ten when Cassandra finally took her leave of Alejandro and went to bed. She was up early on Sunday as was Adriana. They packed and put their bags in one of the vehicles. By eight thirty, they again they had a convoy on the road to go to church in town for the nine o'clock mass.

They met Don Manuel and Ana there and they all sat together. Afterwards, Don Manuel introduced Cassandra to the parish priest who was very friendly yet humble. He was a man from a working class family and very aware of social class.

After saying their goodbyes, Alejandro, Cassandra, and Adriana headed back to the city. Cassandra suggested they have lunch at the embassy residence. Adriana accepted and Cassandra phoned ahead so Pedro would be alerted. After lunch, Alejandro and his aunt left.

Cassandra was sitting in the library of the embassy residence with Amanda when Novio came in.

Cassandra said, "Have a seat. Would you like a drink Novio? We were just about to imbibe."

"I think so; the usual?"

Cassandra called Luis and he brought them each two fingers of fine Tennessee sipping whiskey over ice.

Cassandra asked, "How are things at the house?"

"Quiet. They guys used the time to install surveillance equipment and alarms."

Cassandra said, "Good. I will have my things moved there tomorrow."

Novio said, "Your fiancé knows his stuff. His command of the attack showed him to be an experienced professional"

Cassandra knew that was high praise coming from Novio.

Novio asked, "Did we get Castillo?"

Cassandra shook her head no.

Novio sipped his drink, "I heard he was slippery, but we'll get him eventually."

"We always do. I'd rather it was sooner than later."

Novio said, "Understood."

Cassandra said, "Carmen has not lost her touch."

"No she hasn't. She's a natural born shooter."

Amanda said, "You have a good team, Novio."

Stan came by and Cassandra asked, "Want a drink?"

Stan took a seat, "Sure thing. That looks good."

Luis came quickly with a drink for him.

Stan said, "I heard you added one to your body count."

Cassandra shrugged, "I must have some kind of record for ambassadors."

The group laughed at that.

Cassandra finished her drink and said, "I'm tired and I'm going to turn in. Make yourselves at home and have some more of that fine whiskey if you are so inclined."

She went upstairs and turned in.

Monday morning she was at her desk when Juan came to her office. Carol announced him and he came into Cassandra's office.

"Good morning, Ambassador."

"Good morning, Juan."

Juan took a seat and Cassandra asked, "What is on your mind?"

"I'd like your permission for two things. First I'd like to have a Thanksgiving dinner for the staff and make it a real party. I know it's only a week away, but I have it all planned and I only need your approval. Secondly, I'd like you to approve the date for the official opening. I am suggesting the first Friday in December for a reception. It is short notice, but the other embassies are starting to come back and I think we should be first out of the gate. Thirdly, I'd like to have a Christmas party for the staff."

Cassandra considered the dangers of a reception. There were risks to her credibility, but also if they could pull it off without incident it would be a further step forward.

She stalled to consider it by asking, "How much will it cost and do you have a budget?"

Juan handed her a folder. Cassandra opened it and looked through it. When she finished she initialed the sheets with a hand written note "approved". She handed the file back to Juan. "Make sure to give Carol a copy."

Juan asked, "Will you speak at the Christmas party?"

"I won't be there. This is not for distribution, but I will be on vacation."

Juan said, "My lips are sealed. If you have nothing for me, I will get back to it." He got up and was almost to the door.

Cassandra said, "Juan."

He turned around.

"You are doing a good job."

Juan smiled, "Thank you, Ambassador." He left with a bit more spring in his step.

Cassandra called Carol on the intercom, "I'd like to see Bob and Stan. Please arrange coffee for when they come."

"Yes Ambassador."

Twenty minutes later they came to her office and Luis was just ahead of them with a tray on which was a coffee pot, cups and light pastries which he put on the coffee table. Luis left and closed the door as the two men entered.

Cassandra said, "Good morning, gentlemen," and got up from her desk and went to the sitting area. "Please have a seat."

Bob said, "We heard about your weekend excitement."

Cassandra poured coffee and said, "I just wish we'd gotten Castillo. That is not the reason I called you in. I am moving to the house today as my confirmation vote is being held soon. Further, I will be gone between Christmas and New Years. Alejandro and I will be married at the family compound in Coral Gables. That is not for public consumption."

Stan sipped his coffee and Bob said, "With you staying off the embassy grounds, it is more likely any attack on you will occur at one of your homes."

Cassandra said, "Yes. They are unlikely to try it at the estancia again after what happened on the weekend. The town's folk will also be leery of strangers now. Novio and his team will provide security outside the compound. When I'm here, I'll be your responsibility Bob. I will sleep at the house and I intend my schedule here will be very irregular."

Stan said, "Good idea."

Cassandra said, "If something goes wrong at the house, we'll head here first chance we have. I'd like to do everything I can to keep that from happening. Perhaps you can put some of those nighttime teams out to patrol the neighborhood in the shadows to make sure no one is lurking around. Let Novio know what is happening. We might catch some terrorists before we have to kill them and information is critical. I want Castillo. What do you think?"

Bob said, "So you are going to be bait?"

"Yes."

Stan said, "It might work. They won't be expecting it."

Cassandra said, "If you think it's a good idea, I'll tell Alejandro so his men don't get mistaken for terrorists."

Stan smiled and Bob shook his head in disbelief.

Bob said, "This is like Alice in Wonderland stuff."

Stan said, "Welcome to my world, Colonel."

Cassandra said, "Then it is settled. Now for the fun stuff; the grand opening reception will be held the first Friday in December."

Bob said sarcastically, "Oh, that will be fun."

Cassandra said, "We'll need some officers in dress uniforms and a number of turned out marines of various ranks in dress uniforms visible. We'll need to be on high alert as I expect we'll have a lot of dignitaries on site. Juan will have the agenda, Bob, so you will need to coordinate with him. That evening, I would like some of our recon people roaming the shadows in the streets of the neighborhood. Do you have any questions?"

Bob said, "How many guests are we expecting."

Cassandra said, "I don't know. We'll have to see who confirms, but it will probably be fifty to a hundred."

Bob looked at Stan, "We'll need to confirm identities. Can you help us with briefing material and photos of the people on the guest list?"

Stan said, "No problem."

Bob looked at Cassandra, "I have no other questions."

"Well then gentlemen, I leave it all in your capable hands."

The men left and Cassandra phoned Alejandro. He answered, "Good morning, my love."

"Good morning, handsome. How is your schedule looking today?"

"It is light and I could get away to have lunch with you if that is what you are going to ask."

Cassandra said, "It was. I need to talk to you about some things; some are personal, some not."

Alejandro said, "So do I."

"I can have Pedro fix us lunch. How about at twelve thirty."

"I will be there."

The call ended and Cassandra called Pedro and told him Alejandro was coming and she would need lunch for two served in the sunroom. She then called Carol in and told her about the Christmas vacation plans. She also asked her to help Juan with the reception guest list and invitations. She then headed for her suite in the residence.

Cassandra thought she did not have all that much to pack. She was almost finished by eleven o'clock, but found she had a little more than she had brought. She called Carol to arrange another suitcase and garment bags for her gowns. She then sat and watched the local news on TV waiting for what she needed to arrive. When it did, she finished her packing quickly.

She was in the sunroom when Alejandro arrived. He came directly to her and kissed her on the cheek, "It seems like an eternity since yesterday. I confess I have a bad case of love sickness. Enrique has been joking about it."

They sat and Luis came with soup. Luis left and went into the hall. Alejandro said the blessing and they started eating.

Alejandro said, "What have you to tell me."

Cassandra told him about the plan. She ended with, "I don't want to be looking over my shoulder the rest of my life.

The danger is there, but I'd like it out of the way on our terms not Castillo's."

Alejandro said, "It makes me nervous, but it is necessary. I agree to the plan, but I would like my men to do the shadow patrols. I have some very good people who I trust."

Cassandra said, "Agreed. Compromise is necessary in a relationship."

Alejandro smiled.

Cassandra said, "I formally invite you to the official opening of the embassy reception on the first Friday in December. Informally, I want my handsome fiancé there."

Alejandro said, "I will be there in both capacities."

Cassandra said, "Good."

Alejandro said, "Now I have news for you. Your intelligence people are not as good as they would like to believe."

Cassandra tilted her head and asked, "Why do you say that?"

"Castillo never left Mexico. It was a man who looks very much like Castillo, but it was not him. He is here in the city. His rendezvous with the ships was a ruse."

"Then we really need to be on our guard."

Alejandro nodded, "Yes, my love."

"It is all the more reason to tempt him with the baited trap."

Alejandro sighed, but did not disagree. Cassandra could tell he was torn. She said, "Sometimes an artificial lure catches the fish."

Alejandro said, "I would like that better."

"Unfortunately, some fish will only bite on the real thing."

They finished the soup and Cassandra said, "We are finished Luis."

Luis came and took the bowls away.

Alejandro said, "When will they be going to the estancia?"

"I will ask them to start the process tomorrow. I'm afraid our quiet meals here will come to an end. I will eat with the rest of the staff."

Alejandro said, "I cannot keep them on the Mexican government's payroll once they leave here. They are presently double dipping as you say. What they are presently getting though will be offset by the fact that you have apparently agreed to pay them more than they presently earn and will be providing housing and a better environment for their families."

Cassandra nodded understanding.

Luis brought the main course and Alejandro told her as they ate about the progress of the factory construction. He also gave her an envelope.

He said, "We identified all the men who attacked the estancia, but one. Perhaps your people will be able to identify him. The transcripts of the interrogations of the two survivors second session are in there as well. I have no doubts one is an Iranian agent."

Cassandra said, "I will pass this along."

They finished lunch talking about the upcoming wedding. Cassandra walked Alejandro to his vehicle and he kissed her chastely before leaving. She watched him leave then went to her office and asked Carol to ask Stan to come up.

Cassandra was sipping coffee when Stan came in. He closed the door and asked, "What is up?" He took a seat opposite Cassandra.

Cassandra handed Stan the envelope, "This is information on the attackers. Alejandro's people at CISEN could not identify one of them."

Stan said, "I'll see what I can do."

Cassandra said, "Alejandro says Castillo is not in Venezuela, but here in Mexico City. He says the man in Venezuela is a look alike."

Stan said, "Then he is an identical twin. We got a good photo of him in Venezuela and it was verified against another photo we had."

Cassandra said, "What do we know about Castillo before he became a visible player? Are we sure his name is even Eduardo Castillo?"

Stan said, "We have nothing before he came onto the radar."

Cassandra said, "Then Castillo is likely an assumed identity"

"Yes."

Cassandra added, "And he could actually have a twin brother. Having a twin brother the enemy doesn't know about could be very useful."

"That is an understatement." Stan paused, "Two of them would be an intelligence nightmare. It would explain why we have had trouble keeping track of him or them."

Cassandra said, "Then our working assumption is that there are twin brothers at work."

"I'll let Washington know about our theory."

Cassandra said, "I told Alejandro about our shadow patrol idea. He thought it was a good plan. He will be providing his best people to do that, so we had better stay out of their way."

Stan said, "Understood."

Cassandra said, "Do you have an idea how we can find out who the Castillo brothers really are?"

"Tell Alejandro. He has the resources to search out records of the birth of male twins."

Cassandra nodded, "I will do that this afternoon. Please make sure Novio gets enough from the special fund to pay for the upkeep of his team."

Stan said, "Will do," then got up and left.

Cassandra got on her computer and did some basic research from the web.

Cassandra called for Luis and Pedro and they came to the office. They had never been there before, but seemed comfortable being there.

She said, "Please have a seat." The men sat and she continued, "The time has come to make the move to the estancia. You may have the next seven days to pack up and get moved. Teo is expecting you." Cassandra took out cash and gave each of the men a bundle of pesos, "This is for moving expenses and your pay for the week you are moving."

Pedro said, "Thank you, Excellency," and Luis added, "Gracias."

Cassandra smiled and said, "God speed. You may take the rest of the day off."

The two men left and Cassandra called for Novio. He came into the office several minutes later and Cassandra said, "Have a seat." She told him about the roving shadow patrols Alejandro's people would be doing, but that they would keep a block away from the house. She also asked him to have her bags and clothes put in the vehicles. She went and sent a message to Washington that she had officially moved out of the embassy.

The team went to the house and Cassandra's bags were moved in and she unpacked. She then went to the patio to talk to Novio. He was sitting at a table sipping on a bottle of Mexican beer.

She sat down and said, "Is everyone settled in."

"Yes ma'am. Jace is customizing a HK53 for your use."

Cassandra said, "It will be good for this suburban environment, but I'll want something heavier at the estancia."

Novio said, "Understood."

Cassandra said, "We don't have any cooks on the team and we need one."

Novio said, "Yeah. We'll get tired of grilled burgers and the like quickly."

"I have one spot left open; any ideas?"

"Not really. In the past we've been short term in and out. I can find one that will fit in though."

Cassandra said, "I'll leave it to you. I just need a name and number and I'll request him or her."

"I'll make some inquiries. Can we use the pool when we are here?"

"Yes and Carmen and Anita can stay in the house."

Novio said, "I suppose it would make sense to have them in the room with the twin beds."

"Yes."

Anita approached and Novio said, "You and Carmen will stay in the house; the bedroom with the twin beds. Tell the team they can use the pool when we are off duty, but only two at a time."

It was unsaid, but understood that even when they were "off duty" they stayed near their weapons. Things could go sideways very quickly.

Anita smiled and said, "Understood. I'll pass it along." She walked away.

Cassandra went into the house and called Alejandro. He did not answer and she left a voice mail that it was important business and she needed to talk with him. She called his official number and was told he was not available. Cassandra made a decision.

She went to Novio, "Tell the team we are going out and to saddle up."

Cassandra's unexpected arrival at Alejandro's office building created quite a stir. It wasn't so much that she was the U.S. Ambassador to Mexico, but rather that she was the fiancée of the second most powerful man in Mexico. She was quickly taken to a comfortable room to wait for Alejandro where some staff members were very hospitable.

Cassandra waited fifteen minutes for Alejandro and would have waited longer. He finally came into the room and came and kissed her on the cheek.

He sat down and said, "It must be important to bring you here like this."

Cassandra nodded, "Is it safe to talk here?"

Alejandro said, "Let's go to my office." He offered his arm and they went to his office. Once they were seated with the door closed Alejandro asked, "What is it?"

Cassandra smiled, "I am told it is likely that Castillo is not one man?"

Alejandro looked at her with some surprise.

She added, "I have been given intelligence which seems to indicate that Castillo is actually two men; identical twins.

That is why there are always conflicting reports about where he has been seen. We know little of Castillo's background before he came out of nowhere and it is probably an assumed identity."

Alejandro said, "Are your people certain?"

"I am told the probability is extremely high. You have the resources to search for male twins. If their real identity is established then we can track them."

Alejandro said, "It explains a lot and doubles the danger. I will have my people look into it. Since we know Castillo had his base of support in the drug trade, we may be able to come up with something."

Cassandra said, "I wanted you to know right away. Considering this, if we have reports of him in two different locations, we don't have to discard the possibility of one of the sightings."

"It doubles our chances of catching one of the twins."

Cassandra said, "Perhaps we'll get lucky."

Alejandro said, "You sure made the staff here scurry showing up unannounced. I found it quite amusing until I realized it must be something important."

"It was. I wanted to see you. This Castillo thing was just the excuse I needed."

Alejandro laughed.

Chapter 16 – Confirmations

Cassandra flew to Washington on Wednesday as she was to appear before the Senate Foreign Relations Committee regarding her confirmation. Cassandra stayed with her parents Wednesday evening and appeared before the Committee on Thursday afternoon. Given the press Cassandra had received the questioning was for the most part very civil. Those related to her qualifications were handled delicately given her intelligence experience that no one wanted to get into in any depth.

Those from her father's party made sure to ask questions regarding her very public achievements. Cassandra understood the political posturing and its necessity. She put on a smiling face and endured the process with grace. There were some questions regarding the state of the Mexican political and economic conditions. There were only few tense moments when two opposition Senators challenged her.

The first started out with, "I understand you have made some personal investments in real estate and businesses in Mexico."

Cassandra answered, "That is correct, Senator."

"Isn't that a conflict of interest given your position?"

"No Senator. I invested my own money based on my belief in the underlying soundness of the Mexican economy. I have had investments in Mexico since I came of age. It is no secret my mother's family has had business interests in Mexico since just after the Second World War. I have inherited a share in some of those family businesses and from time to time have increased my investments there. "

Cassandra did not volunteer that she also had business interests in the U.S. and Spain.

The Senator said, "Yes, but don't you have inside information because of your position?"

Cassandra answered, "Would you please clarify Senator. I don't see any connection between my work as ambassador and my personal decision to invest. I am not aware of any information from my official position that gives me privileged information."

The Senator said, "What about the deal you brokered for munitions for oil?"

"I have no investments in oil stocks or oil futures, Senator. I believe that transaction benefitted both countries and businesses in both of them. I am proud of that achievement."

Several of the Senators noisily showed approval.

Another opposition Senator asked the question no one else dared to. The truth was he had few Hispanic voters in his district and so felt he was the one to ask, "Don't you think your engagement to the Mexican Secretary of the Interior presents a problem?"

Cassandra should have been more diplomatic, but decided to be direct, "What could possibly be the problem Senator? As far as I know, the Government of Mexico is both a good neighbor and ally and that our ties are becoming even stronger in recent months. Perhaps you could clarify the question for me?"

There was laughter in the chamber. The committee hearing went on for a while and ended with a vote of the committee to recommend to the Senate her appointment be confirmed. The vote would take place the following week.

One of her father's officials told her it was pretty much now a "slam dunk".

Cassandra left the room knowing she would have to return to Washington the following week to watch the confirmation vote; it was expected. Cassandra went to have dinner with her parents. They talked about the upcoming wedding and the logistics for housing the guests.

Early Friday morning, Cassandra's plane left for Mexico City. She was surprised and delighted to find Alejandro waiting for her when she was passed through customs at the airport. In spite of the fact they were in a very public place and there were security agents all around, Alejandro kissed her and she knew a camera flash went off.

Alejandro said, "I missed you."

Cassandra blushed ever so slightly and smiled, "I am glad to be back."

Alejandro said, "We must have lunch together."

"I would like that."

They went to the vehicles with Amanda and the security people taking strategic positions to protect them. The little convoy left the terminal and headed for the city center.

Alejandro said, "We think your intelligence people were right about the twins. We have identified the two men and it was relatively easy as there were only two sets of identical twins which are still alive and were high up in drug organizations before the Castillo alias was first used. There is a nationwide manhunt underway for the Soto Gomez twins Alano and Alberto. They most certainly know now that we are after them."

Cassandra said, "A cornered animal is the most dangerous."

"Yes. Please be extra careful. I have extra men with Adriana."

Cassandra said, "We need to be extra vigilant at the official opening at the embassy. I think we should stay in the city this weekend."

Alejandro said, "I agree. The trip would provide too many opportunities for an ambush. It might be wise if Adriana were to stay away from both of us."

"Agreed and I will spend a quiet weekend at home so I can rest up."

Alejandro said, "The best place to attack would be in the crowd at church."

"Then we just stay away."

Alejandro said, "Agreed. During the Friday reception at the embassy I will set a trap for the twins in the blocks around the embassy and the house. They may try to get in as a guest or service worker."

Cassandra said, "There will be no service workers. Our military chefs will prepare the food and it will be served by men and women in dress uniform."

Alejandro said, "And the guests will be checked carefully."

"Yes. It would be helpful if there were helicopters keeping the airspace above the embassy clear."

Alejandro smiled and said, "I will talk to our friend Carlos to see if he could do you the courtesy."

Their conversation was broken by a radio signal. "Everyone be on alert. We have two fast movers coming up on us."

Alejandro ordered, "Have the trailing vehicles block the lanes. We need to find a defensible place." Alejandro's orders were relayed and the lanes of traffic behind them were suddenly blocked by four of the security vehicles running abreast doing below the speed limit.

Cassandra heard gunfire. She saw the ideal place and pointed and Alejandro saw it at the same time she did. The two vehicles not blocking traffic took the exit and drove behind the concrete barriers where the road repairs were being made on the crossroad. The vehicles stopped quickly and everyone quickly got out. They had a clear view of the off ramp.

Cassandra yelled, "I need a heavy weapon."

Several assault rifles came out of the back of the SUVs and both Alejandro and Cassandra took one and extra clips. They took positions behind the concrete barriers with the security team and covered the off ramp. The four vehicles that had been travelling slower and blocking the highway came down the ramp and veered off in both directions. Their bullet resistant shells were pock marked from small arms fire and one of the self sealing tires was going flat.

The two following vehicles drove right into the trap. The driver of the first car realized the mistake and slammed on his brakes halfway down the ramp. The trailing car reacted slowly and rear ended the first car. Men jumped from the cars and

Cassandra saw one man raise a rocket propelled grenade launcher and then all hell broke loose.

Both Alejandro's and Cassandra's people opened fire. Cassandra saw the rocket propelled grenade streaking to her right and opened her mouth and hit the ground. Alejandro instinctively reacted and fell on top of Cassandra. The grenade hit the top of the vehicle to their right and exploded. Jagged bits of the roof flew everywhere then the vehicle started to burn. Cassandra and Alejandro had been protected from the blast by their vehicle which was between the explosion and them.

Alejandro jumped up and started firing again and Cassandra followed his lead. Several of the agents were spraying the wounded attackers who were still attempting to fire on the party. Cassandra heard a siren as the gunfire ceased. Alejandro pulled Cassandra along the barrier away from the fire ducking low behind the barriers. The found a place between two barriers forming a wedge and went to ground reloading their weapons.

Cassandra said, "This is an unexpected welcome."

Novio came toward Cassandra and took up a defensive position. Several of her team came to them and Carmen and Seve were helping Shaun who had a leg wound. Soon Cassandra and Alejandro were surrounded by a security perimeter.

Novio said, "Antonio, bring the undamaged vehicle to provide cover."

Antonio ran ducking to the vehicle and speedily backed it up to where they were and swung it around the tires squealing. They now were in a triangle of relative safety. The team was taking up positions covering all directions. Alejandro's men were now collapsing on their position bringing wounded and taking whatever cover they could.

Only the one vehicle was now drivable. The first ambulance came into view and Alejandro said, "Be careful. This might be another trap."

Cassandra thought it was good her fiancé was paranoid. The thought then hit her it wasn't paranoia if they were really out to get you. The ambulance stopped and Alejandro's captain of security called out for the ambulance men to get out with their hands up. Instead the ambulance sped away.

Alejandro pointed to one of his team and yelled, "Go after them," and four of his men jumped in the only running vehicle and went off in pursuit. The remaining security people repositioned themselves.

Cassandra said, "I hope one of those guys shot to pieces is Alberto or Alano."

Alejandro said, "I hope we are that fortunate."

A radio call came in and Cassandra could not hear what was being said. A soldier came to Alejandro, "Sir, the ambulance has been stopped. The four men inside resisted. Two are dead and two are wounded and in custody."

Alejandro nodded.

Another radio message came in and it was a Mexican military unit approaching. They did not want to draw friendly fire so were checking in for clearance. When the military vehicles arrived Alejandro said, "I have to stay. You should go to the embassy."

Cassandra said, "I will wait to hear from you," and hurried away to be loaded with some of her team into an armored Mexican military vehicle. It sped off as part of a small convoy headed straight for the U.S. Embassy.

Cassandra called ahead and when the duty phone was answered she said, "This is Ambassador Crossing; Eagle One. The Embassy is to be placed on full alert and locked down. This is not a drill."

The answer was a curt, "Yes ma'am." Cassandra heard the sound of the new alert sirens going off in the background. The operator said, "One moment for the duty officer."

The phone was answered in a moment, "This is Captain Cable."

"Justin, get the place locked down tight. We were attacked on the way from the airport."

Justin said, "Yes ma'am."

"I am on my way back with the Mexican Military. We are about twenty minutes out."

"Understood."

The duty operator came back on and Cassandra could hear the new alert sirens at the embassy still going off. The operator asked, "Do you need any assistance, ma'am?"

"No, just standby in case I call again."

"Yes ma'am."

Cassandra terminated the call and then called the house. The call was answered almost immediately. Cassandra recognized Anita's voice and said, "Anita be on guard. We were attacked on the way from the airport."

Anita said, "Understood."

Cassandra hung up and turned to Novio, "Where is Shaun?"

"He is being taken for medical treatment and one of our people is with him."

"Very good, did we sustain any other casualties?"

Novio answered, "No, boss."

Cassandra noticed the Mexican lieutenant riding with her was looking at her strangely and she smiled and said in Spanish, *"You'd think by now they'd have learned not to mess with us."*

The soldier's smile broadened and he said, *"Si Excellency. It is unwise to tempt Ambassador Death, no?"*

Cassandra laughed as did her team. The Mexican officer's smile broadened.

They arrived at the embassy without further incident and Cassandra cleared the little convoy to enter the compound. Once inside, she got out and invited the Mexican military to stay for refreshments, but the lieutenant said he had orders to return and so the little convoy left.

Cassandra went and sat down in the living room of the embassy. A soldier came and asked, "May I get you something, ma'am."

"Yes, please. Two fingers of whiskey with three ice cubes."

The soldier said, "Coming right up."

The Colonel came into the room with Stan and Cassandra asked, "Would you like to join me in a small libation?"

Stan said, "I never turn down fine Tennessee sipping whiskey."

Bob nodded, "I concur."

The soldier came back with Cassandra's drink and she said, "Would you bring the Colonel and Stan one please."

The soldier said, "Yes ma'am," and hurried off to comply.

Stan said, "What happened?"

"We saw the trap coming before they could spring it and they got the worst of it. Shaun was wounded and is getting medical attention. Alejandro stayed at the scene."

Bob asked, "How many of them were there?"

"There were twelve; eight in attack cars and four in an ambulance that tried to sucker us after the initial firefight. I don't have the casualty report."

The soldier brought the two drinks for the Colonel and Stan.

Bob sipped the whiskey, "This is very good."

Cassandra said, "Alejandro identified the twins. They are Alano and Alberto Soto Gomez. CISEN has a major manhunt underway."

Stan said, "Good."

Bob asked, "How long do you want us on full alert?"

"Until I hear from Alejandro and then we'll go to yellow until after the reception on Friday. I'm going to have to stay at the house this weekend. With Shaun out of commission and the heightened threat, I'd like six of your best to augment Novio's team."

Bob said, "No problem."

Cassandra's phone rang and she answered it. Alejandro said, "Well we got lucky. We have Alano in custody. He was in the ambulance. He is wounded, but he'll live. He's in surgery now. Nine of the twelve attackers are dead. They had four IEDs about a hundred yards past the exit we took."

Cassandra said, "It was good we took the exit we did." She knew firsthand the destructive force of an improvised explosive device referred to as an IED. They might now be dead if they hadn't turned off the highway.

Alejandro said, "Indeed God was with us."

Cassandra asked, "What about casualties?"

"Your man Shaun has been treated. They will keep him overnight. I lost a man and have three wounded.

Cassandra said, "I'm sorry for the loss."

"The man I lost was a good one and was with me for a long time."

Cassandra said, "I will be at the house."

Alejandro said, "Alberto is going to want revenge badly now that I have Alano."

"I know. Be careful and you might want to increase the guard on Adriana."

"Yes. I will call you in the morning."

The call ended at Cassandra said, "They have Alano."

Stan said, "That may bring Alberto out. He will want revenge. While he's plotting against us, we will be looking for him."

Cassandra said, "Yes and Alberto may do something reckless. Shaun has been treated and they are keeping him overnight. He has company."

Bob said, "I will make sure we are on yellow alert. I'll round up six to augment your security team."

Cassandra nodded and added, "We'll need transportation as our armored SUVs are all shot up. I think we can risk using armored military vehicles to go to the house if we wait until after dark. Two will fit in the garage."

Bob smiled, finished his drink and left.

Chapter 17 – Unfinished Business

Cassandra's plane landed in Washington five minutes ahead of schedule the following Tuesday. The Secret Service people were waiting for her and Amanda as they were passed through customs. They were taken to a limousine and went directly to the big white place Cassandra's mother and father presently called home. Dorothy greeted Cassandra and Amanda with a hug and a welcome.

"You will have a busy day tomorrow. Why don't you unpack and then we'll have dinner. I don't think your father will be back until close to bedtime. He has a very heavy schedule today."

Cassandra said, "Yes, mother. We'll go unpack."

The women had an enjoyable dinner together. Cassandra had brought photos of her Mexico City house and showed them to her mother. After dinner, the women sat around drinking wine and talking. Craig was still at work when the women turned in.

The next morning, Cassandra went to meet with Ed Cook downstairs and left with Amanda. Her father was already at work on just a few hours sleep. Cassandra's meeting had been arranged in the White House where it would be held away from prying eyes. When Cassandra arrived, she was told the Director of National Intelligence was running late, but was on his way. She was led into a room, but Amanda was asked to wait in the hall.

Ed arrived only a couple of minutes late and said as he entered the room, "Hello, Cassandra."

Cassandra got up and said, "Good morning, Ed," and they shook hands then sat down.

One of the general's staff closed the door and Ed said, "That was a nice piece of work figuring out that Castillo was actually twins. We now have eyes on Alberto. He is still in Venezuela."

Cassandra said, "Someone really wants to get Alejandro and me. I'd like to know who that is because it was part of the deal to get the weapons."

Ed said, "We think it was what you represent as much as who you are. Your positions and relationships make you and Alejandro good terrorist targets on so many levels."

Cassandra said, "What is it you want, Ed?"

"I want you to promise not to offer yourself up as bait. There is sufficient danger to your person without doing that. In short, stop acting like an operative. It is too dangerous to the national interest at this point if you go down. Your father and Chas are concerned as am I. Given your background it was felt you might be more inclined to listen if it came from me. Think about the political and diplomatic consequences of your being assassinated in Mexico."

Cassandra thought about it for a moment and realized her mistake immediately. She said, "I was thinking like an intelligence agent, not a diplomat. That was a mistake. I promise."

Ed said, "That was easier than I thought it would be."

Cassandra said, "It is just the reality of the situation. I have a new role and I'm learning on the fly."

Ed smiled and said, "You will be glad to know we are increasing the size of your security detail."

Cassandra just nodded.

Ed said, "I will have orders to that effect sent to Captain Vega so the additional personnel will be in place when you return."

Cassandra said, "Thanks, Ed."

He smiled and got up, "Now that my mission is accomplished, I can go assure the Commander- In-Chief of your cooperation."

Cassandra said teasingly, "It seems you see him more than I do these days."

She didn't know why she did it, but she surprised the general by putting her right hand on his right shoulder. He seemed surprised, but then smiled. Cassandra left the room and returned to the president's quarters. Her father came for lunch and they had a little family time.

In the afternoon, Cassandra was in the senate gallery for the vote on her confirmation. As expected, it passed handily on a party line vote and without much fanfare. Cassandra was then taken to meet with Chas. She arrived at his office to be told the secretary of state was delayed in a meeting with the president. Cassandra was served coffee while she waited.

Chas arrived twenty minutes late and came through the waiting room and greeted Cassandra with, "I'm sorry I kept you waiting, Cassandra."

Much to everyone's surprise Cassandra hugged him lightly and to drive the gawking staff crazy she said, "I'm so happy to see you, Uncle Chas."

Chas started laughing when he saw the jaws of his staff drop. He said, "Come into my office. We have a lot to talk about." He turned to his secretary, "Please bring us some fresh coffee."

Chas shut the door and said, "Oh but you made my day, Cassandra. I'd love to hear the rumor mill by this afternoon."

Cassandra said, "It was fun. The people around here are much too serious and stiffed necked."

They had no sooner taken chairs in the sitting area then there was a knock on the door. Chas said, "Come."

His secretary brought in a coffee tray and asked, "Will there be anything else, Mr. Secretary?"

Chas said, "Not for now, Evelyn," and she left closing the door behind her.

Cassandra started pouring coffee and asked, "What are your orders?"

Chas smiled, "I understand you are having a reception on Friday evening to officially reopen the embassy."

"Yes."

"And the Venezuelan Ambassador will be there."

Cassandra said, "He has indicated he will attend."

"Perhaps you could drop a not too subtle hint during a private moment that we would frown upon anyone attempting to destabilize the government of our neighbors to the south. You might advise him unofficially that there was some talk of major military retaliation over the special cargo smuggled into Mexico and war was a very close thing. You should also say another subversive attempt might lead to the hawks having their way and the countries involved being leaked to the world along with certain evidence of the involvement followed by military action. The price of three ships being turned back is a small price to pay to avoid such a possibility."

Cassandra smiled, "I will do that."

Chas said, "Coming from you I'm sure the Ambassador from Venezuela will take the message to heart and pass it along."

"I would assume so."

They had finished their coffee and Chas said, "I have another meeting."

Cassandra got up, "Thank you, sir."

Chas smiled, "You are welcome, niece."

They both smiled and Cassandra left. That evening she ate dinner with her family. Her father and mother, sisters, and Cal and Maggie were present. Cassandra showed the family photos of the Mexico City house and they talked about the upcoming wedding.

The next morning, Cassandra and Amanda were on a plane headed for Mexico surrounded by ten very fit men and women who had just been assigned to the American Embassy in Mexico City. They had all been privately introduced at the terminal before boarding. Though they were all dressed in civilian clothes, these were the additions to Cassandra's security team.

Cassandra and her team were cleared directly through customs and got into six new SUVs and headed for the embassy. Novio was in the vehicle with Cassandra and Amanda.

Cassandra asked, "Where did the new vehicles come from?"

Novio said, "They were shift driven from the U.S."

The drive to the embassy was uneventful and once there the new security people were integrated into the team and armed and outfitted with body armor. They all ate a meal in the cafeteria and Cassandra left Novio to figure out how to work out the logistics and scheduling for the new team members. She went to her office.

Cassandra met with Juan and Carol to get an update on the reception progress. Everything was on track. Next she met with Bob and Stan and discussed the security arrangements for Friday. When they finished she called Alejandro.

He answered, "Hello, my love."

She said, "Hi, handsome. I'm back and everything went as planned."

Alejandro said, "I know. What time do you suggest I come tomorrow evening?"

"Please come at six and we will have some time to have coffee and talk before the reception."

On Friday there was a flurry of activity at the embassy. There had been a conscious effort to have the highest security while keeping most of it out of sight.

Stan came to her office about ten in the morning. He was announced by Carol and when he came in he closed the door.

Cassandra said, "Hello, Stan. Do we know where Alberto is?"

"It is confirmed he is still in Venezuela. Something is going on because he has been going to meetings and spending a lot of time cooling his heels."

Cassandra said, "What do you make of it."

"We think he has lost a lot of credibility. It may be that they know Alano is in custody and are concerned about what he will give up."

Cassandra said, "I will need a mini-microphone transmitter for tonight. It needs to be something I can turn on and off. I want you to record it and make a copy for Bob and Alejandro."

Cassandra told Stan about the message she was to deliver to the Venezuelan Ambassador unofficially.

Stan said, "It is about time we had somebody in charge who has some cajones."

Cassandra replied, "I agree with the thought, but I think I would have been more diplomatic."

Stan said with a smile, "Well, you are a diplomat now."

Cassandra smiled and said with good humor, "Go on and go back to the basement."

Stan smiled and said, "Sure thing, boss," and left.

Cassandra spent the day in her office studying the files on all the major players who would be attending. She had done the initial study during travel and downtime over the last week.

She went home about four o'clock after being assured by Juan that all the preparations were complete. As she dressed for the event, Cassandra felt confident she would remember what was required. It was a very formal affair and she had a case containing the sashes and medals she had received from the Presidents of Mexico and the United States respectively. Attached to one sash was a micro listening device transmitter. She would slip the sash on at the embassy and hang the medal from a ribbon around her neck. She wore very fashionable shoes that were comfortable and without much of a heel as she would be doing a lot of standing.

She went downstairs to wait for Alejandro. He arrived ten minutes early. She met him at the door with, "Hi, handsome."

Alejandro smiled, "Hello, my love," and kissed her lightly.

Cassandra thought she would melt then shut down her emotions. Tonight was not the night for letting her emotions rule her.

Alejandro said, "You look stunning, cielito lindo."

"Thank you."

They went inside and sat in the living room. Coffee was brought out and served and they both took sips.

Cassandra said, "It should be an interesting evening."

"Yes, it should. Our countries have a lot at stake."

Cassandra said, "Yes. An incident free evening will go a long way to assuring the international community."

Alejandro said, "Enrique asked me to thank you for taking this risk. You have little to gain if it is successful and credibility to lose if it goes wrong."

Cassandra said, "That is true, but we are in this together."

She then proceeded to tell him she would be slipping away to have a private word with the Venezuelan Ambassador.

Alejandro didn't ask what she would say and Cassandra didn't volunteer, but only said, "They need to be warned unofficially of course."

Alejandro handed her an envelope. "It is a list of overseas agents Alano knew about. There are certain connections and bank accounts I am sure your people will be happy to know about."

Cassandra said, "Thank you, love. I think we should be leaving."

They arrived at the embassy compound on schedule and without incident. Cassandra put on her sashes and medals then asked Alejandro to accompany her as she made a last minute inspection. She found everything was satisfactory. She excused herself and went to the communications room where she opened the envelope and examined the contents. She drafted a short message and had it transmitted as highest priority. She made sure the confirmation of receipt came before returning upstairs.

Cassandra ignored protocol and Alejandro stood next to her as she welcomed the guests and mingled as everyone drank champagne served in crystal flutes. Cassandra's field training served her well and she was able to address all the dignitaries by name. She kept sneaking glances at the Venezuelan Ambassador and noted he was living up to his reputation as a boozer.

It was much later as she and Alejandro moved through and among the guests Cassandra spotted the Venezuelan

Ambassador standing in a corner alone glaring at her and Alejandro.

Cassandra turned to her fiancé, "Excuse me for a minute, dear."

Cassandra adjusted her sash turning on the recorder as she walked to the Venezuelan Ambassador and said, "Good evening, Excellency Gomez Morillo."

He gave her a look that could kill and looked around before saying, "Let's not pretend we are friends shall we."

Cassandra said, "Unofficially, I would like nothing better than to be attacked right here by my enemy and kill my attacker with my bare hands."

Cassandra looked at the Ambassador.

The Ambassador lost his cool arrogance and for a moment a hint of fear appeared. He said, 'What do you mean?"

Cassandra pressed her advantage, "My government will take any interference by foreign governments in Mexico very seriously; deadly serious. We know how the special cargo was transited into Mexico and we almost went to war over it and if one of those bombs had gone off our enemies would have been decimated. If a certain three ships are not headed back to the Horn of Africa without unloading, certain proof will be released to the world and I am sure the next time I meet my enemy I will get a medal for doing what I would like to do."

The Ambassador was now sweating, "How dare you threaten me and my country?"

Cassandra smiled, "Excellency what are you talking about? I did not mention you or your country. Your reaction is very interesting and I take it you confess these are your crimes."

The Ambassador leaned forward and called Cassandra some very nasty names then stormed away and left the embassy.

Alejandro came over, "I take it things went well."

Cassandra said, "Yes, I think so."

The rest of the evening was about polite conversation and sipping cocktails and beverages as well as eating fancy finger foods. In diplomatic terms it was a success. It would also turn out to be a strategic success as well. After two hours the guests started to leave and by hour three all had left. There had been no incidents.

Cassandra took a seat and Alejandro sat beside her as the crystal flutes and plates and various items were collected and the rooms were cleaned. Bob came and sat down. Cassandra noted that he looked different in his dress uniform; somehow more serious.

Cassandra asked, “Would you gentlemen like coffee?”

Bob said, “Yes please,” and motioned to a waiter, “Would you bring us some fresh coffee.”

The man said, “Yes, sir,” and hurried away.

Bob said, “I saw the Venezuelan Ambassador left early.”

Cassandra smiled, “I think it was something I said.”

Bob nodded.

The waiter brought coffee and they each took a cup and sipped from it.

Alejandro said, “This is very good.”

Bob said, “Yes, it is.”

Stan came into the room and passed a thumb drive to Bob and Alejandro.

Cassandra said, “I ask you to treat this audio recording as classified, Bob.” She turned to Alejandro, “Please ask Enrique to keep this a secret. It may become useful later.”

As the two men pocketed the drives Alejandro’s cell rang. He picked it up as the others listened to one side of the conversation, “Yes. Very good! Yes and let me know what you find out. Was Alberto with them? Did the other teams stay in the shadows? Good work.”

Alejandro turned to Cassandra, “It seems my men have captured some nasty men who planned to ambush us when I took you home. They are being taken to be interrogated, but unfortunately Alberto was not with them.”

Cassandra asked, “Do you have a replacement team in place.”

Alejandro said, "Yes. There were four teams patrolling and this required only one."

The drive home was uneventful and Alejandro walked Cassandra and Amanda to the door and opened it. In the entry way Cassandra said, "Goodnight, my love."

She put her hand on his cheek and kissed him. The physical and emotional reaction she experienced was intense. She moved away and smiled. She was at a loss for words.

Alejandro said, "I am thankful Christmas is not far away."

Cassandra nodded agreement and Alejandro turned and opened the door, then left. Cassandra shut it and turned to see Amanda smiling.

Cassandra had found her voice, "What?"

"He has it really bad for you."

Cassandra smiled and said, "Yes and it is mutual, so that is why we are getting married."

Cassandra went upstairs and went to bed. She slept like a log. Alejandro came with Adriana for lunch on Saturday and they spent the day sitting around the pool talking, swimming, and napping under the umbrellas. Cassandra spent the weekend at her home resting up.

Monday morning, she woke to her phone ringing. The sun was not yet up. She swung her feet off the bed and picked up her cell, "Hello," before realizing it was her satellite phone that was sounding. She picked it up and keyed in her code and said, "Crossing."

"Good morning, Ambassador."

Cassandra said, "Good morning, Mr. Secretary."

Chas said, "It seems your little talk with your unfriendly guest had unanticipated results. Two of the vessels are headed back to their point of origin. It seems the presence of one of our carrier groups off the coast of Venezuela combined with your meeting has caused some people to take notice. The third ship is apparently preparing to leave port. None of the vessels apparently offloaded."

Cassandra smiled, "That is good news." She had not been told about the carrier group, but knew that her father was behind that. He knew when and how to send strong signals.

Chas said with what seemed to Cassandra to be an upbeat tone, "It seems you are a natural if somewhat unconventional diplomat. You may have found a new calling."

Cassandra was still half asleep and blurted it without thinking, "Oh great."

She had meant it to be sarcastic, but it had apparently not come out that way or Chas had decided to interpret it as he chose.

Chas said, "I'm glad to hear you are so enthusiastic. I am sure your friend the Mexican President will want to talk with you. Have a good day." The call ended.

Cassandra's phone rang again and again she entered the code and said, "Crossing."

"Good morning, Cassandra."

"Hi, Ed, what's up?"

"I wanted to tell you the information you sent was an intelligence diamond mine and we are mining like crazy."

Cassandra said, "Well it is a good analogy because miners work in dark places."

Ed ignored the remark and said, "We also have information that your friend Alberto has been asked to find a new home. It seems he has become a liability. Unfortunately, we do not have a forwarding address, but we have unconfirmed indications he was on one of the ships."

Cassandra said, "Well that is interesting."

Ed said, "Apparently Alberto is going elsewhere to start over."

Cassandra said, "He will probably be shocked to find his Swiss bank account is empty."

Ed laughed, "The money we confiscated will fund our off the books operations south of the border for some time. I have to go now. Be careful." The call ended.

Cassandra was now fully awake. She decided she might as well get ready and go to work. She rolled out of bed and went to her exercise equipment and did her workout before showering and getting dressed.

The call came to her office at mid-morning and it was Enrique's office inquiring if the Ambassador could come for lunch with the president. Cassandra of course agreed. Her little convoy arrived a little early and she was taken to a small room where she was greeted by Maria who came and hugged her.

"Cassandra it is so good to see you. I have missed you."

Cassandra said, "It is mutual. However, the danger has put a crimp in my social life."

Maria smiled, "Adelina is at her estancia. We talked this morning and she is looking forward to seeing you."

Cassandra said, "I think things may now be returning to normal."

Maria laughed, "Which normal?" She took Cassandra by the arm and led her toward the set table.

Enrique came through the door and hugged Cassandra, "Hello, my friend. Please, let us sit."

They all took a seat and Enrique motioned to a waiter who brought wine and then left. Enrique started with, "I enjoyed the little recording you sent me."

Cassandra smiled, "I doubt as much as I enjoyed making it."

Enrique laughed and Maria smiled.

Enrique said, "I heard that a carrier fleet was conducting exercises of the coast of South America these last few days."

Cassandra said, "Yes, that is true."

"Those kind of military exercises are very costly."

Cassandra smiled and looked at her friend, "Yes, but they must be conducted somewhere. You never know when a message has to be sent."

Enrique added, "I have been told that certain vessels have left to return to other ports."

Cassandra said, "It seems so. It may be that Alberto is on one of them, but that is just speculation."

Enrique said, "I did not know that."

"Apparently he has worn out his welcome."

Enrique said, "That is indeed good news. Both personally and officially, I thank you for what you and your country have done for Mexico."

Cassandra smiled, "You are most welcome. Thank you for the note." Cassandra sipped her wine and added, "This is very good."

Maria said, "It is one of my favorites."

The conversation turned to personal matters and how the estancia was coming. Cassandra had to admit she was anxious to go see the progress. As Christmas was approaching, they discussed going to the estancia's next weekend and shopping in town for artisan's work for gifts. It was agreed. The lunch lasted almost two hours.

Enrique finally said, "Well I have a meeting to go to so if you will excuse me." He got up, leaned over and kissed his wife on the lips and they lingered for just a moment. Cassandra thought it was a touching scene. Enrique came around the table and kissed Cassandra on the cheek and left.

Maria said, "After all these years, my world still revolves around him."

Chapter 18 - Finally

For the first time in as long as she could remember Cassandra was nervous. This was unlike anything she had ever done. It wasn't that she had doubts; she didn't. It was just that she was not used to having so much emotion in her life and it had upset her balance; a balance she had worked so hard to maintain.

She was now wondering if that balance had been a part of a false sense and if it had emotionally stunted her. As with all things in her life, she was determined to face the possibility head on. Her only option was to turn back and she didn't want to do that.

Adelina brought Cassandra out of her thoughts when she said, "You look beautiful."

Cassandra looked into the full length mirror and said, "I do look good, don't I."

The woman in the mirror was wearing a sleek knee length white dress with veil and white shoes. She looked every bit the beautiful and sexy bride. It seemed strange to Cassandra that she had never really seen herself as sexy, but at that moment she realized she really was. She just wasn't athletic; she was beautiful. She smiled at the image. She wanted to savor this moment of realization, so she could relive it when she was old.

The flash brought her back to reality. The photographer was very good and Cassandra had forgotten she was there.

There was a knock at the door and Molly opened the door and said, "Come in dad."

Craig Crossing entered the room, "It is time. Let's get this show on the road."

The women lined up. Cassandra's youngest sister Katie then Molly then Adelina took their positions and Cassandra fell in line behind them. Craig went down the stair case first and the women followed. At the bottom of the stairs Craig offered his daughter his arm and the procession started.

Cassandra walked through the living room of her parents Coral Gables home and glanced at the painting on the wall that she had given her parents for Christmas. She looked at her father and he smiled. She had been noticing details about the home for several days that she had missed before like the family pictures spanning the years and the mementos.

They went out onto the back lawn and Cassandra's heart seemed to skip a beat when she saw Alejandro standing and waiting for her. Her father brought her to where Alejandro was standing with his best man Carlos. There was a private TV camera broadcasting a live feed so Enrique and Maria could watch the ceremony.

Cassandra's father had arranged for one of the Supreme Court Justices to solemnize the wedding and thus avoid any conflict over the nature of a religious service. To Cassandra the ceremony seemed to take no time at all before they both had wedding bands on and were declared married. Alejandro lifted her veil and kissed her and this time he did it passionately.

Cassandra thought her body was going into full fledge fight mode. Her heart beat was racing and her blood pressure was up and her body was releasing adrenalin. Suddenly she realized non fighting parts of her body seemed to be heating up and reacting in ways she felt were extremely pleasing. She knew they were making a spectacle and she didn't care.

They broke apart to clapping and she walked arm in arm with Alejandro along the red carpet that was spread on the grass and into the big tent that had been erected on the lawn.

The reception was fun and the family and friends danced and ate and drank. The newly married couple enjoyed the festivities, but they were not reluctant to leave early to catch the plane to start on their honeymoon. As they were being driven to the airport Cassandra was looking forward to her new life with her husband. She wondered how much her previous life would intrude on the new. It was a question she would have to wait to find out the answer to.

www.ingramcontent.com/pod-product-compliance
Lightning Source LLC
Chambersburg PA
CBHW070530260626
47161CB00002B/328

* 9 7 8 0 6 1 5 7 3 3 1 2 8 *